David Michie was born in Rhodesia, educated in South Africa, and has worked in public relations for fifteen years. Specialising in strategic planning, he has consulted for several of London's biggest public relations agencies. His first novel, *Conflict of Interest*, quickly achieved international success. He now divides his time between London and Perth, Western Australia. *Pure Deception*, his second novel, is currently available in Little, Brown hardback.

Visit David Michie's own website at:
www.davidmichie.com

Also by David Michie

PURE DECEPTION

CONFLICT OF INTEREST

DAVID MICHIE

WARNER BOOKS

A *Warner* Book

First published in Great Britain in 2000
by Little, Brown and Company

This edition published by Warner Books in 2001

A CIP catalogue record for this book
is available from the British Library.

ISBN 0 7515 2956 7

Typeset in Goudy by M Rules
Printed and bound in Great Britain
by Clays Ltd, St Ives plc

Warner Books
A Division of
Little, Brown and Company (UK)
Brettenham House
Lancaster Place
London WC2E 7EN

To Koala, with love

ACKNOWLEDGEMENTS

My heartfelt thanks to: Dr Graham Duguid, for his greatly-valued expertise and suggestions in dealing with medical issues; Alex Singleton, for providing such authoritative knowledge of the workings of the criminal mind; my agents, Lizzy Kremer and Ed Victor, for their wise counsel and generous support; and my editor, Hilary Hale, who made this a much better book than it would otherwise have been.

Know all things to be like this:
As a magician makes illusions
Of horses, oxen, carts and other things,
Nothing is as it appears.

BUDDHA (From the *Samadhirajasutra*)

PROLOGUE

———

The businessman with the cheque for £5 million looked awkward. Despite being Chief Executive of the world's largest sportswear manufacturer, and a revered business guru, Nathan Strauss had never been one for slick sound-bites in front of rolling television cameras. Contrived gestures and pre-scripted lines just weren't his style. In fact, there was something about Nathan Strauss's very indifference to his public image that some people found deeply charismatic.

Not that the occupant of Suite 901 of the Dorchester Hotel was one of those. Instead, he watched the television news item on the Starwear donation with a familiar mix of compulsive curiosity and self-reproach. As the camera focused in on the two men sitting at the table, the Distress Line logo emblazoned behind them, phrases like 'the unprecedented size of this donation' and 'considered by his peers to be a leading voice on corporate ethics' sounded through the verbiage of the report. The story of how Nathan Strauss had created Starwear, now the world's biggest brand after Coca-Cola, was briefly recounted. Previous donations made by the Strauss family to the arts, medical research and a variety of charitable causes were listed. All this time Nathan Strauss dabbed at his perspiring forehead with a white handkerchief, before adjusting the heavy horn-rims on his prominent beak.

Then the telephone rang. 'Nat, it's me.'

'Madeleine,' his tone was warm.

'You're on the box. BBC 1.'

'Yeah. I'm watching.' He fiddled with the remote control, turning down the volume.

'I just wanted you to know the girls and I are so proud of you,' she told him fondly, 'but I'll let you go now so you can follow it.'

'Madeleine –' he stopped her before she rang off, evidently in no great hurry to end their conversation, 'you know, um . . . you know I'd do anything for you, don't you?'

The pause at the other end was one of puzzlement. Her husband wasn't usually given to sentimental expression. But, thought Madeleine, maybe his visit to Distress Line that afternoon had moved him to this uncharacteristic, but welcome tenderness.

'Of course I know.' Then, wondering how to respond, she said simply, 'I love you, Nat.'

'Love you, too.'

Replacing the receiver, Nathan Strauss watched himself as he moved to the lectern on which the single page of his speech awaited him. His public relations man, Mike Cullen, had offered to have the speech ghosted, but he had declined, wanting to write it himself; this speech was too important for PR. Now, the small group of Distress Line staff, volunteers, and news reporters watched him closely as he brushed back a stray forelock of his greying hair and leaned closer to the microphone.

'Nearly all of us suffer from depression at some time in

our lives,' he began, 'but there can be nothing worse than the appalling finality of a man who believes he has no alternative but to take his own life. "Why?" is the question we always ask afterwards –' he paused, before shaking his head, 'but there is only ever one person who truly knows the answer.'

As always, it didn't matter at all that his speech lacked clever wordplay, or that his jacket was dishevelled and tie askew; he spoke from the heart and his conviction was compelling. In the semi-dark of his hotel room, Nathan Strauss followed the words of the speech he knew almost by heart to its conclusion: how he believed it was the duty of every company to give something back to society; the work done by Distress Line and the high value he placed on it. And his final line: 'I believe we *all* have a responsibility to give choices to those who find themselves in despair.'

There was the applause and whirr of flash-cubes as he handed over the cheque for £5 million to the Director of Distress Line. A TV news reporter wrapped up the item, saying how Distress Line would use the donation to improve counselling facilities throughout Europe. Then it was back to the newsroom and an item on Northern Ireland. Getting up from the armchair, Nathan walked over to a drinks cabinet, pouring himself a single malt with ice. Behind him, framing the open doors that led out to his ninth-floor balcony, gold damask curtains swayed in the early evening breeze.

Half an hour later, Park Lane was a chaos of wailing police sirens and the flashing lights of emergency-service vehicles. A gathering crowd was already pressing up against the hastily erected police cordon. Paparazzi were moving into position on the roofs of nearby cars and vans, adjusting their telephoto lenses for the most saleable picture of the night.

The alarm had been raised by a motor salesman from a nearby BMW branch who'd been walking along the pavement. The body had tumbled down only metres in front of him, and had bounced several times with such sickening force that the motor salesman hadn't even bothered to stop, rushing instead into the hotel lobby to report the incident, before being overwhelmed by shock. Hotel security had been on the scene within seconds, laying a dark blanket over the shattered, bleeding body as their colleagues hurried up to Suite 901 where they found the half-finished glass of whisky.

When the police arrived on the scene a few minutes later, they identified the body as that of Nathan Strauss, husband of Madeleine and father of Sarah and Rebecca, Chief Executive of Starwear, a man whose personal net worth was estimated at £5.3 billion, and wearing the same suit he'd had on earlier in the day when presenting Distress Line with its largest ever donation. Police said an investigation into the cause of his death would be launched, but foul play was not suspected.

1

_____

Chris Treiger would never forget the eight words that changed his life. He'd been working late at the office, one night in early July, when the phone rang. As soon as he heard the ebullient voice at the other end, he'd wondered how to cut short the call. Bill Brewster, a high-pressure PR head-hunter, had been hounding him for weeks about a phenomenal career opportunity, paying vast sums of money, for which he was ideally suited. Chris had heard it all before. At thirty-two years of age and MIRA's youngest director, he got calls from recruitment agents every month – and with offers a lot more appealing than working for some PR shop.

Chris had already told Brewster he wasn't interested. But the head-hunter was back – and making a virtue of his persistence. He didn't usually try to change people's minds, he declared, it was just that in this case the fit was so perfect he would be doing Chris the greatest disservice if he didn't at least suggest that Chris reconsider. Wasn't it worth an initial meeting?

It was then that Chris had made his tactical error. 'It might,' he conceded, looking out at where the summer sun still burned above the horizon, even though it was past eight o'clock, 'but I'm really up against it right now and I don't have time to run all over town—'

'Well, you wouldn't have to.' Brewster was triumphant. 'Lombard is just two streets away from you.'

Chris was wondering how to regain control of a conversation which had gone off the rails when Brewster came out with his eight, life-changing words – eight words to which Chris had returned many times in his head, marvelling at the perverse logic of them. Eight words, in the form of a question, to which there was only one possible answer: 'Isn't your career worth a hundred-yard walk?' Brewster had asked.

Chris hadn't given the interview a lot of thought by the time he was due to go into Lombard. Of course he'd heard stories about the agency. Who hadn't? But he'd done nothing to prepare for the meeting. In fact he was irritated with himself for caving in to Brewster's hype, and couldn't see how anything Lombard might come up with could be of the slightest interest to him. He was doing well for himself at MIRA, and even if the money wasn't brilliant, his career was rewarding in other ways, which was more than could be said for most of his former Oxford contemporaries.

While they had been cramming at intensive training courses run by Goldman Sachs in New York, or Andersens in Chicago or McKinseys in Piccadilly, Chris had signed up with the polling company MIRA. Market Intelligence and Research Analysis was a global organisation whose voter surveys gave it a high public profile; around election time, no article about voting intentions was complete without the latest MIRA polling result. As one of MIRA's brightest new recruits, Chris had soon found himself involved in the more intellectually challenging aspects of the business. In fact, he'd devised a new way of defining voters according to attitude and lifestyle, which had been hailed as a break-through by the market research industry – and quickly branded the MIRA Psychographic Map™ by his employers. It had attracted a level of interest Chris found extraordinary. Political parties from all over the world had soon been hammering on his door, and so too had all the other players in political drama: spin-doctors, advertising agencies and newspaper columnists. Chris soon found himself being quoted in the press and invited to speak at conferences. He'd be phoned at all hours of the day and night by political reporters chasing a soundbite, or an appearance on TV. His clean-cut good looks – clear, blue eyes, closely cropped dark hair, sensitive features – and his personable delivery made him a popular commentator.

Chris's bosses at MIRA had given him his own office and an impressive title, and commissioned him to devise psychographic maps for companies and brands. Despite his relative youth, he had become regarded as something of a guru among MIRA's expanding client base, his divinatory powers sought by captains of industry and those who advised them. Chris relished the role and played it for all it was worth. He became adept at forming the kind of pronouncements that attracted greatest interest from clients and the media – which had also prompted the steady stream of head-hunters to call. But his remuneration at MIRA was a frustration; even as a director, and one of its highest paid executives, his earnings didn't begin to reflect the new business he'd brought into the firm.

Traditionalists on the MIRA Board clung to the notion that salary was a product of age and experience, and saw in Chris a bright young man with ideas well above his station. He, meantime, saw no reason why contribution to profits shouldn't translate directly into personal reward. A parting of the ways might become inevitable – although Chris had never, for a moment, thought that salvation was to be found at Lombard.

Even though Lombard was the largest and most powerful PR firm in the City, with more FTSE 100 companies than any other, Chris had no interest at all in being a PR man. And if he had, Lombard would never have occurred to him as a place to work. For quite apart from its size and influence, Lombard and its founder, Mike Cullen, had a reputation about which Chris was decidedly ambivalent. 'Cullen has created the Hitler Youth of PR' he remembered someone once saying. The phrase had stuck with him – it seemed to sum up all that he'd subsequently heard about the agency.

Mike Cullen had founded Lombard on the simple premise that to build up the best client list in the business you had to hire the best people in the business – no matter how much they cost. It wasn't long before the stringent requirements Lombard demanded of potential employees came to be known in City circles, and the term 'Lomboid' gained currency. To be a Lomboid was to be extremely good-looking and have immense charm, to possess a first-class degree and a capacity for ferociously hard work. To be a Lomboid was to be fluent with figures, charismatic in presentations, and brilliant on paper. To be a Lomboid was to be supremely self-confident, with a firm view on every major political and economic issue, as well as familiarity with the menu of every up-market eatery in London. To be a Lomboid, in short, was to be as much like Mike Cullen as possible.

Lomboids didn't just act the same – they dressed the same too. A formal dress code applied, with the PR world's Adonises dressed in dark suits and white shirts – always dark suits and white shirts – from Mike Cullen's preferred tailor and shirt-maker in Savile Row and Jermyn Street respectively. The Aphrodites meantime wore Donna Karan as standard kit.

The consultancy Cullen had created in his own image had soon acquired a mystique which major City players couldn't help but notice. As Cullen's storm troopers marched through boardroom after boardroom, their diplomacy and intelligence and winsome good looks sweeping an array of blue-chip companies into their arms, even those who cracked jokes about Lomboids did so nervously. Because there was something about Mike Cullen's unswerving self-belief, fostered in all those who worked for him, which was patently self-fulfilling.

Lombard *did* things differently. Lombard consultants never travelled anywhere by taxi. A limousine service provided a chauffeured Jaguar to ferry the demigods to and from client meetings. When Lombard held its annual staff party, it didn't bring in caterers to circulate Bollinger and crab-meat vol-au-vents, it sent all its staff to party in New York – First Class. And while middle-ranking clients were treated to lunches in Terence Conran diners and Marco Pierre White gastrodomes, Britain's most powerful corporate warriors were entertained in Lombard's own penthouse dining room, where spectacular views of Tower Bridge afforded an appropriate vista for the even more triumphal creations of the full-time chef Mike Cullen had poached from Kensington Palace.

And then there was the secrecy. While other PR firms like Brunswick and Financial Dynamics rarely told newspaper reporters much about themselves, Lombard, predictably, took things a step further; it refused all interviews. No one working for Mike Cullen was under any illusion that the merest hint to a journalist about even the most anodyne aspect of life at Lombard was grounds for instant dismissal. In more than fifteen years at Lombard, Mike Cullen had not once been quoted in any trade or national newspaper. Lombard refused even to allow its name to appear in industry league tables – even though its fee revenue would have easily placed it in the top slot. Lombard conducted no advertising. It had no company brochure. So insistent was its pursuit of invisibility that its name didn't appear on its own stationery, which provided only an address and other contact details. Lombard consultant business cards were similarly anonymous. And enterprising journalists who tried to mine for information at Companies House, where every limited company in Britain is obliged to lodge its annual accounts, soon found that no trace of it was to be detected – Lombard had been incorporated within a convoluted trail of off-shore arrangements so that it was not required to submit a single piece of paper to any place of public record.

The effect of this extreme secrecy was, naturally, fame of the most potent kind. In an industry of mammoth egos, to seek no attention was far more effective than shouting from rooftops. Because nobody knew what went on at Lombard, they could only speculate. When Lombard's golden *wunderkinden* were sighted in the back of their racing-green Jaguars, whispers would circulate about which company they were moving in on, where they were about to strike next. PR rivals, with little inkling of the nature of the beast they were up against, had only rumours with which to second-guess their competitor – and there were rumours aplenty, of the most terrifying kind.

Chris recalled some of the tales of Lombard mythology the evening he made the notional hundred-yard walk – which turned out to be three hundred yards, and why was he not surprised? – for his appointment with a Lombard director, Kate Taylor. After being screened by uniformed security guards behind a black marble desk – a lot more rigorous, he couldn't help noticing, than the usual security check – he was shown through to Lombard reception. It was a vast, softly lit, sumptuously furnished atrium, which appropriately gave no impression at all of the kind of organisation that moved behind its burgundy moiré walls. The impression it *did* give was one of hushed reverence, confirming the notion that this was the hallowed ante-chamber to an organisation of immense, unseen influence. Glancing round at the symphony of magnificent oils, gilt-framed mirrors and damask curtains, Chris couldn't but be impressed. The subdued semi-darkness deepened the effect of brooding power, and was interrupted only by two shafts of light, beaming down from a vaulted ceiling on to the immaculate blonde heads of the two *Vogue*-like glamour girls at Reception.

Inviting him to make himself comfortable on one of the sofas, they phoned through for Kate Taylor. No sooner had Chris made himself comfortable with the *Financial Times*, however, than one of the receptionists called over to tell him there was a change of plan – instead of Kate Taylor, she announced in an expensive, Roedean accent, he was to meet the Chairman, Mike Cullen. Well, this came as a surprise, thought Chris, the prospect of suddenly finding himself face to face with the legendary PR man making him feel, by turn, self-conscious then irritated. So what if it was Mike Cullen? He wasn't interested in PR and he didn't want the job anyway.

Minutes later he was in the lift, going up to the Boardroom on the fifth floor. As the doors slid open, he stepped into a room dominated by floor-to-ceiling windows, offering a panoramic view of Tower Bridge, the Thames, the City. Dusk was falling and with no lamps turned on in the room, one couldn't escape a sense of sweeping omniscience looking out on a scene of such history and splendour. Mike Cullen was standing by the window at the far end of the room, and turned towards the lift as Chris appeared. He was taller than Chris had thought he would be, and broad-shouldered, a lustrous crop of silvering hair brushed back from well-defined, handsome features. His suit was dark charcoal and his shirt was indeed white, with a button-down collar and the Windsor knot in his tie as crisp as though he had just stepped out of his dressing room. On his way up Chris had wondered if Mike Cullen would strike him as Machiavellian or arrogant or intensely driven. But as Cullen stretched out his hand towards him now, Chris realised he hadn't reckoned on the PR man's charm. Mike Cullen possessed an aura of such openness and familiarity, it was as though they had already known each other for years.

Cullen offered him a drink. Had he wanted the job, Chris supposed, he would have asked for something soft. But as he didn't, he opted for gin and tonic. Cullen splashed out two large measures from a blue bottle of Bombay Sapphire. 'How did you find our recruitment man?' he enquired, clunking blocks of ice into the crystal tumblers.

'Very . . . insistent,' Chris responded.

'Why we use him.' Cullen brought over the drinks. 'But I'm very pleased you decided to come.' He sat opposite Chris, raising his glass before sipping. 'You probably think that working here is a bit tangential to what you're doing at the moment,' he began, 'but the point is, I'm not offering you a job in PR.'

Chris was taken aback by Cullen's directness. Not that he had any intention of showing it.

'Do you know the first dictum of our business?' Cullen leaned towards him confidentially. '"Know Thine Enemy".' He regarded Chris closely. 'Of course, all our clients start off thinking PR is about getting them a good press. But that's less than half the story. Managing the way the media deal with their competitors is just as important. But to get there, you first need to know about competitor plans, strategies, how they're seen in the market –' he gestured broadly, 'all the stuff you know inside out.'

It was a train of thought Chris hadn't expected. He wondered where Cullen would end up.

'I saw the work you did for Glaxo. Very impressive.'

How on earth had he got hold of that report? It had been top secret and completed only the week before.

'We'd like to do work like that for all our clients. We want to create a new role here, a new team, to feed into the rest of the business at the highest level. To cut to the chase, I want you to be Lombard's first Director of Research and Planning.'

As Cullen leaned back in his chair, regarding him contemplatively, Chris realised his own surprise arose as much from his own undeniable curiosity as from Cullen's unexpected frankness. Not that he could really take the offer seriously. After a pause he responded thoughtfully, 'Intriguing idea. But I like the polling side of my job too much. It's not something I'd want to give up.'

'We wouldn't want you to.' Cullen shook his head. 'It

would do our lobbying business no end of good if Lombard became an authority on voter intentions. Bring over your political team, lock, stock and barrel.'

Chris couldn't suppress a grin at the audacity of the notion. He could picture the looks on the faces of the MIRA Board as he announced that, as of the next month, MIRA's most profitable research unit would be decamping *en masse* to Lombard.

'That would be fun,' he admitted now, 'but even so, most of the work here is financial – and I've never seen myself as a City man.'

Cullen fixed him with a droll expression. 'You're not a Lomboid, huh?' He raised his eyebrows. 'That regimentation stuff is all crap, you know. It's true that everyone who works here is very bright and very articulate and very hard-working. But they're not all the same. They don't,' he pulled a face, 'all wear dark suits. Take a look round our consumer division, it's like a fashion show down there. And the lobbying boys are pinker than the Sydney Mardi Gras. Our success is based on synergy. Horses for courses. We don't need another City suit – we've plenty of those already. What we need is someone with your analytical skills to bring discipline to the way we carry out research for our clients – the kind of stuff that's your bread and butter at MIRA.'

Chris's expression was noncommittal. There was an undeniable logic to what Cullen was saying, but the whole notion of joining a PR agency was just too foreign for him to seriously consider. Nursing his gin and tonic, he asked, 'So which clients, hypothetically, need planning work?'

'All of them, at some point in their corporate life cycle. But there's a few with more immediate needs. Starwear is one.'

Chris looked up sharply. A month earlier he'd done a company image survey for Starwear. The findings had been extraordinary, demanding further analysis, but the client had said no. Budget overrun. Chris had found *that* hard to believe. He doubted the results had ever found their way up the organisation to its ultimate boss, billionaire guru Nathan Strauss.

Now he told Cullen evenly, 'I did a project for them, not so long ago.'

'I know,' Cullen nodded. 'Nathan told me about it.'

'Pleased he got to see it.'

'He saw it all right. So did I. We were very impressed with your analysis.'

Chris raised his eyebrows. *What else had these guys seen?* 'Didn't you agree the issues I uncovered deserved further work?'

'That's why you're here. It was Nathan who suggested we speak to you.'

This time, Chris didn't even try to hide his surprise. The idea that a business leader as lofty as Nathan Strauss was taking a personal interest in him took him completely unawares.

'Both Nathan and I think what's called for is more than just another MIRA project or even two projects. It's an ongoing process of refinement. Nathan respects your judgement and would very much like you to work closely with him – as you know, the subjects you touched on are near and dear to his heart.'

Chris could no longer pretend that Cullen wasn't pressing all the right buttons. Nathan Strauss was not only one of the world's wealthiest businessmen, he had also achieved a unique status as a pioneer in the area of corporate ethics.

Quite apart from having created Starwear, whose distinctive star icon was now instantly identifiable all over the world, he had also been one of the first, back in the mid-nineties, to pick up that public opinion was moving sharply against the 'greed is good' business maxim of the eighties. It was Strauss who realised that, for reasons of hard-nosed profitability, companies had to become more environmentally sensitive, more accountable to those who consumed their products, more transparent in the way they managed such things as directors' salaries and share options. Despite the fact that vast wealth separated him from the hopes and fears of ordinary mortals, Strauss's sensitivity to public opinion was acutely developed. It was he who had first coined the phrase 'enlightened self-interest'.

While competitor PLCs were badly damaged by revelations about fat cat salaries, secret share deals, deforestation, ozone damage and a wide array of other green issues, Starwear moved ahead of the times. At Strauss's instigation, the company had produced two reports, the first on why companies needed to be more transparent and accountable, and the second on why they needed to improve their environmental performance. Dubbed 'Starwear I' and 'Starwear II', the two reports had soon become touchstones for corporate governance, not only in Britain but throughout the world, and their titles quickly became shorthand, referred to by journalists and businessmen alike. Unlikely as it seemed for a hugely rich, untelegenic, middle-aged Jewish man with an American accent, Nathan Strauss became famous as a champion of consumer concerns.

The main reason for Chris's frustration when he'd finished his project for Starwear was that he thought he'd uncovered a new wave of consumer concerns – this time about child labour in developing countries. Television documentaries about street urchins of Calcutta being sold to sweatshop factories to work away their childhoods in appalling squalor had inflamed public opinion. Were any of the garments retailed in Britain made this way? How did they know the origins of the branded sweatshirts and trainers and golf-peaks they wore? In the past, Starwear had been accused of buying from sub-contractors who used child labour – but Nathan Strauss had soon stamped out the allegations. Chris knew from his recent analysis, however, that public concern was becoming more widespread and deeper felt. And companies like Starwear, manufacturing huge quantities of their output in developing countries, were first in the firing line.

Without doing more in-depth research, it was impossible to decide how exactly to manage the issues. More work had to be done – and he had wanted to do it. He'd been unable to fathom the 'budget overrun' response, but now as he sat opposite Mike Cullen he began to see a much bigger picture. And as he thought about the prospect of working, in person, with Nathan Strauss, Cullen seemed able to read his mind.

'You know, Chris, there aren't many career opportunities of this kind that come your way. It's not just another research job. It's about doing something that really matters, something that will have a positive effect in the outside world. And we're not talking only Starwear – this work could have a much broader impact on corporate policy in the UK and beyond.'

'Starwear III?'

'Exactly. Global employment policy. Community relations in developing countries.'

'Ambitious.'

'Nathan's a radical thinker. You've seen what he's done already.' Cullen was expansive. 'You'd enjoy working with him. Not only is he the most valuable client this firm has, he is also by far the most stimulating. And, you know, Nathan and I share the same basic philosophy.' He paused significantly. 'What goes around, comes around. Do unto others as you would have them do unto you. Enlightened self-interest. It's very important to me that everyone here shares those values.'

Chris nodded.

'With our help, Nathan and his brother Jacob have turned Starwear into the world's most aspirational sports-wear brand.'

'Jacob's the American brother?'

'That's right,' Cullen nodded. 'Very commercially-minded.'

What Cullen didn't say was that he was a very different character to Nathan. Far less well-known in Britain than his Anglophile sibling, images of Jacob Strauss from across the Atlantic were of a handsome athlete who lived the Starwear brand, and whose sporting talent worked in coun-terpoint to Nathan's intellectual prowess.

Across the semi-darkness, Cullen studied Chris for a few moments before he said, a note of caution in his voice, 'I don't want to paint a misleading picture of what it's like working here.'

Chris let the assumption pass.

'You'd find Lombard very satisfying intellectually. But it's also a lot of hard graft. People put in very long weeks – sixty to seventy hours is about average.'

Seventy hours was on the low side if any of the stories Chris had heard were true. Apparently one Lombard director had arrived at work one Monday morning and didn't get home till the following Saturday afternoon. The few hours he'd slept each night had been on meeting room sofas – every day he'd sent his secretary out for a fresh shirt and underwear.

'The reason Lombard is best,' Cullen continued in an important tone, 'is because we hire the very best people and every single one of us is utterly dedicated to our clients.' He paused for emphasis. 'But their dedication is well rewarded. Lombard salaries are more than double the average pay of other City consultancies. No one here over the age of thirty earns less than a hundred thousand, and most people over thirty-five take home more than twice that. Performance bonuses paid in December have been well above forty per cent of salary every year we've been in business. And once you're a Board Director, which you could be after three years, shares are automatically allocated to you, free of charge. I believe in securing everyone a stake-holding, that way no one feels tempted to leave. And it's not a nominal holding. The minimum amount allocated per person is point two five per cent of the equity per year. Lombard is currently valued at a hundred million.'

He could see from the look in Chris's eyes that his interviewee was making the desired calculation, and gave him a moment before confirming, 'Quarter of a million pounds. Per year. There isn't a director here who isn't a multi-millionaire.'

Despite himself, Chris couldn't help being impressed. He'd known Lombard was a big payer, but had no idea it was on this scale. In seven years he could be a millionaire. By the age of forty he'd have enough money to retire.

Cullen had talked around the subject of money, but

hadn't got to the nub of it. Chris knew that was deliberate. On his way over here, when the idea of joining Lombard hadn't seemed even remotely attractive, Chris had decided that if the subject of money arose, he was going to be coolly indifferent. He'd even come up with a put-down line: 'I'd rather think about the job first,' he was going to say, if invited to discuss terms and conditions. He'd certainly had no intention of bringing the subject up himself. But now, as Cullen asked him, 'Any other questions?' cool indifference just didn't seem an option. The kinds of figures Cullen was talking about couldn't be further removed from the modest wage from MIRA on which he'd never be comfortable, let alone rich. What's more, he'd been taken completely unawares by the revelations about how his recent project for Starwear could lead to him working with Nathan Strauss directly. No doubt about it, the Lombard offer was a million miles away from what he'd expected.

And then there was the Cullen factor; Chris had been completely unprepared for his openness and enormous charm, even though he knew the PR man had all the skills of a modern-day Merlin, and knew exactly how to use them for his own ends. Chris found himself saying, 'What kind of package are you offering?'

In the lengthening shadows of the Boardroom, Cullen seemed to relax back in his chair. 'A basic of a hundred and twenty thousand. As I said, the bonus has never been less than forty per cent. I can't promise what it will be in future years, but this year we're targeting around fifty-five per cent.'

Chris did his best to conceal the rush of excitement sweeping through him. £120k. That was double his current salary. Possibly plus another sixty grand. MIRA paid no performance bonus. He'd known, in theory, that he was worth a lot more than MIRA was paying, but here it was, being offered to him on a plate. And a job he didn't entirely dislike the sound of.

'At your level,' Cullen continued, 'your company car would be a fully-fuelled BMW 7 series – top of the range. And Lombard would pay the equivalent of seventeen and a half per cent of your salary into a personal pension of your choosing.'

Chris nodded. *Not even the Chairman of MIRA drove a prestige car. Getting this job would be like winning the lottery.*

'We look after people here,' Cullen was continuing, 'because we expect a lot from them. It's important you're sure you'd want to make the commitment.'

Chris nodded, aware that the tables had now ever-so-subtly turned. At which point Cullen said, 'We find that our consultants who have settled home lives are happiest. You're married?'

He asked it as though it were a given. Chris shook his head. He wasn't even dating anybody at the moment – not that he could see what his private life had to do with Mike Cullen.

'Seeing anyone?'

'No one to speak of.'

Cullen nodded once, pursing his lips. 'The long hours can be difficult—'

'I don't have any competing interests, if that's what you mean,' Chris told him in level tones, 'and no skeletons in the cupboard.'

'Fine.' Cullen smiled. 'I'm pleased that's settled.'

He said the words, Chris couldn't help noticing, with a sense of relieved finality.

*

In the days following his meeting with Cullen, there were times Chris wished he did have someone special to talk things through with. Not that he'd mulled over the Lombard offer all on his own. It was far too important for that. Using the high-level network of contacts he'd built up at MIRA – City analysts and business journalists, others who'd had dealings with Lombard and Starwear – he'd made some carefully placed enquiries. What came back confirmed his impressions. Lombard, a different agency altogether from the one that had been sold to Buchanan Communications several years earlier, was widely acknowledged for having the most impressive, blue-chip client list of any agency in Britain, and Mike Cullen was the colossus of financial PR. While its culture of invisibility was the source of some jesting inside the Square Mile, the agency was respected nonetheless. It had achieved its unique status purely on the basis of its reputation. As for Starwear, Nathan Strauss's track record spoke for itself.

Chris realised that he was being made an offer with all the right credentials, all the stimulation he could hope for, and money beyond his most fanciful dreams. So what was the downside? Long hours. Stress. No longer being the big shot of the company. But wasn't it time for a new challenge?

He'd had several more conversations with Cullen on the telephone, and another visit to the agency to meet potential colleagues over a drink. Then there was the final showdown at MIRA over a lucrative new survey he'd launched, from which he was denied any form of profit-share; he'd never forget the shock on his boss's face when he told him he was resigning. There was frantic footwork in the days that followed, as fellow MIRA directors proposed radical changes to his remuneration package which, only a month before, would have left him ecstatic. But it was too late now. Chris had made up his mind and there was to be no turning back. Plus, he'd already persuaded his political polling team to join him in three months' time – not that the MIRA Board members knew anything about that yet.

He'd also found a new home for himself. Visiting friends in Fulham for an early summer barbecue, he'd been passing an estate agent's 'Open House' and had decided, on impulse, to have a look round. After his dark, basement studio in Islington, the Fulham place was magnificent. Large, spacious, light-filled rooms. A master bedroom with *en-suite* bathroom, and two spare rooms, one of which would convert to a bay-windowed study. But best of all, steps from the sitting room balcony led up to a sweeping roof terrace that looked directly out across the Hurlingham Club, with its manicured lawns and rolling parklands. The rhododendrons were in full, purple majesty, and around the perimeter of the gardens, pine trees swayed back and forth in the late-afternoon breeze. It was the kind of view that made you feel you were in the middle of the country.

Judith would love this, he found himself thinking involuntarily – before checking himself. She hadn't been a part of his life for seven years, and he irritated himself by letting her haunt his thoughts. Their romance had blossomed at Oxford, and had continued when he'd moved down to London to start work. Intense though it had been at the time, and heartbroken though he was when it ended, it was all in the past. The very distant past, at that. Anyway, why did he keep going back in his mind to Judith? He'd had several relationships since, with wonderful, sassy, intelligent girls. There'd been breathless days and sultry nights since Judith, just as there would be again.

Now as he stood on the Fulham balcony, surveying the wooded grounds and flowering shrubberies before him, he decided it was time to open a new chapter. Making a rare, impulsive decision, Chris decided to buy the property then and there.

A week before his September start at Lombard, Chris met a few friends for a celebratory drink on HMS *Queen Mary*. He was standing at the bar, waiting for a fresh round, when the TV up in the corner caught his attention. Trevor McDonald was reading the *ITN News*, behind him a picture of Nathan Strauss.

'Can you turn that up, please?' He nodded towards the TV.

'Sure, mate.' The barman hiked up the volume.

The news bulletin had moved to a woman reporter outside the Dorchester, behind her a phalanx of ambulances and police cars. It had been shortly after seven o'clock that evening, the reporter explained, when the body had been found by a motor car salesman. Chris felt a sudden dread as the image of a stretcher, covered in a dark blanket, was carried into the back of an ambulance. Only that afternoon, Nathan Strauss had handed over a £5 million donation to Distress Line, the organisation that specialised in helping those who felt suicidal. It was, she declared, a horrific irony that within hours of the donation, Nathan Strauss had himself committed suicide . . .

As Chris stood at the bar, the noise of the festivities rising behind him, he felt suddenly dizzy. Slapping two notes down on the bar, he hurried towards the Gents, where he found a cubicle and stood, forehead pressed against the steel of the porthole catch, trying to take it all in. Nathan Strauss dead. It was just too overwhelming to absorb. What on earth would drive someone like him to suicide? And who would take over at Starwear? Working with Nathan had been a large part of the reason for his interest in Lombard – a very large part. Since that first evening with Mike Cullen, he'd spent many hours mulling over the future, and how he'd work with Nathan. Now this. He knew he would never have accepted Cullen's offer if it hadn't included being the prime creator of Starwear III. The big bucks, the bonus, the BMW, even his new flat now seemed tawdry and trivial. But it was too late now to go back: he'd burnt his boats at MIRA, and without Nathan Strauss his supposedly glittering new career at Lombard could be a short-lived cul-de-sac. With a lurch of emotion that was to become familiar over the coming months he realised he'd made a terrible mistake.

He left HMS *Queen Mary* a short while later, no longer in the mood to play. As he walked towards Big Ben, past lamps looped like pearls along the embankment, he was so deep in thought he failed to notice the man walking about fifty yards behind him. The man with the narrow face, hooded eyes and camera case slung over his shoulder, who glanced watchfully about him as he followed Chris along the pavement. The same man who had spent the last two hours on the bridge of the HMS *Queen Mary*, shooting off a roll of film.

Everyone who'd arrived at Chris's drinks party had been faithfully captured and digitally stored for future retrieval. It had been one of his more enjoyable assignments of late, thought Harry Denton. He'd even managed a couple of quiet pints, thanks to the Lombard new boy.

2

Judith woke to the shrill bleep of her alarm clock, and fumbled for several moments in the semi-dark before finally silencing it. Then she flopped back on to the pillow, closing her eyes. She was exhausted; her head throbbed; her mouth was dry and foul as a sewer. She was desperate for one of the cans of Coke she knew were in the fridge, but the kitchen was down three flights of stairs; it seemed a very long way away. Blinking open one eye, she scanned the small bedroom with its strewn clothes and tipped-out handbag, before closing it again, events of the night before seeping back into her consciousness.

Last night had been a mistake. Not just a boozing, smoking, four-hours-of-sleep mistake. Worse. It had been a Ted Gilmour mistake. She hadn't slept with him, thank God. She'd only made that mistake once before, and she suspected she'd had more than Carlsberg in her pint glass that particular night. But she'd spent the whole bloody evening with him. She dully remembered the smoke-filled interior of The Mitre, steaming in the late-August heat. He'd chosen the pub in Farringdon, where he was meeting some analysts from Merrill Lynch who worked nearby. A few of their colleagues from *The Herald* had started off there too.

But as the evening had gone on, first the analysts had left and then, one by one, the other journalists, leaving just Ted and her. There'd been a lock-in and the two of them had stayed on into the early hours. She'd needed a shoulder to cry on.

Now she grimaced metaphorically, as she remembered that, some time well after her fifth or sixth, tears had indeed been shed; God – why did she humiliate herself like that? Through the all-engulfing hangover she recalled Ted hammering his fist on the table between them – 'Alex Carter is the most arrogant shit on Fleet Street,' he'd cursed with feeling. And therein lay both of last night's problems. Alex Carter, City Editor of *The Herald*, Britain's biggest-selling broadsheet newspaper, was indeed an arrogant shit. He was also sadistic, pompous, sexist, idle, blatantly favouritist – and her boss. Fleet Street, on the other hand, had ceased to be the centre of gravity for national journalism over a decade before – before Judith had even started her career, in fact. But Ted Gilmour still talked about Fleet Street, every reference to it only serving to underline their age difference – only one of many reasons that made the idea of a relationship with him unthinkable.

Her mind slowed way down when she was hungover. Instead of the usual flurry of unrelated mental chatter which perpetually swept through her mind, the morning after the night before she would survey each idea with an alcohol-induced passivity which reduced everything to numbed, slow motion. Not that she wanted to relive the events of yesterday afternoon in slow or any other kind of motion. But she found herself drawn ineluctably back to the moment that Alex Carter, having hit his post-Savoy Grill low, appeared in the doorway of his office and,

bellowing across the newsroom, demanded she present herself to him instantly.

It was a well-known fact in the office that Carter's
approach to managing his female staff was a simple, binary
one; it was either frolicking or bollocking. Women were
either sex goddesses or useless bitches. Summoned to his
office they could expect to be flattered and flirted with, or
to be heaped with sardonic acrimony. From his tone of
voice, even before she'd got to his office door, Judith had
had no doubt which this afternoon's session was to be.
She'd felt her stomach turn.

'Output.' Carter slammed the door behind her as she
stepped inside. 'What's yours been? Two, three pieces in the
last fortnight?'

'We have five different investigations underway—'

'And I have a paper to fill. Twelve pages of business
news a day. This newspaper carries the most comprehensive
business supplement of any broadsheet. There's no place for
passengers.'

'We're pushing ahead as fast as we can. Investigative
journalism—'

Carter strode behind his desk and dropped into his chair.
He was a short man with a short man's complex, a large,
balding head, glittering, dark eyes and a fat bum. Lard-arse,
they called him.

'Of course, I know nothing about investigative journalism,' his mouth twisted into a disparaging sneer, 'I'm only
the City Editor, what the fuck do I know about it?'

Judith couldn't think of anything to say, so she said nothing. She stood there, meeting his blazing resentment with a
blank expression until he finally said, 'You need to cultivate
more contacts. I've already spoken to you about this before.'

'Yes, Alex.'

'If you're serious about a career in journalism you've got to get out there. Circulate. Make yourself available to people.'

She knew precisely where this conversation was heading. And she despised him for it. How dare he question her commitment to journalism? Only nine months before, when she'd still been at *The Guardian*, she'd been fêted as one of their brightest stars. She'd even been the youngest recipient of an industry 'Scoop of the Year' award for her investigative piece on the American Tobacco Corporation. But for week after week now, Carter had been so disdainful of her writing, so relentless in his carping criticism, there'd been moments she'd begun to wonder if she really was as good as she'd always thought. Carter just didn't seem able to accept the fact that investigative work required far more time and effort than standard news reportage. Of course, he paid lip-service to the idea. During her job interview he'd waxed lyrical on the specialist demands and abilities required of investigative reporters whom, he had told her over a glass of the aptly named Meerlust Rubicon in a glistening City brasserie, he regarded as the *crème de la crème* of the industry. But when it came to the crunch, Carter didn't accept the realities of investigative reporting. He was only interested in word count. A thousand words a day to be precise.

'Supporting right-on causes might have served you well when you worked down the road,' he jerked a disparaging thumb in a northerly direction, 'but when you work at this level we expect a lot more from you. There's no place for slackers.'

'I work longer hours than most in the department.' Judith wasn't going to let that one past.

'Then where's the output?' He raised his shoulders, before gesturing to the notice-board running down his office wall, to which copies of that week's *Herald* were always pinned. 'A feisty twenty-year-old from a provincial rag would be more productive. Quite frankly, we're hugely overpaying you if all you can come up with is an average of two hundred words a day.'

Then go hire yourself a feisty twenty-year-old to lech all over, you slimy ponce, she felt like telling him. But she didn't. Instead she'd replied, 'If they're the two hundred words that make people buy the paper—'

'My, my, aren't we grand?' he pouted, 'and I suppose Alison MacLean's articles are just padding?'

'Alison MacLean does different stuff to me.'

'You know,' his voice was sing-song, 'I don't think I'd ever have noticed that if you hadn't pointed it out.'

It wasn't the first time he'd compared her, unfavourably, to Alison MacLean. Two years younger than she, Alison had been plucked by Carter from the obscurity of *The Herald* library several years before, and now she had bylined articles in the paper every day – sometimes several of them. Not that she actually *wrote* the articles. Oh, no. What she did was lightly edit the ceaseless flow of press releases faxed to the City desk by public relations agencies throughout London, and present the results to Alex Carter as the fruits of her labours.

When she'd first stumbled on Alison's *modus operandi*, a week after arriving at *The Herald*, Judith hadn't known what stunned her more – her colleague's audacious reproduction of PR feeds, complete with spin, or Alex Carter's unquestioning acceptance of the material she'd supposedly created. But Judith had soon learned that the reason for

Carter's unhesitating use of PR-generated stories was, quite simply, because he was utterly dependent on them himself. On more than one occasion she'd read through the impressive ruminations of his City Editor's daily column, only to discover he'd reproduced, word for word, a PR briefing note. And she'd frequently heard him on the phone practically commissioning pieces from various spin-doctors who were, of course, only too happy to provide a few hundred words containing oblique plugs for their clients.

The idea that there might be some kind of objective analysis, or primary research of a story, rarely seemed to cross Carter's mind. Which was one of the two main reasons why Alison MacLean epitomised his notion of the perfect female journalist. The other was a lot less cerebral; Alison MacLean dressed like a tart. Plain-faced and with an unremarkable figure, hers was a case of wild overcompensation. Judith had never seen her without a face thick with make-up, and clothes that would bring a blush to the cheeks of the most brazen street hussy. Her wardrobe seemed to consist of nothing but crotch-length minis and thigh-hugging jodhpurs, skin-tight blouses, see-through tops, black stockings and suspenders . . . in short, Alex Carter's most cherished fantasies. No matter what she wore, she made sure to reveal both cleavage and visible pantyline, with G-strings her favourite – and Alex Carter's too, thought Judith bitterly, judging by the amount of time she spent in his office flashing her fanny.

There had been moments, especially in the last few weeks when Judith's professional self-esteem had hit rock bottom, that she'd wondered if she was being a fool for not playing the game. Perhaps she too should take up editing press releases, if only to get Carter off her back. Maybe if she invested in a short, black leather skirt and knee-high boots, his views about her journalistic prowess would also change? But no sooner did she find herself thinking along those lines than she'd wonder, how could she even think of being so unprofessional? How could she allow a man who thought that journalism meant editing press releases to have such a degenerative influence on her? So what if he just happened to be her boss.

Now, Carter regarded her balefully. 'I expect more stories from you, Judith. Either a lot more stories, or much bigger stories. So you want to take your time over things? Fine. Just make sure they're big enough to warrant it. If not, we'll have to find you a home somewhere else in the department.'

It was the first time he'd used that threat, but she instantly knew what it meant. The City desk produced monthly survey 'supplements' on various industries and countries. They were, in truth, nothing more than a vehicle for *The Herald* to sell extra advertising, and the articles they carried were overt, PR puffery supporting the advertisers. No one liked writing supplements, but it was entirely at Carter's discretion who did. And that fact made the supplements desk *The Herald*'s Gulag Archipelago, with next step the Jobcentre. Supplement writers rarely lasted long, a couple of months at the outside, and then they disappeared, rarely to surface in national journalism again.

'You probably think I'm a bastard? Well, it's just that I have high standards. I expect a lot of my staff.' Carter now adopted his Mr Reasonable demeanor. 'I know you can do it. I wouldn't have hired you if I didn't think you were up to it. I just don't see the commitment.'

'I *am* committed,' she tried to seem forceful, but it came out sounding weak.

'Well, start proving it to me,' he raised his eyebrows, 'and be quick about it. I want big stories. Big, big stories. It's your job.'

Lifting his telephone receiver, he began dialling. Her audience, it seemed, had come to an end.

Everyone hated Alex Carter. Just her luck, thought Judith, to end up working for the most despised City Editor on any national paper. Later, at the pub, when she'd replayed that afternoon's conversation to Ted, he'd had plenty of his own venom to unleash – there were few journalists who hadn't had a run-in with Carter. Brutish, egotistical Carter. Carter, whose intellectual idleness was exceeded only by his social ambition; he had married the daughter of an earl and, from time to time, was to be found on the Society pages of *Tatler*, noxious little toad that he was. Carter, Ted had declared, hadn't had an original thought in years – and he didn't care. So long as he had bright PR men to do his thinking for him, and glistening socialites to massage his titanic ego, what did it matter?

It was comforting for Judith to be reminded that she wasn't alone in her persecution. In a way, she appreciated the reality check. But, in another way, it only made her despair all the more; what was to become of her journalistic career which, until just recently, had held such promise? Ted had already suggested a transfer to his department. As Features Editor of *The Herald* he was, like Carter, an editorial head, but running a features desk was a less prestigious, and certainly a less well-paid position, than that of City Editor. As much as Judith appreciated Ted's offer, she knew that moving to Features would be wrong – wrong for her reporting career which had been spent, so far at least, investigating big businesses; and wrong for Ted, whose evident interest in her she just couldn't reciprocate.

Ted was always stimulating company over a drink at the end of the day, and was unstintingly chivalrous and attentive. She respected him as a journalist and, having seen him fill six pages of newspaper in just two hours, she admired his creativity and contacts. But that was it. There were no blue moons, red roses and gypsy violins in the relationship for her. It wasn't only the ten-year age difference, which didn't have to be a big deal, although Ted's journalistic reminiscences sometimes made it so. It was, more basically, that she just didn't fancy him.

She'd made this quite clear the very first time he'd hinted at his romantic intentions. 'You're not really my type, Ted, and I'm sure if it wasn't for the three double gins, I definitely wouldn't be yours,' she'd tried the firm but tactful approach. But then she'd gone and complicated the situation by sleeping with him. She still couldn't believe herself capable of it and kept on wondering if maybe Giles Ayling from Advertising Sales didn't have a case to answer. Giles, who with his public-school bray, Hugh Grant hairstyle and pea brain couldn't have been less her type, but who had monopolised her company during the evening in question. One minute, she'd been feeling pleasantly mellow, at the bar of *The Herald*'s local in Wapping, then, hardly any time at all after returning from a visit to the Ladies and taking another sip of her drink, she'd felt the almost physical sensation of sinking into a trance state. She did remember pushing away Giles Ayling's face, which loomed suddenly close to her own, before Ted had appeared. There had been something of a tussle, then she'd been gliding out of the door on Ted's arm. Next thing she remembered was waking up in a strange bedroom next morning, with the melodic strains of 'Oklahoma', in Ted's surprisingly well-modulated baritone, wafting out of the bathroom. She'd run a hand down her body, feeling her nakedness. Oh, shit.

She'd spared him the embarrassment of telling him she didn't remember a thing, but after that it had been more difficult than ever trying to persuade Ted that their relationship should remain on a just-good-friends footing. Now, as she awakened to discover the assault of the night before once again laying siege to her body, the prospect of a sweet, wet Coke and two Nurofen began to outweigh her desire to remain under the duvet. Climbing out of bed, she donned her bathrobe and made her way downstairs.

Half an hour later, she was a woman transformed. Bright-eyed, Ysatis-scented, and headache gone, she stood in her underwear, blow-drying her hair. At twenty-nine she still had a good figure, despite years of alcohol abuse and smoking. Her breasts continued perkily to defy gravity, and she retained her slender form and a hand-span waist, even though she was always shoving junk food down her neck. At school she'd been nicknamed 'Pix' and she was still light on her feet, her dark hair was cut short, and her large, dark eyes were still brightly inquisitive. She was lucky, she knew, not to have turned into a bloated, hacking wreck. From time to time she'd make a resolution to quit smoking, cut down on drinking, even return to swimming, which had been her *raison d'être* as a teenager. But the pressure-cooker of work since joining *The Herald* meant that by the time she finished each night it was at least half past seven and she felt she deserved a very hard-earned drink and a fag.

Climbing into her working gear, with no compromise in

the tight black skirt direction, she checked her watch and decided she had time for a quick breakfast. Having already discovered the fridge was bereft of milk – thanks, no doubt, to gay Simon, her flatmate – she rushed downstairs and out of the front door, heading for the local newsagent.

She'd been a loyal J. P. Patel customer for seven years – ever since moving to London. She'd always flat-shared in the same part of Earl's Court and in that time had visited the corner shop practically daily, at all hours and in every condition. After about three years, when she'd established herself as a permanent resident, as opposed to part of the transient tide of colonial youth that washed through the area, Sanjay Patel had started to greet her. By year four she was on first-name terms – not just with Sanjay, but also with Gita, Sanjay's wife, Amala his mother, Gautama, Devi and Harsha his three children, and Kirana and Pradeep Kahn, Sanjay's sister and brother-in-law – all of whom lived above the shop.

Sanjay had been curious why she always bought a copy of every newspaper; after she told him she wrote for *The Guardian*, it didn't matter how early in the morning she went down for milk or a box of fags, he'd always scanned the paper and had a ready critique of whatever she'd written, which he made sure she heard, whether she wanted to or not. He treated her as his own personal celebrity, adopting a protective, fatherly air, tut-tutting about her boyfriends, her lax attitude to personal safety, her diet, while, with uncharacteristic largesse, surreptitiously providing her with much-needed credit at the end of each month.

For all his illiberal views and idiomatic English, however, Sanjay's heart was in the right place. Last year he had rescued two nephews from appalling circumstances after their parents, Sanjay's brother Hamid and his wife, were killed in a factory fire in India. Paying for their air fares to Britain, he'd taken them into his already overcrowded home and was bringing them up as though they were his own. Judith had followed the rescue of Nandan, nine, and Sohan, seven, who had mysteriously vanished on the night of the fire, and whom Sanjay had feared dead until, several months later, he heard a rumour that they'd been seized by a Delhi businessman in lieu of debts supposedly owed by the boys' father. For five months Nandan and Sohan had laboured as child slaves, weaving carpets, until their outraged uncle had come to the rescue.

Now attending the local school in Fulham, having to learn English and a completely foreign culture, their lives weren't easy. Judith had always had a soft spot for the two boys, who often helped in the shop. She marvelled at the way they were adapting so quickly.

Judith stepped into the shop and made her way to the refrigerator at the back. Sanjay and Nandan were unpacking newspapers at the counter.

'You all right?' queried Sanjay, as she returned, holding out money for the milk.

'Fine,' she nodded, smiling at Nandan.

'Nothing today?' he tapped a pile of *Herald* newspapers awaiting delivery.

She pulled a face. 'You're getting as bad as my boss.'

'How is that fat bastard?' Sanjay asked with feeling. Once, she had explained to him how the business desk was run, and described Carter's predilection for short skirts and PR puff. Since then, Sanjay hadn't had a good word to say about *The Herald*'s City Editor.

'Never changes,' she told him now. 'More stories. More cleavage. I really don't know what to do.'

The moment she said it, she wished she hadn't; it was an opportunity Sanjay couldn't resist. Puckering up his lips, he assumed an earnest expression, the prelude to a well-intended, but superfluous homily. 'Sometimes the answers we seek', he intoned solemnly, 'are right beneath our very noses.'

'Yeah,' she took her change from Nandan and made her way to the door, 'I'll remember.'

Trudging back up the road to her flat, she couldn't help reflecting – *if only it was that easy.* If only the next exposé was beneath her very nose. For in the unforgiving greyness of the morning, another ten hours in the office looming ahead of her, Judith knew she needed a story, and a big one, if she was going to survive.

3

Merlin de Vere dumped his briefcase and grocery bags in the hallway of his Dorset cottage and walked across the semi-darkness of the sitting room, sweeping aside the full-length curtains before unlocking the sliding glass doors behind them. Then he stepped outside. At eight p.m. on the last Friday in August, the sun was high above the horizon, its slanting rays reflected up from the sea in a shawl of shimmering silver. Built near the edge of a promontory, the cottage was surrounded by the sea; out on the balcony, all you could hear was the wash of the surf against the cliffs below, the cries of seagulls wheeling overhead.

Resting his hands on the balcony rail, Merlin closed his eyes, drew in a deep breath and exhaled slowly. This was something of a ritual for him; a private ceremony each Friday evening after the drive down from London at the end of another manic week in the City. Standing motionless, he would let go of the constant clamour of thoughts demanding his attention. For a few minutes, the sun warm on his face, he would just be.

Dorset was his escape, his safe harbour from life as an analyst with American merchant bank, J. P. Morgan. As much as he thrived on the high-octane charge of the City, the big money and big risks that dominated his every waking moment during the week, he also needed to get away from it. This was the perfect retreat. An hour and a half down the motorway and he was in a different world, a world that comprised all the usual pastoral pleasures – walks, pubs, country serenity – as well as a place where he could indulge in his favourite hobby, yachting.

For the past few months, since they'd started seeing each other, Denise had been coming down for weekends too. She ran her own catering company in the City, her life a frenetic whirl of boardroom breakfasts, lunches and cock-tail canapés; she liked keeping the weekends simple, just as he did. More often than not, she had a function to run on a Friday night, so she'd drive down to join him early on Saturday – as was the case this weekend. Friday nights were usually his own, which suited Merlin just fine. So rarely alone, he relished the solitude of his cottage by the sea.

After a few minutes out on the balcony, leaning on the rail and soaking up the familiar tranquillity of the view, he stepped back inside the cottage. And froze. Two hooded strangers were in the sitting room. The moment when he became aware of them seemed to last a heart-stopping eter-nity. The one closer to him, shorter and stockier in build, was holding a hunting knife with a seven-inch blade directly to his face. The other – taller, further away – was already moving behind him, sealing off the balcony. Directly ahead of him, Merlin took in the open front door through which they'd come, his briefcase and groceries on the hallway floor. His car, a sports Mercedes, was parked a short distance from the front door.

Eventually he breathed in again. 'Just take it.' His voice was hoarse, almost a whisper. 'The key's still in.'

He could feel his heart thumping, blood thundering through his head, his mouth dry with shock.

The man with the knife was glancing about.

What the hell did they want?

'My wallet's in the briefcase,' he managed.

Please God, keep that knife away!

Then the taller of the two men was standing directly in front of him. Merlin could see little behind the mask except the angular lines of his face, the dark glint of his eyes.

'Just do as we say and you'll be fine.' The accent was South London. There was something familiar about the hood. 'Any trouble—' he gestured towards the other man with the knife. 'Do we understand each other?'

Merlin nodded once.

Every moment seemed to spin out for ever as shock passed in giddying waves through his body. Then the taller man was barking orders.

'First you can unpack these.' He gestured towards the hallway floor.

Merlin was uncomprehending. 'Wh-where?'

'Don't fuck with me!' There was instant violence in his voice. 'The fridge! Cupboard! Wherever you put things!'

Merlin stumbled forward in bewilderment, collecting up the bag of groceries and taking them through to the kitchen, to the left of the front door. With the two men standing to either side of him, he placed the bag on the kitchen table and began to take out the items he'd bought that afternoon. There was the food for brunch to go in the fridge: eggs and tomatoes, onion and mushrooms, orange juice. As he put away each item he observed his trembling fingers as though they belonged to someone else. The banality of putting away groceries while two hooded thugs threatened him was surreal. If he hadn't known for certain this was in deadly earnest, he might have wondered if it was some kind of bizarre practical joke. *Why didn't they just grab the car, his money, and go?*

There was bread for toast in the morning; a chicken biryani from Marks & Spencer's he'd bought to microwave for supper; a six-pack of Budweiser; two bottles of wine. He glanced again at the taller man who stood, hands behind his back. *Where had he seen the mask?*

'Don't look at me! Move it!'

When he'd finished putting the fruit in a wooden bowl, the taller man gestured towards the hallway with his chin, 'Where do you keep your briefcase?'

'In the spare room.'

'Do it.'

As the man pointed down the corridor, Merlin noticed his hands were covered in thin, skin-white rubber, the same as the mask. And it clicked into place. It was a clean-room suit – the kind used in laboratories and high-tech factories. Merlin had seen people wearing them on his visits to clients' electronics plants. He'd been told they ensured that not a single trace of the wearer could ever escape: not a hair; not a flake of skin; not a fingerprint. They were DNA-proof.

'Hurry up!' ordered the other, as they made their way down the passage, Merlin's hand damp around the briefcase handle.

In the spare room he'd set up a trestle table with a computer for those weekends when work was unavoidable. Now he placed the briefcase under the desk.

'That's where you usually keep it?'

'Yes.'

'Now strip off and get into your wetsuit.'

Merlin stared at him in disbelief. The shock of it all was quickly changing to adrenalin-powered fury. *These guys weren't small-time burglars. But who in Christ's name were they? And how did they know he had a wetsuit?*

'What the hell is going on?' The words came out in a screech.

Suddenly the two men were each side of him, pinning him to the wall.

'Just do what we tell you,' the taller man menaced, face pressed close to Merlin's, breath stale with beer and cigarette smoke, 'or I promise, I'll fucking kill you.'

Merlin began taking his clothes off, dumping them in a pile in the middle of the room. Heart pounding in his chest, he wondered how he could get away from them. *Who were these people?* His mind raced as he recalled the threatening telephone calls he'd taken on his mobile phone. *'Be very careful,'* anonymous, well-bred voices had told him, *'you're playing with fire'*. As an analyst he was used to anger and threats. He'd had sinister calls in the past. On the basis of his advice, major companies could fall out of the sky. The preferred means of persuading him to reconsider his view usually involved lunch with the Chairman in some smart, West End restaurant. But physical intimidation? How Neanderthal could you get?

Now he'd stripped down to his jocks and made a move towards the back of the door from which his wetsuit was hung. He'd had one idea to get out of this. It was a long shot – but the only shot he had.

'Off.'

'But I don't ever—'

'Off!'

Removing his final layer, he was filled with furious indignation. He reached towards the wetsuit. Would this work, he wondered? Work or not, he had to try. Instead of taking the wetsuit off its hook, he seized a golf club from the bag which hung behind it on the back of the door. It was a five-iron and he swung it with all the wild force he could muster, so that it curved through the room, smashing the knife from the hand of the shorter thug and sending the taller one diving for cover.

Then he ran. Out of the door. Down the corridor. Into the hallway and towards the car. If he could get to the car and lock himself in before they caught up . . . But maybe they'd taken the key out of the ignition. They probably had. He'd better set off across the clifftops and hope he could outrun or outsmart them.

It was a moment's indecision, but it cost him his escape.

The shorter man had already grabbed him by the shoulder. 'I'll fucking smash you! I'll fucking smash you!' he kept repeating in a hysterical scream.

Then the taller one had caught up on the other side and seized him round the chest. 'Len – leave off!'

The three of them halted, panting, in the driveway.

'He needs his fucking head kicked in.'

'Leave off. Just get him back inside.'

They'd turned and were heading back towards the front door.

'I tell you, he needs—'

'Len!' The tall man cut him short. 'We can't have any marks.'

In that moment, the truth became suddenly and terrifyingly clear to Merlin de Vere. They'd made him pack away the groceries so everything looked normal. The clean-room suits meant there wouldn't be a single trace of their presence left behind. Now, 'We can't have any marks.' It all added up to the same thing. He knew, now, they were going to kill him. Tomorrow morning, when Denise arrived, she'd find him dead – and it would look like an accident. Just what kind of accident, he couldn't possibly have imagined.

Chris waved his new staff card at the peak-capped gauleiters behind the marble security desk, and strode into reception. It was six weeks after his first meeting with Mike Cullen and five minutes to eight on Monday, September 1 – his first morning at Lombard. Eight was the time Mike had told him to be there, in a tone that implied a gentle start to the day. When they had discussed working hours in detail, Mike had said he really didn't mind when Chris came and went so long as he got the work done. But, he repeated, Chris could expect seventy-hour weeks when things were busy. And Chris assumed, correctly as it turned out, that things were busy all of the time.

Chris didn't have a problem with long hours or early starts. He'd got into the habit of arriving at MIRA early to put in 'quality time' before colleagues started arriving and the phones went mad. But as he discovered now, by eight o'clock Lombard was already in full swing, with clients in reception, couriers rushing out deliveries, the switchboard lit up like a Christmas tree. To be first in at Lombard he'd have to show up a lot earlier. Quite how early, he had yet to find out.

Moments after he reported to reception, the lift doors slid open, and out stepped a tall, svelte brunette who walked directly towards him. Arm outstretched, with a certain formality she introduced herself to him as Charlotte Oxted, and told him she was to be his secretary. Chris smiled, but not too broadly, as he followed her back to the lift, thinking how she was, every inch of her, what he expected a Lombard woman to be like. Dark, shoulder-length hair framed her flawless features and she possessed the manner of a polished professional even though Chris estimated her age to be about twenty-five. Encased in a sculpted black suit and richly coloured scarf which set off her dark colouring to perfection, it wasn't only her looks, Chris realised, which set her apart, it was also her manner. There was a certainty about her, an absence of self-doubt, almost as tangible as her beauty. It was an impression instilled by good breeding and elegance, and the Lombard agency ethos of simply being the best. It was an impression that was initially daunting but which, if Chris's past experience was anything to go by, was only part of a more complex and immeasurably more interesting whole. For the moment, however, impressions were all, and so he played his polite best. Making small talk on the way up in the lift, he quickly established that Charlotte had obtained a degree in classical history and lived, appropriately, just off Sloane Square. He'd also established that she arrived at work at seven-thirty every morning, 'in time for the stock market opening'.

He'd known his office was to be on the fourth floor, but hadn't been aware of the significance of this until they arrived. 'This is the executive floor,' she told him in a smoky voice.

As they stepped out of the lift, Chris couldn't fail to be impressed by the wide, deep-pile carpeted corridors, the wood-panelled walls bedecked with tapestries, and the softly lit semi-darkness which lent the floor an air of hallowed reverence.

'On the other side of the lifts', she said, gesturing, 'are the client meeting rooms. If you want to use one, I'll need to book it for you.'

'I see. And whose offices are along here?'

'Human Resources. Finance. Mike has his suite at the end.'

Chris noted the way she purred the name 'Mike' – boldly familiar, but with a certain respectful distance, too.

'What about Kate Taylor?' he asked. Apart from running Lombard's mighty financial PR department, Kate was to be his 'Personal Manager' while he found his feet.

'Second floor, with the client servicing teams,' Charlotte told him. 'The fourth floor is for directors with an agency-wide remit.'

She paused by a door long enough for him to note its brass plaque announcing: 'Chris Treiger, Director of Research and Strategic Planning' before opening it and showing him in.

Chris couldn't help being astonished; never, in his wildest dreams, had he imagined he was to occupy such an imposing office. It was huge, and had an imperial grandeur about it that was guaranteed to overawe. The far end was dominated by a massive mahogany desk, while to his right was a meeting area – where a Chesterfield and two armchairs were arranged about a polished coffee table. Behind them, discreetly in the corner, a television screen blinked the current share prices of Lombard clients. An Egyptian marble fireplace dominated the centre of the wood-panelled room which was hung with gilt-framed oil paintings of seascapes. Behind the desk a window looked out across the City, the dome of St Paul's visible on the horizon.

Judging it would be a mistake to react too effusively, all he said was, 'Very nice.'

Leading him through the soft-lit shadows of his office, Charlotte pointed out two boxes of business cards bearing his name which awaited him, and showed him how, at the press of a button, a computer screen appeared from the desk top, its keyboard accessed by flipping back a wooden panel.

'You use Windows?' she queried.

He nodded.

'You have your own laser printer under here,' she opened a cabinet running along the wall beside the desk to reveal an array of technology, 'along with your mobile telephone and charger. Numbers are as marked.'

Chris put his briefcase down.

'We've registered you an e-mail address. You'll find all the details printed on your business cards. You had about a dozen e-mails in your in-tray when I checked half an hour ago.'

'Right.'

'We operate a clear-desk policy throughout the agency. Because of the sensitivity of the documents we handle, they must all be locked away when you leave the office in the evening. Your filing cabinet', she opened a cupboard to reveal four drawers of hanging files, 'is locked when you turn this key. Level One security. I also have a safe in my office for any reports that are Level Two security.'

'Fine.'

'Level Three security only operates on the third floor. You'll find an explanation of it all in the Corporate Identity

manual, which I suggest you read.' She tapped a laminated
file in his cabinet with a perfectly manicured nail.

'Suggest' Chris took to be an order, rather than a recommendation. 'OK.'

Charlotte caught him glancing about the room. 'The pictures are all movable. We have a roaming art collection – as
you probably know, Mike Cullen collects young artists.'

'I didn't.'

'Quite an aficionado. He also supports a few art chari-
ties. But if there's anything you'd like changed, just tell me
and I'll arrange a showing of some alternatives.'

Chris nodded.

'I've left out this morning's press cuttings of all your
clients.' She gestured towards a neat pile of folders on the
corner of the desk. Then, glancing at her watch, she noted
briskly, 'Your agency tour with Kate starts at nine. That
gives you forty minutes to get settled. If you'd like a coffee,
there's a percolater in my office.' She gestured towards a
door to the right of his desk. 'Do help yourself at any time.'

'Thank you.'

As she made her way out she paused for a moment at a
cupboard by the door. 'Oh. There's one last thing.' She
opened the cupboard to reveal a top-of-the-range Starwear
tracksuit, Starwear trainers and a Starwear peaked cap, all
assembled in pristine condition. 'Starwear joining kit. If
they don't fit I'll order replacements.'

Chris allowed himself a droll smile. 'Very generous of
them.'

'Everyone in the agency gets a set,' Charlotte told him.
Then, returning his amused expression, 'You're on the team
now.'

*

He watched her as she left the room, once again pondering on her intimidating mix of sexual appeal and ruthless efficiency. She was, no doubt, the kind of girl who could be relied upon to juggle a dozen urgent projects while taking dictation, printing out financial statements and answering the phone. A top-drawer PA who couldn't be more different from his former assistant at MIRA with her haphazard secretarial skills.

In every respect, in fact, Lombard couldn't be more different from MIRA, and as Chris sat for the first time in his large, black-leather, swivel desk-chair and glanced about his new office, he couldn't help contrasting it with the one he'd left behind the week before. MIRA's offices had been mostly open-plan – a nightmare for concentration – and even though he'd been given his own box in the corner, the partition walls were so thin they might as well not have existed. All the office furniture had been at least a decade old; scratched wooden desks supported ancient computers, grimy with the wear of many years, their wires dangling in untidy coils behind every desk. The strip lighting and wall posters now seemed even more shoddy and downmarket compared with the ambiance of rarefied sophistication that prevailed at Lombard.

But the overwhelming impression at MIRA had been that of paper; everywhere you looked there had been computer print-outs, research reports, lever-arch files and assorted stationery. From floor to ceiling, shelf after shelf had heaved with research documentation. Detailed scrutiny of his new office, however, revealed not a single clue to indicate what kind of activity occurred here. No doubt, it was all part of Lombard's greatly valued secrecy. Was it the same with every other office in Lombard, he wondered, or only the executive floor? And what was with all these security levels?

He reached over for the client folders Charlotte had looked out for him, flicking through a list of blue-chip names until he came to the folder marked Starwear. Removing it from the others, he recalled his last conversation with Mike Cullen. It had been shortly before nine, the morning after his evening at HMS *Queen Mary*. He'd still been in bed.

'I thought I should be in touch with you in light of last night's developments.' Cullen was calm and clear.

Chris had again felt the stunned disbelief he'd experienced when he'd watched the news broadcast about Nathan Strauss's death.

'It's come as a deep shock to us all. Nathan wasn't only one of our most valued clients, I also counted him as a close friend.'

'Have the police said anything more?'

'No. And until the inquest is held, there's not a lot to say about it. But life goes on and we've had to make contingency plans.' Cullen's voice was serious. 'Obviously, everything I'm telling you is confidential. There'll be an emergency Starwear Board meeting tomorrow afternoon, the earliest the various members can fly in from different parts of the world. I've been in touch with every director and it seems certain that Nathan's brother Jacob will step into the breach. We need to reassure shareholders on both sides of the Atlantic by the time trading starts on Monday that there'll be continuity.'

'Jacob?' Chris thought a moment. 'Do people over here know much about him?'

'Not right now,' replied Cullen. 'It's something we'll work on.'

After a pause Cullen had got to the real point of his phone call. 'Look, I know how much you wanted to work with Nathan. And I wouldn't try to pretend to you that Jacob is another Nathan Strauss. But you're still an important part of our plan – a very important part. If anything, we'll be needing you even more. Nathan was a thinker. Jay is an action man. He'll need you around to do a lot of thinking for him, and so will I – I want you to know that.'

'Thanks.' Chris was rubbing his eyes. 'I must admit, I'm not sure what to think.'

There was a moment before Cullen said sympathetically, 'We're all a bit like that at the moment. But we have to keep going, taking the vision forward – it's what Nathan would have wanted. And, you know, Jacob is very keen to take Nathan's plans further; in some ways he's even more radical. I'll be introducing you to him at an early stage.'

Once again, Cullen's inherent assumption didn't pass Chris by, the PR man evidently looking for confirmation that Chris was still joining Lombard in spite of what had happened. Chris had been mulling over exactly that until the early hours of the morning, and he'd always come back to the same thing; he couldn't go back to MIRA. Now, after a long pause he murmured, 'I look forward to it.'

'Good. You'll like Jacob. He's a real champ.'

It had been flattering to be called by Cullen personally. At home. And so soon after what had happened. Their conversation had left him feeling reassured, but also daunted. When Cullen had told him at their first meeting how important his job would be to Lombard, he'd assumed it was all part of the usual 'talking up' interview game to get him interested. Of course, Chris knew it was a big job, but he hadn't guessed that his taking it was of such personal importance to Cullen. After that Saturday morning telephone call it was clear he was part of a much bigger game plan. And for the first time he found himself hoping that he'd be able to deliver whatever it was that was of such significance.

That same feeling returned now as he found himself behind his desk on the executive floor of Lombard, panoplied in mahogany and leather. 'From those to whom much is given, much will be expected.' The words returned unbidden from his childhood. So what was Cullen expecting? What did he have that was so important to Lombard that it merited an office two doors away from the Chairman?

Chris opened the 'Starwear' file. It contained press releases and newspaper coverage from the fortnight since Nathan's death. The first release announced the appointment of Jacob Strauss as Chief Executive Officer. It noted that ever since Stefan Gregory Strauss had set up the textile business, first in Germany in 1927, then, after the family fled Nazi Germany, in America exactly ten years later, a Strauss family member had headed the company; Jacob's appointment was in keeping with this tradition. Along with the press release, Chris found some biographical notes on Jacob Strauss, for the benefit of British journalists who had had no contact with him before.

Like his older brother, Jacob, forty-seven, was a Harvard graduate. But while Nathan had distinguished himself academically, the centre of Jay's world had always been the sports field. An enthusiastic all-rounder, he had not only represented his university at distance running and gymnastics, he'd also been selected for the Harvard tennis team in his final year. On leaving university he hadn't joined the family firm, which in those days had yet to break into sportswear. Instead, he'd worked for a variety of sports-related businesses and tournament organisers, before setting up two businesses of his own eight years ago. Reflecting his personal interests, Ultra-Sports retailed up-market sports equipment through four outlets in Manhattan, Miami, Palm Springs and Beverly Hills. The other business, Trimnasium Inc., manufactured home gym equipment designed for busy executives who didn't always have time to go elsewhere for a workout.

His entrepreneurial genius, said the 'Notes to Editors', was widely recognised, and three years earlier he had been invited on to the board of Starwear to head its subsidiary, Starwear International, which manufactured sports garments throughout the world. Divesting himself of Ultra-Sports and Trimnasium Inc., he had focused all his energies on the leisurewear factories based in developing countries. After a year of intensive travel to India, Pakistan, Thailand, Taiwan and Singapore, he'd unveiled his 'Quantum Change' programme, which had dramatically increased outputs of targeted factories through improved efficiencies. The result of Quantum Change was now widely known: from being Starwear's biggest liability, Starwear International had become the company's most profitable operating subsidiary, outstripping even its home operation, Starwear America, as well as the other main subsidiary, Starwear Europe.

Jacob's impeccable credentials made him the clear successor to Nathan. Looking now at the press photograph of him, which had appeared frequently in the media over the past few weeks, Chris couldn't help thinking, not for the first time, how very different he looked from Nathan.

Instead of his brother's ascetic angularity, Jacob, pictured in a tracksuit jogging through Central Park, had open, engaging features. While Nathan's height had had a sparseness to it, Jacob was broad-shouldered and solidly built. But it was their eyes which revealed most; behind their spectacles, there was a certain shy distance to Nathan's. Unencumbered by any lenses, Jacob's were bright, perspicacious, confident. Chris didn't doubt for a moment that Jacob Strauss would prove to be a PR dream.

Turning to another press release, he read the announcement that Starwear would not be moving its global headquarters from London. As a company with dual listings on both the New York and London stock exchanges, and operations which extended around the world, Starwear had mushroomed far beyond its original, modest roots in West Virginia. By far the majority of its production was now in south-east Asia, and while textiles sales for America and Europe were about even, the opening up of Eastern European markets meant that future growth prospects were more likely on the European side of the pond.

Looking at the press coverage, most of it had, of course, focused on the tragedy of Nathan's death and the compelling mystery which still surrounded it. There had also been a lot of company news – the share price fall of eighteen per cent immediately after trading opened the Monday following Nathan's death, then the announcement that Starwear strategy remained unchanged, pushing shares back up again by nine per cent. The announcement of Jacob's appointment as CEO had been subject to little analysis so far, although news of his Quantum Change programme was widely and positively reported. The only negative commentary had been a piece in *The Daily*

Telegraph, written by senior correspondent Jim Ritchie, which attributed the Quantum Change success to McKinsey, and which questioned the relevance to Jacob's new position of his prior businesses selling sports gear and gym machines.

At nine sharp, there was a knock on his door and Chris looked up to see Kate Taylor. He'd met Kate on his second visit to the agency for drinks in the Boardroom and had taken to her immediately. Bright-eyed, dark-haired and the quintessential English rose, there was a vivacity about her – and yet a fragility too – which he had found instantly engaging. And, as the director in charge of financial PR at Lombard, she was also extremely shrewd. When she'd told him she was to be Chris's 'Personal Manager', a role which required her to be his mentor while he found his feet at the agency, he'd been delighted.

'Ready for your grand tour?' she asked him now with a smile.

'Of course.' Getting up he made his way over to her.

'Executive quarters suit you?'

Gesturing at his office, he grinned. 'Great office. But why me?'

'Oh, Mike probably just wants to keep an eye on you.' Although she made light of it, it was a thought that had already occurred to Chris and made him feel uneasy.

'We'll start at the beginning,' she said as they made their way to the lift. 'First floor. Ground floor only has Reception and Security.'

They hadn't spoken since Nathan's death, and on the way down Chris said, 'I remember you saying you worked very closely with Nathan.'

'It's been very sad,' she met his eyes, 'not to mention a

hard slog trying to reassure the market that Starwear is still a good buy.'

'You've started working with Jacob?'

She pulled a face. 'Trying. Only, I haven't even met him yet. Mike recruited a new account director called Elliott North from New York to make Jay feel at home. But Elliott's in protective mode at the moment and it's hard to get anywhere near Jacob.'

'Quick hire?'

'Didn't go through the usual channels. You see, Elliott's worked for Jay Strauss for years in America. He's often come over here to advise on Starwear International business. He has, what can I say, a very different style of operating.'

The lift doors opened and Chris was hit by the tidal wave of noise rolling down a lengthy, open-plan office. Windows ran along the right-hand side of the building, offices down the left, and the area in between was a vast runway of frenetic activity at clustered desks, with Lombard consultants calling out to each other and talking excitedly into telephones, hurrying towards screeching fax machines with papers flying in their hands. Press releases were being hastily composed at computer terminals, while other consultants were vigorously debating tactics around the coffee percolator.

Noticing his surprised expression, Kate told Chris, 'It's called the Pit. It's where the foot soldiers work.'

Chris couldn't help contrasting it with the silent sanctitude of the fourth floor.

'It's not always quite as noisy as this. But we've an *Evening Standard* deadline in forty-five minutes and there's all the morning announcements to get through.'

As they began walking past the desks Chris asked, 'How is it all arranged?'

'Account handling teams. Each group', she gestured towards a cluster of desks, 'looks after an average of eight or nine clients.'

'And what do they do for them?'

'This floor is all financial and corporate PR. We get the best possible coverage of our clients' financial results in the press and also try to persuade analysts to write up favourable reports. Analyst reports are critical, because they're the basis on which most of the shares traded in London are bought or sold.'

They sidestepped a group of secretaries bitching over the water dispenser.

'Things round here get especially hectic in March and September,' Kate continued. 'That's when most of our clients report their interim and annual results.'

Chris nodded. 'I heard a story about some guy who didn't go home for a week,' he told her in a tone of disbelief.

'That was Andy.' She pointed out a tall, darkly handsome man who had a beard shadow and drawn face even though it was just after nine. 'Actually, he had a sleepover last night.'

Chris absorbed this information without comment. Even his friends who worked in merchant banks seemed able to return to their homes at night – even if it was sometimes in the early hours of the morning. He didn't think he'd ever come across such incredibly long hours in his life.

As though picking up on his concern, Kate said, 'It's only really during corporate takeover battles when that kind of thing happens. You have to concentrate huge amounts of time in war meetings and analyst briefings and putting together bid and defence documents.'

Chris nodded.

'It's usually a very bonding experience – you really get to see your clients' true colours. I really got to know Nathan during the Strauss bid for Royalmaine. He often used to camp in the flat upstairs.'

'Didn't know there was one.'

'Penthouse floor, above the Boardroom. Access to it is jealously guarded.'

'Who lives there most of the time?'

'That's very much at the Chairman's discretion.' She delivered a significant glance.

Walking past a consultant who was on the phone to a journalist, Chris overheard him say, 'We don't want that story about our client to appear—' and then moments later '—but I *do* have an alternative. There are some very interesting developments going on over at Southside which you ought to know about. I can fax something over to you – nobody else has seen it yet.'

Turning to Kate, Chris wanted to know about that other, much-circulated story about Lombard. 'I've heard stories about Lombard telling potential clients that you control the media?'

This time, he really did expect her to dismiss this much-vaunted piece of Lombard mythology. So he was all the more astonished when, leading him into what was evidently her office, she closed the door behind them and told him, looking him straight in the eye, 'We do control the media. That's what our clients pay us for.'

He didn't try to mask his surprise, 'But . . . I mean, how can you tell a reporter what to run?'

She gestured towards a chair as she unpinned a sheaf of papers from her noticeboard and handed it over to him. 'That's how.'

'Client list?'

She nodded.

He read down the list of names – a roll-call of Britain's biggest and most powerful industries, the sort of companies that were always in the news.

'If a reporter pisses us off, he'll never hear from us again. He'll never get a single piece of information on any of those companies.'

'But surely he can call them direct?'

She shook her head. 'We're the gatekeepers. It's in our terms and conditions when we sign up a new client. If we represent a company, it has to be on the basis that all media calls are referred to us.'

'What about the quotes you read in the paper, you know, the Managing Director of some company talking about an issue—'

'We write all client quotes according to a predetermined strategy. Of course, we arrange interviews from time to time, but those are carefully scripted.'

'I'm sure journalists love you.'

She grinned. 'But, hey, they need us! Look at all the holes there'd be if we weren't in business.'

She opened up the business section of *The Herald*. Highlighter had been liberally applied to articles throughout the section. 'Those are Lombard stories,' she told him.

'That's amazing . . . over thirty per cent of the business section.'

She nodded. 'We could do the same for any other quality newspaper.' She looked at him significantly, eyes narrowing. 'We *are* the best PR agency in Britain.'

Later, they went up to the second floor, the home of Lombard's consumer division, which was a similar maelstrom of activity. There was a very different buzz up here, more raucous and exuberant, with consultants in trendy clothes, music playing from the design studio at the far end, and TV monitors tuned to half a dozen different stations. Marilyn Rhodes was the larger-than-life Director in charge and Chris met her briefly. She was tall, shoulderpadded, with big, blonde hair, and her striking, Amazonian good looks were clearly matched by a streetwise cunning.

'We're in the business of fad creation. We invent trends – trends to sell our clients' products, whether it's toys or tampons, vodka or video games.' It was evidently a well-rehearsed line.

'How do you get the media to take an interest in Starwear?' asked Chris. 'You couldn't really threaten never to send them another press release on tracksuits ever again.'

Marilyn had drawn herself up to her full six feet and two inches, and regarded him sternly. 'Well, they just don't get access to the celebrities who endorse our clients' garments. They don't get to interview the likes of Leonardo. Ever. Or meet Evander Holyfield or Tiger Woods. Or go to a party with Cindy. Or a dozen other razzle-dazzle names you could think of. Our clients pay celebrities very large amounts of money to endorse their products. It's true the average hack doesn't give a shit about the products, but he'd let you shove a red hot poker up his bum for the chance of an "exclusive" celebrity interview lasting five minutes.'

Kate was listening with an ironic smile. 'Marilyn is the

only PR person I know who dictates front-page headlines down the phone to journalists.'

'Starwear is a consumer PR's dream,' Marilyn enthused now. 'The logo is simple – and *everywhere*. The name of the brand lends itself to endorsement by celebrities of all kinds – sports, entertainment, you name it. And because it's famous as an American brand, there's the tie-in with the Stars and Stripes. Owning a pair of Starwear trainers is very aspirational if you're a teenager in some south-east Asia slum.'

Just then, Marilyn's secretary appeared with a large, black board on which press cuttings were mounted. 'You wanted this urgently.'

Marilyn glanced briefly at the board. 'Too much black space,' she said. 'Take them all off, blow them up by twenty per cent, then remount them.'

Chris couldn't help chuckling at the audacity of it.

Marilyn met his expression with a vulpine look. 'Little trick to boost the column-inch ratings.'

Lombard's political lobbyists were based on the third floor and the mood here was different again – one of *sotto voce* conversations, knowing humour, and lashings of eau de Cologne. Several of the consultants, mostly male, had a decidedly effete air about them – Chris couldn't help wondering if all the stories he'd heard about Westminster's gay mafia were true. Nicholas King, who headed up the division, had the air about him of a benevolent headmaster to whom absolutely nothing would come as a surprise.

He asked Chris which clients he would be working on, and when Chris mentioned Starwear he nodded approvingly. 'Nathan was very good at public affairs,' he murmured, 'very discreet. Never bragged about his victories, which is why Whitehall always listened to him.'

There was a pause before he went on to murmur, 'We're going to have to educate his younger brother. They do things differently in the States, you know. Spend their lives buttonholing Congressmen.'

'You mean you never use the old cash-for-questions gambit?'

'Good heavens, no!' King regarded him indulgently. 'By the time legislation comes up in the House of Commons, you've missed the boat. We get in a lot earlier, when civil servants are still drafting bills. Those men from the Ministry are surprisingly amenable to a good argument over a good lunch.'

Also on the third floor was the Lombard library – like everything else in the agency, bigger, better and more comprehensive than anything Chris could have imagined. Library shelves were packed with so many books, reports and reference works that it looked better resourced than any business reference library.

'You'll find back issues of all the national press on CD-Rom or microfilm,' Kate pointed in the direction of one set of shelves, 'and of course if you ever want Reuter cuts or Mintel reports or any of that kind of stuff, this is the place to come.'

Chris shook his head. 'Setting this place up and maintaining it must cost Lombard a bomb. Do any other PR agencies have—'

'No chance.' Kate shook her head. 'We can afford it, just like we afford everything else we do that's different, because the hourly charge-out rates for Lombard consultants are double the industry average.'

'And your clients?'

'Pay happily, because we give them something that no other PR agency in this town can.'

'Media control?'

'You've got it.'

Behind the library, occupying a space even larger than the lobbying unit, were banks of computer operators working behind terminals.

'Are they part of the lobbying group?' he asked.

Kate glanced through the solid, tinted-glass wall that divided them from the library. 'They're part of every group in the agency. They keep close tabs on everything that's happening in every British newsroom, and quickly tell us if there's anything going on we should know about. They might look just like a bunch of hackers, but they're really our "X Factor" – they give us the edge over all our competitors.'

'Must be pretty well connected?'

'Exactly.' She met his eyes meaningfully. 'And strictly off limits to the rest of us.'

Chris recalled what Charlotte had mentioned. 'Level Three security,' he murmured, 'access authorised only by Mike Cullen personally. Read it in the Corporate ID manual earlier.'

'You *have* been conscientious,' Kate smiled.

Turning to make their way back to the lifts, Chris asked, 'So what are they called, these X Factor people?'

'Monitoring Services,' Kate replied. Then, as a figure approached them from a distance, 'And here is Mr Monitoring Services himself.'

He was much older than most Lombard employees, fifties maybe, shortish in build, his pear-shaped body clad in tweeds. His complexion was sallow, with dark liver blemishes. Not only did he look a lot different from anyone else Chris had met at the agency, he also had a very different manner, seeming hesitant, even reluctant as Kate gestured towards him now. 'Come, meet our newest recruit – Chris Treiger, Research and Planning Director. Chris, this is the Head of Monitoring Services, Bruno d'Andrea.'

Chris reached out to shake his hand, noting how d'Andrea's eyes met his for only a split instant before he was glancing away again. They were large and heavy-lidded, so that even in that flash of contact they seemed bizarrely omniscient.

'Pleased to meet you,' said Chris.

'Likewise.' D'Andrea abruptly dropped his hand. Then he was making his way towards the Monitoring Services door, searching in his pocket for a key card.

As Kate and Chris made off, she whispered under her breath, 'Bit of a cold fish, but an incredible operator.'

'Been here long?'

'Almost since the beginning,' she met his look of enquiry. 'If anyone knows where all the bones are buried, it's Bruno d'Andrea.'

Chris smiled quietly to himself. He was always amused by the metaphors people used to make their colleagues – and their jobs – sound somehow more darkly glamorous than they really were.

Just after ten-twenty that night, Elliott North swiped his card through the electronic security lock to Monitoring Services. He strode swiftly past the rows and rows of computer stations, now in near total darkness, towards the only source of light on the floor – the desk lamp shining in Bruno d'Andrea's office.

Dark-haired, moustachioed, his steel-framed spectacles flashing in the shadows, North had received d'Andrea's message on his pager less than half an hour earlier: '*Guardian* has the story'. Only four words, but all that was needed for him to excuse himself from the dinner he was co-hosting for a visiting Italian client with another Lombard director at Le Palais du Jardin. Climbing in a Lombard Jag, he'd ordered the driver back to the office with all haste.

Now, before he'd even reached d'Andrea's office he demanded, 'What have they got?'

'Everything.' D'Andrea looked up from behind his desk as North appeared in the doorway.

'Shit!'

He regarded North impassively, his heavy-lidded eyes seeming even larger in the darkness.

'How's it looking?' demanded North.

D'Andrea didn't bother answering. Instead he pushed an early edition of the next day's front page across the desk.

North scanned the main headline: *City high-flier in kinky sex death.* 'Christ Almighty!' he sat down opposite d'Andrea, rapidly digesting the contents of the article. The body of Merlin de Vere, a £400,000-a-year analyst with merchant bank J. P. Morgan had been found at his Dorset cottage, it reported, after what appeared to be a kinky, auto-erotic experiment which had gone wrong. Dressed in a black, rubber wetsuit covering both body and head, and legs bound together with a pair of his girlfriend's stockings, de Vere had been discovered with his head in a dustbin of two-week-old, rotting rubbish. He'd died of asphyxiation. Police had found substantial quantities of sado-masochistic pornography both at his Dorset cottage and downloaded on the computer in his London flat.

The article went on to report how de Vere's body had been discovered by his girlfriend, a City caterer, when she arrived at his cottage to spend the weekend with him. Currently being treated for shock, his girlfriend had said nothing except that she was simply unable to believe her boyfriend capable of the state in which she'd found him.

There was a paragraph on how de Vere was described by colleagues. 'A loner,' said one, 'never a man to follow the herd. Constantly challenging convention, which is a very useful quality for an analyst to have.' 'Something of a recluse,' said another, 'rarely joined his colleagues for a drink at the end of the day, and couldn't wait to escape town at the end of the week.' The outlines of a portrait began to emerge – de Vere as the compulsive oddball, the social misfit – perhaps, the implication seemed to be, the manner of his death wasn't so surprising after all?

The article ended with a line-up of high-flying achievers who'd died in similarly sordid circumstances, including the late Conservative MP Stephen Milligan, who had been found under his kitchen table, asphyxiated, in his mouth a segment of orange containing amyl nitrite.

The article was better, a whole lot better, than what North had feared. But it was still early days. Scanning it over once again, he glanced up at d'Andrea who was watching him. 'No mention of the police. What are they up to?'

'The usual. It appears forensics have been in but didn't find anything,' d'Andrea spoke in his customary monotone. 'The coroner's report will be available in due course. It will confirm death by asphyxiation.'

'As long as that's all it confirms.'

North met his gaze. Ever since he'd arrived in London there had been tension between the two men. He put it down to hierarchy. Before he'd got there, d'Andrea had been the undisputed Prince of Darkness at Lombard. Despite his deliberately modest-sounding title, 'Head of Monitoring Services', in reality, d'Andrea was Mr Intelligence, the eyes and ears and, on occasion, invisible hands of the whole operation. Then along had come North, fresh from America, with his own ideas about how to deal with sensitive issues. D'Andrea resented the imposition, but there wasn't much he could do about it; he knew Elliott North had long been Jacob Strauss's confidant, and Jacob Strauss was not, in any circumstances, to be irked.

North ignored d'Andrea's expression of distaste. 'Nice touch, wasn't it,' he bragged, 'downloading stuff on to his home PC?'

D'Andrea said nothing.

'We also made sure we had his fingerprints all over a stash of S&M material in the cottage.'

Then, looking d'Andrea in the eye, 'What had he dug up on Jay?'

'Nothing on his computer at work. At home we found a few files which we downloaded then deleted.'

Reaching down to a drawer, he retrieved an envelope containing computer disks which he handed over to North.

'He'd got a fair way down the road on previous business stuff,' d'Andrea continued.

'Personal life?'

'Hadn't looked.'

'Good,' North slumped back in the chair with relief,

'looks like I've put out the fire . . . on this occasion.'

Across the dark shadow of his office, d'Andrea met North's challenging expression, his mouth forming a bitter smile. 'I can't emphasise strongly enough our extreme reluctance for agency staff to involve themselves in this kind of activity,' he said evenly.

'And I can't emphasise strongly enough the importance of my client to Lombard,' countered North.

'That's never been in dispute. What's in dispute are the tactics employed. What works in America doesn't necessarily do in Britain.'

North pulled an expression of amused disdain. 'Oh, really? Exactly what alternative did we have with de Vere?'

'We could have had him switched from the manufacturing brief at J. P. Morgan,' d'Andrea wearily repeated an evidently much-rehearsed argument.

'And how long would that have taken?'

The other shrugged.

'It's all about timing, and time is something we don't have much of.' North rose, about to leave the office. At the door he turned and asked, 'Tell me about Treiger?'

'What about him?'

'Precisely.' North fixed him with a baleful stare.

After a pause, d'Andrea shrugged. 'Squeaky clean.'

'You told me that a fortnight ago. What have you got on him in the meantime?'

D'Andrea leaned back in his chair. 'Chris Treiger is a hard-working young man with a keen desire to impress you all. He's been telling all his friends he expects to work twelve to fourteen hours a day at Lombard.'

'What about his personal life?'

'We'll make sure he doesn't have time for one of those.'

'He told Cullen he's not in a relationship, but I can't believe he's not balling someone.'

'It happens.' D'Andrea pursed his lips.

'I need to be sure. What level of monitoring have you got him under?'

'Standard.'

'Extend it. Pick up his home phone calls. Have him followed weekends. Get me some dirt – I might just need it.'

'If you tell me where to start digging—'

'Just watch him.' North gestured impatiently. 'Keep close tabs on his every move. If you told me he gets shit-faced with his mates every Friday and has a bit on the side I'd be a lot happier.'

Then, pausing reflectively, he said, 'It's always the quiet ones, you know, that end up causing the most trouble.'

A fortnight into the new job, Chris[...] touched the ground. Every morning[...] and every evening late. Very late. For some[...] function had never existed prior to his arrival,[...] hard to believe the demand for his services. Wh[...] the research and planning around here before?[...] there was any question of him passing up on any p[...] He was still the new boy with everything to prove.

Every morning he'd get out of bed at five forty-five, t[...] a shower, get dressed and be in the office by seven[...] Breakfasts and lunches were snatched affairs on the run; bagels and Danish pastries from the Lombard kitchen, sandwiches from the Prêt à Manger round the corner, all eaten in the brooding semi-darkness of his office while he worked at his computer. Days would end at eight, nine, ten o'clock – on several occasions, way past midnight – six days a week. Sundays he might take some work home with him, or go into the office for a few hours in the afternoon. It didn't matter when he arrived or when he left, however, there was always someone else in before him and someone who'd be staying later. Downstairs in the Lombard basement car park, there was always a handful of Saabs,

4

's feet had scarcely
had been early
one whose job
he'd found it
'd done all
Not that
ojects.
ke

...us of retainers
...e the figures he'd been
...MIRA look like small change.
...n't countenance taking on a client
...han £10k a month, and most were on £20k
what's more, all the contracts were open-ended so
that if Lombard consultants spent more time on an account
than was covered by the monthly retainer, every additional
hour was charged. Charge-out rate denoted status within
the agency; junior consultants were charged out at £100 an
hour, Account Directors at £250, Board Directors at £350
and the ultimate spin-doctor himself, Mike Cullen,
weighed in at a hefty £1,500 an hour – the highest rate
charged by any PR man in the country. Chris's own charge-
out rate was £300, to be reviewed after his probationary
period. On his very first day, Charlotte had, with customary

efficiency, tutored him on the vagaries of electronic time sheet keeping, and had told him that he would be expected to record at least fifty chargeable hours a week. Ten hours a day of billable time seemed an ambitious figure to Chris, but he soon discovered that most consultants clocked up far more than that; sixty and seventy hours a week were common, and hundred-hour weeks were by no means unusual. During results seasons, the consultants in Kate Taylor's Financial PR team frequently worked round the clock, ignoring weekends and handing in time sheets in the hundred and twenties.

Time sheet keeping, as Chris soon learned, wasn't just some administrative chore. It was Lombard's Holy Grail. Consultants were expected to input the hours they worked each week by the Tuesday of the following week. Then every Friday, the total schedule of hours worked was reviewed by Lombard's directors, listed against each of their names. The arrangement wasn't overtly to encourage competition, but in reality the different directors at Lombard were perpetually trying to outdo each other in their bid to clock up more man hours per week, with bigger teams of consultants hiking up higher average charge-out rates. Financial competed with consumer, political was pitched against environmental as each of the Lombard directors vied for a bigger share of the fee income – to which their personal profit share was directly linked.

Pay-out time came twice a year and was always a big event, according to Charlotte. Twice a year, always on a Friday morning, every Lombard director would go up to the fifth floor to listen to the Finance Director report on company results. Total revenue, operating costs and company investments were reviewed. But the real interest was how big a bonus each of the directors was going to collect.

In the past five years, no Lombard director had earned less than a £100k bonus for any six-month period. Often it was way above that figure. Kate Taylor had herself collected £450k after a particularly gruelling but lucrative half year, in which three of her clients had, with Lombard's advice, successfully fought off hostile takeovers. After each of the directors had been told how much money they had made, staff bonuses were decided over a sumptuous lunch prepared by a former royal chef. No expense was ever spared at these celebrations where the freshest of wild Scottish salmon, the most succulent scallops of veal and the most orgastic of pavlovas were all washed down with copious quantities of Louis Latour claret, Californian White Grenache and, of course, the ever-proffered Bollinger.

Then, over the vintage port and cigars, the performance of every member of agency staff was reviewed and a bonus awarded. Billing hours were, of course, at the heart of all this, but other things counted too. If a consultant was cruising at sixty hours a week, but was directly responsible for bringing in a new £300k client, he could expect at least a £30k pat on the back. Conversely, the ninety-hour-a-week Lomboid whose client had been gobbled up in a takeover could expect little but sympathy – and a not-so-subtle hint that it was time to polish his new business shoes. All the time individual bonuses were debated, Mike Cullen's secretary went to and fro, inserting figures into letters that had already been prepared. The process could take two, three, four hours.

And then the gods would descend from the Boardroom, envelopes would be handed out to all staff, and the agency would erupt in an orgy of celebration. And like everything else, when Lombard celebrated, it did it bigger and ballsier than anyone else. Brand new Ferraris, Maseratis and MGs would be summoned from sports car dealerships in the City, to be delivered, in a gleaming line-up, outside Lombard offices that very afternoon. Weekend Concorde trips to New York would be hastily arranged. Property deals would be struck, with seven-figure loft conversions changing hands, sight unseen. Bonus Fridays were one of the few times of the year when clients found their advisers at Lombard unusually difficult to get hold of.

Chris was inputting hours into his time sheet for his first week when Charlotte poked her head round the door.

'Everything OK?' she enquired.

'My first time sheet,' Chris pulled a face.

'Ah. You're in creative mode then?' She stepped into the room and walked to his desk.

Charlotte and he had relaxed into a convivial relation-ship after he'd bought her dinner one night when she'd stayed till nine-thirty. He'd quickly discovered that behind the carefully cultivated image of relentless efficiency and impossible glamour, Charlotte – now Lotte to him – had a decidedly risqué sense of humour. After a fair few glasses of wine, droll observations about colleagues had been exchanged, and personal lives shared. Back in the office next morning, things had changed between them in a subtle, but important way.

'I'm supposed to be creative?' he asked now.

'Once you've been here a couple of weeks I'm sure you'll be billing the most incredible hours,' she grinned.

Chris leaned across his desk, speaking *sotto voce*, 'You mean, double-billing?'

'Double-billing?' She adopted an expression of mock-contempt. 'Think big.'

'I see.' Chris smiled.

'Let me introduce you to the concept of Lombard Time.' She met his eyes with a twinkle. 'You see, there's other PR agencies' time, and then there's Lombard Time. Because people who work at Lombard are cleverer and better connected and more effective than everyone else, we get things done in half the time. But that doesn't mean we only charge them for half our time. We charge them the full whack – that's how we make our money.'

Lombard Time, Chris soon learned, was a tacitly agreed concept throughout the agency. However many hours consultants worked, their time sheets recorded even more. A morning's work drafting press releases translated into a full day on the time keeping sheet. A ten-minute telephone conversation was marked down as an hour.

But along with this discovery, Chris also came to learn just why Lombard clients were prepared to pay so handsomely for the services of their PR agency; media control was what Lombard boldly declared it could provide, and media control was what clients got. Lombard virtually ran the City desks of most national newspapers, feeding them most of their stories which would appear, with all the right nuances, in the next day's papers. Non-business news would be fed through to the domestic news editors, the political or environmental editors, appearing with apparent effortless ease in articles and columnist reviews. Consumer stories would be placed in Sunday supplements, lifestyle magazines and TV programmes. Despite being well versed in the ways of the media before he joined, even Chris was amazed at how much of what passed for 'editorial' comment and reportage was material that had come directly off Lombard desks.

And if there was one thing Lombard was better at than getting good stories into the papers, it was keeping bad stories out. Blood-letting in the boardroom, analyst jitters, sales slumps after new product launches; all these were the stuff of headlines that none of Lombard's clients ever wanted to see – and rarely did with the well-oiled Lombard machine at their disposal. Lombard executives would use the leverage of their massive client list, without compunction, to lean on journalists who were tempted to stray beyond what was deemed desirable. What's more, they always made sure they had at least one tempting tale to offer by way of a replacement, if negative mentions could be avoided altogether.

At the heart of Lombard's frenetic media management was Monitoring Services. From behind the Level Three security barrier on the third floor would flow a steady stream of missives and telephone calls throughout the day to various Lombard staff. 'Alex Carter at *The Herald* is planning a piece on generic drugs for next Monday', a note might read, 'Plug for one of your pharma clients?' Or 'ALERT! Sue Horley at *Guardian* writing damaging piece on Elpane Industries. Urgent call.' Lombard consultants would quickly swing into action, neutralising damage and exploiting whatever opportunities presented themselves.

Chris couldn't but be impressed by the efficiency of the operation and, in particular, by the accuracy of Monitoring Services' notes.

'How on earth do they do it?' he'd asked Kate Taylor, when a briefing meeting had been interrupted by a telephone call from Monitoring, advising one of Kate's staff that his client was about to be roasted by *The Times*.

'That', she'd looked at him pointedly, 'is something none of us is encouraged to investigate too closely. It's their job to get us the edge over everyone else – including the media.'

Intense, money-driven competition was the energy that propelled everyone at Lombard. It was the reason Mike Cullen had picked him to work as Research and Planning Director. And work he did. In two weeks he'd put in more assignments than he had in six at MIRA. There were journalist audits, analyst trackers and corporate image studies. He commissioned focus groups, panel studies and ad hoc quantitative projects.

But of all the projects Chris was working on, he never had any doubt about which was the most important; he'd been briefed on it his very first day, an assignment so secret it was to be referred to only by its code name: Project Silo. Summoned along the corridor, and through an ante-room where Cullen's secretary Rosa and her assistant presided over a flurry of fax machines, photocopiers and word processing, he was shown into the Chairman's office. It was his first visit and he couldn't but be impressed. One floor beneath the Boardroom, Cullen's office was at the end of the building, and the entire end wall was glass, floor to ceiling, providing what must be the most breathtaking view of Tower Bridge of any office in the city. Walking into it was like stepping into a spectacular landscape painting.

He paused for a moment, transfixed where he stood. To his left was Cullen's desk and an arrangement of armchairs. A TV monitor displayed current share prices, the Starwear price prominently displayed. To his right was a huge stretch of rosewood at which Cullen and another man were sitting.

Looking up at him, Cullen smiled. 'It's one of the most expensive views in London.'

'I can believe it.'

'But worth every penny.' Cullen met his eyes. Large, imposing, he conveyed that same winning combination of reassuring *gravitas* and familiarity that Chris had found so compelling the first time they'd met. As Cullen pulled out a chair beside him and gestured that Chris should come across, it was as though they'd been colleagues for a very long time.

'Chris, I'd like you to meet Elliott North.'

The other rose to his feet and shook Chris's hand across the table. He was dark and wiry in build, and Chris noted the curious intensity of his pale, blue eyes which blinked behind a pair of steel-framed glasses. Unusually for a PR man, he sported a neatly trimmed, almost military moustache. Chris remembered what Kate Taylor had said about North's overzealous protectiveness of Jacob Strauss – she had made him out to seem almost obsessive. Not that there was any sign of that now. North was cordiality itself.

'You'll remember the conversation we had about Starwear when we first met,' Cullen started off the proceedings.

'Starwear III. I've actually done some work on it.' Chris tapped a folder of papers he'd brought up with him.

Chris caught North glancing in surprise at Cullen.

Cullen noted the folder, clearly impressed. 'Quite a lot of work, by the look of it.'

Chris acknowledged the compliment with a nod. 'Just some positioning papers and a draft contents outline.'

'Great initiative. I'm sure it'll be useful.' Cullen looked over at North. 'Hasn't been with us a day and he's already drafting major policy statements.'

Across the desk, North chuckled.

'Starwear III still has a high priority,' Cullen continued. 'We'll want to put ideas together in a month, maybe two. But the tragedy has forced us to reassess our priorities. There's a planning project we need to get under way before then which is both important and extremely urgent.'

North was nodding, seriously.

'As we discussed last time,' Cullen went on, 'Starwear has always been at the forefront of defining what constitutes good corporate citizenship. "Doing the right thing is the right thing to do" – all of that. But recently we've been running into problems.' He gestured to Elliott North to continue.

'Some of Starwear's rivals are not playing fair,' announced North.

Chris raised his eyebrows.

'They're taking advantage of the transition time, as Jay finds his feet, and are hell-bent on inflicting maximum damage.'

'What kind of damage?' Chris had opened a briefing pad and was taking notes.

'Mud-slinging. Rumour-mongering. People out there are trying to make out Jay is incompetent, weak – there are some very nasty allegations circulating. And they're using dirty tricks on the marketing side, to seize market share. We're still waiting for details on that from the client. But it all adds up to a pretty worrying situation.'

Chris met his eyes with a look of surprise; mud-slinging and dirty tricks was the last thing he'd expected to be briefed on when he'd been summoned to Cullen's office. North was clearly disturbed by it all. Chris noticed his temples darkening to a deep shade of red.

'Sounds desperate.'

Beside him, Cullen agreed, 'It is.'

'Who's behind it?'

'Bob Reid and Ed Snyder.' North's glasses flashed across the table.

Chris raised his eyebrows. The CEOs of Starwear's two biggest competitors had never struck him as that kind.

'Reid's a desperate man. Profit forecasts are looking sick for Sportex right now. But Snyder's the real worry. Used to be a director of Starwear and still owns substantial Starwear stock. He's a real wild card that one.'

Cullen glanced over at the Starwear share price on his office terminal.

'The point is, these guys are inflicting damage. But we hardly know anything about *their* operations. The only market intelligence we have about Sportex and Active Red is anecdotal. We need to be a lot more systematic.'

'Competitor analysis?' queried Chris.

'Exactly,' both men chimed, before Cullen continued, 'We want you to find out everything there is to know about these companies – shareholders, chains of command, marketing activities. How we can use the Starwear brand to maximum effect.'

'In particular,' added North, 'we want to know a lot more about what Reid and Snyder are up to.'

Chris glanced up, hesitant. 'This goes beyond the usual territory of market analysis.'

They both nodded.

'We could get a certain amount of information through desk research, but we'll probably need to do some other stuff,' he mused. 'Is there a budget on this?'

North shrugged. 'It's open. Tell us what you need.' Then,

fixing Chris with a significant expression, 'Be imaginative in getting the information. Don't leave any stones unturned.'

Chris absorbed this seriously.

'And we'd like the report in four weeks. Mid-October.'

'No problem.'

Cullen pushed his chair back from the table and turned to Chris. 'This is a priority project, Chris. A lot is hanging on it.'

It was clear that he didn't only mean a lot for Starwear; the project would also be the test of him.

'The information we're dealing with here is highly sensitive. We don't want you to mention it to anyone else in the agency besides Charlotte. I suggest we give it the code name Project Silo.'

'Uh-huh.' Chris wrote it down.

'As a general rule,' Cullen met his eyes across the desk, 'you know, of course, there must be no talking shop outside the office. Even the most casual asides are open to misinterpretation. So, it's best to say absolutely nothing. Not about clients, not about colleagues, not about anything that you do.'

There could be no mistaking his gravity.

Chris was nodding with equal seriousness when Rosa appeared. 'Mr Cullen, your five o'clock is in the Boardroom.'

'Thanks.' Cullen got up to leave. 'A copy of the report to each of us, please, in four weeks.'

*

Mike Cullen looked up from his desk as Rosa stepped into his office. Rosa had been with him since Lombard began twelve years before in a single, serviced office suite, and knew more about the agency and its clients than most of the bright young things who worked on the floors below. She also knew Mike Cullen's every mood, and had an intuitive understanding of when to offer advice, and when to hold back; what to say, and how to say it. It was, she often used to think, almost like a professional marriage.

Mike Cullen had certainly changed her life. She'd been at a very low ebb when her husband had walked out on her when she was in her mid-forties, leaving her with two teenage children. A regular churchgoer, she had been introduced by her priest to another member of his congregation, a man who helped provide Sunday School outings for under-privileged kids, and whose handsome, open features she could hardly have missed. Mike Cullen had explained that he was starting a new business and was looking for a secretary. Would she be interested?

Since then, Mr Cullen, as she still insisted on calling him, had rewarded her loyalty, not only in purely financial terms, but also by allowing her to take on an assistant to carry out the more routine secretarial work. He trusted her to look after personal arrangements, as well as Lombard business. And to take care of matters like the one in hand.

'I just wanted to check this with you before sending it to *City News*,' she said, holding out a single sheet of paper. It was headed 'Condolences' and the message was short but poignant: 'Merlin de Vere. One of the City's brightest and best. A respected colleague whose wisdom and friendship will be sadly missed. Sincere condolences to Frances and family. From Mike Cullen and all at Lombard.'

After reading the message, Cullen handed it back to her. 'That's fine.' He spoke quietly. 'You'll circulate it round the agency?'

'Right away.'

He was shaking his head. 'I had lunch with him just a couple of weeks ago. It's a tragedy. A real tragedy. His mind was so . . .' He gestured with his right hand, holding the tips of his fingers and thumb together, '. . . he was right there.'

After a pause, he looked up at Rosa. 'Has there been an announcement about a funeral?'

'Not yet.' She shook her head. 'I expect the inquest . . .'

'Yes.' It would be another week at least before his family was able to bury him. 'When the date's announced, you'll organise things, will you?'

'Kate Taylor and you will be going?' she confirmed.

He nodded. 'And a personal cheque donation to their charity. What do you think – five hundred?'

'That would be more than generous.'

'No word to anyone. Wouldn't want people to get the wrong idea.'

'Of course, Mr Cullen.' She bowed out of his office.

The wrong idea, to which he was referring, was the one that circulated about his personal wealth. Masterful though he was at keeping his clients in the public eye, Rosa had always known that Mr Cullen hated having the spotlight on himself. He avoided all personal publicity and, in particular, had a visceral aversion to being thought of as rich. Which was why all the charitable donations he made – and they were always generous – went unnoticed, except by those who benefited directly from them. Her employer, Rosa often used to think, was the most private of men. Deep down underneath, she believed, he was really quite shy.

5

———

Merlin de Vere had been one of Judith's best sources in the City. Not that he was leaky – though he was less of a closed book than some of his peers. It was more that he'd had his own views which he wasn't afraid to share; views that usually ran contrary to the rest of the market, and that frequently turned out to be right. Forthright and controversial, Merlin de Vere had always made for good copy.

Judith had been calling him for a quote since she started on *The Guardian*, having quickly discovered he was someone she could call at any time of the day or night for his angle. Since those early days, they'd both seen each other through changes in jobs. A symbiotic friendship had grown up between them. Operating in different parts of the same, closed world, there was always plenty of information to exchange – and they had learned to trust each other.

So when the news of his death had come out, a week ago, Judith had been more than simply scandalised. While most others responded to the circumstances of his 'accident' with a voyeuristic shiver, she'd been left feeling bewildered and strangely hurt; she'd never so much as suspected a dark side to Merlin. Had the super-intelligent, witty and cultivated man she'd thought she'd known been leading a double life all along? Because, within hours of the first Reuters report of his death, rumours had been churning through the newsrooms of the City; Merlin de Vere had choked himself to death on methane. He'd been surrounded by hard-core S&M magazines. He'd had his head in a refuse sack of two-week-old garbage, including the rotting carcass of a seagull. He'd shoved a dildo up his ass.

No matter how saddened and curiously betrayed she felt by the news, Judith realised that her feelings were as nothing compared to what Merlin's girlfriend must be going through. After the funeral at St Columbus's, last Friday, she'd greeted Denise Caville outside the church afterwards, but could think of nothing to say. There simply weren't the words to express what she was feeling. Instead, she'd simply given Denise a hug and whispered, 'I'm so sorry.'

Now, as she stood in Denise's Wapping flat that September evening, looking out over the broad, blue-grey sweep of the Thames, she was still wondering why Denise had invited her. She had phoned the day after the funeral saying there was something she wanted to talk to her about – could Judith visit her at home? Judith had been surprised and mystified. Why did Denise, whom she'd never met before the day of the funeral, want to see her? Half a dozen possibilities had been occupying her thoughts ever since that brief conversation, none of which, she was soon to learn, had any relevance. Denise brought over a glass of wine for each of them, and sat opposite her at the large picture window of her sitting room.

'I'm glad you could come so soon,' she began, the dusk skyline reflected in her sunglasses. 'I wanted it to be you because I know Merlin trusted you. With information, as well as other things.'

Judith nodded. There had been many times in the past few years when she'd been privy to news from Merlin that would have made a front-page scoop, but which she hadn't used until he'd given her the say-so. But did Denise suspect she knew something about his sexual other life?

'You see, the full story of his death hasn't been in any of the newspapers.'

Judith raised her eyebrows. 'There've been plenty of tabloid stories.'

'Which are mostly true . . .' Denise bit her lip. 'The stuff about the porn and the dildo and the seagull – it was all there.'

Judith was astonished by her frankness.

'But there were other things which very few people know about,' she continued, 'things which tell a very different story. You see, Merlin didn't die in some bizarre S&M "experiment". He was murdered.'

Judith sat back in her chair, eyes narrowing. 'You've talked to the police?'

She nodded. 'And they've done sweet FA of course. Which is why I wanted to speak to you.' She took a sip of her wine before speaking softly. 'I know you'll be thinking that I'm just looking for some other explanation because the truth is too painful. But it's not like that at all.'

Judith nodded.

'I want to give you the real story, or at least the part of it that I know, because I know you won't twist what I say.'

'Denise, I feel very privileged, really I do. And grateful to you for thinking of me. But the thing is, I'm not a crime reporter. I cover business stories.'

'This is a business story,' Denise assured her. 'Judge for yourself.' She paused for a sip of wine, before beginning, in a slow, clear voice, to tell Judith the story of what she'd found when she'd gone down to Merlin's Dorset cottage the previous Saturday.

It had been almost noon when she had arrived, later for her than on most Saturday mornings because she'd had to go into the office to clear up some invoicing which needed to be done by the end of the month. She had parked her car behind Merlin's, and gone into the cottage. From the moment she'd stepped inside the front door, she'd realised something was different, though it took her a moment to work it out; the clock had stopped. It was a mahogany grandfather clock, and had been in the de Vere family for five generations. Merlin had always been in awe of the fact that, despite its age, its time-keeping was still precise – so long as it was wound up regularly. A creature of habit, Merlin would always wind the clock before attending to any other chores in the cottage. On a summer's evening, Denise told Judith, when he arrived at the cottage, he would usually open the sliding glass doors at the front, spend a few minutes out on the balcony, then return inside to wind up the clock. But when she'd got there the following morning, the clock was stilled into silence.

Calling out for Merlin, and receiving no reply, she had assumed he was outside, or had gone for a walk. Then she'd taken her overnight bag down the passage to their bedroom – and had been hit by the stench coming from the bathroom. It had taken her several minutes to fully take in her discovery. What she found inside the bathroom was like a scene from the sickest pornography imaginable. After pulling back the wetsuit mask to confirm the body inside was Merlin, she'd gone straight to the telephone to call the police.

The police had kept her out of the way while they removed the body and dusted the house for fingerprints. Finding nothing to suggest the death was suspicious, they'd later asked Denise if there was anything outside the bathroom that was out of place. She'd told them about the grandfather clock right away. Then, after she'd gone through the kitchen, she mentioned finding a bottle of red wine in the fridge. Merlin, she said, was a bit of a wine buff, and one of his firmly held principles was that red wine should always be served at room temperature. Not so long ago, after a chilled red wine experience in a pub, and an argument with an irate Australian, he'd told her that people who put red wine in the fridge should be shot. So what was an expensive bottle of claret doing nestling beside the orange juice inside the fridge door?

Notes had duly been taken by a police officer. Then later that day the police had escorted her back to London, making sure she was safely home before they went on, with some Met colleagues, to search Merlin's flat for any signs of unusual activity. They'd found nothing untoward, and their search had included a scan of Merlin's computer records – which was when they'd opened a file containing a huge quantity of explicit S&M video clips. All this they reported to Denise later, although she was still too paralysed by shock to know what to make of it.

'I didn't even try to sleep that Saturday night after Merlin died,' she told Judith now. 'I was so shaken up I couldn't stop thinking about it all, knowing that there was something very, very wrong. Then just before dawn I had this sudden thought, *I must check Merlin's computer against the disks*.

'You see, Merlin had his computer crash on him a couple of years ago, losing everything on the hard drive. Since then he's been paranoid about losing stuff – the problem is, he's pretty hopeless with anything technical. So when he discovered I used to be a computer programmer, we came to this arrangement that every Wednesday evening I'd go home to his place, make back-up copies of everything on his computer, and keep the disks in my private safe, for extra security. So at dawn on Sunday, I went to his flat, booted up the computer and checked my back-up disks against what was on his hard drive.'

Judith followed what she was saying intently.

'The analysis showed two differences. First off, all the porn stuff was new—'

'You mean it was downloaded since—'

'The Wednesday night before he died. Correct.' Denise looked at her significantly. 'I happen to know he had a late-nighter on Thursday, only got home at about one-thirty a.m. And he left for Dorset straight from the office on Friday. So when was he supposed to have got hold of the stuff?'

She shook her head, less bewildered, Judith couldn't help observing, than outraged.

'The other thing was an entire missing directory. It was there on Wednesday night, gone by Sunday morning. Merlin could never bring himself to delete files – he might transfer them to the trash can, but he could never delete a single one of them, let alone an entire directory.'

She regarded Judith carefully. 'I would say those two differences are quite significant.'

'This missing directory—' Judith began.

'That's where I need your help. You see, I don't understand it. There are pages and pages of accounts. I have the feeling Merlin was on to something – something very big, involving a lot of money – and someone very powerful was determined to stop him. I know this must all sound like a huge conspiracy theory, but there are just too many things that don't add up.'

'All the financial information, do you know what company it's about?'

'There are several. They seem to be US-based – nearly all the figures are in dollars. But I noticed one name kept on coming up as a director, something like Jason Strauss.'

'Jacob Strauss?'

'Yes. That was it.' She raised the glass of wine to her lips. 'Who is he?'

Later that evening, Judith sat in her Earl's Court bedroom, working at the dressing table which doubled up as her computer desk. Bottles of cosmetics and miscellaneous beauty accessories had been hastily shoved aside to make space for an ageing and cumbersome IBM, which she used now to scroll through the files that had mysteriously disappeared from Merlin's computer. Somehow, Merlin had got hold of the trading figures of both Ultra-Sports and Trimnasium, the two privately owned companies Jacob Strauss had established years before he joined the board of Starwear. Having annotated the reports, he'd scanned them into his computer. Judith didn't think she'd ever found companies' financial accounts such compulsive reading – especially in light of the highlights and annotations Merlin had made while going through them.

She had never written about the Strauss brothers in the past, at least not in any detail. Like most London-based journalists, of the two brothers she knew quite a lot about Nathan, but nothing of Jacob. When she thought of Starwear the company, as opposed to the brand, she instantly conjured up an image of Nathan, the philanthropist, who had died in such tragic circumstances only a few weeks before. Of course, she knew that Nathan's younger brother was Starwear's golden boy in America, whose good looks and sports accomplishments made him an icon in the US. And she'd followed the news of Jacob's appointment as the global CEO of Starwear after Nathan's death. But that was the full extent of her knowledge.

Now though, moving the cursor down page after page of financial records, she did recall an editorial meeting at *The Herald* about a week ago. Alex Carter, sitting at the head of the table in a fug of cigar smoke, had brought up the subject of Jacob Strauss. Given his imminent arrival in London to head up Starwear, said Carter, *The Herald* should carry a profile on him. It was then he'd made the comment that had stuck in Judith's mind: 'I want something sensitive and supportive,' he'd said. Sensitive and supportive. The phrase was so utterly out of character for Carter that it had firmly stuck in her mind. A hagiography about St Jacob had duly been pieced together from various PR briefings by – surprise, surprise – Alison MacLean. Judith hadn't paid it much attention, but she did recall that Jacob's pre-Starwear career had involved the hugely successful creation of two sports-related businesses – the businesses whose accounts she now found herself scanning.

But the figures set out here told a very different tale from that retailed in Alison MacLean's profile. According to the accounts for Ultra-Sports, a chain of four upmarket sports equipment shops with outlets in Manhattan, Miami, Palm Springs and Beverly Hills, the profits made from all four stores had been almost entirely swallowed up by shrinkage problems in the Manhattan store. Hundreds of thousands of dollars' worth of equipment had, it seemed, simply vanished without being paid for, from Ultra-Sports on Fifth Avenue. Merlin had made a note on the accounts: 'Shrinkage – or theft?' It wouldn't have been the first time that shrinkage had been used as an explanation for the systematic rifling of the tills by a cash-hungry owner, thought Judith. Not that Jacob Strauss had any room for complaint in the income department. Merlin had also highlighted the section in the accounts which showed he'd drawn off a salary of $250,000 – well beyond what Ultra-Sports could support. At the end of the Ultra-Sports accounts, Merlin had summed up what it all meant in just two phrases: 'Cash strapped. Zero capital.' He'd also tapped in the name 'William van Aardt – Partner' and put a large question mark against it. Judith made a note to find out more about Mr van Aardt.

While the Ultra-Sports accounts told a very different tale from the success story Jacob Strauss claimed, the Trimnasium figures were even worse. A different file revealed that Trimnasium had never recouped the huge research and development costs incurred bringing the product to the market. In fact, its total income was barely enough to cover its rapidly rising advertising costs, as an increasingly desperate management tried to boost sales. It seemed that every lifestyle magazine and supplement, not to mention all the major health and fitness media in America, had carried Trimnasium advertisements for an intense period of two years. But the sales just weren't there. Merlin had made some notes of a conversation he'd had with a J. P. Morgan colleague in New York. 'Trimnasium product OK, but $$$', the notes read. 'Other products more functionality and less $$.' Merlin's own summary was equally concise: 'No market intelligence prior to launch. Absence of strategy – product stillborn.'

Far from proving Jacob Strauss's entrepreneurial genius, a phrase Alison MacLean had used in her 'sensitive and supportive' profile, Ultra-Sports and Trimnasium were text-book cases of greed and incompetence. Not that Alison MacLean was the only journalist guilty of swallowing Jacob Strauss's public relations hook, line and sinker. Scanned into another file was US press coverage announcing the sale by Jacob Strauss of both Ultra-Sports and Trimnasium to a privately owned, Panama-based holding company called Sprintco. A photo-opportunity had evidently been set up on the slopes of Aspen, Colorado, showing Jacob, resplendent in that year's skiing apparel, celebrating the company sales with bottles of champagne. Perhaps he *was* an entrepreneurial genius, Judith thought now, persuading anyone to buy the two companies from him. Ultra-Sports's finances were precarious, and Trimnasium was a sinking ship – if due diligence had been carried out by any buyer, how in God's name had Strauss pulled off the deal?

Merlin had circled the name Sprintco and put a large question mark beside it. The unknown identity of the buyer made the deal all the more suspect. The American press, oblivious to the real health of the two companies, had read-ily accepted Strauss's explanation that the buyer, a wealthy individual trading under the name Sprintco, had made it a condition of the sale that his anonymity must be protected.

So no names were mentioned by Strauss, and no figures either, although he hadn't discouraged estimates between $100 million and $150 million for the two companies – figures which, in light of the accounts she had just scrutinised, Judith realised were pure fantasy.

She got up from her dressing table, lit a cigarette and paced about her bedroom, a dozen questions leaping to mind. Questions like: who was the buyer behind Sprintco? Was it just a shell company set up to enable Jacob to make an apparently successful exit from two companies that would otherwise have gone bust? Had Nathan known about the disastrous state of Jacob's business affairs? If he had known, why did he appoint Jacob to such a senior position on the Starwear board?

There was no question that this material was explosive – especially in light of Jacob's recent appointment as CEO of Starwear. Once she'd double-checked Merlin's sources, Judith knew she had an exposé that could potentially out-scoop anything she had ever done before. It was more than just a business story – Denise was right. As Merlin would have known only too well, once the truth about Jacob's early track record was revealed, it would have an instant and catastrophic effect on Starwear's share price. The company would be blasted out of the blue-chip league and into mortal danger, ripe for takeover as long as Jacob remained in the top slot. Jacob's own reputation and career would be in tatters. Criminal enquiries would be opened against him in the States. Having so recently become one of the most powerful players in the global corporate world, Jacob Strauss would face immediate public humiliation and financial ruin.

Realising just how high the stakes were, and how

desperate Jacob Strauss must be, the idea of a fatal accident to conceal the truth didn't seem so incredible. How better to silence the man who threatened to destroy you than by arranging an accident in a remote part of the country? The more outlandish, the better the distraction. Mulling it over apprehensively, Judith became convinced that Denise was right – Merlin had been murdered. She also realised that if she pursued this story she'd be putting herself in serious jeopardy. *But how had they found out that Merlin was on the trail of Jacob Strauss? And what were the chances they'd discover she had picked up on it too?*

As she paced her bedroom, she knew she faced a major decision. The safe option would be to let this story go; to accept that she'd be venturing into deep and treacherous water, which could easily overwhelm her. Not for one minute did she underestimate the danger she'd be putting herself in. Giving up an investigation was something she'd never yet done, something that smacked of defeatism. But was it worth risking her life to find out what lay behind the glossy image of Jacob Strauss?

Dr Ellen Kennedy had been in a state of unusual excitement ever since returning from her September walking tour of the Lake District, two days earlier. For as long as anyone could remember, Dr Kennedy had been a permanent feature of life at St John's College, Oxford. Generations of students had come to share a fondness, not to mention a high regard, for their college's most eminent economist. Though her bright eyes, apple cheeks and grey hair drawn back in a neat bun gave her the look of everyone's favourite grandma, students soon learned never to underestimate her rapier-sharp intellect or widely broadcast intolerance of sloth. Following her return from the Cumbrian mountains, the diminutive figure of Dr Kennedy, in her sensible woollen check skirts and flat walking shoes, could be seen moving through the corridors of the college even more briskly than ever.

The cause of her newfound energy, apart from long walks in the bracing air, was an item of post she'd discovered among the large quantity accumulated during her fortnight away. It was a letter more replete with promise than any she had ever received before. Claude Bonning, whom she'd met several times in his capacity as President of Family First, had written inviting her to join the Executive Council of GlobeWatch, an organisation recently set up to promote good corporate citizenship by major multinational companies who operated throughout the world. Claude himself was the new organisation's founding Chairman.

It wasn't the invitation itself that intrigued Dr Kennedy. Every year she received more requests to join the bodies of worthy causes than she cared to think about – requests that she invariably declined, through pressure of work. It was, instead, the more tangible offer that accompanied the invitation.

'Funded by a large and growing number of multinational companies,' Claude Bonning had written, 'GlobeWatch will not be just another talking shop, strong on rhetoric but offering no solutions. Instead, we intend to pursue a full programme of research, policy-formulation and publishing, independent of our sponsors. In particular, a sizeable budget has been allocated to research and policy formulation in the area of child labour, and we very much hope you will consider directing initiatives in this area.'

Child labour had become a subject very close to Dr Kennedy's heart in the past few years. During her long career as an economist, issues faced by developing countries had increasingly preoccupied her – and more and more, the problem of child labour. Perhaps it was that she had found, at last, an outlet for her maternal instincts which had eluded expression through all her long years in academia. Perhaps it was that, as an educationalist, she felt strongly that children denied schooling were denied a future. But there was no doubt she felt more passionately about child labour than she had about any other issue during the course of an illustrious career – and she had probably done more to bring the issue to public attention than any other academic in Britain.

She had published papers on the subject and delivered lectures at conventions worldwide. She had visited regions in Pakistan and India, where some of the worst excesses occurred, with TV cameras, appearing in a documentary series on Channel 4. She had spoken out at legislative think-tanks in London and Brussels and Washington DC. But despite all she'd done, she was frequently overwhelmed by the knowledge of all that still needed to be done. And the perennial problem in doing it was always the same; there was never enough money. Never enough to monitor the extent of the problem in every country where children were exploited. Never enough to bring the issue fully to public attention. Lack of funding was something Dr Kennedy felt acutely – every month that went by consigned untold thousands of children to the abject misery of enslavement.

During her recent holiday, she'd had plenty of time to think. Charged as she was with new ideas, the arrival of

Claude Bonning's letter really couldn't have been better timed. Although it begged a particular and intriguing question: just how sizeable was 'a sizeable budget'? Excited though she was by the prospect of fresh research funding, on her first day back Dr Kennedy hardly had a moment to think about the letter, swept up in the usual demands of university life – student tutorials and final exam assessments, Fellows' meetings and the usual college administration. She was only just beginning to get back to her usual routine on her second morning in college, when her telephone rang. Claude Bonning announced himself.

'Ah, Mr Bonning! How good of you to ring. I received your letter when I got back from holiday yesterday.' Sitting at her desk, she retrieved the letter from her in-tray. Glancing over it again, she noted it was dated a week before. 'I'm sorry I haven't had a chance to reply.'

For a few minutes they discussed the Family First conference at which they'd last met and where Dr Kennedy had made a keynote address, before Claude Bonning moved the conversation on to GlobeWatch, explaining the contents of his letter.

'It certainly is very interesting,' Dr Kennedy responded after hearing him out. Then, with typical acuity, she observed, 'But it seems a little strange to me that big companies would want to sponsor research, the results of which could damage their own profitability.'

There was a pause at the other end before Bonning replied, 'It may seem like a contradiction, but I suppose you'd call it enlightened self-interest. The companies sponsoring GlobeWatch really are committed to environmental protection – it's not just window dressing for them.'

Dr Kennedy pursed her lips in thought. Far be it from

her to begin an argument with a man she both liked and respected – and one who could prove to be a research benefactor – but she couldn't help remaining sceptical about the motives of big business.

At the other end, Claude Bonning came to the point. 'I realise if you've just got back from holiday, you probably haven't had much time to think about it,' he said, 'but I'm keen to find out your initial response.'

'Yes, I'm afraid it's been hectic since I got back,' Dr Kennedy told him truthfully. Then, for the sake of her negotiating position, 'At the moment I'm inundated with requests.'

Just because she was an academic didn't mean Dr Kennedy lived in an ivory tower. Having studied the world of commerce most of her life, she well understood the benefit of creating an impression of scarcity – in this case, of her time. Although, behind her unpromising words, she was far less hard to get than she pretended. Last night, as she was preparing for bed and, for the first time that day, had had time to think about Claude Bonning's letter again, she'd allowed herself the giddy pleasure of speculating on how much the 'sizeable' research budget he'd mentioned might be. Eight to ten thousand pounds was about the minimum amount required to embark on research of any substance. Fifteen-thousand-pound annual grants were fairly common, although she hadn't yet managed to attract any sustained funding at that level for her own child labour studies. But if she could secure fifteen thousand a year for at least two years, that would enable her to hire a top-rate, part-time researcher, do the travelling she'd hitherto been prevented from carrying out, and put into action some of the ideas she'd had while walking in the Lake District. Fifteen thousand would be good, very good. And of course, if 'sizeable' meant more than fifteen, and went up to, say, twenty thousand, well that would be exceedingly good. Why, on twenty thousand pounds she could hire a full-time researcher and . . .

Dr Kennedy had checked herself there. No point getting her hopes up. Speculating about what the budget may or may not be wasn't going to help matters.

Now Claude Bonning told her, 'I would never have thought to bother you with GlobeWatch if there hadn't been a decent research budget.'

So, she thought, 'decent' was now added to 'sizeable'. She could contain her curiosity no longer. 'Has a research budget been finalised?' she asked.

'It'll depend, to a large degree, on the programmes you propose to carry out. A figure of fifty thousand has been pencilled in, but it could go much higher than that if you were able to present a compelling case.'

The conversation had now left the realms of Dr Kennedy's dearest wishes and had broken into the stratosphere of wild fantasy. But she didn't miss a beat.

'Compelling case?'

'If you were to assemble proposals that were endorsed by the GlobeWatch Executive Council, which I don't think would be a problem given your stature in this area, we might be able to improve that figure by a further twenty or thirty thousand pounds.'

'Yes, research costs are rising all the time.' Dr Kennedy was, by now, on autopilot.

'All the same, the GlobeWatch's budget is much higher than average.'

'Of course it is Claude, and I'm most grateful to you for thinking of me. I'm certainly very interested and I'd like to reflect on the idea in a little more detail. I'm sorry to delay things further but would you mind if I call you back with a firm decision in a day or two?' She didn't want to seem too keen.

'That would be fine.'

He repeated his telephone number. 'Look forward to hearing from you.'

Dr Kennedy replaced the receiver, her head spinning. Fifty thousand. Possibly eighty. It was more than the total she'd spent in the past ten years. This would be a boost to the child labour issue such as it had never had before. As she thought of all the programmes she'd be able to carry out, she felt emotion welling up inside her, a powerful mix of joy and gratitude which tugged at her lips and threatened her composure; it was the best news of her career since she'd been appointed a Fellow of St John's.

In a celebratory mood, she glanced up at the clock on her study wall. Eleven-fifteen a.m. She had a strict rule that she only ever allowed herself a small glass of Bristol cream sherry after twelve noon. But today she decided to throw caution to the wind. Making her way over to her drinks cabinet with a veritable skip, she seized the sherry bottle, poured herself an immodest quantity of her favourite tipple and, about to take her first sip, caught her own reflection in the glass of a favourite watercolour. She raised her sherry glass in a toast. 'To Claude Bonning,' she said aloud, 'you dear, *dear* man.'

Bonning put down the telephone receiver and stared at it for a few moments before raising his eyes with a weary expression. Across the table from him, the other removed his headphones.

'Well?' asked Bonning.

'It's very important to us that she says yes.'

'She'll say yes.'

'She sounded underwhelmed.'

'She's like that.'

'And we can't afford more than a hundred grand.'

'I heard you the first time. And the second. And the third.'

'Doesn't hurt to be reminded.' Elliott North hated academics. They were all so damned pompous; so full of intellectual conceit. They thought they were cleverer than everyone else and that somehow they deserved to be admired because of their higher intelligence. Seeing Bonning squirm gave him a decided pleasure.

Bonning rose to leave. 'I'll be in touch in a couple of days' time when I hear back from her. So you can stop calling me at home at eleven at night.'

North shook his head. 'The calls won't stop, Claude. Like we told you at the outset, getting Kennedy on board is just the beginning. What we're really after is first prize. The gold star. *Cum laude*. Whatever you people call it.'

'And as I told you at the outset, unlike you I'm not into mind control. I can assemble persuasive arguments; I can work for consensus. But you're dealing with some highly intelligent, independently minded individuals with their own agendas. The best I can do is lead them towards a certain conclusion.'

'You'll have to do a lot better than that if you don't want your sister splashed all over the tabloids.'

From the brown envelope beside him, North extracted a photograph and flicked it over the desk top towards Bonning. It was a photograph of an attractive young woman taken in Montreal. Picking it up, he stared at it, shaken, before suddenly wondering if it was North's only copy.

'Why don't you take it home?' North asked, as though reading his thoughts. 'Stick it on the mantelpiece. Show the kids. In fact, I've an even better idea. Why don't you run it in next month's Family First magazine?'

It was a long while before Bonning finally met his eyes, with a shake of his head. 'You're a sick bastard.'

'Oh, Mr Bonning, "Judge not lest ye be judged."' North rose from the other side of the table and walked over to open the door. 'Isn't that the phrase you folks use at Family First?'

6

There was something odd about Elliott North, decided Chris. More than just odd. As the Lombard lift doors slid shut in front of him, and he descended from the fourth floor to the basement garage at the end of another fifteen-hour day, he searched for the right word for Elliott North. 'Sinister' was maybe overdoing it, 'eccentric' altogether too tame. He had to mull it over a few moments before he knew he had it; the word was 'unsavoury'.

He hadn't noticed so much that first time they'd met in Mike Cullen's office. North had seemed rougher around the edges than most other Lombard consultants, but Chris hadn't seen any great significance in that. During subsequent encounters, though, he'd picked up something more. Working flat out on Project Silo, he'd been using every trick in the book, and calling in all the favours he was owed from MIRA days to obtain all the information he could on Sportex and Active Red. So far he'd uncovered no sign that either company was, as North had suggested, waging a dirty tricks campaign against Starwear. What he *had* found, however, was evidence of cash-flow problems at Sportex, and distribution failures at Active Red – information that would be invaluable in planning Starwear's future strategy.

In the course of his research during the past three weeks Elliott North had visited him several times. Each time he'd used the same phrase: 'Are you digging up the dirt?' Chris hadn't been sure how to react at first: the competitor research was revealing, but he didn't see himself as being in the business of digging up dirt. Maybe that was just North's way of putting things. So this evening when North had stepped into his office, Chris had told him about the findings on Sportex's liquidity problems and Active Red's failure to secure several major distributors. North had seemed interested – but not *that* interested. Instead he'd asked about Bob Reid and Ed Snyder – the respective CEOs of Sportex and Active Red. How had the two of them screwed up, he'd wanted to know. What skeletons were rattling in their cupboards?

North was missing the point. The personalities of Jacob Strauss's counterparts might be titillating, but what *really* mattered was coming up with ways that Starwear could exploit the operational weaknesses of its rivals, and flex its brand to maximum effect. Mike Cullen had said as much himself.

It was as if Elliott North was out of sync with the rest of the agency and had his own agenda for Starwear which was different from the one everyone else was following. One of the first things Kate Taylor had told Chris about Starwear was that the agency was committed to a Four-Point Communications Strategy. She'd shown him a summary consisting of four goals highlighted with bullet points:

- To establish Jacob Strauss's credentials among Starwear's key audiences.

- To ensure the Textile Bill, about to be debated in Parliament, was amended to protect Starwear's interests.
- To achieve recognition for Starwear's human resources management in developing countries.
- To generate maximum benefit from Starwear's annual results, to be released in a few weeks, which would show record profits.

All of that made sense to Chris, even though he didn't understand the rationale behind every point. So where was Elliott North coming from with all this talk about skeletons in cupboards?

The lift doors opened and he stepped into the basement garage. Walking over to his car, he heard footsteps on the concrete behind him and turned to find Kate emerging from the stairwell. 'Came down the lazy way,' he smiled.

'You're a few floors up from me.' She approached him, looking in her handbag for her keys. 'Things going OK?' She glanced up.

It was a couple of days since they'd last spoken.

'Very well,' he confirmed. Then, lowering his voice, 'Pulled in some great stuff on the project whose name I dare not speak.'

'Excellent!' She knew he was working on something confidential for Mike.

They were walking together towards where their cars were parked, just a few yards away.

'And otherwise – things OK?' she asked.

He nodded, although she detected a hesitancy in his expression.

'But?' she prompted.

They carried on walking till they had reached her car, a midnight-blue Saab convertible. Kate was looking up at him now with an intensity that made him wonder if he should have left this alone. Although, even on his first day she'd signalled her own reservations about Elliott North.

'Well I – I don't want to make a big deal out of this . . .'

'Just say it.' She was insistent.

'It's Elliott. Maybe it's just me but he seems somehow *different* . . .'

She was shaking her head with a smile. 'In a few weeks you won't be quite so diplomatic.' Then, catching his embarrassment, she reached out to touch his arm. 'It's not just you.' She glanced about the basement garage to make sure they were alone. 'I haven't felt comfortable about him ever since he arrived.'

Kate evidently wanted to confide. He was flattered. 'How do you mean?'

'Well you know what everyone in the City thought about Nathan? That didn't just happen by accident. That happened because we managed his relationships. We made sure he was out there, pressing the flesh with analysts and reporters. They got to know him well and respect his views. So when they needed an angle on an industry story, Nathan was the head honcho they turned to.'

Stepping closer, she told him, 'A couple of weeks ago I wrote to Jacob, suggesting an analyst briefing. Nothing formal. More an evening drinks meeting, with Jacob making a ten-minute presentation, you know, "different man, same strategy", the kind of thing the City wants to hear. Next thing I know, Elliott North is marching into my office wanting to know what I'd been thinking of, writing the letter, why Jacob needed to meet analysts out of results season, etc., etc.'

Chris raised his eyebrows.

'I couldn't believe it at first.' Kate was animated before checking her voice and glancing about them again. 'I explained what the idea was. North said he thought it was a waste of time. I told him Jacob had to meet and greet if he wanted to build up the kind of rapport that Nathan had had. He stormed off. Then I started thinking – why the hell do I need to justify myself to Elliott North? *I'm* in charge of Starwear's financial PR.

'But things get worse.' Kate paused for a moment to take breath. 'Two days ago I took a call from Steve Evans at the *FT* requesting an interview with Jacob. Steve has always been a friend of Starwear's – very on-side. I phoned Jacob recommending we go ahead with the interview, but he wasn't in, so I left a message with his PA. This time I get an e-mail from Mr North. He's heard about the interview and wants to restrict the area of questioning. I e-mail him right back, saying that's crap. Telling someone of Steve's stature there are no-go areas is like waving a red flag to a bull.

'The interview was yesterday afternoon, and I went to Cavendish Square to meet Steve and take him upstairs to the CEO's office. The drill is, after a few minutes of polite banter, I leave them to it, then call both parties later in the day to see how it was for them. So, I take Steve upstairs, and who should be sitting there with Jacob, but Elliott North. What's more, when I signal it's time to leave, he sits tight.'

'Did he stay—'

'The entire duration.'

'And what did Steve make of it?'

Kate rolled her eyes. 'He just thought it was bizarre. He liked Jacob – liked him a lot. He's particularly impressed with all the Quantum Change stuff. But he said North just sat there in silence, wringing his hands like some dyspeptic Ayatollah.'

'Was that the phrase he used?' Chris chuckled.

'It was.' But her amusement soon faded. 'I can't operate with a control freak double-guessing me.'

'You've spoken to Mike?'

She nodded. 'He said "patience". North's not used to working in a structured operation. Mike says he's got to learn to let go.' She pulled a face. 'He's also got to get right off my back.'

Chris was contemplative for a moment before he asked, 'Insecurity?'

She shrugged. 'Could be.' Then, consciously adopting Personal Manager mode, she said, 'I don't want you feeling uneasy about Elliott. He's a displaced person right now, but he'll sort himself out.'

Chris took a step towards his car.

'He's new to London. Probably just needs a good . . . social life.' Kate made light of it, delivering a meaningful smile which intended more than she said.

Chris grinned. 'I guess.'

He was still grinning as he drove his car up the ramp of the basement garage and into the street. 'Social life' indeed! He hadn't had one of those for a while. His last girlfriend, Sophie, had been an on-off affair which had finally fizzled out six months before. It had been more his fault than hers that things hadn't worked out – she'd got tired of always being the one to make the running.

Reflecting on his love life, his thoughts inevitably turned to Judith. Judith, Judith, Judith, his *grande passion*. The reason, he knew, his subsequent relationships with other women had never lasted very long; Judith had spoiled him for them. There were times, in his darker moments, when he wondered if he'd ever feel about anyone else the way he had about Judith. There had been such intensity, such passion, he sometimes doubted anyone could expect to have that more than once in their lives.

They had met at Oxford – he in his final year, she in her first, but both visiting the same professor for weekly discussions on American literature. Judith, with her lithe, petite frame and dark, tousled hair, caught his eye, but it hadn't been love at first sight. The emotion came later, when they'd both gone to listen to a debate on the future of the novel, and found themselves, afterwards, continuing the discussion late into the night. It was her passion he was drawn to more than anything. With Judith, there were no half measures. What she felt, she felt and expressed strongly – something which Chris, who'd been brought up in a culture of reserve, found utterly captivating. Later, they'd laugh about how intensely they'd discussed Hollywood, the Internet and literacy standards. They'd circled round each other for several weeks, each wishing something would happen, but fearing the possibility of rejection – unexpressed emotion rising ever greater each time they met.

Then at the end of Michaelmas term, shortly before they were due to leave for Christmas, they found each other at the same carol service at St John's, followed by a *glühwein* party in Tom Allwood's rooms. It remained in Chris's memory as an evening of ultimate enchantment, beginning with the candlelit ritual in the chapel, enjoyed for the first time with someone who provoked feelings in him he hadn't known he possessed, and carrying on through an evening's festivities suffused with promise. At the party, he and Judith stood in one corner, so absorbed in each other they could scarcely break away to refill their glasses. Until it was time to leave, then they'd slipped into their coats and walked the frosted, cobbled streets, aglow with good feeling, willing on the moment they were alone in his room, inhibitions dissolved.

The next six months had been the most intense and ecstatic of Chris's life. Somehow he managed to do enough work to pass his exams. Then came the summer vacation when the two of them travelled to France together on what had felt, at the time, like a glorious, extended honeymoon. On their return, Judith had helped him choose and decorate the flat in Islington. Once she'd finished at Oxford in two years' time, they decided, she would join him in London.

For a while the arrangement had worked well, as they weekended together, either at Oxford, which Chris loved, or in London, where together the two of them made the city their own. But Judith, who had been a supporter of environmental causes since before she arrived at university, became more and more involved in green issues. There were so many of them: energy emissions and the ozone layer, rainforests, passive smoking, food additives, whaling, child labour, nuclear waste. Fundraising and campaigning became an increasingly important part of her life; Chris found himself with the choice between seeing less of her, or joining in.

To begin with he'd hoped that by his holding back,

Judith would come to find a balance between campaigning, and the time she spent with him. But as their weekends together grew fewer and less easy, he began to realise that he'd misjudged: environmental issues had become too important to her to compromise. Instead of seeking balance, she sought instead complete immersion in her cause. When she told him, on their last weekend together, that she had started seeing Clive Slater, a Greenpeace activist who'd formed a protest group at Oxford, Chris had been devastated.

Now, as he headed towards Fulham, he thought about how, for the first time in years, he could let go completely of unwanted ties to the past. His new home had nothing to do with Judith. Unlike Islington, where there hadn't been a corner of the place that didn't hold some memory of Judith, the Fulham house offered a completely fresh start. There was no reason why Judith should ever set foot in the place.

Of course, seeing her wasn't something he could completely avoid – they had Oxford friends in common and would find themselves at the same parties. He'd probably see her in a few weeks' time at Bernie's birthday bash. And, as always, he had strongly mixed feelings about the prospect. He couldn't deny a decided *frisson* of excitement at the prospect of seeing her again. She still made his heart beat faster when she stepped into a room and, crazy though it seemed seven years after their break-up, he supposed that deep down he still held on to the enduring hope that maybe . . .

But on the other hand, what if she arrived with some ardent suitor in tow? What kind of a mood would she be in, and how would she act around him? There had been several times, in the past couple of years, late at night, and after a lot of alcohol had been consumed, when her behaviour had been very much less than loving towards him. In fact, at one New Year's Eve party she'd raged at him, memorably, for being an 'anally retentive pillock'.

Hostility, he'd reassured himself afterwards, was supposed to be better than indifference. But even so, he knew he had to find a way to let go. His feelings for Judith were still unresolved, and the best way to resolve them was to find someone else to take her place in his life. But who?

At the end of the Boardroom table, Elliott North doodled in the margin of his notepad while Kate Taylor discussed what she'd been doing on Starwear's behalf in the previous week. The regular Starwear Traffic Meetings were a total pain in the ass as far as he was concerned. Maybe it was important for all the others at Lombard to make sure they didn't tread on each other's toes – 'communications synergy' was the phrase they used in front of clients. But when it came to his own operations, the less they knew about them, the better.

In New York, the agency he'd worked for had given him a completely free hand to do whatever needed doing to keep Jacob Strauss happy. Nobody questioned where he went, what he did or why he did it. But early on, Cullen had told him that approach wouldn't wash at Lombard. Even though Starwear was by far and away the biggest PR client in the country, and Lombard's prize account, people in London, said Cullen, expected accountability. Transparency. They wanted to be in the loop.

Which was why he would find himself sitting round a table and going along with the game, in the company of

Kate Taylor, in charge of Starwear's financial PR, Nicholas King from lobbying, Marilyn Rhodes, consumer affairs, and Tim Wylie, corporate. And of course, Mike Cullen in the Chair. His own remit had been labelled, after much deliberation, 'Special Projects'. It was suitably vague and all-encompassing. It meant he could still get involved in anything he wanted. And he liked it, because as far as he could see, what he did was special; all the rest was mere housekeeping.

Now the Taylor woman was reporting back on the results of an Analyst Audit that had been carried out. All the initial impressions of Jacob Strauss were favourable, she was saying now. Little did she know, she had him to thank for that. Had de Vere been allowed to busy himself at J. P. Morgan for much longer he would have produced a report that torpedoed Starwear below the waterline; the damage would have been impossible to repair.

Next on was Nicholas King, who'd been trying to persuade MPs that the new Textile Bill, soon to be debated in parliament, needed an amendment. In the past, the Government had offered a range of financial incentives to foreign companies investing in Britain, incentives that gave them a financial advantage over their local competitors. The new Textile Bill was intended to level the playing field, removing the incentives to foreign-owned companies like Starwear. It would have a big impact on Starwear's bottom line – and share price.

'What we're telling Members,' King said now, 'is that without an amendment protecting sportswear manufacturers, this Bill is bad for Britain, and bad for the industry. We need to encourage responsible management.'

He looked round the table over his half-moon

spectacles, clearly relishing his role as the architect of Starwear's parliamentary defence.

'The Bill is bad for Britain because existing incentives have resulted in over £8 billion of investment in the past decade, and 30,000 jobs in the sportswear industry. Take the incentives away and companies like Starwear will simply relocate to other countries who are only too happy to provide financial inducements.

'It's bad for the industry because, contrary to popular belief, not all Starwear profits go in their shareholders' trousers. Starwear spends an average of £40 million a year in Research and Development, creating products which their competitors instantly copy. Take away the R&D and stagnation hits not only Starwear, but the industry as a whole.' He delivered a perverse smile.

'What level of support are you getting for the arguments?' asked Cullen.

Across the table, King's smile froze over. 'Well, Mike, we're up against numbers. The Government's got a Whip on this and want to be seen as champions of free competition.'

He removed his glasses and rubbed his eyes. 'I'd say our chances are very much less than fifty-fifty.'

Cullen nodded seriously, making a note in the margin of his Agenda. 'You'll keep up the pressure?'

'Rest assured, by the time the Bill is debated, there won't be an MP who isn't familiar with our line.'

'Responsible management,' muttered Elliott North.

King glanced over at him with an expression of mild surprise. 'Indeed.'

Now Cullen turned to North with an enquiring glance. He was always last on. After a slug of black coffee he began. 'Just one thing. Some new think-tank, GlobeWatch, is about to be launched. Claude Bonning, President of Family First, is assembling a high-powered council to run the operation. Their main thrust is to monitor the activities of global businesses in labour relations, with a close eye on the manufacturing activities in third-world countries.'

Around the table, the others were following him intently. Then Marilyn Rhodes asked, 'Who's behind it?'

'Interesting you should ask.' North shot her a glance. 'Independent. I guess they'll be out with the begging bowl soon, looking for sponsorship. And I'm proposing we make a healthy donation.'

'Whose budget?' Tim Wylie flinched.

Mike Cullen cut in before North could reply. 'Let's not get ahead of ourselves.' He continued calmly, 'But we wouldn't, obviously, put our existing obligations at risk.'

Now Mike glanced around the table. 'Anything else?' he queried.

After a moment's silence, Wylie mentioned, 'On my way down to this meeting, Monitoring Services handed me a note. A journalist has been calling all over the Starwear operation, here, the States, even Jaipur, with questions about the Quantum Change programme.'

Having returned to the margins of his notebook, North abruptly stopped doodling. 'What's his name?' he demanded.

'It's a her, actually,' said Wylie, 'Judith Laing. *Herald*.'

'One of Carter's. What do we know about her?'

'She used to be at *The Guardian*.' Kate Taylor glanced around the table at everyone except North. 'Specialises in investigative stuff. She's done a couple of big corporate stories at *The Herald*, but she's only been there about six months.'

'Shall I arrange the usual briefings?'

Wylie had a well-worn routine for Quantum Change journalist briefings. It involved a video presentation and handsome information satchel containing glossy reports on how Quantum Change had transformed Starwear's fortunes.

Cullen paused for a moment before he said, 'If she's an investigative type, the usual treatment might backfire.'

North was nodding.

'Get her over to Cavendish Place. Set up for her to meet the top brass in International Division – Lester and Eaglesham. Tell them to give her an in-depth briefing. We need full co-operation.' He glanced across at North as he said it.

'Absolutely,' agreed North.

At the bottom of his list of action points North wrote the name 'Judith Laing' in capitals, before underlining it. Twice. He didn't like the sound of this at all. Whoever this Judith Laing was, he needed to find out all about her, pronto – where she came from; what she was on to. And make sure she got stopped in her tracks.

7

Judith strode into Alex Carter's office and, with a flourish, presented him with a four-page article. Wearing a new, black, wrap skirt which revealed rather more of her legs than other garments in her wardrobe, she leaned across his desk at a particular angle so that her womanly assets, delectable in Wonderbra, were presented to him at eye level.

'Two thousand incisive words on the information vending industry,' she announced.

For a moment, Carter was uncharacteristically bedazed. Then he leaned back in his chair and regarded her carefully before saying, 'My, my! We have turned over a new leaf.'

Judith shrugged. 'You know the old saying, "If you can't take the heat, don't stay in the kitchen."' She cocked her head. 'I'm staying.'

'I'm pleased you've taken my comments on board.' There was a hesitance in Carter's voice, as though he half suspected her of setting him up. 'Delighted, in fact.'

'It's already paying dividends,' she responded encouragingly.

'Indeed, it is.'

Judith had had five bylined features published in the past three weeks. She hadn't actually originated them, of

course; she'd got a couple of PR spinners to churn out articles, which she redrafted, quoting a few extra sources, and,
tra-lah, presented Carter with his precious 'output'.

Now Carter looked her up and down with undisguised
relish. 'I can see you're working your way to becoming a
highly valued member of the City desk,' he grinned.

She returned the smile, amused by the transparency of it
all. 'I don't just want to be valued,' she told him, running
her hand down her thigh, 'I want to be the best.'

Carter's tongue flicked briefly across his lower lip. 'No
harm in setting high goals,' he told her.

Strutting her way across the crowded newsroom, she
headed towards her desk. Her new wardrobe had provoked
mixed reactions from her colleagues, from bewildered disbelief to pure venom in the case of Alison MacLean, who'd
slipped in the City Editor's ratings ever since Judith had
adopted her new approach. In fact, Ali darling had cor-
nered her in the Ladies' a fortnight before, after the first
outing of her wrap skirt.

'You may think you're getting ahead,' Alison had murmured poisonously, her own mini so high it barely covered
her crotch, 'but let me warn you, as a friend, you're playing a
dangerous game. Alex is fickle as fickle can be. You're flavour
of the month one minute, then he dumps you the next.'

'Really?' Judith supposed she should feel sorry for her
colleague, but pity was an emotion hard to feel with a long,
red talon wagging in your face. 'How long do you think I've
got?' she asked, wide-eyed.

'Got?'

'As flavour of the month. I mean, are we talking literally
here?'

Alison was caught off guard by this line of questioning. She stepped back. 'One month. Maybe two.'

'Oh, well. That's all right then.' Judith was casual.

An expression of deep puzzlement passed over Alison's features.

'That's all I need,' Judith told her.

'Why?' Alison was suspicious. 'Are you leaving?'

'Leaving?' Judith snorted. 'I'm not leaving, I'm getting promoted!'

Alison shook her head with an expression of self-righteous indignation. 'You know, you're even more arrogant than I gave you credit for,' she told Judith. 'You're more likely to be fired than promoted.'

'Well, if I am fired,' Judith delivered a withering glance in the direction of Alison's mini, 'at least I'll have more than a fanny pelmet to fall back on.'

Back at her desk, she removed the plastic wallet containing the Jacob Strauss investigations from her handbag. In the end, she hadn't been able to resist her journalistic impulse to follow up this story. She had decided to proceed – but with extreme caution. She was keeping her notes on disk – she certainly wasn't risking leaving them on any computer. When she'd told Alison MacLean that two months was all she needed, she hadn't been joking. That was as long as she'd given herself to finish her investigations; she couldn't keep up this charade with Carter for ever. The idea of doing an Alison to buy time and keep Carter off her back had come up over a few pints with Ted Gilmour. She suspected Ted had his own motives for urging her in the direction of her new wardrobe, but that was another story. The point was, for the past three weeks, since her meeting with Denise Caville, she'd been editing press releases and flashing plenty of cleavage, and Alex Carter had been sweet as pie, with not a harsh word exchanged. For the moment, at least, her position on the City desk was secured.

In the meantime, having double-checked Merlin's sources, she now had enough to run a story that would be the lead business piece of the week. It would no doubt be picked up by the US media and turn into an even bigger story in America, where Jacob Strauss was so much better known.

But Judith had already decided against that course. Apart from its being lazy journalism, every instinct told her that Jacob Strauss's rapacious greed and managerial incompetence hadn't come to an abrupt end once he'd joined Starwear. The full might of Starwear's promotional machinery may have kept his activities concealed, but that didn't mean there weren't other ways of getting to the truth.

Besides, Judith reckoned she knew where to look. When Jacob Strauss joined Starwear, and until his recent appointment as CEO, his title had been President of Starwear's International Division. At the time he'd been brought on board, Starwear divided its activities into three geographic territories – America, Europe and 'International'. It was this latter category to which Jacob had been assigned, and Judith wondered if Nathan had put Jacob into International on the basis that it was where he could do least harm. Five years before, International Division had comprised a miscellaneous assortment of factories and markets, including developed countries such as Japan and Australia, as well as the developing territories of India, Thailand and Indonesia.

As manufacturers the world over began the stampede to set up factories in developing countries, where labour was significantly cheaper than anywhere else, Starwear's International Division suddenly acquired a new importance; a decision was taken by the Starwear Board to shift as much production of Starwear products into the developing world as possible. The trouble was, few of the existing production plants in developing countries were equipped for huge production volumes. Which was where the Quantum Change programme came in. Calling in Forbes, the management consultants, Jacob Strauss had asked them to come up with a way to transform Starwear's production processes, as quickly and painlessly as possible. Forbes had toured all the Starwear sites involved and retreated to their cerebral majesty before presenting a two-inch-thick document which gave detailed recommendations on what ought to be done. The figures showing production improvements looked impressive.

Quantum Change had been duly implemented. And for a worrying few months afterwards, it looked as though the huge costs of the multi-country operation had been entirely wasted. Far from sharp increases in productivity, there was actually an overall decline, with labour problems and mechanical breakdowns temporarily closing down some of the factories. Behind the scenes, Judith learned from a contact at Forbes, there had been furious rows between senior Forbes consultants and Jacob Strauss, with both sides blaming the other for the potential catastrophe threatening not just International Division, but the whole of Starwear. Three shadowy off-shore companies, Zillion, Kraton and Quivelle, had been buying up Starwear shares in huge numbers. They were obvious front operations – but no one knew for whom. Judith had discovered all three were incorporated in the Isle of Man and owned by Swiss-based trusts – their true ownership was impenetrable. Jacob Strauss had been paranoid that Ed Snyder, a sportswear rival and former Starwear director who already held substantial stock, was about to mount a hostile takeover.

For a period of several months, Jacob Strauss disappeared from public view, leaving Nathan to reassure Wall Street and the City that Quantum Change 'teething problems' would soon be dealt with. And, after a worrying transition period, true enough, the turnaround occurred. International Division came back from the brink to triumph. Not only were Forbes's upbeat productivity forecasts met – they were comfortably exceeded. Fears of takeover abated and Jacob Strauss now emerged as the man who had transformed Starwear International, and Quantum Change was regarded as the model of future sportswear manufacturing.

It was about a year later that, for the first and only time, rumours started circulating about Starwear and child labour. At first, the story had been confined to gossip on the trading floors and second-hand sources. Then a tabloid newspaper had run a story that was careful not to accuse Starwear directly, but did report on the rumours about 'a major sportswear manufacturer'. It was at that point that Nathan Strauss had insisted Starwear respond to the whispering campaign before it started gaining any credence. Judith had read the media statement issued by Nathan, which said he was outraged by the suggestions of employment practices that ran completely against all that Starwear stood for. She had also watched an interview of Nathan, over and over. Run by Bloomberg news service at the time of the press release, the high point of the inter-view showed Nathan delivering his message to the camera with rabbinical severity: 'Starwear has never used child labour,' he declared, 'and never would use child labour. The very idea of it is an abomination. Those who are spreading these lies, and bearing false witness, will have the full weight of the law to answer to.'

He couldn't have put it any plainer. And his statement had the desired effect: there had never been another word about the child labour issue. Judith was struck by the lack of curiosity on the part of analysts and journalists about why it was that Quantum Change had over-delivered on even its own heady forecasts. Had it under-delivered, of course, there would have been close questioning. Flaws would have been found, blame would have been attributed, heads would have rolled. But over-delivery was great for profits and, so long as it continued, everyone seemed happy to go along with the explanation that it was all because of Jay Strauss and his Quantum Change programme.

Judith decided she needed to know more about Quantum Change, and confidentially phoned Jo Ayreshaw, her contact at Forbes, and formerly one of her brightest contemporaries at Oxford. Jo quickly told her that Forbes couldn't hand over any information about Starwear for which the company hadn't given formal approval. But, she also said, the Quantum Change model had proved to be such a success that Terry Derwent, the Forbes director in charge of the programme, had done the rounds of several business schools, lecturing on what had been achieved for Starwear, with the company's full approval. As a result, there was already detailed information about Quantum Change available.

A trip to City University, one of the business schools Derwent had visited, and a search of the library, soon produced a number of documents which Judith, after standing in the library's interminable photocopying queues, eventually took away with her and studied in painstaking detail. At the same time as pursuing this line of investigation, Judith had also tried the official channels. She'd telephoned about half a dozen different people at Starwear, under the guise of researching a straight piece on Change Management. She had to exercise extra care not to arouse any suspicions, she knew, but the change management people in London, the Starwear International headquarters in New York, the operations divisions of Starwear in India and Thailand and Indonesia had all given her the same response: all journalist calls are to be referred to our PR agency. And the agency looking after Starwear in London? Lombard.

In the five years she'd been a national journalist, Judith knew enough about Lombard, both directly and through reputation, to give the agency a wide berth. Not because Lombard couldn't be relied upon to produce a highly sanitised version of reality for her to write up. It was just that, once having come to the attention of the Starwear account handler at Lombard, she'd never hear the last of it. Lomboids had a reputation for relentlessness without equal. Any journalist expressing the remotest interest in a client would be chased and harried and leaned upon until the right form of words appeared in the newspaper. And if the right form of words didn't appear, then the future prospects of a journalist getting access to any of Lombard's many other blue-chip clients were slim, to say the least.

It wasn't future access that concerned Judith right now.

It was the far more imminent prospect of harassment. She had no desire to have to fend off telephone calls from silver-tongued PR-ettes, trying to merchandise their version of events. If they so much as suspected that her line on Starwear was going to be less than positive, they'd start jumping, not only on her, but on Alex Carter too – and, while she carried out her investigations, that was a complication she could well do without.

She was still trying to work out how to get a door at Starwear to open when, to her enormous surprise, she had received a call from the secretary of none other than Matt Lester, Operations Director of Starwear International. Mr Lester understood she had been making enquiries about the Quantum Change programme; would she care to visit Starwear's Cavendish Square headquarters, next time Mr Lester was in town, for a full briefing?

Judith collected up the plastic wallet of carefully selected Quantum Change documents she had removed from her handbag, slipped them in her briefcase, and made her way across the noisy newsroom. Having got Alex Carter off her back, at least for the moment, she could disappear off to meetings without any questions being asked. Downstairs, she made her way out of *The Herald* building, walked up to the main road, and had to wait only a few minutes before flagging down a taxi. 'Cavendish Square,' she told the driver.

If it was important to make sure that Lombard didn't get wind of her investigation, she reckoned, it was even more important to keep Alex Carter in the dark. As the black cab purred its way along the Embankment, she thought how, even in these miniskirted, Press Release-driven times, she was still skating on thin ice with Carter. He could turn on her at any moment – Alison MacLean had been right about that. If it suited Carter, she could suddenly find herself consigned to the supplements desk without explanation. If Carter benefited, she could arrive at work one day to find her investigation of Jacob Strauss had been hijacked. Eager though she was to share her discoveries and suspicions, and to have the benefit of someone else's perspective, she realised that, right now, silence was her best counsel.

Starwear's Cavendish Square headquarters were a model of restrained elegance. Established by Nathan Strauss, the global high command for Starwear was accommodated in a magnificent Georgian building, decorated with an understated sophistication which was a testament to the former Chief Executive's taste – and that of his wife's. Judith was surprised to find that Starwear's entire executive offices comprised just three floors – and quickly realised that the company's huge operational staff must be based wherever the organisation had factories or distribution hubs.

It wasn't long after arriving that she was shown up a sweeping staircase, decorated in stately-home style with huge oil paintings, to a meeting room in which two dark-suited men were waiting. Matt Lester was tall, broad-shouldered and blond-haired, the whiteness of his shirt seeming to emphasise the darkness of his tan. Greeting her with a slow, Southern accent, he radiated laid-back confidence. With him, short and bespectacled, was Dr John Eaglesham, Vice-President of Operational Planning and, on first impressions, thought Judith, clearly a propeller head.

It was only a few minutes before the two of them had slipped into the Matt and Dr John routine, a presentation of Starwear's Quantum Change programme which they'd evidently delivered many times before. It began with a six-minute corporate video, showing various Starwear factories in the developing world, before and after the 'QC' pro-gramme – a distinction which was nothing if not impressive. That was followed by ten minutes of Dr John, explaining the rationale for the programme, and explaining how it had been implemented, with the aid of trade-off analyses, flow charts and performance models. Then Matt Lester, whose handsome good looks were, Judith suspected, matched by an extremely well-developed ego, talked about the impact of Quantum Change on Starwear as a brand, and how it made the company virtually impregnable in the market.

It was a slick performance, the video imagery well supported with detailed documentation, and all delivered with an upbeat, almost evangelical zeal which left no doubt that QC was the best thing that had happened to Starwear in recent years. Judith absorbed all this, and when invited to ask questions afterwards, followed up on some of the aspects mentioned in the video before Matt Lester handed over a VHS copy for her file. While she was interested, it wasn't the reason she'd come here today. But she knew what game was being played – she was every bit as capable of playing it herself. Which was why she declined to reveal her cards when asked if she had any questions.

It was only after they'd finished with questions and had spent a few minutes informally chatting about the manu-facturing industry in Britain that Judith asked, while sweeping her papers up into her briefcase, 'By the way, am I right in thinking your QC factory in India has eight pro-duction lines?'

Both men nodded in unison. 'Correct,' replied Lester.

'And the India income figure in the latest Starwear Annual Report – that's the product of your QC factory in Jaipur, is it?'

'The Jaipur plant is our only operation in India,' Dr John nodded.

Judith clicked in the catches of her briefcase, lifted it off the table, and paused, about to leave. 'It's just that I was reading a Forbes report about Quantum Change, and it said the maximum output of any QC production line is 1,200 units an hour, or 9,600 across all eight lines. But your annual report suggests an output nearly double that.'

Lester didn't hesitate. 'Well the Jaipur plant has exceeded all expectations.'

Judith noted the furrowed brow of Dr John Eaglesham. She nodded. 'So I understand. But double the output? Forbes must have got it badly wrong to have underestimated—'

'Forbes's forecasts weren't that far off,' Eaglesham interjected. Then, looking up at Lester, 'There were other factors which inflated the income figure for India in the latest report.'

'Yeah,' Lester was nodding now, 'proceeds of a disposal.'

'Oh?' Judith nodded for him to go on.

'When we originally bought Hydrabull Textiles, to get into India, we acquired a whole load of stuff that was peripheral to our main business. Last year we sold off some property.'

Judith was heading towards the door. 'Must have been quite a big sprawl.'

Lester was running fingers through his hair. 'I guess. It was some . . . office block in Delhi.'

*

Five minutes later, Dr John Eaglesham regarded his colleague across the room with a furious expression. 'Why in Christ's name did you say that?'

'Don't get heavy with me, John. You were doing the prompting.'

'Prompting about a disposal, not stuff about an office block.'

Lester shook his head. 'I couldn't just say "a disposal" and not tell her what it was.'

'I thought the plan was that we'd say we'd get back to people—'

'If I said I'd get back to her, she'd have got suspicious. Why wouldn't I know about the disposal of a ten-million-pound asset?'

Eaglesham turned and stared out of a window overlooking Cavendish Square. After a pause he said, 'We'd better tell Elliott North. Damage containment.'

'I don't think that's such a good idea.'

'Not for you, maybe.'

Matt Lester's position as Vice-President of Operations had been tenuous ever since the Forbes débâcle. The last thing he needed now was for Jacob Strauss to get wind of the fact that he'd mishandled the briefing of a potentially difficult investigative journalist.

Striding over to Eaglesham, Lester seized his colleague by the shoulder and wrenched him round so that they were facing each other. 'You listen,' he seized him by both shoulders and shook him as he spoke in a furious, choked voice, '*don't* even *think* of threatening me. If it wasn't for me, you'd still be number-crunching at Deloittes. *I* put you where you are. I made you! And if I go down I'll make *fucking* sure you come down with me.'

Eaglesham's face had gone suddenly ashen as Lester held him, like some quaking prey, in his powerful grip, before he threw him back against the boardroom wall with a thud.

After a few moments, Eaglesham pulled himself up from the wall with as much dignity as he could muster, straightening his skewed spectacles and fumbling with his tie. He looked aghast in the full force of Lester's fiery resentment.

'Anyway,' Lester towered over him, 'how's she going to find out?'

To doctors and the nursing staff of The Monastery, Claude Bonning was a popular and much-admired figure. A regular visitor, every Wednesday, come rain or shine, to the private nursing home for the mentally ill, the President of Family First would come to spend time with his sister Jeannie who had been at The Monastery for longer than nearly all its serving staff. Claude had brought her over from Montreal more than twenty years earlier. The poor dear had completely lost her mind and her memory – except for brief glimpses of her early childhood in Montreal, which would appear as sharp images through the mists, she had no idea where she was or how long she'd been there.

That particular Wednesday in early October, he arrived at four p.m., as usual, driving his car past the sweeping lawns and rhododendron borders, towards the magnificent, mock-Gothic building, before making his way inside, and down the familiar passage to Jeannie's ward. It was at the front of the building, overlooking the lawns and their magnificent flower borders, vibrant with autumn colour. Jeannie was sitting staring vacantly out of the window, a TV soap blaring in the background.

'Hello, my dear.' He kissed her on the cheek.

'Oh, hello.' She looked up at him. 'Have you come to take me for my walk?'

'Of course I have.'

He often wondered how much she recognised him; if she knew who he was. He wondered if she'd know him at all if he went away for two or three months. But it was too depressing a subject to dwell on, so he would focus only on the here and now.

'Would you like to walk with me today, or go in a wheelchair?'

'I think the wheelchair – it's such a nice day.'

'Yes, isn't it.'

Having helped her into the wheelchair, he manoeuvred her out through the French doors and on to the path which wended its way through the beautifully landscaped gardens. It was so peaceful out here in the gardens. Every time he visited her he couldn't avoid the irony of his own observation that it was a wonderful place to think – but thinking was the one thing of which Jeannie was completely incapable.

As he pushed her along the pathway, the slanting rays of an autumn sun were warm on his face.

'Well, Jeannie,' he told her after a while, 'it's caught up on me, at last.'

It had been a possibility from the start, of course, and in the early days when he'd just started seeing Launa, his wife, the problem had preoccupied him greatly. But the longer he'd been married to Launa – and they'd just celebrated their eighteenth anniversary – the more remote the possibility seemed. Then the call from Elliott North, a bolt out of the blue which brought it all back into horrifying definition.

'I always hoped it would be our little secret – just you and Launa and me. And Him upstairs, of course,' he chuckled sadly, pushing the chair through an arch in a hedge and out to where the gardens were wilder, less constrained.

'I can't think how it could have come out. They must have investigated me, looked into things. But you know, my darling, I still think I did the right thing. There *was* no reason anyone needed to know you're my wife. You made me promise, when we married, never to leave you, and it's a promise I've always kept. Launa understood. She wasn't worried; she cares for you too.'

Jeannie began humming the theme tune from the TV soap that had been on in her room.

'But there are people who wouldn't understand. They wouldn't see past the legalities. And in my position with Family First, it's not just the personal and professional disgrace, it's the organisation I'm worried about too. How would it recover? I can see the headlines now. "Bigamist". That's the word they'd use.'

They came to a park bench, where he parked the wheelchair and sat down, taking one of her hands between his own.

'I didn't see what I could do, except go along with them,' he said. 'I haven't wanted to tell Launa – she's so happy at the moment, building a life for herself with the children off her hands. And now this. Oh, Jeannie, what am I to do?'

As they held each other's eyes, he wondered, with the same sharp pain that he'd felt so very many times in the past – did she understand anything at all of what was going on?

Then something caught Jeannie's eye. 'Oh look.' She pointed.

A large box kite was flying high overhead, a long tail of coloured ribbons dancing beneath it.

'It's a kite,' Claude told her.

'Yes. A kite.' She looked back at him. 'I feel like a kite.'

Elliott North's flat in Onslow Gardens was part of an exclusive square of grand, Edwardian homes, with doric columns, bay windows, and balconies overlooking the private garden around which the houses had been built. In this South Kensington sanctum of establishment money, the aura of privilege and wealth was as inescapable as the luxury vehicles which occupied the residents' parking bays – Jaguars, Audis, Grand Cherokee Jeeps.

North's own flat was no mere bachelor pad. It had three spacious double bedrooms with *en-suite* bathrooms, a study lined with mahogany shelves from chair rail to ceiling, a dining room he never used, and an unusually large sitting room with French doors leading out on to the balcony. The flat had been furnished throughout in the finest taste, and with the benefit of a generous budget, by a well-known interior decorator just off the King's Road. Kevin McLeod had attended to everything, from wallpaper to furniture to soft furnishings, including a pair of magnificent damask curtains in the sitting room, which swept with theatrical majesty from a high, tassled pelmet, down to the floor, secured at either side by tie-backs, to allow late-afternoon sunlight to flood into the room.

North hadn't seen the flat when he bought it. Nor had he been at all involved in its interior decoration. Starwear's London office had seen to all that, couriering over papers to sign and briefs to check over, to which he had paid scant attention. For the fact was, North had very little interest in the niceties of his living arrangements. He didn't care if he lived on the first or second floor, or whether his bedroom was blue or yellow. That kind of thing meant nothing to him. His only concern had been location; so long as his home was no further than a five-minute drive, or a twenty-minute walk from The Boltons, he would be happy enough. Because, in that ultra-exclusive residential enclave, a magnificent, four-storey detached mansion, which boasted one of the few remaining private ballrooms in London, had been recently acquired, at a cost of £5 million, by Starwear's new Chief Executive Officer, Jacob Strauss. Jay had arrived from New York with his wife, Amy, and family; their two teenage daughters would be flown back to America every term until they completed their schooling. For the next few years, at least, London was to be home for Mr and Mrs Jacob Strauss.

North sat in his sitting room wearing a burgundy velvet dressing gown and scanning his laptop for e-mails. He'd never really been big on clothes, but the dressing gown was something he was proud of because Jay had given it to him about three years ago in New York. He still clearly remembered the day in Saks. Jay Strauss rarely ventured anywhere near a shop, all his stuff was bought for him. But that particular day, they had been caught up in traffic in the back of Jay's limo, when the gown had caught Jay's eye from across the sidewalk. Urging him out of the car and into the store, Jay had walked right in, demanded he remove his suit jacket and try on the gown for size, before buying it for him on the spot.

'I'm not saying there's anything less than satisfactory about your physique.' Jay had touched North's hand. 'It's just that there are moments when it's useful to have something to wear that's not a suit.'

North knew exactly which moments he was referring to. The next time one of them came along, he had slipped into his new, quilted, velvet dressing gown, provoking great admiration from Jay. North had become so attached to the garment, in fact, that when the time had come for him to pack his belongings for the move to London, it was one of the few items he insisted on bringing over with him – most of his wardrobe being shipped over a few days later.

It wasn't only the luxuriance of it which made North fond of the gown – it was also the fact that Jay Strauss had bought it for him. For while Elliott North had long-since resigned himself to the fact that he was one of society's outsiders, one who lived on the fringes of normal intimacy, on the subject of Jay Strauss his feelings ran very strongly indeed. The bond between them was as compelling and intimate and reciprocal as could be. And he never, for one moment, forgot whom he had to thank for his success.

That spark of mutual recognition had been there from their very first meeting. At the time, North had been running his own PR agency out of a shabby office in Brooklyn. North Media claimed specialism in 'marketing and corporate communications', a term deliberately designed to mean all things to all people. He called it an 'agency', but in reality it was just him, a telephone, a coffee-stained PC, and a box of index cards on which were written the names of a few dozen not-very-important in-house PR managers and local businesses whom North hoped might, in time, become his clients.

North Media had come about by necessity rather than choice. While his peers had always found North abrasive and unfathomable, his awkwardness hadn't mattered so much when he was at the very beginning of his career in PR. By the age of twenty-eight, however, he'd been expected to meet clients and establish rapport, to create the chemistry needed for new business wins. He hadn't been a success in this department, and it was on the grounds of 'poor interpersonal skills' that his employer, Ketchum PR, had let go of him. Hence North Media, and the hand-to-mouth subsistence it provided. He had one retained client, a small, local insurance broker whose fee just covered the rent, and added a couple of other small-time regulars. Apart from that, he'd take whatever one-off projects he could get.

Then one day he got a call out of the blue from Douglas Cameron, Corporate Communications Director of Starwear. There was a project he might be able to help them with, Cameron told him; would he be available for a briefing at Starwear HQ later that day? All the time he was talking to Cameron, North was getting more and more excited. And curious. How was it that the PR head honcho of one of the world's biggest brands had decided to call him in? North had never written to him to solicit business; he wouldn't have wasted the stamp. What, in Christ's name, did he have of any interest to a heavy hitter like Douglas Cameron?

Later that day he'd presented himself at the reception of Starwear Tower, on Madison, wearing a fresh shirt and tie bought specially for the occasion. Escorted up to executive offices on the penthouse floor, he was met by Cameron in a modern boardroom replete with Starwear iconography and float-framed photographs of major Starwear events. No sooner had Cameron sat him down with a cup of coffee, however, than the Corporate Communications Director had excused himself, returning to the room a few minutes later with Jacob Strauss himself. Mr Strauss would brief him directly, explained Cameron, before wishing North a good day, and bowing out of the room.

Jacob Strauss's dazzling good looks were, in the flesh, every bit as compelling as when North had seen him on television. It wasn't only the tanned blondness, the sensual smile, the athlete's body. It was also the way he held himself, his every movement imbued with as much poise as though he were still on piste; North couldn't help being bowled over by his charisma. Jay quickly explained how it was he who had asked Cameron to set up this meeting. One of North's fliers had come to his attention, the one outlining North Media's services, and showing a photograph of 'Elliott North, Chairman'. He'd thought the flier was well put together, he told North, and wondered if North Media would consider producing a flier for one of their new trainer lines?

Who was going to say no? From the moment Jay had explained what he had in mind, North suspected there was an ulterior motive; in Jay, he'd seen something of himself. And sure enough, in the ensuing weeks, as the two of them saw more of each other, that initial spark of recognition developed rapidly into a full-blown sexual adventure. North had embarked on the most thrilling journey of his life. Both men, of course, had to exercise extreme care. Jay Strauss was so high-profile that his every appearance in public was a potential media event, and Starwear security men monitored his every move. He was a married man, and the leader, in America at least, of a sportswear firm that put healthy families at the heart of its promotional campaigns. Scandal could not be allowed to touch him.

Over the next two months, things changed dramatically for North Media. During dinner in a private suite at The Plaza, Jay put a proposition to Elliott North which he had no difficulty accepting. Starwear's long-established public relations agency in New York was Hill Stellar, one of the largest operations in the country. What Jay proposed was that North sell North Media to Hill Stellar. It would look strange, Jay explained, if he was seen to have continual contact with a one-man operation in Brooklyn. Under the auspices of Hill Stellar, however, their level of contact could be as high as they liked without raising the slightest suspicions. What's more, although he would work out of Hill Stellar's offices, he would continue to run as an autonomous business unit, working exclusively for Jay. North's only question had been about Hill Stellar: what if they didn't want to buy North Media? Jay had only laughed.

'You just leave that to me,' he'd assured North. 'We spend so much with those guys every year they'll do exactly what we tell them to. Besides, one way or another, I'll be funding the purchase. So, what do you say to a million dollars?'

A short while later, Elliott North bought himself an apartment on the Upper East Side. He also became the proud driver of a Porsche, courtesy of Hill Stellar, and enjoyed all the benefits of an American Express – Gold Card – expense account. Gone were the days of chasing after business. When he wasn't involved in an assignment on behalf of Jay Strauss, which soon became most of the time, he was keeping an eye on the other Starwear activities being run out of Hill Stellar. Quickly discovering that his close contact with Jay conferred a special status on himself, he learned that he barely needed to raise his eyebrows about an idea and it was squashed flat. The merest hint that Jay might like something was quickly translated into fully worked-up proposals. For the first time in his life, Elliott North had power; he had truly relished terrorising the staff of Hill Stellar.

This happy state of affairs may have long continued. But there were several security lapses and word began to get out. Rumours started flying about the place, and it was only his own efforts, and that of a privately commissioned firm of fixers, that succeeded in keeping stories out of the media. He and Jay had to adopt a very low profile until the dust settled. After six months, they were still wondering if things were safe when Nathan committed suicide; at an emergency meeting held the afternoon that the news came through from London, it didn't take them five minutes to decide that Jay should move to London when he was appointed Starwear's new CEO.

There were complications with North's transfer. Hill Stellar's equivalent in London, Lombard, had a strong relationship with Nathan Strauss lasting many years. Jacob Strauss was virtually unknown, and while that had certain advantages, it also meant that Elliott North, as Jay Strauss's spin-doctor *numero uno*, didn't carry nearly so much clout among his PR peers as he had in New York. What's more, though Jay Strauss had got Mike Cullen to take on his special adviser without much persuasion, it wasn't quite the same deal he'd struck with Hill Stellar. Now, North was regarded as part of Lombard's Starwear team – but he'd never been a team player. Not only did he have Cullen breathing down his neck these days, he also had to deal with the likes of that ponce d'Andrea. Then there was the Taylor woman, in it completely over her head.

He could do without having to deal with the Lombard lot all the more because, as he found out soon after arriving, British journalists were far more likely to run around printing hugely damaging stories than their American peers. Unlike America, where the dollar was Almighty, and success to be worshipped, he discovered that in Britain, success was a source of resentment, and tall poppies were there to be cut down. If the risks involving Jay and him were big in New York, they were ten times bigger in London. All of which meant that their affairs had to be conducted with the utmost secrecy and vigilance. A point that Jay, judging by his increasingly wild demands, had completely failed to understand.

Now, as he sat in the sitting room of his Onslow Gardens flat, the laptop resting on his velvet-gowned knees, North scrolled through incoming e-mails. Part of his vigilance was to keep close tabs on individual journalists who could cause trouble, and deal with them if they got out of line. It was the strategy which had protected Jay – and him – in New York, and which was imperative here, although d'Andrea was less than enthusiastic about seeing through the results of his monitoring – as the de Vere exercise had shown. That time, he'd had to take matters into his own hands.

Reaching an incoming e-mail from Monitoring Services, North noted the subject title: Judith Laing. He quickly opened it. Following that week's traffic meeting, the alarm bells ringing in his ears the moment Tim Wylie had mentioned Judith Laing's activities, North had gone straight to Monitoring Services to demand a biographical update.

As he scrolled down the information they'd sent him, he became even more perturbed. Judith Laing was trouble, there was no doubting it. First of all she was very smart – North knew you didn't get into the British equivalent of an ivy-league university without serious intellectual fire power. Second, she was anti-establishment. Reading through a list of articles she had penned while at *The Guardian*, including the scoop for which she'd won an investigative journalism award, North decided she was a hardened leftist. Big business was her natural enemy. All her important pieces had been about environmental disasters, or third-world exploitation or discrimination in the workplace – she was no armchair commentator, or newsroom hack. But worst of all was her commitment. As he scrolled through her earlier associations at Oxford, he groaned loudly; Greenpeace, Friends of the Earth, Women First, NUSEA – she'd been involved in them all at some time. According to d'Andrea's note, she'd even had an affair with the President of NUSEA who was in her year.

The idea of her sniffing around Starwear was a nightmare made real. Cullen's charm offensive might be enough to see her off, but he doubted it. He'd had to deal with a dozen Judith Laings in his time. And if she kept on digging, as she probably would, he wouldn't be left with any choice but to bring a permanent end to her enquiries. D'Andrea would go ballistic, just as he had over de Vere. He'd fiddle and fret and talk about having Laing transferred to some other remit at *The Herald*. But North felt no compunction at all about ordering the final solution. There was simply too much at stake to risk anything different; as long as Judith Laing remained alive, she could surface from nowhere and blow them all out of the water.

He was mulling this over when the telephone rang. 'You're ready?' asked Jay, as always dispensing with preliminaries.

'Sure.'

'Half an hour?'

'I'll put the champagne on ice.'

'You do that, sport.'

'I'll be waiting for you . . .'

8

Chris's office was in darkness apart from the pool of light thrown by his desk lamp. That had been burning till midnight, and usually after, every night this week, and the week before, including Saturdays. In the hours after seven p.m., with the support staff mostly gone and the phone no longer ringing, he'd devoted more concentrated energy to Project Silo than he had to any report in his entire career. Subsisting on a diet of strong, black Brazilian from the percolator in Charlotte's office, and hastily snatched burgers from a nearby Burger King, Chris had never worked so intensely in his life.

But he reckoned he'd got the results. Five and a half weeks after joining Lombard, he'd pulled together more comprehensive profiles of Sportex PLC and Active Red than had ever existed. He'd picked over analyst reports, he'd mined Companies House and scrutinised the two companies' financial records in forensic detail. There was the original research among market commentators, the brand analysis, the in-depth market segmentation, and the biographical detail on Bob Reid and Ed Snyder distilled from a dozen sources.

Chris reckoned he'd spent two hundred and forty hours

on Project Silo. At his charge-out rate of £300 an hour, that equated to a project fee of seventy-two grand – plus all the research expenses passed through with a twenty per cent mark-up, which would push the project well over a hundred and fifty grand. The final result of which now sat on the desk in front of him, two inches thick, complete with Executive Summary, Appendices and final amendments. Lotte would input his final commentary in the margins tomorrow morning. Tomorrow afternoon, Friday, he'd hand in the report to North and Cullen. Then it was the weekend. Bernie's party. Time to play.

He glanced at his watch – nine-fifteen p.m. He'd take a half day, he thought wryly. He cleared his desk, beginning with the Project Silo report which he took through to Charlotte's lock-up filing cabinet – Level Two security. Then there were all the other papers that had to be secured in his own filing cabinet, leaving his desk in a state of vacant anonymity. After shoving the remaining desk-top items into a drawer, he was finally unhooking his jacket from its hanger and slipping his arms into it, when he heard voices coming down the corridor outside.

Strange. Since Mike had left, an hour ago, he'd thought he'd been on his own on the fourth floor. Now he recognised one of the voices as North's.

'. . . later than I thought,' North was saying, as Chris appeared at his office door. 'I'll have to get you back right now.'

'Not before you get him his new tracksuit.'

Glancing down the corridor, to where the stairs leading up to the penthouse suite were usually behind locked doors, Chris saw the figures of North, his back towards him, a schoolboy in uniform and, to his great surprise, standing in the penthouse entrance, none other than Jacob Strauss.

As Strauss caught sight of Chris he smiled, before giving the lad a playful punch on the shoulder. 'Top of the range. The full works plus kit bag.'

Both North and the boy, catching sight of Strauss's expression, turned now to Chris.

'Working late?' remarked North.

'Guess why.' Chris stepped out of his office.

'You already know who this is.' North nodded towards Strauss. 'Jay, this is Chris Treiger, Lombard's new—'

'I know.' Strauss moved towards him, arm outstretched. 'The planning guy. I'm very pleased to meet you.'

'And this is Dale.' North nodded towards the schoolboy, who shook Chris's outstretched hand, awkwardly self-conscious.

Having waited with such anticipation to meet the legendary Jacob Strauss, now that the moment had come, it took Chris by surprise. Strauss was wearing, appropriately perhaps, a Starwear tracksuit and socks, a towel round his neck, having evidently just showered. But even in his *déshabillé* state, thought Chris, Jacob Strauss was more handsome in real life than in his press photograph. His macho good looks were of the classic variety – tall, blond, and muscular in build, he had open, friendly features and a dazzling smile. But it wasn't only his looks that conveyed charismatic appeal, there was also something in his posture, the way he moved with an easy, athlete's grace, which held the eye. He had that special air about him of having known the best of this world. Chris found it hard not to stare at him.

Strauss gestured that Chris should pause for a moment,

before turning his attention back to the kid. 'Give me five, big man,' he held out his hand.

The boy reached up, striking Strauss's hand with his own. 'Can I have one of the Blue Galaxy tracksuits?' he asked excitedly.

Strauss laughed. 'Of course. You can have any damn kind you want, Dale. Elliott will sort you out.'

'Sure thing,' said North.

'And tell that friend of yours, we'll also sort him out with a Blue Galaxy when he comes in.'

'OK.'

The boy turned, as Elliott North gestured down the corridor towards the lift. He must be about ten, eleven, reckoned Chris, and wearing a school uniform – grey trousers, purple blazer, a purple cap with gold emblem – Chris knew he'd seen the uniform before, but couldn't place it. As the boy waved goodbye, it struck Chris that he was such a good-looking kid he might be Strauss's own. He had smooth skin, almond-shaped eyes, the same open features. But Chris knew that Jacob Strauss had two daughters, both in their teens.

North and the boy stepped into the lift. Strauss nodded in their direction. 'Charity thing. Starwear sponsors the school, you know, free sports kits, that kind of stuff.'

Chris nodded.

'You have a moment?' Strauss started down the corridor, taking Chris's availability for granted. Cullen's office would have been in virtual darkness had it not been for the rising moon, which cast the room in eerie silver. Strauss didn't bother trying to find a light, instead he walked over towards the window and turned to face Chris, Tower Bridge resplendent behind him, and the moon floating silver above the river. Chris couldn't help thinking how effortlessly Jacob Strauss seemed to find himself in the right place at the right moment.

'So,' he looked over at Chris with an expression of bright enquiry, 'how is it all going?'

Chris paused, 'You mean—'

'The research. Project Silo.'

'Project Silo's going very well.' Chris was as impressed that Strauss could be bothered to remember the coded reference as he had been earlier when Strauss had recognised his own name. Obviously, Project Silo was a subject near and dear to his heart.

As though reading his thoughts, Strauss said now, 'Critical part of the plan, Chris.'

He nodded. This was strongly reminiscent of Mike Cullen.

'You'll have it ready soon?'

Chris hesitated. He decided against saying 'tomorrow' – Elliott North and Mike Cullen would want to see the report first. Instead he said, 'Next week.'

'Great.' Strauss turned and glanced, distracted, out of the window, before striking right fist into left palm. 'Great! You've dug up plenty of stuff about those bastards at Sportex and Active Red?'

'Yes, sir.'

Chris hadn't called anyone 'sir' since leaving school, but it seemed suddenly natural now he was talking to the handsome, charismatic and American Jacob Strauss.

'Oh, I can't wait to read it – can't wait!' enthused Strauss. 'You know Snyder learned it all at Starwear. He stole the QC programme and ran off to copy it at Active Red. As for Reid, the guy's a complete crook.'

Chris knew all about the cash-flow difficulties at Active Red, but wouldn't exactly have described Snyder as a crook. Instead he told Strauss, 'He certainly runs his operation close to the wire.'

'Close to the wire!' Strauss laughed dryly, as he met Chris's eyes across the room. 'You Brits are masters of understatement. Anyway, the chickens will all come home to roost when the amendment comes up.'

Studying Strauss closely across the dark shadows of Cullen's office, Chris couldn't help being surprised. Quite apart from the simple but undeniable magnetism of his physical presence, which took some getting used to, Jacob Strauss seemed far more personally caught up in the machinations of Starwear's commercial enemies than any CEO he'd ever worked with in the past. Bob Reid and Ed Snyder clearly stirred his emotions. What's more, Chris was amazed how confident he seemed about the outcome of the Textile Bill amendment. In the past fortnight, Chris knew, Nick King and the boys from lobbying had been frenetically lobbying every MP and senior civil servant in the DTI they could, rehearsing all the arguments in favour of an amendment. But it wasn't looking good. By the time a Bill got to the House of Commons, it was already too late. What's more, as a Government-sponsored Bill, the chance of provoking back-bench rebellion was remote. Didn't Strauss realise that things over here were different from on Capitol Hill? Besides, what did Project Silo have to do with the Textile Bill amendment? The two were completely unrelated.

Uncertain how to respond, Chris simply said now, 'We certainly live in interesting times.'

Strauss shook his head with a grin. 'Lombard sure is a

refreshing change after all the bullshit I get from Hill Stellar. You just get on and do the business.'

'We try.'

Strauss was moving back across Cullen's office towards the door, with his easy, leonine poise. As they made their way back towards the lifts, he repeated, 'Can't wait to read your report.'

Chris nodded. 'I'm just putting the finishing touches to the Executive Summary.'

'Oh, I wouldn't bother. I'll be reading the whole thing.'

Pressing the lift call, Chris turned with raised eyebrows. 'That's very unusual sir, for someone at your level?'

'Why wouldn't I want to?' Strauss retorted with a grin, looping the towel from round his neck over his arm with a flourish. 'I'm going to lap up every last detail.'

A few minutes later, Chris was behind the wheel of his BMW and heading west along the Embankment, Nina Simone playing on the CD. Something about his encounter with Strauss disturbed him. Jacob Strauss may have been every bit as charming and charismatic as he had expected – and some – but the encounter had left Chris ill at ease. Strauss seemed a man more driven by emotion than by commercial imperatives. North had kept asking him about 'digging up the dirt', and he'd picked up a similar preoccupation from the Starwear boss. Unlike his brother Nathan, whose *modus vivendi* was one to which Chris had felt attracted, Starwear's super-icon seemed more street-fighter than strategist.

He was still mulling this over when he turned left into New King's Road, not far from home, heading in the direction of Parson's Green. Up ahead of him a red Ferrari had pulled over by the kerb, bringing the inside lane of traffic to a bottleneck. Drivers caught behind the Ferrari were nosing into the right-hand lane. Well behind the action, Chris watched as the Ferrari's passenger door flipped open and out stepped a kid in school uniform, hurrying across the pavement towards the entrance of a large, Victorian building. Chris saw the purple blazer and cap.

As he drove past where the car had pulled up, Chris glanced over. Even though the driver's head was turned, he recognised the profile. He hadn't known North drove a Ferrari, but it didn't surprise him. What did surprise him was that the mighty Starwear was giving handouts to kids from a little-known Catholic orphanage in West London – an orphanage to which many thousands of pounds' worth of tracksuits and trainers could be donated without Starwear benefiting in any definable way.

Chris often drove past St Stephen's Home for Boys at the weekends – there'd be schoolboys swarming everywhere in ubiquitous purple. He always felt sorry for the kids, knowing that none of them had homes and families to call their own. Now he remembered what Strauss had told him.

'Charity thing,' he'd said. 'We give them free sports kits, that kind of stuff.'

As he turned right into Harwood Road, Chris thought again about his first impressions of Jacob Strauss. Maybe there was also a human side to him. Maybe he shared a sense of altruism with his late brother, Nathan, even if he expressed it differently. Maybe you couldn't always tell by first impressions.

Across town, in the Virgin Heathrow Upper Class lounge, Matt Lester grimaced as his mobile telephone sounded.

Enjoying a shoulder rub from a luscious young masseuse amid subdued lighting and Baroque cadences, he had been starting to unwind. Now work called.

'Matt, it's Elliott. I'm not disturbing anything?'

Sitting forward in his chair, concern clouded the Starwear director's face. Elliott North was the very last person from whom he wanted to hear. Quite apart from his suspicions about North, whom he thought of as Rasputin at the court of Strauss, he was feeling vulnerable about his latest encounter with the press.

'I was just wondering how things went with Judith Laing?' North enquired, nosing his Ferrari homewards down the King's Road with one hand, while holding his mobile phone to his ear with the other.

'Oh, standard stuff. John and I ran through the usual presentation.' Lester knew he hadn't handled the interview well. He'd handled it disastrously, if the truth be told. The encounter had been on his mind ever since – and he'd been trying to work out damage limitation to cover his ass.

'Any curved balls?' North wanted to know.

'Not really. She did mention production figures. Nothing we haven't handled in the past.'

Long before North had called, Lester had decided he would neither volunteer anything but, if pressed, nor would he deny it. That way, no one could later accuse him of lying. 'De-emphasising', he believed, was the term used by the PR boys.

At the other end, North was suspicious. As a heavy-hitting investigative hackette, fireside chats with company directors weren't Judith Laing's style. Either she'd gone Mary Poppins, or Lester wasn't telling the whole truth.

'What sort of production figures?' he wanted to know.

Lester closed his eyes and raised a hand to his forehead. This was exactly where he didn't want to go. 'The ones we announced in the last annual report. She'd somehow got hold of the Forbes forecasts and worked out the discrepancy. But I stuck to the line we agreed. I told her our returns for last year were inflated as a result of a disposal.'

Now North was seriously alarmed. If Judith Laing had gone nosing around Forbes, she was obviously researching Starwear in detail. Christ knew how far she'd got.

'You said a disposal, huh?' he confirmed.

'That's right.'

North could detect uncertainty in Lester's voice. Or was it guilt?

There was a pause before he responded, 'You did the right thing, Matt. Exactly the right thing. The disposal line was what we agreed.' North knew how to reel in the self-absorbed fat cat.

'That's what I thought.'

'I'm sure you charmed the pants off her,' he was congratulatory, 'you've always been good with young lady reporters. We should send all the hackettes to you.'

Lester chuckled with relief. The danger had passed.

'What's she like?' asked North curiously as he stopped at a red light, 'I've never actually met her.'

'Oh, she's bright. Perky. Quite a cute little thing.'

'I bet.'

'Big eyes.'

'All the better to see you with, my dear.'

Lester laughed slyly.

'I'm glad it went well. Any idea when she's going to write something up?'

Lester shrugged. 'She seemed a bit vague about that.'

'Yeah, whatever,' North had his end-of-conversation voice, 'good contact for us.'

'Exactly.'

'Oh, the disposal thing,' North sounded casual, 'I don't suppose she wanted anything more specific?'

It was the dread question. But the way it came out, Lester didn't feel so bad about answering it. Hadn't North just told him he'd taken the right line?

'Yeah, she did. Just, you know, when she was walking out the door.'

When the real questions get asked, thought North. Like now.

'I said it was some office block we'd acquired with the Hydrabull properties.'

'Uh-huh.'

'I mean, she's got no way of checking out a story in the middle of India.'

'Too late if she has,' North's tone was ambivalent. 'So long, Matt.'

North snapped shut his mobile phone and threw it on the passenger seat. Fuck it! The bitch was on their trail. Christ knew how she'd got on to it. But he'd have to do something about her immediately. Find out how much she'd got – and stop her getting any more.

Picking up his mobile again, North pressed a memory-dial number. It rang just twice before being answered. 'Sol,' said North, 'hack problems. Her name's Judith Laing, *Herald*. She's sniffing around our Jaipur operation. You know what that means.'

9

Judith unlocked the passenger door of her once lime green VW Beetle, and climbed in. Ever since her close encounter with a Cherokee Jeep on Holland Park Avenue while shooting a red light – running late, no change there – the driver's door had ceased to open. So she had to take the scenic route in, which involved a certain amount of calisthenics getting over the gear shift. But eventually she'd find herself, irked and flushed, behind the wheel, cursing Alex Carter, *The Herald*, her booze-and-cigarette lifestyle, and journalism for paying so badly she couldn't afford a better car. Here she was, all dressed up and places to go – and Bernie's parties were always lavish affairs – stuck in a beat-up old bomb which the AA mechanic had described as a 'death trap'. She hadn't sent it in for repair, because she didn't have the money. Or maybe she did – but spending it on a car just seemed a complete waste.

Turning the key in the ignition, she was relieved when the engine unleashed its distinctive, throaty roar. Pulling out into the Finborough Road traffic, she leaned back in the bucket-seat. She supposed her job did have its compensations. At least it was interesting – at the moment, very interesting indeed – if also unnerving. As she'd suspected, Starwear had been unable to explain the discrepancy between the figures in their own annual report and the Forbes documents. Worse still, they'd lied. Prince Abdul Narish of Hydrabull Investments had laughed when she'd telephoned him to ask if he'd sold Starwear an office block as a package with the factories at Jaipur.

'I specialise in industrial property,' he had declared, in a plummy, Eton accent. 'You can look at my property portfolio in the Delhi land register any time. Domestic and commercial property just isn't my bag.'

Judith duly had the register checked, finding the Prince as good as his word. At no time had he ever owned the office block Starwear claimed they'd bought from him – and later sold at a substantial profit.

Without Starwear so much as suspecting a thing, in four weeks Judith had gathered enough material for a major exposé. And it was one that would not only exhume a whole lot of skeletons Jacob Strauss had thought he'd long-since buried, but also provide evidence that in the past six months Starwear had misled its shareholders about the origin of seven million pounds profit – a jailable offence. But she still wasn't ready to run. There were too many unanswered questions – like, where had the money really come from? Why the cover-up? How high up had the decision been taken to cook the books?

Finding out the answers to these questions, she knew, would be the most perilous undertaking of her career; especially if they were the answers she suspected. She'd come up with a theory that seemed far fetched at the moment – but experience had taught her that when big money was at stake, anything was possible. The scenario she'd put together went something like this: Jacob Strauss's business ventures, launched in his twenties and thirties, had each come unstuck. He is saved the humiliation of bankruptcy only by a private sale to a company no one's ever heard of. Plus the only person who knows the realities of his finances, his partner William van Aardt, is found hanging from his belt in his Vermont shed the week after Jacob bails out. A hasty inquest returns a suicide verdict, according to a piece in van Aardt's local paper, which Judith had tracked down after an exhaustive media search.

Next, Jacob appears on the Starwear Board – didn't Nathan know the reality of his brother's business failures? – and is given the job of heading up International Division. No great shakes there until, in line with its competitors, Starwear decides to move its manufacturing operations into developing world countries, using cheap labour. Jacob Strauss gets Forbes to tell him what to do, but when the Forbes plans are put into action, there are problems; problems which no one seems able to fix.

Strauss gets desperate. The share price is tumbling and someone's taking a position in the company, buying up shares through off-shore investment entities. Strauss knows he can't count on big brother to protect him from Starwear shareholders. So he comes up with his own plan to boost productivity. He secretly subcontracts a whole lot of Starwear production to local factories that can turn the gear at a fraction of the cost – because they use child slave labour. Bingo! The graphs head up and he's back in business. Maestro of Quantum Change. While Nathan Strauss is banging on about corporate ethics, brother Jacob has thousands of street urchins chained up in sweatshops eighteen hours a day churning out Starwear apparel. When word seeps out about child slaves, Jacob vehemently denies it all. Nathan refutes the charge on national television. The question is never asked again.

So much for the theory. When it came to hard evidence, however, Judith could only prove that money was coming from somewhere in India besides the Quantum Change factories. What she couldn't prove was that that 'somewhere' involved child labour. Previous reports about Starwear's exploitation of children had appeared in only one tabloid newspaper, eighteen months earlier. Judith had tried to track down the Asian correspondent who'd written it, but he'd moved off his post, no one knew where. What Judith needed was fresh evidence for herself – but she realised that, even if she remained in Carter's good books, a flight to India to investigate a hunch was as likely as a trip to Mars. So, she'd have to come up with Plan B.

In the past couple of days, she'd hardly had any time to think about it. She'd been too busy keeping her nose clean and generating column inches. And right now she didn't feel like thinking about it because she wanted to have fun; time off from Starwear and the anxieties of coming to the wrong people's attention; time off from *The Herald*; from the incestuous relationships of the newsroom; and from Ted Gilmour in particular.

The two of them had had a stand-up row the night before in the Gents of The Slug and Lettuce. Very edifying. There'd been the usual Friday night drinking binge with a whole gang of them from work. Ted had had a few, and so had she, when he pulled her aside and told her he'd booked a weekend away for the two of them at some stately home in Wiltshire.

Another time she might have let him down gently, or laughed him off as a hopeless romantic. But not last night.

Last night she'd been in a bad-time-of-the-month, end-of-a-long-week and, worst of all, back-from-a-three-hour-lunch-with-Alex-super-lech-Carter frame of mind. So, she let him have it. He'd told her to calm down – big mistake. She'd told him she wasn't calming down for him. He'd tried escaping to the toilets. She'd followed, castigating a row of gaping, urinating City suits for being ruled by their dicks instead of their brains, and lecturing that when a woman says no she means no.

She had, of course, been utterly unreasonable. She'd have to apologise to Ted on Monday. But would Ted misconstrue the apology to mean she really *was* interested? Lordy, lordy, better not even think about it. Why was it her relationships always became so fraught? Like her relationship with Chris, who would probably be coming tonight. They'd both been part of a group that used to congregate in Bernie's rooms at Oxford – even then, Bernie had wangled himself superior accommodation, lucky sod – shooting the breeze into the early hours. Bernie had always been a natural focus for social activity both at Oxford and afterwards. In recent years, it was at his parties, more than anywhere else, where she and Chris had met again; and where she'd found herself behaving every bit as irrationally towards him as she had last night to Ted. Stoking up tensions that needn't exist. Biting his head off. Why did she do it? Who was he to her except a well-intentioned, if conventional man, who'd been her lover in the long-distant past? This evening, she decided, she really should make more of an effort.

Arriving in Bernie's street, she found a space on a single yellow line. Bernie had a typical terraced home, but inside it felt like a palace. He'd had several walls taken out to make fewer, more expansive rooms that were ideal for entertaining. In particular, his sitting room was a cavernous, rag-rolled triumph of luxuriant red. Looking up now from her car, she saw the front door open, and the party already in full swing. Twisting her rear-view mirror down, she checked her appearance – a final smudge of lippie, a last brush through the hair – before twisting herself back across the gear stick on to the passenger side. She was wearing black leather pants and a black halter top, no fancy labels but still she looked pretty svelte; at least the wardrobe she'd acquired for Carter's benefit had other uses. She slammed the Beetle door shut, and there was an ominous rattle before she discovered the lock was no longer working. The key went in, but it just wouldn't turn. She tried, punched the door, tried again. Then, flinging the key into her handbag, she strode off in disgust. Who'd want to break into the bloody thing anyway?

Chris ran his index finger along the polished bonnet of his BMW as he walked down the short driveway of his house. It was the first Saturday since he'd joined Lombard that he hadn't gone into the office; the first Saturday he hadn't had to work on Project Silo, and he felt great. After a late lie-in – eight a.m. was the height of hedonism now – he'd spent the morning wallowing through the newspapers over brunch at a local brasserie. The afternoon had been spent watching cricket and cracking open a few cans of lager in front of the box. He'd also tidied away a few things into cupboards around the flat. His future study, in particular, had been in a state of chaos. He'd planned to throw out a whole lot of old sports stuff when he moved from Islington, but his mother had delivered a lecture along the lines of 'It might be rubbish to you, but there are a lot of people who'd be thankful for it.' She'd persuaded him to donate the stuff to a charity instead . . . only he hadn't got around to it yet. Now, freshly shaven, showered and shampooed, he was on his way round to Bernie's.

Bernie lived a ten-minute walk away; a pleasant walk on a mild, mid-October evening like this. Even so, for a few, brief moments Chris had thought of driving – before admitting to himself that the only reason for doing so was to show off the new car to his mates. Which wasn't a very good reason at all. In particular, he supposed he wouldn't mind Judith seeing it. But then, that sort of thing didn't impress Judith – he should know.

The first few weeks after she'd announced she was seeing Clive Slater had been a painfully schizophrenic time for him. There were moments he just wanted to block her completely from his mind; if he didn't think about her, he'd get over it more easily. But then there were other occasions – like most of his waking moments – when he would have done anything to change her mind.

When she'd broken up with him, she'd said she wanted them to stay friends. All very civilised. So it was as a friend he'd taken her to L'Artistes Assoiffé, with its candlelight and parrots and luxuriant intimacy; as a friend he'd secured tickets in a box at the Royal Albert Hall to watch a Proms concert, followed by dinner at the top of the Hilton in Windows on the World. There'd been the expensive gifts. The desperate efforts at *bon vivant*.

But of course, in taking her to all the kinds of places Clive Slater could never afford, Chris was only making matters worse. Money was not the currency that impressed her. Like anyone else, she enjoyed the things that money could buy, but it wasn't her aphrodisiac. Chris doubted that had changed. Now, as he set off for Bernie's place, a cooler-pack of assorted alcohol in his hand, he thought back to his last phone conversation with Bernie, who had seemed almost apologetic when he told Chris that he'd also invited Judith to the party. Poor chap. Their friends from Oxford still tiptoed around the subject even though it was all ancient history. If Judith turned up tonight he wouldn't avoid her, but nor would he seek her out. The last few times they'd met, she'd been decidedly prickly – he didn't need that in his life.

Besides, tonight he was in top form after handing in Project Silo. Yesterday afternoon just after four he'd delivered copies to North and Cullen. At four-thirty he'd taken Lotte down to the local wine bar for celebratory Taittinger. Christ knew, they deserved it.

Now he was looking forward to getting a life; seeing people, going places. When he arrived at Bernie's house, Chris made his way straight through the house and into the garden, where his host – large, ebullient and check-shirted – was surrounded by a bunch of the other guys in the late-afternoon sunshine.

'Hey, hey, hey – its Mr Psychographic Mapping!' Bernie called out as Chris made his way towards them.

'No – the Invisible Persuader,' cried another.

'Not exactly,' Chris pulled a face, as they looked up at him. 'What's going on?'

Tom Allwood, a university friend and now stockbroker, was twirling a golf club. 'Bernie's new toy.'

'Business aid,' Bernie corrected him with a grin.

The recent acquisition was a golf-drive practice net set up a few yards away. It didn't only catch balls, it also measured their speed; inevitably a competition was in progress among the men, which Chris soon joined.

Cocktails were a regular feature of Bernie's parties. Exotic and dangerous concoctions would circulate in a variety of vivid hues, topped with tropical fruit and paper umbrellas. As more friends started arriving, Bernie retreated indoors to mix drinks in his well-stocked bar. Singapore Slings, which, he insisted, were the very acme of the art, were soon being downed, Jimi Hendrix belted out through the speakers, and the party started to swing. It was a great mix of people, Chris thought, moving up from the lawn to the verandah. He was happily into his second drink and talking to a very tasty art director from M. & C. Saatchi. Blue eyes, long legs and mind on a different planet – where did Bernie find them all? Apart from the regular Oxford crowd and work associates from Salomons, there was a fair sprinkling of less conventional types at the party: an actor who made regular TV appearances in *The Bill*; a hypnotherapist who'd helped Bernie kick smoking; an art director, Carole, who claimed she couldn't draw to save her life, but who, thought Chris appreciatively, could be forgiven any multitude of sins with a body like that.

Food began appearing some time after nine. Bernie could always count on a bevy of willing female friends, including his long-suffering girlfriend Trisha, to produce a lavish buffet for his parties. Chris had collected a plate and was reaching out for an avocado Ritz when he found himself hip to hip with Judith.

'Hey!' he greeted her carefully.

She'd arrived when he was out on the verandah. Out of the corner of his eye he'd watched her coming into the sitting room. He'd always liked her in black; somehow it seemed to heighten her edge. And tonight she looked as desirable as ever. Almost as a reflex action he had checked to see if she'd brought anyone with her. Hadn't looked like it.

Now their greetings were restrained. None of the hugs and kisses they had for other friends of the opposite sex. It was easier this way.

'How's it going?' asked Judith.

He met her eyes. Long enough to seek innuendo, without assuming the intimacy between them which no longer existed. She seemed straight-up.

'I'm fine,' he nodded. Then, glancing down over her, 'You're looking very well.'

'You too.'

'Oh, I don't know. Haven't seen much of the sun lately.'

They moved down the buffet.

'Working hard?' asked Judith.

'Yeah. Big project on the go.'

Her glance was empathetic. 'Know the feeling.'

A couple of times over the meal he was aware of her glancing over at him. Once, they caught each other's eyes and exchanged smiles; he never knew what to make of her. Then Bernie marched through from the freezer with a massive crystal bowl filled with Dom Pedro, a concoction of vanilla ice cream and whisky he'd come across on a trip to South Africa, which he was insistent everyone quaff in large quantities. The accumulation of alcohol was soon loosening tongues and inhibitions. And in Bernie's capacious sitting-womb, with its comfortable sofas and subdued lighting, the intimacy was inescapable.

After the food and desserts came yet more cocktails. The tide of good feeling rose with the night and, at some point, dancing started out on the verandah – just the Pet Shop Boys and a few couples to begin with. Then Trisha hauled out Abba and turned up the volume; the blast from the past was a sure-fire way to engender good feeling. And as Abba was succeeded by Wham and then Sade, it wasn't long before just about everyone in the room was up there, strutting their stuff – a vertical expression of a horizontal desire.

Things were passing by in a cheerful, alcoholic blur. Inevitably a circle had formed on the dance floor and Chris was swept up in it, linked arm-to-arm on each side. Judith was there too, directly opposite, and as the circle swirled round, amid much gaiety and high spirits, they looked over at each other, laughing without restraint. For a while it was as though nothing had changed between them, thought Chris. It was as though time hadn't passed. Was this some kind of game she was playing?

There was, as usual, a good crowd at Bernie's, and as soon as Judith arrived, she was corralled into a corner by Sebastian Hayes – conversational sparring partner since lazy, student evenings at The Trout. The cocktails were flowing thick and fast. Voices rose. Everyone round her was getting quietly smashed, and she reckoned she might as well do the same. Catching sight of Tina Aldren, she crossed the room.

'I thought you were in the middle of Africa?' They exchanged kisses.

'Back on holiday,' replied Tina.

'Rhinos doing OK?'

'Stormin' Norman's a proud dad yet again.'

'You little Cupid!' She reached over and squeezed Tina's cheek.

At college they'd hung out a lot together, the two of them very similar, both petite, and equally outspoken to compensate for their lack of height. Tina had always been the more gregarious of the two – one of those people whom everyone liked to confide in. She'd surprised them all by taking a job with Andersen Consulting, where she'd flown very high, very fast, for five years, then she'd surprised them all even more by throwing everything up and heading to Zimbabwe to help in a breeding programme of the endangered black rhino.

She didn't spend much time in England these days. Even so, she seemed to know more about what everyone was doing than most of Judith's London friends. Now the two of them exchanged news and gossip over the obligatory Singapore Slings, Tina telling Judith about her boyfriend, the tobacco farmer, and Judith filling Tina in on Alex Carter and Ted Gilmour. As usual, they ran through all their closer friends and acquaintances, inevitably coming to Chris.

'So, you're still being a cow to him?' Tina grinned.

'Not deliberately!'

'Moo!' The other pulled a cheeky face. 'Mooo!'

'It's not like that.'

'I'd say calling him an anally-retentive pillock was pretty bovine.'

'That was years ago,' Judith was defensive, 'and he knew I didn't mean it.'

'Ah. Clairvoyant, is he?'

'Anyway,' Judith ignored the barb, 'I'm sure he's not too worried about that now he's got his new piece of fluff.'

'He's seeing someone?'

'You tell me.' She gestured towards the verandah. She'd

noticed him talking to some tall, slim, blonde number. Well, whoopie-do.

Tina raised herself up on her tiptoes. 'You mean Carole Keheyan?'

'The blonde.'

Tina delivered a droll smile. 'That's Bernie's boss's girlfriend.'

'Oh.'

'Funny. For a moment back there your eyes seemed to go a vivid shade of green.'

'It's not like that. Really.' Rewriting history, she'd long since decided, only ever led to tears.

When she met Chris at the buffet table she tried to be friendly, but he seemed wary. After their previous encounters of the past few years, she really couldn't blame him. So she ate supper with Tina and Sebastian and some of the others from the old crowd, friends she saw less frequently these days, and whose company she valued all the more. Then Bernie laid on his doctored ice-cream dessert, and things got very mellow, which was when the dancing started and they were all out on the verandah *I do, I do, I do-ing* at the tops of their voices.

The dance circle that formed had Chris and her directly across from each other. But it didn't feel awkward. Caught up in the mood, as they whirled and kicked through the music, it was just a bit of uninhibited, if slightly inebriated fun. Then the music got funkier and the circle broke up. Judith spent more time circulating and watching with the others while Bernie staged an impromptu fireworks display. Then some time around midnight she noticed Chris doing the rounds, saying his goodbyes, and decided to slip away herself.

Minutes later, she was lighting a cigarette as she made her way down the street to her car. The evening had turned cool, and her pace was brisk. Retrieving the car key from her handbag, she slipped it into the passenger door lock and tried to turn it. No movement. Then she remembered what had happened earlier in the evening, and how she'd ended up leaving the door unlocked. Only now, when she tried opening the door, it wouldn't budge. Slipping the key back in the lock she fiddled with it. Maybe she *had* locked it earlier, without realising. There was some movement when she used the key. But not enough to get the door open.

She shook the handle and punched the door. This was all she bloody needed! The early bloody hours of a Sunday morning; every cab in London crawling round the West End; and she was a very long walk from home. It made her want to scream with frustration. 'Christ Almighty!' She tugged at the handle with as much force as she could muster.

Hearing footsteps on the pavement she looked up. Oh, shit, of all people.

'Trouble?'

'It won't open.'

'And . . .' he gestured to the driver's door.

'Accident,' she cut in, before he could ask, 'I've been using this side . . . till I got it repaired.'

Chris quickly took in the situation. He tried the lock a few times, and gave the door around the handle a few solid thumps. Then he straightened up. 'Looks like a taxi,' he murmured.

There was a moment before he gave her a reassuring smile. 'A locksmith will sort it out in no time,' he told her.

'I'd offer you a lift home myself, but I only live round the corner.'

She looked down at her feet. 'I'm way over the limit anyhow.' Then stepping away, she met his eyes again. 'You moved?'

He nodded. Was he imagining it, or was she being less hostile this evening? Probably all the booze. The cocktails were also affecting him more than he realised, because before he'd even thought about what he was saying, the words were coming out of his mouth. 'You can call a taxi from my place, if you like. Have a coffee or something while you're waiting.'

She managed a half-smile as she glanced away. 'Thanks.'

They walked the short distance back to Chris's home, Judith's high heels loud on the midnight streets. Conversation was safe and low-key; it had been a great party, they agreed. Bernie had been the life and soul. Some things never changed. After nearly ten minutes, Chris was reaching inside his jacket pocket for a set of keys, his footsteps slowing. As he made his way towards a short flight of steps leading to a front door he stepped past a BMW, sleek and gleaming in the street light. She couldn't help observing the proprietorial glance. Unlocking the door, he showed her into a large and beautifully proportioned hallway.

'Moved up in the world,' she couldn't resist saying.

He didn't know how to respond. Her tone seemed admiring, but with Judith it was hard to tell. So, as he led her into the sitting room he replied, 'Haven't been in long. Just a couple of months.'

As they both looked round the room at the pictures and pieces of furniture he'd brought with him from Islington he continued, 'Most of the stuff's from the old flat. But I've still a lot of work to do, decorating the place.'

Handing her a few minicab cards, he pointed towards a telephone by the sofa, before leaving her to make her call. He went through to the kitchen, filled the kettle and got things ready for coffee.

In the sitting room, Judith soon ordered a cab but, as she called through to Chris, there would be a twenty-minute wait. Getting up from the sofa, she folded her arms in front of her and walked slowly around the room, taking in the pictures, the souvenirs – so many things as deeply familiar as they had been long-forgotten, until this moment. How many hours had she lain cocooned in their duvet in Islington, she wondered, staring up at that Monet print they had bought in Covent Garden? And the calabash from her week's holiday in Jamaica – there it was, perched in a corner; why in God's name had he kept all this stuff? She'd cleared out any mementos from that period in her life years ago.

She wanted to reach inside her handbag for a cigarette, but supposed she shouldn't smoke in here; it wasn't her house. Instead, she wandered through to the kitchen, where Chris was spooning Nescafé into two mugs. On the wall by the fridge she found a pinboard the two of them had started together in Oxford, still holding so much of the memorabilia: the menu from a Magdalen College dinner; the May Ball invitation – it was where they had first met Bernie; a champagne cork on which she had written '*Je t'adore*' in red biro on a romantic weekend in Paris.

'You still have this,' she nodded, touching the board.

'Mmm.' Chris glanced across at her. They had avoided eye contact – direct, lingering inspection – for years. When they had met, by force of circumstance, it had all been momentary encounters and sidelong glances, as though they couldn't bear to reveal anything of themselves to each other. But now he held her gaze, searching for her intentions – and could find none. Not so much as a flicker of the old emotion. Nothing to suggest they'd ever been more than casual friends. Perhaps he expected too much. He poured hot water into the two mugs and, as they made their way back to the sitting room, he began to realise that inviting her to his home had been a mistake.

'So . . .' he sat opposite her on one of the sofas. *How were they going to kill time till the taxi arrived?* 'You've got just under twenty minutes to tell me about the past four years of your life.'

She laughed self-consciously as she leaned forward, holding her mug in both hands and blowing on to the surface of the drink. Then she began, telling him about her move to *The Herald*, and about the titanic ego that was Alex Carter. She mentioned her place in Earl's Court; her attempts to quit smoking.

'And how's Libby?' Chris asked.

'Still driving people crazy.'

He laughed. Judith's mother was a cranky old thing, known in the Cotswold village of Tetbury as 'a personality'. Having lost her husband in a car accident, she'd suddenly found herself, in her mid-thirties, with a family of three young girls to bring up, single-handedly. She'd taken to trading in antiques, a business in which she'd done very well, but not without ruffling a few of the local feathers.

Judith told Chris the family news, and answered his questions about some of her other friends he'd lost touch with. Of course, there was one question more than any other he wanted her to answer. He wondered if he should hold back, and wait to see if it came up in conversation. But time was short. So, in as neutral a voice as he could manage, he asked her.

'You seeing anyone at the moment?'

Meeting his eyes, she shook her head. 'You?'

'No. Even if I wanted to, I've no time. Specially since the new job.'

'You left MIRA?'

He was surprised she didn't know. He'd just assumed . . . 'I'm now looking after Research and Planning at Lombard.'

Judith was taken aback. Eyes widening and eyebrows raised, she put her coffee mug down on a side table.

'I know, I know,' he assumed an air of nonchalance, 'the devil's work.'

She sat back in the sofa. 'I never take calls from Lombard PRs,' she told him matter-of-factly, 'so what does a planner do? Sounds as Machiavellian as the rest of the operation.'

Chris pulled a droll smile. 'Hardly. I basically find out what people think of Lombard clients. I look at all the financials of clients and their competitors, corporate strategy, brand positioning – that kind of thing.'

'Like analyst reports?' Judith thought of Merlin.

'Exactly. But for the benefit of the clients who commission them.'

'Sounds very analytical.'

He nodded.

'You enjoy it?'

'Only been there six weeks, and I've been too busy to even think about it. I was getting stale at MIRA. I needed to move on.'

After a pause he added, 'It's strange the way things turn out. I never thought in a million years I'd end up working in the City.'

'Especially not for Lombard.' She couldn't help herself; she was more than simply surprised by the revelation. It seemed to Judith that Lombard had half of the national press in their pocket. And even though she'd managed to give the agency the slip, by fixing her meeting with Lester and Eaglesham, she had never, for a moment, underestimated Lombard's power.

All of which made her feel very wary of Chris's new job. She couldn't help thinking there had to be more than money to lure him into that den of crooks.

Leaning back in the chair, she asked him curiously, 'So, which clients do you work on?'

As Chris looked across at her, Mike Cullen's words thundered in his ears. *There must be no talking shop outside the office. Even the most casual asides are open to misinterpretation. So, it's best to say absolutely nothing. Not about clients, not about colleagues, not about anything that you do.* And here he was, sitting opposite an investigative reporter from one of the country's most powerful national newspapers; a reporter who also happened to be the woman who'd meant more to him than any other. What was he to say?

After a pause he said noncommitally, 'Just about all of them.'

Judith nodded. 'That wouldn't include Starwear by any chance, would it?'

'Yeah,' he was casual, 'I've done some work for them.' He wasn't about to blurt out anything he'd regret later on; and definitely not that he'd done a major investigation for them.

Across from him, Judith was chewing her lip. She always used to chew her lip when she was anxious.

'Why the interest in Starwear in particular?'

Suddenly, she felt she needed a cigarette. She reached into her bag for a pack of B&H Lights.

'Mind if I . . .?'

He shrugged.

Getting up, she walked across to the window where she lit a cigarette in rapid, jerky movements, exhaling loudly. 'You've only been at Lombard six weeks, right?' she asked him.

'Right.'

'You work on all those different clients, right?'

'Right.'

'And there's nothing you've come across at Starwear that you consider . . . ethically questionable?'

He was genuinely surprised. And pleased he could deal with this in a way that Mike Cullen would have applauded. 'Quite the opposite. Starwear is one of the most straight-up companies I've ever dealt with.'

'Christ help us!' Judith took a long drag of her cigarette.

Chris regarded her with the benevolence of a doting father watching his child making mischief. 'Come on, Jude, Nathan Strauss was hardly someone—'

'It's not him I'm talking about. It's his younger brother. Why do you think Nathan topped himself?'

Chris could hardly believe what he was hearing. This was way off the spectrum. 'You're not saying that had something to do with Jacob?' His voice had risen.

'That's exactly what I'm saying.' She was firm.

They held each other's gaze across the sitting room, Chris flabbergasted by her accusation – all the more so

given the calm self-assurance with which she'd made it;
Judith wrestling with all she knew and wondering how
much she ought to tell Chris. Here she was, standing opposite a Lomboid; one who worked on the Starwear account
and probably had dealings with Jacob Strauss.

'Look, I don't have the full picture yet. And what I do
know . . .' She trailed off.

'Yes?' he demanded.

It was a moment before she answered. 'How can I be sure
you won't go running back to Lombard?'

There was a long pause before he asked, in hurt rather
than anger, 'Don't you think you mean *anything* to me?'
Then, trying to be more conciliatory, 'Whatever else you
think of me, surely you know I can be trusted?'

For a while they held each other's gaze. Finally she said,
'I know for sure that Strauss and his cohorts are dangerous
and untrustworthy.'

Chris shook his head. 'Where's the evidence?'

'The evidence?' she flashed back, her voice notching up
several tones. 'There's Merlin de Vere, just for starters.'

'The kinky sex guy?'

'That was a set-up.'

'Some set-up! It's got the police fooled.'

'Damned right it has!'

He was shaking his head, regarding her with rising
anger. How could she believe this crap?

'Are you seriously telling me,' he leapt off the sofa, finding it hard to conceal his contempt, 'that Jacob Strauss
ordered the murder of one of the City's leading analysts?'

'Him or one of his thugs.'

'What was the motive?'

'Merlin knew too much about Strauss,' she shot back,

'like the fact that he's a crook and that every business he's ever run has gone to the wall.'

'That's a bloody lie and you know it!' he exploded, unable to restrain his rage a moment longer. 'I won't have you standing here in my house,' he jabbed his hand at her furiously, 'talking about my clients as though they're a bunch of gangland mafiosi—'

'But they are.' Any thoughts she'd had about treating Chris with kid gloves this evening were forgotten in the tide of indignation that swept her away. 'What's the matter with you – have you stopped thinking for yourself? Just because they give you a BMW do you believe every piece of crap they churn out?'

She wasn't standing for him wagging his finger at her like some complacent fat cat. 'You want evidence? Well, go and look through the accounts of Ultra-Sports. You'll see that your great client had his fingers in the till – five point seven million dollars unaccounted for in the last year's trading. And Trimnasium never even recouped its R&D expenditure. Seventeen million down the pan!'

'A point entirely missed by the financial community on both sides of the Atlantic.' Chris's sarcasm was bitter.

'It wasn't missed by Merlin de Vere.'

'And I suppose Jacob's business associates were all ecstatic about being ripped off?'

'He only had one business partner, William van Aardt,' she sneered, 'and as you all too evidently don't know, *he* was found hanging from his belt in his garden shed, a week after Jacob sold the companies. Strange behaviour for someone who's supposedly just become a multimillionaire.'

At that moment, the doorbell sounded.

Judith took a final drag of her cigarette and flicked the

butt clear of his window, before collecting her handbag, and making her way back through the hallway.

'For God's sake, not a word to anyone. You could put me in serious danger.'

'Don't think you can chuck bombs at me then just walk away.' He was following her, in high dudgeon. 'You've made serious allegations—'

'And I've got a taxi to catch.'

'But you can't just—'

'Watch me!' She opened the front door and gestured to where the cab driver was back behind the wheel.

'I'm calling you to discuss this further.'

'Only after hours,' she insisted.

'I don't see what's wrong with—'

'All Lombard calls are recorded.' She was stalking across to her waiting taxi, slinging her handbag over her shoulder. 'Don't tell me you didn't know *that*.'

Actually, he didn't. And he had no idea if it was true. But as with all her other accusations, Judith had delivered this one with such unshakeable authority that he couldn't help wondering. After watching her taxi rattle down the street, he closed the front door and returned inside, realising that despite being infuriated, yet again, by this latest confrontation with Judith, he couldn't dismiss all she'd said. She was right that he knew nothing about Ultra-Sports and Trimnasium apart from what Lombard had put out; and he'd never even heard of William van Aardt. But what about Merlin de Vere? The notion that the City analyst had been the victim of some corporate cover-up seemed as ludicrously far-fetched as it was perverse. How could it possibly be true?

10

'**B**it of all right, ain't she?' Harry Denton leaned forward as d'Andrea flicked through the photos. It was Sunday evening in The Hounds and Horses, a pub near d'Andrea's home, which he used for meetings with Denton. They were sitting at a small table in the rear corner of the pub, a table almost completely concealed behind a row of fruit machines. D'Andrea paused at one of the photos taken the night before, bringing it up to within six inches of his eyes. Chris Treiger was walking down the street with the girl. No hand-holding, d'Andrea noticed.

'You reckon he picked her up?' he asked, scrutinising the picture.

'Too right, the smooth little sod. I followed him from his place to the party. He definitely went alone.'

'They spend a lot of time together during the evening?'

'Couldn't see much. Bad access round the other side of the house. When I saw him saying goodbye to his mates I skipped round the block as fast as I could. It took about ten minutes. But, hey presto!'

Denton leaned back in his chair, downing a bitter. D'Andrea worked his way through the photos, puzzled. It didn't seem like Treiger's style to pick up women at parties and take them back to his place; he was too buttoned-down. But the evidence couldn't be disputed. D'Andrea came to the shot of the two of them in Treiger's kitchen, the curtains wide open, the lights full on, and the two of them standing very close together.

'Come back to my place for coffee, me darling.' Denton's mouth twisted in a sly smile.

D'Andrea had never found Denton's East End wit even mildly amusing. Denton had long-since decided that d'Andrea was a miserable old geezer. But he paid top dollar.

'And after this?' D'Andrea was waving the photo.

'They went round the other side of the house. But the lounge curtains were closed. I hung around – thought they might go upstairs to his room and give me a free floor show. But when they went up, he closed the curtains straight off, antisocial git!'

D'Andrea looked across at him seriously. 'You're absolutely sure she stayed the night?'

Denton nodded vigorously. 'No doubt about it, guv. After he closed the curtains, the light stayed on about half an hour. Then I went round the front again, thinking I might catch her when she left. By three a.m. she'd still not come out. I called it a night – I'd been up twenty-four bloody hours.'

'Hmm.'

D'Andrea leafed through the photos again till he came to the best one of the girl. She was in the kitchen. The lighting was excellent and it was a direct, full-face shot. As he sat, staring at the picture for a while, he mulled it all over. There was definitely something odd about this. On an intuitive level, he knew the story Denton was telling him didn't stand up. It might be part of the truth, but not all of it. Denton probably didn't know the full story himself.

And there was another thing that bothered him: the girl's face. It looked somehow familiar, as though he'd seen it recently but he couldn't place it. D'Andrea didn't just have a good memory, he possessed a remarkable aptitude for recalling faces, names, dates, biographical details – in his job he needed it. Maybe the girl was just some arbitrary pick-up, but on the other hand, perhaps she had already flickered across the Monitoring Services radar screen. He would soon find out. Tomorrow morning, he'd take the photograph into work and have it cross-checked against a picture library which included over three thousand women in the City, media, and PR industry. If she was anyone on file, he'd soon know all about her.

Knocking back the last of his Bloody Mary, d'Andrea shuffled the photos together, placing them in an envelope which he slipped into his inside pocket. In the same movement, he retrieved a separate, brown envelope, which he handed over to Denton. 'The usual,' he grunted.

'Uh-huh.'

D'Andrea scraped back his chair as he stood up. 'Keep on Treiger's tail and stay in touch.'

Denton glanced up at him with a wink. 'Pleasure doing business with you, guv.'

No sooner had Chris Treiger stepped into his office the following Monday morning than Charlotte was there to meet him. 'Elliott North's been trying to get hold of you,' she told him hurriedly, 'he's rung three times in the past half hour and hasn't sounded friendly.'

He glanced at his watch. Eight-fifteen. Late start. But

with Project Silo out of the way he'd reckoned he could ease up a little for the next few days. He was irritated to be caught napping by North. Picking up the phone he dialled three digits.

'My office. Now,' North ordered him, after he'd announced himself.

Glancing over at Charlotte, he made his way swiftly to the door. 'You're right,' he murmured. '*Very* unfriendly.'

Instead of waiting for the lift, he raced down the stairs. Was North as pissed off as he sounded, he wondered, or was it just Monday morning-itis? And what had provoked him? Nothing he'd done, not that he could think of. Maybe North hadn't had a chance to read Project Silo over the weekend – when he had, Chris expected a rather different reception.

North's was the last executive office on the first floor behind the Pit, which was an open-plan frenzy even at this time on a Monday morning. Chris had only ever been in the office once, and had immediately been as aware of the minimalist décor – white walls, no pictures, functional office furniture – as he had been of the pungent aroma of fruit. North ate fruit throughout the day; discarded apple cores, banana and orange skins steadily piled up in the metal dustbin under his desk, lending the place a ripe miasma. As he stood at the door of North's office this morning, Chris was surprised by the fetid aroma so early in the day.

'Morning, Elliott,' he greeted him.

North looked up, glowering.

Whatever it is that's eating him, I'm not going to let it get to me, decided Chris, as he stepped into the office to sit opposite him. North pointedly stood up and stepped round behind Chris to close his door, before returning to his desk. In the middle of the desk, Chris couldn't help noticing, was North's copy of Project Silo. As he sat down, North slammed his hand on the report. 'What exactly are you trying to prove, turning in this crock of shit?' He fixed Chris with a furious expression.

Chris was so surprised by the reaction that for a moment he didn't know what to say.

'Four weeks,' North's voice rose. 'Four weeks you've had to work on this. Your first major project at Lombard. And all you can come up with is a whole pile of marketing bull-shit!'

Chris's mind was reeling. He could hardly believe North was talking about Project Silo; his best work ever. Shock quickly turned to anger, and when he did eventually speak, he had to fight to keep his voice even. 'I was actually very pleased with the way it turned out.' He looked North in the eye. 'What exactly didn't you like about it?'

'Jesus Christ!' North brought his hand down on the desk with a thump. 'This stuff reads like some academic treatise. What we're after is real meat.'

Chris realised that if he could control his own temper while North lost his, it would be to his advantage.

'What specifically do you mean?'

'Like what has Ed Snyder been up to that he doesn't want anyone to know about? Like where we can hit Bob Reid so goddamn hard he'll never recover?'

'I've covered positioning—'

'Positioning! I want facts; the low-down. All this waffle—' he prodded the report contemptuously, 'is utterly useless!'

Chris cocked his head to one side, before saying

pointedly, 'I beg to differ.' His arctic tone concealed a rising tide of resentment. 'I've identified fundamental weaknesses in Active Red's distribution activity, and negative gearing at Sportex, which no one has uncovered before and which gives Starwear an unprecedented commercial advantage. As for positioning, whether you like it or not the fact is that Starwear is a brand that needs to be revitalised; freshened up. I've shown', he gestured towards the report, 'where the brand needs to go to be repositioned, and how to get it there. No one's ever done that before.'

All the time he'd been speaking, North had fixed him with a long, disdainful stare. Now he was shaking his head. 'You just don't get it, do you?' he said after Chris had finished. 'So let me spell it out for you in words of one syllable. Your job is to dig up all the dirt on Snyder and Reid.'

'What do you think I've just been talking about?'

North flicked his hand dismissively. 'Who gives a shit if Active Red hasn't signed up a few retail chains? What I need to know is that Snyder has been paying bribes to the Pakistani Government for production rights; or that Reid is balling his niece.'

Chris regarded North, dumbfounded. 'I'm a strategic planner,' he replied icily, 'not MI5. It seems to me you need to hire yourself a private dick.'

'Correction,' North placed his elbows on his desk, folded his hands and scrutinised Chris furiously behind his glasses, '*you* should have hired him. We pay you a wedge of money, a very big wedge. You're the research whiz-kid. We give you time, we give you whatever budget you need; you're supposed to work out what needs doing.'

'A private detective?' Chris was incredulous.

'Next you're going to tell me that offends your sensibilities?' North was fiery with contempt. Chris returned his gaze coldly.

'Fact is,' North continued, 'I've already done that job for you. After I read your . . . thesis, last Friday night, I got a guy, Kuczynski, on the case straight away. Gave him the briefing *you* should have six weeks ago. Meantime, I'm gonna have to stall Jay Strauss. He tells me you've already said the report would be out this week?'

Chris couldn't deny that had been an error of judgement. Only, he hadn't anticipated North's reaction. He still found it hard to credit. Now North was shoving his copy of Project Silo towards him. 'Kuczynski will be in touch with you direct. Rewrite Project Silo on the basis of what he comes up with. And don't forget we're running out of time.'

'How do you know he'll come up with anything at all?' Chris didn't even try to conceal his scorn.

'I've used him before. He's expensive,' North eyeballed Chris significantly, 'but at least *he* does the business.'

Chris returned to his office, closing the door firmly behind him. Never in his professional life had he been subjected to such brazen arrogance, and as he returned to his desk, the phrases played back – *crock of shit . . . reads like some academic treatise . . . all this waffle is utterly useless*. If North thought he was going to rewrite Project Silo on the basis of what some private dick had to say, he had another thing coming. Who the hell did he think he was? Mike Cullen's reaction to his report, Chris was certain, would be a very different matter indeed.

He'd always known that North was out of sync with the

rest of the agency. This latest contretemps showed just how far out of sync he was. Worst of all for Chris, if using private dicks was North's *modus operandi*, perhaps some of the accusations Judith had made last Saturday night weren't so far-fetched after all. Even though two days had gone by, the shock of what she'd told him still hadn't receded. Her version of reality was just so completely at odds with what he believed that it had been hard to take in. If it had been anyone except Judith, he would have dismissed all she'd said as some lurid, journalistic fantasy. But it *was* Judith. And he knew her well enough to realise this wasn't a game.

North had finally shown his true colours, decided Chris. His demands weren't just perverse – they also triggered a memory of the night he'd met Jacob Strauss. What had disturbed Chris about Strauss, he recalled now, was the same obsessiveness about his business rivals. Corporate competition was reduced to crude, underhand battles for personal power. It was a mentality utterly divorced from how the rest of Lombard conducted its business. All of which meant that Chris had some homework to do. And fast. He needed to check out some of the accusations Judith had made last Saturday night. He already knew exactly what he was going to do about it.

11

Judith didn't pay any attention to the police car when she first noticed it. Double parked and with blue lights flashing, it blocked a whole lane of Finborough Road, reducing the bumper-to-bumper eight p.m. traffic to walking speed. On her way home from Earl's Court Underground, the Tuesday following Bernie's party, she realised as she got closer that the police car was parked directly outside the front door of number 174. She climbed the short flight of steps up from the road, and found a police constable standing at the open door.

'Evening, madam?' he queried.

'I live here,' she explained, 'top floor.'

He retrieved a notepad from his pocket and glanced down a list of names. 'And you are?'

'Judith Laing.'

'Very good.' He opened the door for her.

'What's going on?' she asked, hurrying towards the stairs.

'My colleague up there will explain.'

She rushed up the six flights of steps to the top flat. The door was unlocked and she could hear voices from inside. Hurrying through the hallway, she turned into the large room they used as a lounge-cum-dining room. It looked like a bomb-site. Every book, picture and piece of paper that had been in the room was now scattered across the floor. Ornaments lay smashed, tables and chairs were over-turned. A bottle of tomato ketchup had been sprayed like graffiti over one wall. In the centre of the scene of disaster, a woman police constable stood taking notes from Simon who stood, ashen-faced, in a short-cropped T-Shirt and blue jeans a size too tight.

As she stepped into the room, the two looked up.

'I'm afraid you've had a burglary,' the WPC explained needlessly.

Judith glanced over towards where the TV, video recorder and CD player used to be.

'They took my camcorder,' Simon whimpered.

'And a lot of other stuff.' Judith looked around with the feeling that she'd been caught in some surreal drama.

'The landlord will have to replace all *that*,' Simon was, as ever, both self-absorbed and theatrical, 'but my camcorder was personal property. Brand, spanking new.'

The WPC exchanged a glance with Judith before trying to reassure her. 'The bedrooms aren't nearly so bad. But I'd like you to have a good look round yours to see if anything is missing.'

Judith turned, making her way down the short corridor. As she did, she suddenly thought of Merlin de Vere. *What if this wasn't just some random break-in? What if it had to do with her Starwear investigations?* She made her way hastily into her bedroom. Her ancient desktop computer stood untouched, dwarfing her dressing table. All the computer disks were exactly where she'd left them. She raised a hand to her chest as she glanced about at the overturned drawers and open cupboards. Tough shit if they'd come searching for jewellery, she thought. She didn't have any of value. Though, as she looked over at her bedside table, she saw her Discman had been stolen. The gold-faced alarm clock her parents had given her when she left for university had been ground into the floor.

She felt emotion well up in her; a powerful and bitter-sweet paradox of relief and anger. The bastards! How dare they invade her private space! She didn't have much – there'd hardly been anything to steal – but this was the only corner of the world she could call her own. Knowing that some anonymous, malevolent thug had been rifling through all her most intimate belongings only hours before, seeing what he could loot and pillage, made her feel vio-lated. As she fought to retain her composure, anger and loss churned inside.

The WPC knocked on the door. 'There's been a lot of it in the area, I'm afraid,' she said, seeing Judith glance about her room with an expression of hopelessness. 'Teenage gangs.'

'Drugs money,' Judith's voice was flat.

'That's about the sum of it.'

'And not a bloody thing we can do.'

'I've left a leaflet on how to improve your security,' the WPC tried to steer the conversation in a more positive direction. 'These sorts of people always pick on the easy tar-gets. The harder you make it for them to get in, the less likely they are to try.'

'How did they get in?'

'Kitchen window.'

Judith looked up with a weary expression; the kitchen window faced directly on to a fire escape. 'And how do you suggest we seal that off?'

'I admit, it might be difficult . . .'

'Impossible, more likely.'

'Yes, well. I can request a Community Liaison Officer comes round to advise you—'

'I'd sooner you catch the bastards who did this,' Judith vented her frustration, 'but I don't suppose you'll be sending round the CID to dust the scene of a domestic burglary for fingerprints?'

The WPC met her eyes with a cool expression. 'Actually, they've already been.'

'Oh.' Judith glanced away, embarrassed. Up till now, she'd always had the distinct impression that apathy prevailed in the Metropolitan Police when it came to 'petty crime'.

'There's a gang that's been active in the Chelsea and South Kensington area,' the WPC was explaining. 'They're getting more and more audacious – there's been quite a lot of press coverage on them.'

Now that she was reminded, Judith did recall seeing some headlines in the *Evening Standard* about burglaries.

'We've identified who they are. Special Branch thought this job was another of theirs. But', she added knowingly, '*I* knew it wasn't, the moment I arrived.'

Judith looked at her, questioningly.

'This gang have their own signature – something that *hasn't* been written about in the papers.'

'And that is?'

The WPC looked away. 'They masturbate on the bed-clothes.'

Judith pulled a face.

'I knew dusting here would be a waste of time,' the WPC sounded firm.

'No ID?'

She shook her head. 'No prints at all.'

'What?'

'Whoever did this job was very professional. Didn't leave a trace behind.'

Judith immediately glanced back at her computer and disks.

'Do you see a lot of this?' she said, chewing her lip. 'Not leaving any prints behind, I mean?'

'Far from it,' the WPC was firm. 'Most criminals don't give a damn. Usually teenage junkies in too much of a hurry.'

It was not the answer Judith was looking for.

'But', she asked, urgently needing reassurance, 'have you seen professional burglaries in the area at all?'

The WPC flipped shut the notepad she'd been carrying, and slipped it into her pocket. 'I've been working this beat for five years, and I've never seen a job like this. It has all the hallmarks of a teenage break-in, but it's been carried out by a very slick operator.'

Judith felt her mouth going dry.

'It's almost', the WPC continued, 'as though this was some kind of copycat operation; a professional trying to look like an amateur.'

Judith met her eyes with a look of desperation. 'But why . . . us?' Her voice was strained.

In the pause that followed, she realised it was a question to which there was no answer. The WPC looked sympathetic as she admitted, 'I really can't say, madam. But I can request—'

'A Community Liaison Officer. Yeah, sure.' Judith glanced about anxiously.

'Would you like a visit?' the other persisted.

Judith shrugged. 'Sure.'

'About this time of day?'

'Any time after eight.'

'I have your details.' The WPC tapped her pocket. 'Someone will be in touch first.'

'Fine.' She wouldn't hold her breath, Judith thought, as the WPC turned and left the room. She wouldn't expect any answers either.

As she stood in the centre of all this mess, she looked around her with a growing horror. What if it was, as the WPC had suggested, a break-in designed to look like a burglary, but with a very different motive? Stepping back to her computer, she was now a lot less certain than she'd been earlier. *They could have come in here and copied every single disk – and she'd never know. They could have downloaded the entire contents of her computer.* Were these the guys who had murdered Merlin de Vere, and dressed up the crime to look like a squalid episode of autoeroticism; the same guys who had made sure William van Aardt had been found strung up?

She fumbled in her handbag for her cigarettes and hastily lit one. Her only consolation, she thought as she exhaled, was that even if they had checked through all her computer files, they would have found she was clean as a whistle. Ditto her computer at *The Herald*. Everything to do with the Starwear investigation was safely stored on three computer disks she kept with her, in the pocket of her cosmetics bag, at all times.

Dropping on to her knees, she began collecting up the clothes and books that had been thrown to the floor. In her mind she went back to her last contact with Starwear – the

conversation with Matt Lester. They must have realised he'd
screwed up, she thought. They must be wondering if she'd
discovered that Lester had lied to her. It was a lie that would
be hugely damaging if reported in the press – a lie that would
send the price of Starwear shares into freefall, and see half
the Starwear Board fired; including, probably, Jacob Strauss.

It was all making sense. As she replaced her lingerie
drawer, trying to block out of her mind the knowledge that
unknown fingers had been searching through it only hours
earlier, she realised what was going on. They were trying to
find out how much she knew; how big a threat she was.
And if she became a problem to them, she had no illusions about what would happen to her. She would join the
roll-call of victims that included van Aardt and de Vere,
and God knew who else. A fatal mishap would befall her –
of that she had no doubt. The question was – what could
she do to stop them?

'I have some disturbing news.' D'Andrea always used the
Boardroom when he needed to impart particularly sensitive
information. Soundproof, and swept for bugging devices
every morning, it was the one room in the building in
which there was no chance of anyone eavesdropping on
the conversation.

Across the Boardroom table, in the late-afternoon shadows, Elliott North raised his eyebrows.

D'Andrea opened the brown A4 envelope in front of
him and took out a photograph which he pushed across the
table. 'This was taken three nights ago. Kitchen of Treiger's
new house.'

North glanced at the photo. 'Who's the girl?' he wanted
to know immediately.

D'Andrea paused before answering. When he did, his voice was quiet. 'Judith Laing.'

North shot him a disbelieving glare, before looking back at the photo, which showed the couple standing close together in a kitchen. 'What the—?'

'It seems they know each other rather well.'

'Tell me something I don't know.' North's face filled with sudden fury, the red marks at his temples deepening several shades.

'I was about to do exactly that.'

'Of all the people he could hit on.'

'Oh, it's worse than that, I'm afraid. Very much worse.' D'Andrea retained his provocative calm.

'How could it be any worse?' North fixed d'Andrea with a savage expression, as though holding him personally responsible.

In the twilight shadows, d'Andrea responded with a look of distaste. 'It would seem the two have been in an on-off relationship for the past ten years.'

North struck the table with his fist with an almighty thump. 'I don't believe it,' he screamed, jumping up from the table and pacing the room. 'Why the fuck are you telling me this now? Why didn't you say anything before we hired the son of a bitch?'

D'Andrea observed North's tantrum with a cool detachment. 'We didn't know,' he shrugged.

'But it's your job to find out.'

'We find out what we can. But when a relationship has been . . . dormant for a period of several years—'

'Judith Laing is turning into a major issue. A week ago I'd never heard of the dumb bitch. Now she's all over Starwear and Treiger.'

'I believe we passed on both those pieces of information,' d'Andrea reminded him evenly.

'Routine surveillance,' snapped North, shoving hands in his trouser pockets as he stood staring out of the Boardroom window. 'Ten years. Like an old married couple, and you never picked it up.'

'Clairvoyance is not one of our specialisms.'

'What's that supposed to mean?'

'What it means', d'Andrea addressed his back, 'is that if there'd been a relationship to pick up, as you put it, we'd have picked it up. But there wasn't. None of Treiger's friends or colleagues knew anything about a girlfriend. The two of them haven't exchanged a single phone call since Treiger started here. There have been no visits or physical contact since,' he nodded at the photo, 'that night. It's my belief that they aren't regularly in touch. But last Saturday night they found themselves at the same party, they had a few drinks . . . and so it goes.'

'And so it goes, huh?' North turned back from the window. 'All very well you giving me this "and so it goes" crap. I've got to patch up a major security leak.'

For a long while, d'Andrea regarded him with a long stare, scratching one of the liver blotches on his hands before saying finally, 'Maybe. Maybe not.'

'What the hell's that supposed to mean?' The welts on North's forehead were burning deep crimson.

'You don't know if anything leaked. We've carried out a search of Judith Laing's flat this afternoon. We also downloaded all the files from her computer at work.'

He paused, observing North's surprised expression. 'Nothing on Starwear.'

'Nothing?' North was disbelieving. Then a sardonic

expression crossed his face. 'Well, how's about that? Next you're going to tell me that she's "squeaky clean". I believe that was the expression you used to describe our great recruitment error?'

'That's not a description I would use in this case,' d'Andrea overlooked the vitriol, once again. 'She could have written straight on to disk and be carrying around any disks with her.'

'Shit.' North raised a hand to his brow.

'Of course, the only way of checking that would be to remove her handbag.' D'Andrea's voice betrayed no emotion. 'But coming on top of the break-in at her flat, her suspicions would be aroused. Anyway, even if we found one set, she might still have back-ups.'

'God Almighty.' North paced the other side of the Boardroom table for a while before wheeling round suddenly to face d'Andrea, eyes blazing. 'I want both of their flats bugged.'

D'Andrea raised his eyebrows. 'Expensive operation.'

'The client will pay,' he spat out the words. 'In the meantime, I'm going direct to Carter.'

'I would strongly counsel against that.' D'Andrea pursed his lips. 'It's something one would contemplate as a final resort—'

'Which is exactly what this is,' exploded North. 'We pay his kid's school fees, don't we? We foot the bill on his holidays. Where's the pay-off?'

D'Andrea shrugged. 'I'm not the PR man. But I have the impression the pay-off is every day he's City Editor. There's a lot of . . . goodwill there. We don't want to blow it.'

Leaning over the Boardroom table, North's eyes flashed behind his lenses. 'You're right,' he snapped, 'you're *not* the

PR man. So why don't you go back to playing hide-and-seek while I take care of the business?'

D'Andrea held his eyes, utterly unintimidated, before shaking his head, slowly. 'You know, Elliott, most of the time it doesn't feel like we're playing on the same team.'

Five minutes later, North was back in his office, dialling a phone number. 'Alex. It's Elliott North,' he announced when he was put through. 'It's about one of your staff – Judith Laing. I'm worried about her . . .'

12

The buildings of Regent's College were ivy-clad red-brick, built among the towering oaks and lush lawns of the park, and evocative of a dreamy yesteryear. Inside the college, its lecture theatres and tutorial rooms were spartan affairs, original wooden furniture rickety from generations of use. Cheap, plastic chairs and Formica-topped tables had been brought into service, their utilitarian charmlessness in stark contrast to the grandeur of their surroundings. It was a world of familiar contrasts to Ellen Kennedy, who arrived promptly at the college at two p.m., having come down from Oxford on the twelve-twenty train. Proceedings were due to commence at two-thirty but, in his letter to members of the GlobeWatch Executive Council, Claude Bonning had explained that tea would be served from two o'clock onwards, to give committee members of the new organisation the chance to meet informally.

Having helped herself not only to a cup of tea, but also to a foil-wrapped chocolate biscuit – surely a superfluous, if enjoyable, extravagance for a not-for-profit body like GlobeWatch? – Ellen spent most of the first quarter of an hour talking to Claude, whom she hadn't met in person for quite some time. He explained to her how the Family First project she had visited several years before had been extended to inner-city areas elsewhere in Britain, and in America too.

Keeping her eye on the door as he spoke, Ellen was expecting a steady stream of executive-sponsor types, with sharp suits and electronic organisers. But as time moved on, to her surprise the only arrivals were people she had already met or knew about from other charity foundations. There were council members from Save the Children, and a medical adviser to the Red Cross. Various ecological experts arrived, including several she'd met at the Royal Geographical Society and, as the noise volume in the room steadily increased, in strode two well-known trade union leaders, with a band of American industrial relations consultants in their wake. Introducing herself to the only young man she suspected might be a corporate donor – fresh-faced, clean cut, and armed with a mobile telephone – Ellen was surprised to discover he was the new press spokesman for Greenpeace! As she glanced around her, she couldn't help observing that it was an impressive cross-section of groups Claude had brought together; she found herself in very good company indeed. Others in the room were, of course, making that self-same observation.

Shortly after two-thirty p.m., Claude took his place at one of the desks arranged in a circle, and thumped it with a whiteboard wiper. 'My lords, ladies and gentlemen. Could I ask you to take your seats, please?'

Obediently, they found themselves places, glancing around expectantly – some in a surreptitious spot-the-aristocrat exercise. Ellen, who had already met Lords Hoyle and Wilthrop in the St John's Senior Common Room, was far more excited by the fact that there didn't appear to be a single business 'minder' in the whole group. That immediately set GlobeWatch apart. In the past, she'd been invited to join all kinds of societies and institutions, only to find that they had really been set up by large companies to provide a convenient fig leaf for their own activities. GlobeWatch was obviously different; you couldn't fool all of these people, could you? As she glanced down the agenda, copies of which had been placed on each desk, she immediately noted point number three, 'Programme Funding'. That, she supposed correctly, was why everyone was here.

Now, Claude was clearing his throat. 'First of all, may I say how delighted I am that you could all attend,' he began.

From somewhere round the table a stray voice chipped in, 'When there's the chance of funding . . .' to general laughter.

Ellen settled in her chair, folding her arms and putting them on the desk in front of her. She could tell this was going to be a good meeting.

Claude began by talking about the objectives of the new group. GlobeWatch was to be a high-profile, well-funded think-tank, advising multinational companies and governments around the world on good corporate citizenship in the areas of industrial and labour relations, and environmental stewardship. Documents describing GlobeWatch's objectives in detail had been circulated a fortnight before the meeting. Claude now invited comments. A number of suggestions were made, which opened up discussion. The less significant word changes were accepted with little debate, while more important shifts in emphasis produced a few lively verbal tussles which, Ellen observed, Claude handled with the consummate skill of a committee veteran, making everyone feel they had won something, while steering through his original proposals intact.

Having dealt with objectives, they turned to point number two on the agenda, Globe Watch strategy, and once again Claude solicited the support of all present to carry out the activities he proposed. Everyone was eager to get on to point number three, thought Ellen, which was why GlobeWatch's objectives and strategy were agreed to with only the lightest debate – no doubt this was a deliberate ploy on Claude's part, since he had drawn up the agenda.

'We've all been involved in organisations of this kind over the years,' Claude said as he moved on to the main event, 'where the wealth of good ideas has been matched only by the poverty of the organisational coffers. It's no use having the vision splendid if you don't have the means to realise that vision. Many of us have also been involved in an even worse scenario – where the funding is there, but because different projects are undertaken on an ad hoc basis, with no reference to each other, there has been no overall momentum. This is why I, personally, am keen to see GlobeWatch get it right from the start.'

Pausing, he looked around the table, meeting the eyes of each of those present. 'As everyone here knows, we have the funding.'

'Hear, hear,' someone applauded him.

'You've all seen the list of corporate donors I've sent out.'

It was a list Ellen Kennedy had studied with care. Over thirty of Britain's biggest businesses had committed funds of over a quarter of a million pounds, making Claude Bonning the veritable Santa Claus of the voluntary sector.

'We're meeting today to learn how those of you seeking GlobeWatch support would use the funding. What we *all* want is to see a set of programmes in place which complement each other. We need to move in the same direction to maximise the benefits.'

Around the table there was much nodding and agreement.

'Each programme sponsor will have the chance to speak. Then, over the next few days, I will canvass the opinion of everyone present and, if there is a general consensus, funding for each programme will be granted, in principle. Any details can be thrashed out at a later stage. If funding is not granted for a particular programme, we may ask the individuals concerned to re-submit new proposals.'

Claude had already explained all of this on the phone to the new Council members. Ellen had asked him in which order people were to make their pitch for funding. Claude had said he hadn't decided, which was when Ellen had requested to go on last. That way, she knew from past experience, she could make sure her own proposals conveyed none of the weaknesses of those that had gone before. And, what's more, having detected the reaction of the group to other proposals, she'd have a far better idea of how to play her own.

Not that she need have worried. They were not all competing for the same money but, rather, seeking mutual approval to go ahead with programmes. As one programme sponsor was followed by another, each enthusiastically outlining the benefits of their ideas, Ellen observed how a dynamic of mutual support was soon established – I'll back your project, if you back mine. The cynic in her couldn't help being amused by it. But, she reminded herself reasonably, these were all devoted professionals; leaders in their fields, men and women like herself, who for years had wanted to move projects forward but had been held back time and time again for lack of money.

When it came to her own turn to present her proposals, she was her usual brisk, sharp-minded self. She'd prepared a brief presentation on the programmes she had in mind and, unlike many of those present, she also had substantial documentation detailing her plans. For many years, ideas for projects she'd dreamed of setting in motion had sat dormant in her filing cabinet, she had simply dusted them off, updated them and had them copied and heat-bound in clear, plastic covers. The authority and passion with which she spoke on the subject of child labour, and the sensible measures she proposed to stop it, couldn't fail to move her audience. When she finished, there was even a round of applause.

After the funding proposals, Claude briefly discussed a GlobeWatch publishing and public relations programme, to run in tandem with those projects that were endorsed by the Executive Council. Time was moving on, it was just after four, and people were beginning to glance at their watches. And then Claude came to the final item on the agenda – the GlobeWatch Awards.

'As I said at the outset, GlobeWatch needs to adopt a high profile if it wants anyone to pay attention to it,' he enthused, ' and one of the most effective mechanisms I've discovered, while at Family First, is running an awards evening. Awards evenings give a focus to things. If one arranges a well-attended media event, one has the opportunity not only to make sure that GlobeWatch becomes well known, but also to reward those companies whose activities represent best practice. It's our chance to hand out carrots, instead of always using the stick.'

There was much agreement around the table.

'I've drafted a number of possible categories for an awards event. Although I suggest we keep things confidential – there's nothing hard and fast about the categories at this stage – I'd appreciate your views.' He waved towards a pile of papers before glancing at his watch. 'I realise it's after four and some of you have to go. But thank you all very much for coming. I'll be in touch with you individually in the next few days.'

There was an excited buzz as the meeting broke up. The combination of generous funding, well-known Council names and a highly effective Chairman gave the proceedings a decidedly upbeat feel, thought Ellen, packing documents into her briefcase. She overheard someone say that more had been achieved in two hours that afternoon than in the past five years put together. She wasn't sure she would have put it quite so boldly as that, but there was no getting away from it – something exciting had started. On her way out, having bade her goodbyes, she helped herself to one of the sheets listing possible GlobeWatch award categories. A stickler for paperwork, she wanted to give the categories her full attention. Not, she noticed, that too many other people seemed to have taken copies.

She arrived at Paddington station with just five minutes to spare before her InterCity train departed. She found her seat, and put her briefcase on the one beside her, then leaned back into the first-class luxury. What a treat! She felt positively decadent travelling first class, but Claude Bonning had enclosed the tickets with his notes for this afternoon's meeting. As the train began to glide slowly out of the station, she found herself being served a complimentary cup of tea and a biscuit. Presently she opened up her briefcase and pulled out the first paper that met her eye. It was the one about the awards scheme. There were no great surprises in Claude's twelve suggested prize categories: Best Environmental Rejuvenator, Best Corporate Citizen, and a list of similar awards leading up to a main GlobeWatch Company of the Year.

What did surprise her, however, was that next to each category except the main one, he had provided a shortlist of three companies, with an asterisked 'winner'. She didn't suppose there was anything very controversial about his selections. But surely it would have been better to invite suggestions from the Executive Council? In fact, now that she thought about it, the whole notion of an awards scheme had been presented as a *fait accompli*. That wasn't like Claude, she thought. He had always been scrupulous about consensus-building. She noticed that against several of the categories, Starwear had been identified as the winner.

She immediately thought of poor Nathan Strauss's suicide and that dreadful business of the child slave accusations. She had met Nathan several times at the Institute of Directors in Pall Mall, and there had been instant rapport. His innate intelligence and awkward self-consciousness had had the strangest effect on her – he'd been the first man she'd thought she could simply *eat*, he was so wonderful. Which was why, when the allegations about Starwear using child slaves in India had come up, she had been deeply upset – until Nathan made his well-publicised statement about it being untrue. An innate sense, deep within her, knew that Nathan could be trusted. That, as far as she was concerned, had been the end of the matter.

So, seeing Starwear appear now as the nominated Best Developing Nations Employer was a decision that appealed. She'd support Claude on that one. It would be her way of doing something for Nathan. As the English countryside began to slip past the window, and the train sped forward in a gentle rhythm, she couldn't resist resting her head back against the well-upholstered seat and closing her eyes. Claude's *fait accompli* regarding the whole awards ceremony might be a little irregular but, she supposed, it didn't really matter. What mattered, very much more, were all the ideas she'd been gathering over the years which now had some hope of bearing fruit. As she fell into a light doze, her dreams were all of programme funding.

Kate Taylor briefed Chris in the back of the racing-green Jaguar that was taking them to the Young Artists' Exhibition in Covent Garden. The idea for the exhibition had been hatched by Nathan Strauss and Mike Cullen seven years earlier. All the finalists whose work was exhibited would be guaranteed a sale, and the winner, as judged by an independent team of art critics, would be awarded a cash prize of £10,000. Nathan had paid for the event personally, Kate explained, and Lombard organised it. It was only one of the many charitable activities in which Nathan was involved, but probably the one that had given him the greatest pleasure. He had enjoyed the personal contact he had with the artists, several of whom had gone on to establish names for themselves after first showing at his exhibition. It was also through the exhibition that Mike Cullen's interest in young artists had developed. Nathan had told him the story of the Francis Bacon painting sold for £150 in the 1970s that had fetched £2 million fifteen years later, and that was all the incentive he needed. Mike's collection had been growing steadily ever since.

Not that art was the reason Chris had volunteered to join Kate that Wednesday afternoon. Rather, it was the Young Artists' Exhibition patron: Madeleine Strauss. Madeleine was known to be a formidable woman, grand in manner and, since Nathan's death, outspoken in her dislike of her brother-in-law. Chris knew that Lombard had tried to set up several photo-opportunities in which she and Jacob appeared together, to present a united front, but she had refused, point-blank.

If he could get her on to the subject of Jacob Strauss, Chris decided, she could be a highly instructive starting point for his investigations. So too could Kate. Turning to her now, he said, 'Had a few drinks with some friends the other night. One of them said something about Lombard phone calls being recorded.'

'Financial division,' she nodded, 'all our calls are taped.'

He raised his eyebrows.

'Self-defence,' she explained. 'We don't want to be accused of leaking inside information. If everything's on tape . . .'

He was nodding. The explanation put rather a different slant on things.

'I don't know about the fourth floor,' she brought her hands together in prayer position and bowed towards him, wearing a mischievous smile, 'but I doubt it. Why? D'you have a problem with it?'

He shrugged, 'Not really. It just . . . came as a surprise.'

'In all the years since Lombard started, we've only had to dig out tapes on two occasions – both during takeover battles,' she reassured him. 'Otherwise, it's not as if anyone ever actually *listens* to you.'

They arrived to the popping of champagne corks, as the first guests of the evening were starting to arrive. Madeleine herself swept in about ten minutes later, tall, solid, and expensively finished, with an immaculately coiffed power-set, and resplendent in black and gold brocade. Kate went over to greet her and make sure she was offered a drink, before performing introductions. She and Madeleine were evidently old friends, and what happened next was a well-practised routine. First, Madeleine met that year's exhibitors, a colourful crew whose clothing ranged from lounge suits to retro-punk. Next, she was introduced to the judges, headed by a suitably servile valuer from Christie's. Then, with Kate on one side and himself on the other, Madeleine set sail round the exhibition, standing before each of the paintings, glass in hand.

About halfway around the exhibition, Kate had to excuse herself, leaving Chris to accompany the *grande dame*. The opportunity he had hoped for.

'My late husband really used to enjoy all this,' she told him, holding out her glass for a refill from a circulating wine steward.

'Yes, Kate was telling me about the artists that started out here.'

She scrutinised him thoughtfully. 'Quite a number. The question is, should one continue?'

He didn't know if the question was hypothetical, or addressed to him. He answered carefully, 'I'm sure Nathan would have liked it to continue.'

'He would indeed,' she agreed crisply, 'but there's the financial side of things.'

Chris looked around for Kate, before spotting her talking to the Christie's man. He only had a short time, he realised. He decided to wing it, 'Perhaps someone else in the family could support it, in Nathan's name, I mean?'

She glanced at him briefly, as though he'd taken leave of his senses. 'There *is* only Jacob,' she said.

'It was just a—'

'Jacob's never had one brass penny to rub against another. He'd never be able to support something like this.'

This was more than he had expected. Much more.

Finding, in Chris, a sympathetic listener, she continued, 'He's never been any good at making money.'

Chris nodded, prompting her. 'Before joining Starwear his businesses in America—'

'Disastrous! He has what I call the anti-Midas touch. Everything he comes into contact with turns to dust.' She sipped her champagne briskly before meeting his eyes. 'I suppose I shouldn't be telling you this, seeing that you work for him.'

'I don't, actually,' he told her smoothly, disguising the tumult going on in his mind, 'I work with Kate, on the financial side.'

'Ah. The acceptable face of Lombard.'

Kate had finished talking to the Christie's man, but had been stopped by one of the other judges. Chris knew he had to press ahead. 'Maybe Jacob', he noticed her expression of distaste when he mentioned the name, 'could get Starwear to sponsor future exhibitions.'

She shook her head fiercely. 'I wouldn't want it. Even if he offered, which he won't, I wouldn't want it. There are personal reasons, which you couldn't possibly know about, why I would never accept anything from that man, directly or indirectly. The whole reason we came to England was to get the family away from him.'

Chris didn't have to exaggerate his astonishment. 'I had no idea.'

'I couldn't have my girls growing up in the same city as that perverse creature. Even New York was too small a place,' she shuddered.

'But all the papers say he's a great family man,' Chris acted dumb, 'who likes spending time with the kids.'

Madeleine fixed him with a withering look. 'You're the spin-doctor, you know how *that* works.'

He adopted a suitably abashed expression, then she murmured softly, 'Other people's kids, maybe.'

He instantly remembered the night he'd first met Jacob Strauss; his surprise at finding, outside his office door, a young boy from St Stephen's.

'If you take my advice,' Madeleine leaned down to check his name badge, 'Chris, the less you have to do with Jacob Strauss, the better.'

He left the exhibition an hour and a half later, soon after Madeleine had departed. Kate and he went their separate ways – she was going straight home, but he needed to collect his car from the office. So he caught a cab to Lombard, and was soon driving himself west through the City. Usually he listened to music in the car. But tonight he wasn't in the mood.

He headed along the river, on the Victoria Embankment and around Parliament Square, thoughts racing as he recalled his conversation with Madeleine. The Jacob Strauss she had described was certainly worlds apart from the Lombard version with which he was more familiar –

and seemed to back up Judith's accusations. But if there was any truth to what Madeleine had said, how was it that Lombard had successfully pulled the wool over the eyes of the whole City of London? And yet there was Merlin de Vere; Merlin, who had supposedly been murdered by agents of Jacob Strauss. It still seemed incredibly far-fetched.

It was as he passed Chelsea Bridge that Chris noticed, some way behind him, a red Citroën ZX Turbo he thought he'd seen pull out behind him when he left Lombard House. Following his usual route home, he noticed the car was still there as he turned left into Fulham Road. Plenty of Fulhamites worked in the City – nothing strange there. Except that instead of coming right up behind him at the traffic lights, the car held back, waiting for another vehicle to come between them.

That was when he wondered if he was being followed. Or was his imagination now operating on overtime? What was he supposed to do – race off and zigzag round a few blocks to see if he could throw off his followers? But if he did that, they'd know he knew. Better to act as if he hadn't noticed. Who were these people?!

The lights turned green. He sped forward, deliberately faster than usual, before heading up Dawes Road – not his usual route. The car was still behind him. Thinking quickly, he remembered the Waitrose supermarket he could go to – make it look as if he'd come here for a reason. He pulled down a side street, heading past cars parked bumper to bumper. At the far end, he pulled into the first free parking space. He stared into the wing mirror. The Citroën had also turned into the street.

He got out of his car and hurried back to the supermarket. As the Citroën continued its slow progress down the street, he was walking right past it in the opposite direction. It was all he could do not to turn back. But he kept his head down and pretended not to notice. He already knew that if he looked in the window of that car, the faces would mean nothing to him. They were just the gofers, the snitches; shadows, he supposed, hired by the likes of Kuczynski.

When he returned ten minutes later, a packet of groceries in his hand, there was no sign of his pursuers. But as he headed back towards Parsons Green the Citroën materialised again, two cars behind him. Just where in hell did they think he was going? And how long had they been tracking him? Hours? Days? Weeks? He racked his brains, trying to think of any place he'd been that 'they' might deem suspicious. But he'd hardly had a life since joining Lombard. It had been to and from the office every day. Except for last Saturday. *Walking Judith back to his place. In the kitchen — no curtains, full lights. Christ Almighty! He had to warn her.*

They followed him all the way home. When he arrived he got out of the car, walked up to his front door, and unlocked it. As he did so, he saw the Citroën out of the corner of his eye: up the street on the left-hand side, headlights killed. He put his keys in the lock, hardly able to wait till the moment he was in, and had closed the door behind him. Then he leaned back against it, staring up at the ceiling. He remembered what Judith had said when she'd stood in this same place last Saturday: *All Lombard calls are recorded. Don't tell me you didn't know that.* His gaze moved from the light fitting in the middle of the hallway ceiling to the light fitting in the sitting room and down to his own telephone. As he stared at the receiver he felt all his certainties, all his assumptions, collapse beneath him.

*

Jacob Strauss lifted the walnut-veneer telephone from its cabinet in the back seat of his chauffeur-driven Rolls Royce. Meetings with bankers had always been a pain in the butt as far as he was concerned, and having just ended the day with one, he thought he'd earned himself some fun. He dialled a number; he didn't have to wait long.

'Party time,' he said when there was an answer.

'I've put the champagne on ice.'

'Glad to hear it.'

'But I've had some problems with the entertainment.'

'Problems?' There was instant heat in Strauss's voice.

'Uh-huh. Access problems.'

'Then pay them more.'

'It's not the money.'

Strauss paused, before saying wearily, 'It's *always* the money.'

'Well, it's usually the money, but this time I've a feeling it's something else.'

In his Onslow Gardens flat, Elliott North's face was set in a frown. Jay's answer to everything was to throw more money at it. But this was a very delicate situation. Enormous discretion and confidentiality were required. One wrong move would blow everything for both of them. Trying to explain that over a mobile telephone, which had all the security of a public broadcast, wasn't easy.

'Those ones we had last time, they were great.' He could hear Jay getting excited at the other end.

'I want the same ones.'

'I know you do. Me too. But, like I say, there's trouble getting hold of them.'

Strauss was getting tired of this. He wasn't used to being told he couldn't have what he wanted. When he spoke, his

voice was filled with anger. 'I thought we had an arrangement?'

'We do.'

'Don't tell me there's someone else getting in there.'

'It's exclusive. Believe me.'

'Then where the hell are they?'

'No one over there has any idea. But I'm going to keep
calling. They've got to come back some time.'

'Damned right they do.'

'And the moment they do, we'll know about it.'

'I'll give their butts a damned good hiding.'

'You'll enjoy that.'

'Hey, too right!' He was loosening his tie when the
thought occurred to him. 'So, have you got something to
put me in a good mood?'

North felt the packet of powder in his jacket pocket. 'Of
course I do.'

'Enough to put us all in a good mood.'

'You betcha.'

'I'm on my way now. We'll get into a good mood, then
we'll party.'

'Yeah.'

'Lots of fun.'

'A whole lot.'

The telephone clicked.

As North replaced the receiver he couldn't help thinking that it was all getting too much. Jay kept wanting more
and more. When they'd first arrived in London, the entertainment had been just like in New York: once every
couple of weeks; discreet; controlled. All expertly handled
through a contact from New York, someone they could
trust. But then the contact had moved out of town. North

had been on his own and he'd had to find a new source. That meant taking risks, and he hated taking risks about this.

Jay knew, of course, but he didn't seem to care. He just kept wanting more: every week, then twice a week. It had turned into a major logistical nightmare. Then there were the drugs. They'd always been part of it, but now it had become every time. It would have been bad enough in New York but here it was much worse because he didn't know his way round town; he didn't have the same network. He couldn't just pick up the phone to one of his fixers and have things done. And having things done, Elliott North knew, was the only reason Jay Strauss hired him.

13

'Judith,' there was relief in his voice, 'am I glad to get you!'

'Where are you calling from?' She was suspicious.

'Bernie's.'

'OK,' she exhaled a cloud of cigarette smoke as she made towards the door of the pub, mobile clutched to her ear.

He glanced round Bernie's study, at the wood shelves and leather-topped desk, the green curtains drawn round the bay window. There was a reassuring affluence, a well-heeled, ordered calm about the place which he very definitely needed right now – along with the Scotch, which glowed in the cut-crystal tumbler in front of him.

When he'd arrived, nerves still jangling from his discovery earlier that evening, Bernie had immediately prescribed a generous helping of Glen Morangie. He had wanted to keep quiet about it all until he decided what to do. But he couldn't pretend to Bernie and Trisha, they'd seen how rattled he was. So he'd sworn them to secrecy and told them he was being followed; he didn't know who by. They had been aghast; wasn't it just a coincidence? He'd convinced them it was not. Why else had he sneaked over the back fence of his own house to get here?

They'd been even more startled when he announced he

needed to get hold of Judith; did they have her mobile telephone number? They looked bewildered – after all the
petulant hostilities over the past few years, what on earth
was going on? Sidelong glances had been exchanged as he
left the room. But from the moment he'd arrived home
that night, he had known he had to make the call. Right
away. From a safe place.

'About last weekend,' he said now, 'we've got to talk.'

'We do?'

'I know I was . . . sceptical about what you were saying—'

'Don't you mean incensed?'

'But a lot has happened.'

'Oh, yeah?'

There was no avoiding her distrust. 'No, really. It has.
I'm not so sure any more. Not so sure about anything.'

The only response from the other end was the sound of
her dragging on her cigarette, before another long exhala-
tion. Then she said, 'Well, sorry not to be bowled over by
the idea of a chinwag, but for all I know you could be at the
office recording everything I say. This could be a set-up.'

'But it isn't. Look, Judith,' his tone was authoritative,
'there's no time to be precious. I can understand how you
feel, but believe me, I'm not playing games. The fact is, you
and I are both in serious danger right now.'

'Why should *you* be?'

'I'm being followed.'

'Oh, really?' she seemed unconvinced.

'I was tailed home from the office tonight. The point is,
I don't know how long it's been going on. They could have
seen us together on Saturday.'

'Well, thank you very much,' she was sarcastic, 'so the
little visit was down to you.'

'What little visit?'

'My flat yesterday afternoon. Petty crime lookalike – stole the video, trashed the place. But it was a professional job. No doubt they've been through my computer files. They wouldn't have found anything.'

Both of them were thinking of Merlin de Vere.

'You know who's behind it?' she asked.

'That's why we need to meet.'

Well, if we *are* to meet,' she was prickly, 'you'd better come unescorted.'

'I have a plan.'

'Yeah. Right.'

'How about this Friday?'

'Get a life!' she snorted.

'Well, you suggest a date.'

'I'm going to need some time.'

'And I need some answers.'

'The thirty-first's free.'

'That's over a fortnight away! *Anything* could happen.'

'Charming. I don't suppose you've worked out just what the hell I'm supposed to do about my personal safety?'

'Actually, I have,' he told her simply. 'You've got to act normal.' His voice was firm.

'Oh, yeah, that's a big help.'

'Just act', he ignored her sarcasm, 'like everything's totally normal.'

A few minutes later, he put the phone down and took a mouthful of Scotch, pulling a face as he swallowed. Taking action helped stave off the knowledge that somewhere out there in the darkness, someone was waiting for him.

And in the meantime, there was the flat. Pulling a Yellow Pages directory across the desk towards him, he flicked through it until he came to an advertisement in the 'Security' section. 'Detection and clearing of listening devices', it read. He glanced at his watch. Nearly ten. But there was a mobile telephone number to ring. It was worth a try.

That same Wednesday evening, Kate stepped into the bathroom leading off her office, and closed the door behind her. She was one of only a handful of Lombard executives with a private bathroom. She'd demanded it be written into her contract before she agreed to join the company. Not that she was driven by corporate one-upmanship or ego. The fact was, she needed a shot of insulin three times a day to stay alive, and she preferred having somewhere private to inject herself.

Though the bathroom did also make for a wonderful retreat when things out in the Pit were going mad. It was a quiet place where she could escape for a few moments of tranquillity when things were particularly manic. And on nights when she was heading straight out to dinner – most nights of the week, in fact – it was nice to have a place where she could do her make-up in private, as she was about to do now.

As she unzipped her cosmetics purse and pulled out a bottle of mascara, she supposed she thought of her private bathroom as one of the perks of her job, like her Saab cabriolet, her flat in Chelsea, her wardrobe of designer clothes.

When she'd started out in PR, in her early twenties, building a successful career had been the most important thing in the world to her. Her father, in his day, had been a leading Harley Street physician, and from him she'd inherited the gritty determination to succeed – to prove she was as capable as he in her own field. Financial PR had provided an excellent choice for someone of her skills. Bright, literate as well as numerate, and a strong communicator, she'd known all along that so long as she worked hard, all the rewards were there for the taking.

She'd started out as a humble account assistant at Lowe Bell, then graduated to an account manager job at Brunswick. By the time Mike Cullen approached her with the idea of setting up a new consultancy, she was in her late twenties and a well-established account director. She knew Mike Cullen from various industry bashes – the IPR City branch, *PR Week*'s annual awards – and she'd always held him in high regard. So when he offered her the chance to join him in a new venture, getting in on the ground floor of an agency that had huge potential, she didn't have to think too hard about it. Those early days at the agency, she often thought, had been among her happiest, because after the initial bedding-down period, Lombard quickly began acquiring big, blue-chip clients, and Kate found herself working harder than she had known she was capable of as Mike's vision of a superlative agency quickly turned into a hugely successful reality. By the time she was in her early thirties, Lombard's success, and her own part in it, was on a grander scale than she would ever have conceived.

Now, in her early forties, however, things looked very different. While Lombard was easily the biggest name in corporate and financial PR, Kate couldn't help feeling that, somewhere along the line, she'd lost the plot. Somewhere in the past ten years, she'd begun to realise that all she was doing in her job was the same thing, over and over again. 'Every deal is different,' was one of her PR mantras. While technically true, the reality was that every deal was just another variation on a small number of well-worn themes.

And she was exhausted playing them. There had been just too many cancelled dinner dates and an increasing number of working weekends; too many late-night phone calls with clients in a panic over hostile takeover bids; too much work and not enough play. In particular, no time for a love life.

Her single status had, over the years, been the cause of enormous heartache for, as well as the lack of time for a relationship, it seemed to Kate that with age came increasing discrimination. There had been moments, more and more frequent in the past couple of years, when she had found herself, late at night or on a Sunday afternoon, feeling a sudden, deep loneliness at the realisation that life was passing her by and that she had no one to share it with.

All of which made her value her relationships with close male friends even more; friends like Jim Ritchie, whom she was seeing tonight. Bastion of the *Sunday Telegraph* City office, Jim was a craggy, charismatic Scotsman. A *bon viveur* with an aphorism for every occasion, Jim also had an encyclopaedic mind from which he would constantly extract arcane gems, as well as embarrassing reminders. Being around Jim certainly kept you on your toes. Had he been a few years younger, and not married with three children, thought Kate, she would certainly have contemplated a happy union with him, but alas . . .

Jim's only vice appeared to be vintage cars – 'my habit', as he described it – an obsession absorbing most of his spare time. Over the years he'd assembled quite a collection, and such was his passion for rally driving that one of his colleagues had written up a diary piece about him which had appeared one Sunday, alongside a photograph of Jim in goggles and cap, much to his chagrin – not to mention the amusement of his media contemporaries.

In the last twenty years Kate and Jim had seen whole tides of people come and go in the constant flux of the City media world they both inhabited. So although she was in PR, and he a journalist, their relationship had for many years gone way beyond the usual constraints. In fact, Jim had been a PR man once himself, after his first job as a reporter with the *Aberdeen Press and Journal*. PR hadn't suited his temperament, however, and he'd moved to a job with the City office of the *Telegraph*, which was where he was when Kate first met him. These days, it was their custom to meet for dinner every few months. There was always some client to whom the meal would be billed – 'journalist briefing' – and Kate made sure her secretary chose one of London's better restaurants. With Jim there was to be no stinting – Kate was always guaranteed a delightful evening.

Her face required only touching up. Standing back from the mirror she brushed her dark, shoulder-length hair, checking her appearance as she did so. She was wearing her new Favourbrook jacket for Jim – a sumptuous affair in burgundy brocade, with ornate, antique-gold embroidery – he always noticed things like that. She never wore much jewellery, although she had always loved the ruby solitaire which hung from a gold necklace around her neck – her thirtieth birthday present to herself.

Then it was time for her medication. She kept her disposable syringes neatly stacked in the medicine cabinet. Breaking one out from its hermetically sealed wrapper, she pushed it into an insulin capsule, extracted the full dosage, held it upright and squirted so there were no air bubbles, all with ease of practice. Inserting the needle into her arm, she pressed the plunger down in smooth motion. She had this operation down to a fine art. She was so good at it, there was never more than a speck of blood, and it hardly even hurt. She'd had years to perfect it, after all.

The diabetes had been diagnosed when she was in her late teens. She'd fainted a few times at school and begun suffering from dizzy spells; it hadn't taken much to work out the problem. The treatment, however, had been a lot harder to accept. As a girl she'd been terrified of needles. Having to inject herself was a trauma she'd just had to come to terms with – there had simply been no other way.

All that was long gone, of course. She'd become so used to it, now she could do it in the dark. It was all so much a part of her life that she rarely even thought about her diabetes. As long as she didn't hugely overindulge in chocolates or desserts, it wasn't even an issue. It certainly didn't stop her enjoying herself.

A short while later she was being dropped off at The Ivy by one of the Lombard Jaguars. The restaurant, much loved by 'the mediahedin' as Jim called them, and showbiz celebrities, was one of her favourites – so much so that she could nearly always command her preferred table, tucked discreetly near the back, but with an ideal purview for star-spotting. As she stepped into the restaurant she saw that Jim, ever the gentleman, was there before her. In all the years she'd known him, he had never kept her waiting.

'Kate, lovely to see you,' he greeted her in his warm, Scottish brogue, as he stood to give her a hug.

Then as she sat opposite, 'I've ordered our usual.'

She glanced to where the wine steward had appeared with a bottle of Dom Perignon. 'Wonderful.' She smiled across at him, warmly.

Conversation was, as always, a medley of the latest inside information, gossip about who was doing what in

City newsrooms, and high-jinks from the world of PR. The champagne flowed freely, a table of Hollywood luminaries pulled up in a stretch limo – grotesquely out of place in the narrow street outside – and all was set for another night at the top. But soon after ordering, Jim took the conversation in an unexpected direction which she found deeply disturbing. They had been discussing Lombard's latest client wins, and which ones Kate would be working on, when he remarked, 'You've taken on some new staff, too?'

Kate nodded. 'We have our first Research and Planning Director. Poached from MIRA.'

Across the table from her, Jim's brow furrowed. 'Aye. And some American. Is it Elliott North?'

'Ah. Yes.' Elliott North was a subject she didn't care to embark on. Now she told Jim, 'I try to keep him away from people I like.'

Jim's eyes twinkled. 'Well, my dear, I'm afraid you didn't succeed in my case.'

She looked over at him, startled.

'I had him on the phone the other day—'

'That's outrageous,' she exploded in vehement underbreath, leaning across the table. 'He knows perfectly well you're my contact. It's marked clearly on the media list.'

Jim raised his eyebrows. 'Well, I get the impression that subtleties of that kind really don't feature—'

'He wasn't rude to you, was he?' She was horrified.

'Oh, no. Nothing like that.' Jim took a sip of his champagne, before his expression turned serious. 'Something potentially much worse.'

As Kate regarded him with a look of apprehension, he told her, 'You'll recall the piece I wrote on Jacob Strauss when he took over as CEO?'

How could she forget it. It had provoked forty minutes of heated debate at a Starwear traffic meeting. Amongst all the press coverage the announcement had generated, *The Sunday Telegraph*'s was the only one that had provided a less-than-enthusiastic analysis, along with the news piece. It wasn't that it was particularly negative; just that Jim had questioned the relevance of Jacob Strauss's prior experience, running small-scale retail operations in America, to his new role as the head of a global organisation. Kate had thought it was fair comment. North had been ferocious in his contention that Jim Ritchie had way overstepped the mark, and should be regarded as Starwear's media enemy number one. For all Kate's efforts to explain that universal adulation from the British press was a hopelessly naive expectation, North just hadn't understood. On the subject of Jacob Strauss, it seemed to Kate, he had gone native. Objectivity just wasn't there.

Now, Jim was telling her, 'The moment he came on the phone, he was banging on about the profile. I thought it was quite positive, myself. I'd mentioned all the sporting icon stuff, the hero status in America, and, and, and. But he didn't see it that way.'

Kate cringed.

'He told me my comments about Jacob's previous business experience were completely unwarranted, and that Jacob's entrepreneurial achievements were widely acclaimed in the States.'

'So what did you say?'

Jim smiled caustically. 'I told him it was very convenient for him that his client had been so successful in a country where I didn't have easy access to business records. That seemed to take the wind out of his sails.'

'Jim, I'm so sorry.'

'I don't know what he expected. Did he think he was going to bluster me into just caving in?'

'I'm mortified,' she said with feeling. Not far beneath the surface, she was also furious; absolutely livid with North for trampling across her patch with such brazen disregard. Relationships with senior journalists like Jim were sacrosanct. How dare he abuse that trust?

In Jim's case, fortunately, North's barracking hadn't had the slightest impact. Now he was telling her, 'You know, I get calls from bleating PRs fairly often. But I would never have expected that kind of conversation with someone from Lombard.'

Kate was shaking her head. 'I don't know how he acted in New York, but he's just not house-trained.'

'Tell me about it,' he agreed. Then leaning across the table he lowered his voice, 'To be frank, I wouldn't have given the subject a second thought if it hadn't been for what North said next.'

Could it get any worse?

'He started rambling about vintage cars, wanting to know how many I had. As you can imagine, by this time I wasn't in a conversational mood. Then he was going on about Jacob Strauss's contacts in sports racing. I told him,' Jim was dry, 'I didn't quite see the connection to Formula One racing.'

Kate was following him intently, dreading what she suspected he was about to say.

'He said that Strauss had connections throughout the motor industry. Deals could be put together to minimise expenses. I couldn't fathom what he was trying to say, to begin with. Then I worked out he was offering to subsidise my habit.'

Kate closed her eyes, and was shaking her head slowly.

'He used this phrase a couple of times, oh aye, "an understanding", he kept saying. After a while I told him, "Elliott, if I didn't know Lombard better, I might think you were trying to bribe me."'

'I just can't believe—'

'He backed off instantly. Some guff about Jacob Strauss having a personal interest in vintage cars.'

There was a long pause while she regarded him across the table, shamefaced. 'Jim, I really am *so* sorry,' she said eventually, 'I just don't know what to say.'

'Oh,' he was dismissive, 'it takes a lot more than that to upset me. What I find so amazing is the effrontery of it all. If you can't bully the journalist into submission, then try a bribe.'

She grimaced. 'You can rest assured I'm going to do something about it when I get into the office tomorrow,' she told him, determined.

'I've dealt with American PRs before,' he continued thoughtfully, 'they've never behaved in such an extraordinary way. What I want to know is, where did he pick all that stuff up?'

Halfway through Thursday morning, Judith was lighting her sixth cigarette of the day in *The Herald*'s smoking room. She'd been spending a lot of time in here recently. Thinking through things seemed somehow easier with a cigarette. Not that there was anything easy about the way she was feeling right now. The burglary two days earlier had left her charged with a cocktail of emotions that were deeply unsettling. Seeing how easily her flat could be broken into and vandalised made her feel vulnerable – at risk in a way she had never felt before. But the same thing also made her furious. How dare they do this to her? What kind of an idiot did they take her for, if they thought she hadn't worked out instantly what was going on? The only grim satisfaction she derived from it all was the fact that she'd cheated them of what they were after. They still had no idea at all what she knew about them. Right now, she was only the more determined to crack the story.

The night of the break-in, after the WPC had left, she'd found herself hauling all the bedclothes off her mattress and taking them down to the launderette. Remembering what the WPC had said about the teenage gang and their 'signa-ture' – even though they weren't the ones who'd broken into her place – had made her feel sullied and revolted. She'd returned home from Sanjay's with an armful of deter-gents and brushes, and commenced scrubbing every surface of her room. She needed to get rid of the intruders; elimi-nate all evidence that any strangers had ever been there.

After the scrubbing there was the vacuuming; the clear-ing out of assorted debris from under her bed; the rearrangement of all the stuff on her dressing table, in her wardrobe, even the furniture in her room. She had to clean it, change it all and make it different. And that was just her bedroom. Moving through to the sitting room, she had found it virtually unchanged from the way she had found it earlier in the evening. Her flatmate Simon had spent the past three hours perched on one corner of an overturned sofa, smoking cocktail sobranjies, and with the phone to his ear, thrilling his friends with descriptions of the chaos, and revelling, in particular, in the ejaculatory details of the local teenage gang. Throwing a brush and pan in his direction, Judith reflected, not for the first time since they'd moved in together, that she'd have to revise her view about a gay man being a girl's best friend.

By the time the flat was habitable once again, it was nearly eleven p.m. She had quickly packed an overnight bag and gone round to her cousin's place in Redcliffe Gardens. She and Michelle would often call on each other in times of crisis. Tonight she was in need of a long, hot shower and a bed for the night; Michelle's sofa was, she decided, preferable to her own bed right now. She needed a night away from it all.

Since then, her every waking moment had been dominated by thoughts about Starwear. And as she stood in *The Herald*'s smoking room, staring out of the window, unseeing, at the view of the river, she was so wrapped up in her thoughts that she didn't even notice when the door behind her opened.

'I thought I might find you in here.' Alex Carter stepped in, resplendent in red braces and bold pinstripe navy trousers. He had never been in here before – she'd always thought of the smoking room as a Carter-free haven – but as he stepped over towards her, he pulled a cigar from out of his pocket, and began the great ceremony of lighting it up. Carter, she had observed before, spent a very long time playing with cigars – rolling them between his fingertips, squeezing them, moistening them, preparing to light them before, at the last minute, hesitating; he spent very little time actually smoking them.

'I was going to call you into my office, but it's just as private here,' he glanced over his shoulder at the closed door, 'and we can indulge in our filthy sin.'

Judith chuckled mirthlessly. The morning after her conversation with Chris, she was still feeling a bit shaky – and in no mood for a confrontation with Carter. Watching him discard the Cellophane wrapper of his cigar, and begin fingering and squeezing it, she felt a strong desire to end this suspense.

'So,' she asked, as he extracted a cutter from his trouser pocket, 'what did you want to speak to me about?'

'Ah, that.' He glanced at her with a cryptic expression as he inserted the end of the cigar into the cutter and forcefully snapped it shut. 'Let's just say that your . . . behaviour over the past couple of weeks has been noticed.'

'My behaviour?' She kept her tone expressionless. She had been out several times on the investigation, although she'd always tried to time her outings when she knew he'd be in a meeting.

'Oh, I know you probably think I'm too caught up in management meetings to notice these things but I actually keep very close tabs on what every member of my team is doing. I notice things.'

'Right.' She took a drag of her cigarette and exhaled. She supposed it could be good news. After all, she'd produced more column inches in the past few weeks than in her whole life as a journalist. And then there was her growing collection of miniskirts. But it wasn't like Carter to make a fuss of his staff. Frolicking or bollocking – those were his two styles. And he already knew she wasn't the type to be frolicked with.

Looking up from where he was examining the clean, cut tip of his cigar, Carter asked, 'Is there anything you'd like to say before I go on?'

Here we go, she thought. *The bastard is going to drag it out as long as possible, no doubt deriving sadistic pleasure from making me squirm.*

'Well, I – I suppose after the last time you spoke to me –

I mean about things in general, output – I suppose after that I've really been trying to . . . work smarter.'

He raised his eyebrows in a look of cynical enquiry. 'M-hmmm. And what else did I say to you that time about working smarter?'

Judith couldn't think of anything. *Why did he always make her feel like a silly little girl?* 'I don't remember,' she admitted.

'I do.' He began tapping the cigar on the side of his gold Ronson lighter. 'I distinctly remember saying that I wouldn't have wasted my breath on you if I didn't think you had what it took.'

'Oh, yeah.' She was now feeling decidedly wan.

'And what you've done has proved me right.' He commenced licking his cigar. There was a gleam in his eye – was he tricking her, she wondered, or was this something positive? 'A few minutes ago, in my office, I carried out an exercise.' His speech was interspersed with sucking and saliva noises. 'I counted the number of articles with your byline in the past week and compared them to a month ago. I also compared them to the output of the other City hacks. Yours is prodigious, Judith. Quite an achievement.'

He was staring at her now as though she ought to get on her knees and unzip his fly in gratitude.

'I have been trying hard,' was all she could say.

'I know you have. After our last conversation you probably thought I was a complete bastard,' he chortled.

'Well . . .'

'Come on, Judith, there's no need to play games. If you felt resentful I could understand. But you see, it was all calculated.' He was reaching his final moment: the cigar, poised between the fingers of his right hand; lighter in his left; the flame; the vigorous sucking; the great cloud of pungent, blue-grey fumes. 'I know every member of my team,' he boomed, his voice thick with smoke. 'I know what you are capable of better than you do yourself. I know when to chide and when to bless.'

'I suppose you do.' She had no option but to agree with him.

'So here you are, one month later and just look at you.' He gave a grandiose sweep of his cigar. 'Sassier. More confident. Output increased – a two hundred and fifty per cent improvement.'

'Thank you.'

He glanced back towards the door before lowering his voice melodramatically. 'And that's why I'm awarding you a pay rise.'

It was the last thing she expected. 'Really, Alex?' she found herself croaking. She rarely used his Christian name. And when she did, it was almost always with a sarcastic inflection.

'Not just some meaningless pay rise, either. Twenty-five per cent. Immediate.'

'That really is . . . wonderful.'

'And because I'm awarding it to you now,' he was relishing the moment, 'your index-linked rise in two months' time will be based on the new salary.'

'I don't know what to say.' She shook her head.

'You don't need to say anything,' he glowed. 'I might be a hard man, but I'm also a fair man. I'm giving you a rise because you've worked for it.'

'Well, thank you very much.' She was stabbing out her cigarette, hands shaky. 'It . . . it really means a lot to me. I've been feeling skint.'

'The lot of the journalist, I'm afraid,' he told her, massaging his Romeo y Julietta again. 'Those of us committed to the craft have to look beyond money for our reward.'

'That's true,' she agreed with feeling. She was immediately searching her handbag for the B&H Lites.

'Some of the stuff you've been doing recently,' he said, stepping closer, 'your passion really comes through.'

'Oh?' She watched his hand suspiciously. Surely he didn't expect a payback?

'That stuff you wrote on North Sea fishing quotas. You gave a balanced picture, but you also argued your case with great conviction. That's journalism at its best.'

As she lit another cigarette, waving the match out, she remembered the press conference arranged by Gorlan Smythe. The PR company had handed out comprehensive briefing packs which even carried pre-written articles. She'd jokingly complained to a Gorlan Smythe director that the articles weren't available on disk. He'd taken her at face value, and had had a disk biked round to *The Herald*'s City office that very afternoon. It didn't seem to bother Alex Carter that an almost identical piece had appeared the same day in *The Daily Echo*.

'Tell me,' he was being all *sotto voce* now, 'are you cooking up anything special at the moment?'

It didn't even enter her head to mention Starwear to him. Not yet. 'Just a few bits and pieces. Interesting lead on ICI.'

'Oh, yes?'

'A cost-of-environmental-management type piece.'

He nodded. 'Sounds promising. Is that it?'

Judith glanced up towards the ceiling. 'It's all I can think of.'

He fixed her with a thoughtful expression. 'It's just that

someone mentioned you were looking at Starwear?'

'Oh. That.' She tried to hold her composure. She had already planned what she would say if the subject ever arose, and had come up with a phrase to use: 'A gentle probing,' she told him. 'Went to see one of their directors, Matt Lester. But I didn't come up with anything definite. Certainly nothing worth writing up at this stage.'

Carter rolled his cigar for a moment, to and fro. 'I must have got my facts wrong.' Irritation had crept into his voice. 'I got the impression you were quite far advanced?'

'Oh no. I haven't even committed anything to paper. I only went in for a briefing.'

He nodded, before taking another drag and exhaling pensively. 'Well, if anything comes up on that score, you'll keep me up to speed?'

'Of course.'

'I need to know – management purposes – if some major piece is likely to materialise.'

'I quite understand, Alex. I'll let you know if . . . if anything comes up. But I doubt it will.'

He was already making his way to the door. 'You do that.'

She watched him through the blinds that covered the glass partition between the smoking room and the outer office. As she followed his progress between crammed desks amidst the frenetic activity of the City office, her heart thundered in her head. Now that the moment had gone, she felt the shock of it pass through her. She'd been discreet. Very discreet. But somewhere out there, there'd been a leak. *How in God's name had he found out?*

14

There was no one on his tail when he set out for work the next morning. He was always in the office early; maybe they just assumed he drove there directly. Which suited him fine. Two streets up from the house he pulled over to the kerb and stepped inside a telephone box. Swiping his credit card through, he placed a call to New York. He knew they were five hours behind London time, and it was still the middle of the night there, but all he needed was the answering machine.

Rick Kane worked for Information for Business – a desk research operation in New York. When Chris had been at MIRA, he and Rick had been in touch on a weekly basis. There was no formal business arrangement, but they were constantly trading favours. Just before he left MIRA, Chris had done more than his fair share of legwork for Rick, getting hold of London-based data sources. Just as well, he thought grimly. Now it was his turn to call in the favours – bigtime.

He left a short message on the answering machine. He was after the accounts of Ultra-Sports and Trimnasium for the last three years they'd been in business. He wanted them faxed to a private number, and no way was Rick to contact him on any telephone except the one he gave. Thank God for Bernie's home office.

After Rick, he called a London number. He could tell that Brett Harrison, his former MIRA colleague, had still been in bed, although he pretended otherwise. He needed an alibi, he told Brett quickly. Could he visit him later in the day – say one p.m.? Brett had sounded bleary and surprised, but had agreed.

Then he was back in his car, driving the now-familiar route to the City. Last night, he'd gone through the whole thing in his mind: visualised where the telephone boxes were; planned what he needed to do – right now and through the day. After getting home from Bernie's he'd analysed what needed to be done, and plotted it all out in detail. The knowledge that he was being pursued made him conscious of his every move. He had to find out what was going on. And fast. He had no doubt that this all had to do with Jacob Strauss and Elliott North. But how long had they been following him? And who else was in on the operation? Exactly who at Lombard could he trust? He had recalled his meeting with Bruno d'Andrea; the sallow face and shifty eyes. 'He knows where the bones are buried,' Kate Taylor had told him. All of a sudden, Monitoring Services had taken on a very sinister complexion.

After arriving at Lombard, he followed the advice he had given Judith: head down and act like nothing was happening. There was no shortage of work to keep him occupied. Lombard had three new client pitches on the go, all of which needed his strategic input yesterday – the usual way. Crisis management, so he had discovered, was a permanent state of affairs in the PR industry. After juggling his commitments so that he could leave the office for a couple of hours without his absence being noticed, he told Lotte shortly after twelve-thirty that he was heading off to MIRA for lunch, followed by a meeting with a former colleague. He would be back by four.

He'd put a lot of work MIRA's way since arriving at Lombard. He knew the research company's strengths and weaknesses better than anyone, and he'd commissioned several major qualitative projects. So there was nothing at all surprising about him heading back to his former employers. Though as he left the Lombard building and took the 'hundred-yard walk' back to MIRA he felt curiously exposed. *Were they following him?* he couldn't help wondering. There were several times when he felt like turning to look over his shoulder. But he resisted the temptation. Who was he looking for anyhow?

Arriving at MIRA reception – an unassuming affair after the sweeping grandeur of Lombard – he reflected that he never could have guessed just how relieved he'd feel stepping into this building. The armchairs had seen better days, the oatmeal carpet might be coffee-stained, but it was as though a heavy burden had been lifted, temporarily, from his shoulders.

Reception buzzed for Brett, who came bounding down the stairs a few minutes later, wearing a bemused expression, and led him off immediately to a meeting room. He wanted to know what was going on, of course. But Chris told him firmly that he couldn't say anything just yet. His seriousness was self-evident, and, to his relief, Brett didn't press him for an explanation. Instead they agreed that if anyone should call for Chris at MIRA, a secretary was to field the call and say she'd pass on any urgent messages.

Meantime, Chris took a MIRA mobile telephone on which he could be contacted.

Within minutes he was making his way out of the back of the building, down a service lane that squeezed, out of sight, alongside the building next door, and which emerged not far from the steps leading down to the Underground. He headed down the steps and was soon on a train travelling west. As he sat, surrounded by tourists, shift workers, anonymous men and women reading their papers, he couldn't help checking up and down the compartment. *But who was he looking for?*

He got out at Earl's Court and took a cab the rest of the way – it was quicker. They might be watching his house, he realised, but he'd just have to risk that. If they thought he was at MIRA, it was extremely unlikely they'd also be in Fulham. At home he quickly changed into his oldest trousers and a scruffy, long-sleeved shirt, both coated with the patina of several years' worth of odd jobs. He added to the disguise with a pair of Reebok trainers and peaked golfing cap, and some ancient, eighties sunglasses, black and locust-like. He went through the cupboard of his future study, and rifled through all the sports gear he'd planned to throw out, separating the stuff with his name on it from the things he was placing in a large black bin liner. *It might be rubbish to you, but there are a lot of people who'd be thankful for it*, his mother had said, thank God for her! Once he'd finished, he went into his garden and, using the MIRA mobile, ordered a local minicab a.s.a.p. Peaked cap down, and glasses disguising his face, he was soon on his way out again.

At St Stephen's he quickly had to orientate himself. He didn't want to go too far into the building, but he had to see the kid. He'd spent half the night racking his brains trying to think of the name. He knew it had been a bit unusual. Then this morning, when he was scanning a new business document, it suddenly came to him: Dale. He was sure that was it. He didn't have the surname, of course. But there couldn't be too many Dales aged about ten at the school.

Inside the entrance from the pavement there was a covered porch leading to a worn and shabby concrete quadrangle at the front and, from each side, through to dank corridors, pungent with industrial disinfectant. Boys in purple blazers were milling about the place, talking at the tops of their voices, in a chaos that made Paddington station at rush hour seem a haven of calm. But, Chris observed, no one seemed to be in charge – which suited his purposes exactly.

He approached a couple of boys about the same size as Dale, who were fighting over a Walkman. 'I'm looking for a kid called Dale. About your height. Dark hair.'

'Dale Nesbitt?'

'Yeah. Know where he is?'

'Probably in the gym,' said one.

'Always in the gym,' chimed the other.

'Bit of a sportsman, right?'

The two exchanged looks. Best not pursue that one.

'So, where's the gym?'

One of them began to explain. He'd have to go through this building, and down that flight of stairs. All too convoluted.

'I tell you what,' he jangled his pockets, 'there's five quid for each of you if you go and get him for me.'

'Right now?' They were suddenly interested.

'As soon as you can.'

As they rushed off, he glanced at the clock above the quadrangle. Eight minutes to two. He shuffled on to the pavement, just outside the entrance. Plenty of purple blazers out here too, as well as lunch-time passers-by and the usual chaos of London traffic. He paced around impatiently, glancing into the entrance every minute to see if the two boys had returned with Dale. The weight of the sports kit began to tear the bin liner in his hand, so he had to pick it up and hold it from underneath.

Then, just before two, a bell sounded, shrill and sustained. The effect was instant. There was a scramble of activity on the porch and pavement, as the purple leaked away. Uniformed figures were hurrying across the quadrangle and down the corridors, quickly emptying the place. Chris was starting to despair when the two boys came running into view with a third in their wake. Thank God it was him.

Chris quickly handed his helpers a crisp £5 note each, which they seized with great excitement before hurrying away. All the time, Dale was studying him with a solemn gaze. Once the other two had left, Chris realised he was now alone in the porch with Dale.

'It's good to see you,' Chris told him, trying to be friendly.

'I've got a class.'

'I know,' he said quickly. 'Look, there's a lot of stuff in here I thought you could use. Sports gear.'

'Why?' The other was wary.

'Why?' repeated Chris. It wasn't the reaction he'd expected. There was a remoteness about the child's expression he found hard to place.

'Why d'you want to give it to me?'

Chris stepped back, trying to be reassuring. 'Look, if you don't want it, that's fine,' he said. 'It's just that I know you're big on sport. Always in the gym and stuff . . .'

There was a pause before the other said, 'He sent you here, didn't he?'

Now Chris couldn't mistake it; it was fear. The boy was scared out of his wits. He took another step back. 'Who d'you mean?' he asked.

'The man with the Starwear. But I don't want his stuff.' The boy's voice was rising, his hands clutching at his crotch. 'I thought he liked giving me things. That's what he said at the beginning. But he just wants to do things to me. I don't want to go back!' he begged.

Chris hated doing this. But he had to know. 'Why not?'

Dale stood there, dark-eyed and suddenly mute, his ten-year-old face filled with horror. The hands holding his shorts were trembling. Then Chris looked down at where he was standing, and noticed the puddle at his feet, growing larger with each second.

Across the quadrangle, a priest had caught sight of him and was striding over, dark cloak billowing in the wind. 'What do you want?' he cried, his mouth a dark gash in the lengthy whiteness of his face.

Chris knew he had to go. Black bin liner still in his hands, he about-turned, running out of the porch and on to the pavement outside. Mingling with the crowds, he rushed to jump on to a number 49 bus that was pulling away from the kerb. He permitted himself to glance back, once the bus was well away. All he could see was the priest's face, an angry speck, at the entrance to St Stephen's.

As he turned to the conductor to buy his ticket, he

reckoned he'd had as many answers as he could stomach for one day.

Judith sat on the District Line, heading home to Earl's Court. She'd been working late, till nine-thirty p.m. As she glanced about at her fellow travellers – four Irishmen in muddied builder's dungarees, a gang of drunken Chelsea supporters, a couple in elegant evening wear, frozen in the corner like scared rabbits – she wondered, not for the first time, what on earth had induced her to choose an antisocial job like journalism. It wasn't only the long hours, though they were bad enough. It was also the constant stress of it. And today, more than most, had been a high-stress day.

The more she thought about her pay rise, the odder it seemed. Was Carter *really* rewarding a few weeks of editing press releases and a change of wardrobe with a twenty-five per cent increase? If that was how it worked, Alison MacLean should be driving a 450 SLC by now. She still didn't know how Carter had found out about her Starwear investigation. It was something that worried her – but there didn't seem any way she could discover how he knew, and certainly no one she could mention it to. But one thing she was sure of was that she was going to get to the bottom of this story. She'd already assembled enough evidence for a major piece that would have the business press chattering for weeks, though she still needed to prove her most explosive theory of all – that Starwear was running child slave factories in Jaipur. And how was she going to do that from London?

She didn't think there was a hope in hell of her getting a trip out to Jaipur courtesy of Carter, even though, in a moment of wild optimism, she'd applied for an Indian visa – just in case. She'd wondered if she might set up something long-distance; *The Herald* had stringers in India. But she didn't know any of them personally. Could they be trusted to keep schtum? Whatever else happened, she didn't want to lose control.

She'd racked her brains for avenues to pursue, and had even called her former tutor from Oxford, Dr Ellen Kennedy, a well-known figure in the campaign against child labour. Although their conversation had been very cordial, Dr Kennedy had been unable to provide any special insight into which companies were believed to be the current offenders. Precisely this kind of monitoring, she said, needed to be done – though she confided that she was hoping to be able to set up a monitoring panel with a grant from a new organisation, GlobeWatch.

During the course of the day, Judith hadn't had time to think about things much futher. Carter, taking advantage of her gratitude for his great munificence, had asked her to do him a 'small favour', and dig out comparative international data on economic cycles. The small favour had taken most of the day, as he well knew it would. On the basis of the figures she'd pulled out, he'd write some insightful analysis for which he'd be showered with compliments. It went with the territory, she supposed, but it meant she was no further on with her own investigations.

She got off at Earl's Court and began walking the familiar route home, past the exhibition hall across the road, and down in the direction of J. P. Patel's. She needed to get a few groceries. Loo rolls had become an urgent requirement and no doubt Simon had been too busy today with his cadenza to buy any. Since the break-in he'd been on the phone almost permanently, wailing about the precious camcorder he'd failed to insure.

Judith stepped into the shop, and picked up a few items from the shelves and fridge before heading for the till. Sanjay was on duty this evening, standing behind the counter while his nephew, Sohan, sat perched on a high stool beside him, poring over an arithmetic exercise. Seeing Sanjay again, she recalled the last piece of advice he'd given her: 'Sometimes, the answer you seek is right beneath your very nose' had been his homespun wisdom. But remembering it now gave her sudden pause for thought.

Pretending to be interested in different brands of cat food, she waited till the two other customers in the shop had left before she went over to the counter.

'This fish quota business is just too terrible,' announced Sanjay as she put her groceries on the counter. Evidently he'd read her piece that morning. 'Those bastards in Brussels,' he continued, keying in the prices of the various items she'd bought, 'how dare they criticise Britain all the time when they let the Spanish get away with blue murder?'

'It *is* dreadful,' she agreed, handing over a ten-pound note.

'I never realised what was going on till I read your piece.'

'Thanks, Sanjay.' She took her change as he began putting her groceries into a plastic bag.

'Front page of the business section. You must be in Carter's good books.' He loved feeling he had the inside track on office politics at *The Herald*.

'I'm doing my best to distract him while I work on another, very big project.'

She lowered her voice, feeling somewhat theatrical, as

she leaned across the counter towards him, 'It's the biggest thing I've worked on in my whole career. *No one* knows about it. But I need help.'

Sanjay met her eyes with a look of conspiratorial enquiry.

'You see, I'm researching a piece on child slaves in India.'

'Here is one.' He squeezed Sohan's shoulder.

'I know. That's why I think you may be able to help. You see, I've got to get hold of kids who've worked on sports clothes.'

'Not carpets?' He was disappointed.

'No. It's got to be sports clothes. I thought that maybe, when you were trying to get the kids out of India, you met other people who also knew about children going missing?'

'Thousands of them are used as slaves.' He was expansive. 'Tens of thousands.'

'But have many been rescued and brought to London?'

'Without a question. You know, Judit, we Indians are a very close community. If I put out the word, I soon find out.'

'It all needs to be—'

'Of course.' He held a forefinger to his lips. 'Hush, hush. I won't mention your name.'

'But you can say that if I get to interview these kids it would lead to publicity.'

'Photographs in *The Herald*!' He thumped the counter with feeling. 'Bring down the oppressors!'

'It'd be better if you don't mention *The Herald*, at the moment,' she cautioned. 'Just say a national newspaper.'

'Of course. "A national newspaper." Sports clothes. You know, if I find many people I will arrange a meeting for you.' His eyes glowed with excitement. 'My brother-in-law has a place in Southfields. There is a big lounge, very, very big. It holds a lot of people. I could bring them all there for you to meet.'

'That would be wonderful,' Judith encouraged him. She'd never asked Sanjay to do anything like this before and it was all very spur of the moment. But he'd always been supportive and asking him seemed to make sense.

'How soon do you think you could make a few enquiries?'

Sanjay regarded her brightly, before leaning down to retrieve a telephone from under the counter, and placing it in front of him with a jangle. 'Stop by tomorrow morning on your way to work,' he told her importantly. 'I have news for you by then.'

Chris stepped out of his front door, locked it shut behind him, and began walking swiftly along the pavement. It was a pleasant evening for a walk and he could do with the exercise. He glanced at his watch. Just after nine. That meant just after four in New York. With any luck Rick Kane would have found something for him. With any luck, when he got to Bernie's, he would find a fax waiting for him – and the truth about Jacob Strauss's management of Ultra-Sports and Trimnasium.

He listened for footsteps behind him, but there were none. He was tempted to turn round to look behind, or to step into an alley and wait. Just to check. To see what they looked like. But for the hundredth time in the past twenty-four hours he warned himself not to do anything so bloody stupid. He couldn't afford to let them know he knew. *He had to act normally.*

As he strode along under the streetlights, his thoughts kept turning to 'them'. Not the spooks on the ground, but the people operating them. Was it the likes of North's private dick, Kuczynski, who was tracking his movements, he wondered? Kuczynski, supposedly so adept at 'digging up dirt', but from whom he hadn't yet heard. Not that he really cared.

Mike Cullen's response to Project Silo had, as he'd expected, been very different from North's. Mike had congratulated him on an incisive and comprehensive report – 'groundbreaking' was the word he'd used. He'd left Chris in no doubt that he'd earned his spurs with Project Silo, proved himself more than equal to his new role. When Chris had told him about North's reaction to the report, Cullen had been taken aback. When he'd mentioned Kuczynski, Cullen had been visibly perturbed. There was no way, he instructed Chris, that Project Silo was to be rewritten on the basis of what some corporate spiv might uncover. Ever the pragmatist, he had suggested, though, that whatever Kuczynski came up with might be included as an appendix to the report – to keep North, and more importantly, Jacob Strauss, happy. It was a difficult 'bedding-down' period the agency was going through with North and Strauss, he'd told Chris. He hadn't had to say more, Chris could read between the lines; Cullen obviously had his own concerns about North and his ultimate paymaster.

Now he stood, waiting for some cars to go by before crossing the street. It had been Trisha's idea that he went round for supper. Late last night, after his calls to Judith and the security company, she'd suggested he drop in the next day after work. Bernie was never home before eight anyway – they could have a meal together. He'd told them his suspicions about his flat. Advance Security had promised to undertake a discreet, electronic sweep of the place later in the week – until he'd had the report on that, he had no intention of using his own phone for anything other than innocuous social calls. Stopping at a Threshers shop, he bought two bottles of claret before continuing the short distance up Bernie's street.

Trisha greeted him at the door. 'Anyone behind you you'd like to invite?' she enquired, as they kissed.

He pulled a droll smile. 'Don't know and don't want to know,' he replied.

She waved him through to the lounge. 'You've had a long fax from New York,' she said the magic words, pointing towards the coffee table, where a sheaf of paper and a bowl of nuts was waiting for him. 'Can I get you a drink while you go through it?'

Chris couldn't help smiling. 'All so efficient. I don't know how Bernie ever managed without you.'

'He didn't,' she said grinning.

'I'd love a glass of wine.'

After she'd gone through to the kitchen, he was about to sit down before he suddenly remembered. He looked through the uncurtained French doors of the sitting room and into the darkness. There were only the backs of other houses, he told himself. Glancing round at the windows, he noted the other curtains were all drawn. Sitting down, he picked up the fax, with its familiar IfB cover page.

'Had to use weasel words to get there,' Rick had scribbled on the front. 'Who would have thought our great sporting hero was such a crook? Happy hunting.'

Quickly turning over the pages, he was soon completely

absorbed in the accounts of the Ultra-Sports chain of shops and Trimnasium home gym equipment, the much-vaunted success stories of Jacob Strauss's pre-Starwear career. Page after page of the accounts of the two companies showed that, far from being massively profitable, Ultra-Sports had actually been on the verge of bankruptcy when it was sold off, and Trimnasium would have gone the same way had it not been for the repeated influx of large sums of cash – 'irregular' was hardly the word for it.

It was the first concrete proof that Judith had been right about Jacob Strauss's business record. Even though Chris had been prepared for sets of accounts that were less than straightforward, these exceeded his most perverse expectations. *Was this the information Merlin de Vere had uncovered? The reason William van Aardt had been silenced? Was this the reality Elliott North was so desperate to conceal?*

Bernie arrived not long after, and Trisha produced a curry with all the side dishes. Curry was usually one of Chris's favourites, but tonight he was distracted: there was too much to think about; it was getting late. And despite the company and concern, he'd felt himself feeling suddenly and strangely dislocated; detached from the reality he'd shared with everyone else – until last Saturday night.

He hadn't long finished his coffee when he decided he'd better be heading off. Slipping the sheaf of pages down his shirt front, he said his thank yous and goodbyes, and started home. The last time he'd walked this way, he thought, had been with Judith. So much had happened since then that it all seemed an age away. His footsteps on the pavement were solitary in the late-night calm, but he still wasn't looking behind him.

As he walked, the knowledge he'd just acquired settled

over him, a heavy and unexpected burden. And he found himself recalling Mike Cullen's words during that first briefing at Lombard: *You know, of course, there must be no talking shop outside the office. Even the most casual asides are open to misinterpretation. So, it's best to say absolutely nothing. Not about clients, not about colleagues, not about anything that you do.*

But what if you discovered your client was not only a fraudulent businessman, but one who molested little boys from the Catholic orphanage? What if one of your fellow employees bribed, burgled, and murdered to suppress the truth? What if the one person you knew you could trust – the person who'd first alerted you to all of this – was the last person in the world you should be talking to?

15

_____

Kate Taylor was still furious when she arrived at Lombard on Thursday morning. None of The Ivy's considerable delectations the night before could compensate for Jim Ritchie's revelations about North. Her position was intolerable; Mike had to do something about it. Dumping briefcase and handbag in her office, she checked through that morning's stock exchange announcements before taking the lift up to the fourth floor.

Rosa was behind her desk listening to Dictaphone tapes when she arrived. Mike was having a breakfast meeting at the Savoy, she explained, but was expected in by nine. He had a nine-thirty meeting to prepare for, she continued, then, seeing Kate's expression, she promised to phone down the moment he got in.

Heading back for the lifts, Kate passed Chris's office. Glancing in, she saw him behind his desk, surrounded by papers. 'Hard at it?' she greeted him.

'As always,' he responded, looking up. Then, seeing her expression, 'You OK?'

One thing she definitely wasn't was OK. 'That obvious, huh?' She glanced at the door leading from Chris's office to Charlotte's room.

'She won't be in till ten,' he told her.

Kate walked over to Chris's desk and sat in a chair opposite him. Then she recounted her conversation of the night before with Jim Ritchie.

Chris sat absorbing Kate's story, noting the heat in her eyes as she described North's meddling and attempted bribery. And as he listened to her tirade of indignation, he kept thinking to himself: *She couldn't be connected to the Jacob Strauss cover-up. It just wasn't possible. As far as she was concerned, North was in the opposition camp. She'd made clear her frustration with North from the start. Now, after the Jim Ritchie dinner, things had developed way beyond frustration. It was clear, from the way she was speaking, this was a resignation issue.*

Meeting her eyes, still fraught with emotion, he spoke evenly. 'All that stuff you sent to Jim Ritchie about Jacob Strauss – it was the press pack I've seen, was it? The one issued when he was made CEO, about all his entrepreneurial successes in America?'

She nodded with a weary sigh.

There was a lengthy pause, then, across the grey, morning light of his office, he asked her seriously: 'Let's say you had this hypothetical client. And let's say you found, one way or another, that you'd misrepresented him to the media – not just exaggerated, but actually put out the complete opposite of the truth.' He swallowed. 'What would you do?'

She was following him closely, wondering about the recognition she'd sensed in him as she'd been telling him about the night before. There had been a resonance there. More than simply a resonance. *Just how hypothetical was this client?*

She sat back in her chair. 'I'd need to know a couple of things first,' she told him now, trying to be matter-of-fact. 'For instance, how reliable was the evidence that what the client said wasn't true?'

Chris nodded. 'Company accounts.'

She raised her eyebrows. 'And did the client knowingly mislead the agency?'

'Very knowingly,' he told her.

There was another pause while she thought awhile. Then she said, 'You know, the stock exchange has certain rules. Distributing misleading information about a publicly listed company is illegal. For starters, the agency would have to resign this "hypothetical" client.'

He leaned forward on his elbows, his voice just above a whisper. 'Even if the client was the agency's biggest – by a huge margin?'

She fixed him with a hard expression, trying to fathom him, before asking outright, 'What are you saying, Chris?'

What *was* he saying? If he told her, maybe she could take it up with Mike and that could be a way out for him. It wasn't as if he'd be breaking client confidentiality. He hadn't done anything illicit to get hold of the information. It was there, in America, for those who knew where to look for it.

'What I'm saying,' he said carefully, 'is nothing that Madeleine Strauss hasn't been saying about Jacob to God knows how many people.'

'There's no love lost there – everyone knows.'

'At the art exhibition she told me that Jacob had the anti-Midas touch. Everything he had contact with turned to dust.'

'Typical Madeleine remark,' she said with a grimace.

'She said he'd never been any good at making money. I couldn't help thinking back to the press pack. I think the words "entrepreneurial genius" were used.'

'Elliott North's words.'

'I couldn't help wondering – just what's going on here?'

She was following him intently, hardly bearing to guess where this conversation was heading.

'It so happens,' he told her, 'that I have a friend in the States who runs a desk research operation. If there's a single sheet of paper that's ever been generated about a company, he's the man to find it. Last night I was faxed the company accounts of Ultra-Sports and Trimnasium.'

He reached into his top drawer and pulled out a sheaf of fax paper which he handed over the desk to Kate. 'Jim Ritchie was being very generous when he questioned the relevance of Jacob Strauss's previous experience . . .'

For a few moments she flicked through the pages in silence. Reading company accounts was second nature to her, but these she had to double-take. She could scarcely believe them. For the past God knows how many weeks, she'd been sending out press packs to her closest journalist contacts, positioning Jacob Strauss as the great sporting icon and entrepreneurial *wunderkind*. Meantime . . .

'If this gets out—' She was shaking her head. 'It explains Elliott North. But if this gets out . . .' She put down the pages and stared at him. 'This changes everything,' she said. Then, glancing back at the pages, 'I'm going to have to tell Mike. This,' she shook the pages, 'this is a hostage to fortune. It's only a matter of time before it blows up in our faces.'

Pushing his chair back from his desk, he got up and walked to the window. He hadn't planned to do what he'd just done. But what had he planned to do? He was sure he could trust Kate. So where was the problem?

'I don't want to be the guy with the smoking gun,' he said when he turned back to Kate. 'I've already had trouble with North over Project Silo.'

He decided not to tell her about child molestation and the kid at St Stephen's. About the faceless drivers following him. About having his house swept for bugs. 'I'm still the new boy here.'

'I'll see to it,' she reassured him. 'I won't mention where I got this.' She glanced at the fax ID number, 'I could have had it faxed over by IfB myself.' Then, meeting his worried expression, 'Trust me, Chris. I won't even mention your name.'

An hour later, when she stepped into Mike Cullen's office, she closed the door behind her and looked over to where he was going through the morning's e-mails.

'Bad news, I'm afraid,' she said when he looked up. 'I've just discovered Jacob Strauss is a crook.'

Mike Cullen's usually untroubled features were clouded as he stood motionless at his office window, deep in thought. Kate's revelations had presented him with a problem, the full implications of which he was still working through.

From the very first time he'd met Jacob Strauss, during a trip to New York, he'd known Jacob wasn't cut from the same cloth as his older brother. At the time, Jacob had been in trouble over the implementation of the Quantum Change programme. Instead of transforming the fortunes of Starwear, Quantum Change had knocked a gaping hole in productivity figures, and seen the company's share price slump to its lowest level in eight years.

At the time, the thought of digging about in Jacob's past hadn't even crossed Mike's mind; he'd had far too many more urgent problems to deal with. Although he'd immediately been suspicious of Jacob's heavy reliance on Elliott North, some nickel-and-dime PR merchant who'd worked out of the backstreets of Brooklyn before Jacob had leaned on Hill Stellar to acquire his 'company', on pain of losing Starwear's business. What exactly was North able to provide, Mike kept asking himself, that Hill Stellar couldn't deliver in spadefuls?

When Nathan had died, it had been much more, to Mike, than a mysterious tragedy. Starwear was Lombard's biggest client, but its significance to him personally went much further. He thought of Starwear as his foundation, the rock on which he had built his agency, and on which he was to build his personal fortune. All his dealings with Nathan had been congenial, stimulating, rewarding. But, under the new regime, all that had changed. From the very beginning, Jacob's assumption had been that the arrangement he'd enjoyed with Hill Stellar in New York would continue with Lombard in London. Elliott North was to be his special adviser, his spin-doctor-without-portfolio, to be accommodated and generously remunerated by Lombard.

Almost immediately, things had gone wrong, throwing Mike's meticulously developed plans into turmoil. The 'bull in a china shop' cliché, he reflected, was barely adequate as a description of Elliott North's impact since his arrival. It was bad enough that he had instantly upset Mike's staff. Once he'd embarked on his crass campaign, demanding universal adulation of Jacob Strauss by senior national journalists, Mike had found himself spending increasing amounts of time firefighting. Soothing journalistic egos and restoring dented pride had always been one of his specialties, but lately he'd become exhausted by the constant need to dampen down the trail of havoc left by North in his wake.

These latest revelations about Jacob Strauss's early career provided yet another, unwelcome twist to the whole, unsavoury affair. Mike couldn't say they surprised him. He'd never rated Jacob's business acumen – errors of judgement were why he'd found himself in such a mess over Quantum Change. But the discovery of yet more skeletons in the cupboard created a new difficulty. Lombard, like any PR agency, traded on providing journalists with access to clients, and credible information on their activities. Take away the credibility, and you were left with nothing. And if Kate had uncovered the company accounts of Ultra-Sports and Trimnasium, it was only a matter of time before any number of journalists did too.

Not only did he have to act, swiftly and decisively over Starwear, he also had to do something about Kate. During the past year or so he'd become increasingly concerned about her. Having been a close working colleague for the past twelve years, he knew her every turn of mood, and it seemed to him that she had become more and more jaded. This latest turn of events seemed like the last straw – there was no telling what she might do next.

It was a tough decision to make, but in the end he knew he had no alternative. He called through for Rosa on his intercom. When she arrived he told her, 'I'm going to have to set up a full agency meeting for eight-thirty a.m. tomorrow week, and I'll expect everyone to attend.'

She raised her eyebrows fractionally. Full agency meetings were rare enough – Lombard had grown too big to summon all its consultants together with any frequency, and the last full agency meeting had been two years ago. But compulsory attendance – she had never known it before.

'I have an important announcement, and I want everyone to hear it directly from me.'

'Shall I make arrangements to use Reception?'

He nodded. 'Good, thanks.'

Suppressing her burning curiosity beneath her customary brisk efficiency, she turned to leave the room.

'Oh, and Rosa?' He caught her on the way out. 'Elliott North. I want him in my office. Now.'

Mike Cullen looked up, his face like thunder, as North came into his office. 'This came to my attention early this morning.' He wasted no time on pleasantries, handing over instead a copy of the Ultra-Sports and Trimnasium accounts. He studied North's reactions carefully, as the other man sat opposite him and, after scrutinising the first few pages in detail, flicked through the accounts with the casualness of familiarity.

'Where did you get these?' he asked, without looking up.

'You might well ask.' Cullen's tone was loaded with anger. 'Kate Taylor gave them to me. *She* got them by telephoning a research company in New York and asking for them. Something which any journalist, *sufficiently provoked*, might decide to do.'

North looked across the desk at him wordlessly, eyes steely behind their lenses.

After a pause, Cullen continued, 'For the past several weeks, my agency has been distributing press packs on Jacob Strauss like confetti, telling all who care to listen about his "entrepreneurial genius",' his lips curled in distaste, 'and all the while—'

'You've always known that Jay is no superman—'

'Damned right I have. I know what a total cock-up he's made of everything he's done since Nathan gave him the job.' Cullen's fury was controlled, and all the more devastating for it. 'What I didn't know and, quite frankly, didn't want to know, was anything about his pre-Starwear activities. I had assumed, from your phrase "entrepreneurial genius" that he'd been at least solvent. This', he prodded the report with his forefinger, 'shows Trimnasium was a no-hoper from the start, and Ultra-Sports a virtual basketcase.'

North regarded his furious expression for a while, before leaning back in his chair with a shrug. 'Shit happens,' he said.

Cullen slammed his right hand on to his desk. 'Not at Lombard!' His voice was heavy with rage. 'It may surprise you to know that there're plenty of Jacob Strausses who've passed through my hands in the past twenty years. Head honchos who've been promoted beyond their ability; overpaid fat cats trading on borrowed glory. Sooner or later, heads roll. You can't hide from the market. That's why we never lie about our clients. We might draw a discreet veil, but we never lie.'

'I don't see the difference.'

'There's a lot of things you don't see, Elliott.' Cullen was devastating. 'In fact, the only thing that matches Jacob Strauss's incompetence as a businessman is your own spectacular incompetence in media relations.'

'I don't have to take this crap from you.' North was getting up.

'You're wrong there, too.' Cullen looked up at him. 'If

you don't get back in your seat, I'll have you escorted off the premises. I can pull the plug on Jacob Strauss and you. One telephone call and you're history. Don't forget that.'

North slouched back to his chair.

'Quite apart from compromising the credibility of my agency,' Cullen continued, mighty with anger, 'your interference has become intolerable. You've been getting under the feet of Kate Taylor, one of the finest practitioners in this agency. Showing up at client interviews – what's the matter with you? Are you trying to make us the laughing stock of the national press? And if that isn't bad enough, I hear you've been making cack-handed attempts to bribe a senior reporter.'

'That was a misunderstanding,' barked North.

'There've been too many misunderstandings, haven't there? Like the Chris Treiger misunderstanding. Here you have an intelligent young man, one of the best planners in the industry, and you blast him out of the sky.'

'I only did that—'

'I *know* why you did it. But you were wrong.' Cullen pointed across his desk. 'Since you arrived, you've screwed with my staff, you've screwed with the national press, and you've screwed with our four-point strategy for Starwear.'

For a long while Cullen glowered across the desk at North who sat, hunched, in his chair.

Eventually, North found his voice. 'So, what d'you want done?' He spoke in barely a whisper.

'That,' Cullen was severe, 'I can sum up in a single word.'

16

'We had a visitor a few days ago,' said the priest from St Stephen's, the one with the long, pale face and hooked beak.

'What kind of visitor?'

'A fellow asking questions. I thought he was from you at first.'

'But what did he look like?'

'I didn't see much of him. Youngish, I suppose. Dark sunglasses. Golf cap.'

'In other words, just about anyone,' the other's tone was acid. 'You said asking questions?'

'He was looking for Dale.'

'Shit! You didn't—'

'It was the lunch break. He gave two of the boys money to bring Dale out to the entrance.'

'I don't fucking believe it! What did he want to know?'

'Not much. I was there straight away. It seemed to me that he was trying to bribe Dale with some sports kit.'

'Oh, yes?'

'Dale said he didn't want it. He thought, you know, it meant he'd be invited out again. He was . . . unable to control himself.'

'What do you mean?'

'His bladder.'

'Christ Almighty!'

'I chased the fellow away.'

'Why didn't you follow him?'

'He slipped out of sight. There were that many people about . . .'

After a pause, the other said, 'You did the right thing to phone me.'

'Do you think it's serious?'

'Very serious. I'll arrange to have him collected tonight. We'll have to move him.'

'Where?' The priest was alarmed.

'Leave that to me. I'll figure it out.'

The message came at eleven a.m. the Monday following his exchange with Kate Taylor. Chris had been in a new business meeting, helping to prepare a client pitch, and had returned to his office when Lotte gave him half a dozen messages. One was personal.

'A guy called Roger called. Said the sofa you were interested in is now in stock.'

'Good,' he'd nodded, walking towards his desk.

'What kind is it?' she asked now.

'Kind? Oh,' he had to think for a moment before gesturing dismissively, 'just a kilim thing.'

That lunch-time he told Lotte he was going out for a sandwich. Often he just ordered down something from the Lombard kitchen, though if he could afford the time he liked to go out to stretch his legs. On this particular occasion though, he had more than roast beef baguette on his mind. Chris glanced at his watch as he approached the shop. A couple of minutes before one-fifteen. He headed towards the fresh fruit section, glancing across at baskets of apples and oranges and bananas. He was reaching out for a Red Delicious when he saw the man he was looking for, a white handkerchief in the breast pocket of his suit. Their eyes met for an instant. Then the other man was taking an envelope out of his jacket pocket and handing it to Chris, who quickly slipped it into his own suit. It happened in an instant. Then Chris went to collect some sandwiches before heading for the tills. He couldn't wait to get back to the office.

Back on the fourth floor, he closed his door behind him before moving over towards his desk, retrieving the envelope from his pocket and tearing it open. The letterhead said 'Advance Security'.

Dear Mr Treiger,
Further to your enquiry, we have conducted an electronic sweep of your property under the auspices of carrying out industrial cleaning of all carpets and curtains. Our sweep identified microphone transmission devices in the following locations . . .

Then followed two and a half pages of line-by-line entries for each room of his home. There were microphones in every single room – even the spare bedrooms he never used; both telephone receivers, of course; out on the balcony. Christ – even the bathroom was bugged.

Having his suspicions had been one thing. But knowing that they were justified was, as he discovered now, quite another. Everything, every damned thing he'd said for the last God-knew-how-long had been picked up. Recorded.

Listened to. That must be why whoever it was had gone after Judith. They'd heard every damned thing the pair of them had said. They knew she had a story. They'd trashed her place trying to find it. They'd probably planted her place with bugs too.

He didn't think he'd ever received such a disturbing letter. All the itemised details of room lights, picture frames, bedside tables – he'd been living in a broadcasting studio without being aware of it. At the end of the letter, Advance Security outlined two courses of action he could take: to have the bugs removed, or to disable them with a blocking mechanism. Chris knew that neither option was really available to him; on no account could he alert his pursuers to the fact that he knew they were monitoring him.

Charlotte came in from her office and took one look at him and the Prêt-à-Manger bag on his desk. 'Something not agree with you?'

'What?'

'Are you okay? You've seemed sort of . . . edgy today.' Not just today, she couldn't help thinking. Since his encounter with Elliott North, a week ago, he'd seemed strangely withdrawn.

Chris met her look of concern for a moment, then suddenly realised this place must be bristling with bugs too. 'I'm fine.' He tried a hearty laugh. 'I don't think this sandwich is really my style. Too garlicky.'

'I'll order something from the kitchen if you like?'

'It's OK, thanks. Maybe later.' He paused for a moment. 'I'm really not hungry any more.'

Seven-thirty p.m. two days later found Judith in her VW

Beetle on the South Circular. She'd had the lock of the passenger door fixed, the driver's side panel-beaten and had paid for a full service and assorted repairs. It had cost her nearly six hundred quid. But she was back in business for at least another ten thousand miles, she reckoned. She'd had trouble getting away from the office this evening. A breaking story about the merger of two oil giants had had three senior staff pulled off their usual briefs, and it was all hands to the pumps. Judith had pleaded a prior engagement with a PR company. Carter hadn't been happy, but couldn't complain. Quite apart from all the legwork she'd done on his behalf in the past two days, she'd also done a count of all *The Herald* business bylines, and found she'd had more than anyone in the past week.

Besides, nothing was going to keep her away from this meeting. Ever since this morning she'd been barely able to think of anything else. On her way to the tube station she'd stopped at J. P. Patel's. As good as his word, Sanjay had not only found families who had pulled children out of bondage in Indian clothing factories, he'd even arranged for her to meet them – tonight. She'd overlooked his assumption that she had nothing already planned. This was no time to be precious.

He'd scribbled down an address on the corner of a day-old newspaper. Looking it up later in her London A–Z she'd found a street in Southfields, a suburb just north of Wimbledon with a strong Asian community. Turning into the street now, she found rows of terraced houses the same as in any other middle-class suburb in the country. As for the meeting, she didn't know quite what to expect, but she thought she'd better plan a few words to say at the beginning. She'd start with child labour as an issue in general, and then talk in particular about companies whose products were sold in Britain. She wasn't going to mention Starwear specifically – she'd seen too many cases where journalist prompting had produced all the right answers to begin with, only to backfire later. She didn't know how well they all understood English. Best to keep it simple.

The house belonging to R. J. Patel looked no different from most of the others on the street. Shortly after seven-thirty she pressed the buzzer. The door was opened by a genial-looking man in a shirt and tie. 'Come in, come in,' he smiled, waving her into the house. 'It's Judith, right?'

She soon found herself in a full-length lounge-cum-dining room, with twenty or thirty people sitting on two rows of chairs that ran down each side. Some were in suits, having evidently come straight from work. Children played on the adults' knees or on the floor in front of them. There were warm smiles and greetings as Judith glanced about them. She couldn't help feeling slightly taken aback, having imagined the meeting would be smaller, more low key. This all seemed very organised. A dining-room chair had been placed in front of the mantelpiece, separate from all the others and clearly intended for her.

'Thank you all for coming,' R. J. Patel was saying, as conversations died down and parents shushed their children. 'This is Judith who works for a national newspaper. She wants to ask us about child slaves in India.' He turned to Judith and gestured towards the chair.

'Thank you very much for giving up your time.' She glanced slowly round the room. There was total silence as she met all those intense, anxious expressions. She'd always felt hesitant speaking to groups, and she felt even more apprehensive as she experienced, here and now, the scrutiny of men and women to whom child labour was not just some shock story they'd read about in a magazine. These were families who'd been through it. Who were going through it still. Desperate families who'd lost their children to the unimaginable horror of enslavement and whose lives, whatever the outcome had been, would always be scarred.

She felt suddenly and unexpectedly humbled being here. Just as well, she thought, that she'd prepared a few words. She spoke about how child slavery in countries like India was coming increasingly to the attention of the media. Then she explained how, for a reporter in London, it was difficult to get first-hand evidence. She told them how she was particularly interested in cases where children had worked on garments which were later sold in Britain – cases that would be relevant to newspaper readers. Then she said, 'Before we start, does anyone have any questions at this stage?'

A large, distinguished-looking man with all the bearing of a maharajah sat at the end of the room. He raised his hand. 'We're very pleased to see you, make no mistake, late is better than never,' he began, 'but why have you people never paid us any attention before?'

Judith was confused.

'We've phoned you to tell you about this. We have written letters. We even sent a press release – but never any interest.'

'It's true,' another woman, elegantly coiffed and wearing a cream sari agreed, 'not even a letter to say you heard from us.'

R. J. Patel now said, 'It's as if the Jaipur Abolitionist Group didn't exist.'

There was much nodding and agreement.

Judith put a hand to her chest. 'I'm sorry, I didn't know . . . did you say something about an abolitionist group?'

'It was started three years ago,' said R. J. Patel, 'by families in Britain whose relatives had fallen into the hands of the slave masters.'

'I'm surprised you haven't heard of us,' said the *éminence grise*, 'everyone in Southfields knows about us.'

'The newspapers didn't even return my photographs,' another woman complained.

Judith glanced across at R. J. Patel. 'There's a press release about this group?'

He nodded, gesturing to a slim, anxious-looking man. 'Bobby, you show her the press release.'

The man reached inside a box file on his lap, before producing a stapled sheaf of papers which he got up to give her. Addressed to 'Editors of the Quality Press' the headline read: 'Jaipur Abolitionist Group Demands Immediate Freedom of Raja Dinesh Pudrah, Bala and Bhanu Patel, Jawaharlal, Prakesh and Nayendra.' An ageing typewriter with a defective letter 'e' had been used, by the looks of it, and the 'press release' was poorly photocopied and ran to six pages, the first of which was a general rant on the abomination of the slave trade. The kind of document, thought Judith, which wouldn't even make it to the editor's desk.

But as she flicked through the pages, rapidly scan-reading, she found, starting on page three, examples of different children, where they had worked and what had happened to them – exactly the kind of first-hand evidence she needed, if she could find kids who'd worked in Starwear sweatshops. After looking through the press release she glanced up.

'I think I see the problem,' she started to explain, as kindly as she could. 'It's all about how you present your case. You see, every day, newspaper editors get about six inches of mail sent to them by people hoping to get in the papers. Most of the press releases get thrown out almost immediately. It's best not to send anything to the editor to begin with, but to the reporter covering that area – like the industrial relations correspondent. But even then, you've got to produce a release that instantly catches the attention. Summarise your story on a single page.'

There was stunned silence as she looked around at a roomful of concentrated expressions – all of the adults present completely absorbed in what she was saying.

'Make no mistake,' she reassured them, waving their press release, 'this is a big story. A very big story. People are buying stuff in the high streets completely unaware that it's been made by children chained to benches in India. It's a bombshell.'

'And you'll help us with it?' asked one of the women.

'Absolutely,' she said. 'You have all the material. It just hasn't been packaged right.'

A murmur of excitement passed through the room. Whatever else came out of tonight's meeting, thought Judith, her trip wouldn't have been wasted. She didn't doubt for a moment that there was a story here. The big question was: would she find the evidence she needed?

Holding up her hand for quiet, she had to raise her voice. 'When I spoke to Sanjay, I told him I was interested in cases where children have worked on sports clothes.'

The man who looked like a maharajah introduced himself as B. J. Singh. Evidently the group's leader, he now told her, 'Everyone here tonight knows children who've worked on sportswear.'

She nodded, trying to suppress her anticipation. 'Were any of the garments major brands that are sold in Britain?'

A few names she'd never heard were called out, and she wrote them down in a notebook. Then Bobby, the anxious-looking man with the box file offered, in a soft voice, 'Starwear.'

'What was that?' Judith looked up at him.

'Our nephew made Starwear clothes.' Next to Bobby, a large, motherly woman in traditional sari gestured towards a child who was lying on the carpet with colouring books. Judith glanced down at the child. He looked about eight years old.

'Does he speak English?' Judith asked.

The child looked up, almond eyes burning in a small, elf face. 'Of course,' he answered.

Judith could hardly believe it. Was she finally face to face with the diminutive figure who would provide the evidence she needed? 'How long did you work there?' she asked the boy solicitously.

'Three years,' he managed, before turning his face away from her.

'From the age of five until he was eight,' his aunt was explaining, 'then he ran away to the police who managed to find his other uncle in Jaipur. Vishnu was one of the lucky ones.'

'Several other children here worked in the same factory,' B. J. Singh was saying now.

'Really?' asked Judith. 'Who?'

There were assorted calls from around the room. This was incredible! There must be at least half a dozen.

'You're all absolutely sure it was Starwear? Not Starwear knock-offs?'

The room was filled with strenuous denials.

'These children can tell fake Starwear just by looking at it,' R. J. Patel told her. 'They know Starwear garments down to the last detail.'

'We had to do it right,' the boy on the floor was looking up at her and speaking again, 'or we were punished.'

Bobby was flicking through all the papers in his box file again, before producing a black and white photograph which he handed to her. It showed three men outside a large, corrugated-iron shed. 'This is the factory,' he told her. 'My brother in India, he took the picture for our group. And this one,' he pointed at one of the men, 'he is the slave master, isn't he, Vishnu?' He showed the photograph to the boy.

The child took one look at the photograph before turning to his aunt, burying his face in her sari.

'It's all right, Vishnu,' she comforted him, 'you're far away now. Safe with us.'

Meeting Judith's eyes she said, 'Every time we go past a shop selling Starwear he is like this.'

Elliott North had thought Cullen was about to try firing him. He'd never seen him so angry – hadn't thought him capable of such elemental fury. Not, thought North, that it mattered a damn. The simple truth was that Cullen *couldn't* fire him – unless he was prepared to put the Starwear account in serious jeopardy. And nothing, he knew, was more important to Mike Cullen than Starwear and his precious Four-Point Plan.

He'd been right, of course. Cullen hadn't tried scalping

him, though he would have liked to. Instead he'd summed up what he wanted North to do in a single word – apologise. After all the storm and bluster it had been pathetic, thought North. Wet and witless. He'd demanded that North do some serious ass-creeping with Taylor and her journalist buddy at the *Sunday Telegraph*. He was also supposed to sweeten up Treiger, whom he'd hardly seen since throwing out his academic treatise; ever since he'd heard he was balling Judith Laing, North had been keeping his distance.

Apologising was the very last thing he planned to do, knowing it was Taylor who'd come by the Ultra-Sports and Trimnasium accounts. As if it wasn't bad enough keeping the hacks in check, now they were being sabotaged from within. He hadn't liked Taylor from the start – and she made it clear she didn't approve of him. The snooty cow thought her 'principles' put her way above him. The problem was that she was the most important person working on Starwear in Britain, with the exception of the Grand Four-Point Planner in the Sky. Despising her was one thing – but she'd become a real problem. Now she knew too much and, like Merlin de Vere, was too close to too many people. Something would have to be done about her, pronto. Something for Solly Kuczynski.

And it wasn't just Kate Taylor who knew too much. As he sat in the darkness of the microfilm viewing cabin in Monitoring Services, rolling film laboriously through the machine and staring at it through his steel-framed lenses, he thought about Jay's private life – and the threat of a serious leak there. Jay's demands had been getting more and more extreme, and it was North's job to make sure his boss's desires were fulfilled – and no one else got to hear about them. But the greater the demands, the higher the risk.

And every instinct told North they'd gone one risk too far. Something would have to be done to contain the leak. Another one for Solly.

It was all getting hectic. Too hectic. Like their last days in New York. But he did have his plans. Sure, things were coming to a head, driving towards an inexorable climax. But he had made arrangements. And part of the arrangements included what to do with someone who'd started out as a mere irritant, but developed into a potentially far more devastating adversary: Judith Laing.

It was all very well for that smug prick d'Andrea to tell him Laing's computers at work and at home were blanks. He'd said the same thing about Treiger. 'Squeaky clean', he'd said, before it turned out Treiger was rooting Laing. Talk about colossal cock-up. When he'd got on to Alex Carter, the guy had acted like he was doing North some huge favour even mentioning Starwear to Laing. He was quite happy to take their money, of course, but ask for something back and he gets all up himself with his lordly airs and graces.

When Carter had finally got back to him, he'd been no better than d'Andrea. Laing had done some 'gentle probing' into Starwear, he said. The kind of thing that went on all the time. Every day his hacks looked at half a dozen different stories, but would only write up one of them – and even that might get spiked if a really big story came along and took the space.

North hadn't thanked him for the sermon on how a newspaper works; he'd just hung up. He'd never operated on the basis of what people said, but on what he suspected them capable of. And he suspected Judith Laing capable of a lot. She wasn't the type to go rifling through Forbes documents, compare their analyses to sets of annual reports, ask Matt shit-for-brains Lester about the discrepancy – and then just walk away from it. No way, José. She'd be right in there, and her investigations would take her exactly where she couldn't be allowed to go. Because where she was heading was more than explosive. Jay's miserable business failures were as nothing compared to India. *That* was meltdown material.

Christ knew what she'd already told Treiger, and what Treiger would do, which was why they were both being watched twenty-four hours a day. The activity reports had shown nothing more suspicious than visits to friends' houses for dinner – all very twinky. Which, in itself, was suspicious. Wouldn't be long now till the game was up, thought North. The final curtain. But, until then, he had to keep a grip on things.

Eventually he found what he was looking for. The record of the deal with Hydrabull Investments, consisting of a wadge of documents, some on Hydrabull letterhead, which provided contact details for the Company Chairman, Prince Abdul. Checking his watch for the time difference – early evening over there – he picked up a telephone receiver and started dialling.

'Can I speak to Prince Abdul?' he demanded when the phone was finally answered after much clicking and long-distance signals.

'Just hold on.'

There was a lengthy pause, during which North gazed into mid-distance, lips pursed with impatience.

Then at the other end, 'Who is calling?'

'John Acker from the *Wall Street Journal*.' The name tripped out with ease of practice.

There was another long pause before a voice came on the line. 'How may I help?'

It was a public school voice – upper-class Indian twit, no doubt. 'John Acker, *Wall Street Journal*, Prince Abdul,' he said. 'Sorry to disturb your evening. I'm just researching a story on Starwear.'

'Yah?'

'The transaction you made when you sold them some property—'

'I expect you've been reading *The Herald*?'

North jumped to his feet. '*The Herald*?'

'British newspaper,' the Prince told him. 'I had a young lady reporter the other day taking just the same line.'

North fought to control his voice. 'I like to find out the answers for myself.'

'Well, as I told her,' the Prince seemed irritated having to repeat himself, 'it was a straightforward agreement. I sold two factories to Starwear. There was no office block involved. She seemed to think a town block worth a considerable amount of money had changed hands. I don't know where this story is coming from but it really is most distracting.'

North raised a hand to his forehead.

'I don't deal in commercial property,' the Prince lectured North, 'only industrial. I hope *The Herald* got it right. What are they saying?'

'Nothing has been published as yet,' North replied now, 'and isn't ever going to be.'

17

Kuczynski had phoned Chris just after Tuesday lunch-time. The conversation had been short and to the point. He'd finished his report. If Chris was available at four he'd bring it round personally. He suggested they meet at a street corner not far from the Lombard building. Chris had agreed; he wanted this over and done with. And he certainly didn't want Kuczynski up in his office.

The weather was ominous that late October afternoon, the sky overcast and with a chill wind blowing through the City. Chris slipped into his coat, pulling the collar up and digging his hands into his pockets. He set out at exactly four, and walked over to the corner where they'd agreed to meet. The thought had occurred to him: *What if this is some kind of set-up? What if they're luring me away from the protection of the office?* He thought of Merlin de Vere and William van Aardt. Then he decided he was being ridiculous. He'd told Charlotte who he was meeting, where and why. If they were going to pull off something like that, they'd hardly do it in broad daylight in the middle of the City – would they?

When the man in the heavy overcoat, Homburg and sunglasses, approached him, Chris could see no sign of the report. After confirming his name, Kuczynski suggested they take a walk along the river.

'Where's the report?'

'In here.' He touched his coat. 'But I thought you'd like to know what's in it, first hand like.'

Chris couldn't deny he was curious. Exactly what had the incisive Sol discovered in ten days which had eluded him in four weeks of intensive research?

They set off past the soaring concrete-and-glass towers of the City on the north side, and upmarket residential apartments on the south. The wind blew up from the river in cold gusts as the afternoon turned deep grey. They had walked on for some time before Kuczynski glanced over at him with a smug expression. Raising his voice above the wind, he told Chris, 'I think you can say we hit the jackpot, old son.'

'Oh, really?'

Chris felt disadvantaged without sunglasses. Not that dark glasses were exactly necessary, right now. He wondered how Kuczynski could see in front of him.

'Not so much on the corporate side. More on the personal side.'

'How do you mean? There *is* only a corporate side.'

Kuczynski glanced back at him, cocking his head to once side. 'Elliott told me to look into personal stuff too.'

Chris shrugged. What was the point of arguing with Kuczynski?

'Expect he forgot to tell you,' Kuczynski was casual. 'Any road up, you won't regret it. I did some sniffing around and I got lucky.' He gestured as though playing a one-armed-bandit, and grinned broadly. 'We lined up the Lucky Sevens. We're talking about some serious dirt.'

Then, reacting to Chris's expression, 'Don't worry, old

son,' he tapped his coat again, 'got it all written down here. But I thought you'd want me to tell you right away. Elliott's always impatient.'

Chris tried to keep his voice even. 'So what did you find?'

'Take Bob Reid. Wealthy cove. Owns a few homes, you know, London, Gloucester, South of France. He also has in his property portfolio a six-bedroom flat in Belgravia.' Kuczynski was clearly relishing this. 'He and Mrs Reid don't live there, mind. Six young ladies with lots of make-up and black fishnet stockings live there. Or, should I say, entertain there every night.'

Chris's astonishment was genuine.

'Full-on knocking shop, old son,' guffawed Kuczynski, whacking him on the shoulder with glee. 'There've been complaints from the neighbours, but never what you'd call "hard evidence", if you receive my meaning. All very posh and tasteful with clientele from the Middle and Far East.'

'You're saying Bob Reid is a pimp?'

'Oooh, now, I didn't say that.' He pulled a sardonic smile. 'But I would say that he derives an income from immoral earnings.'

'So, Bob Reid may have had no idea when he rented out his flat that there were hookers moving in.'

'All in the telling, isn't it?' He winked. 'All in the telling. "Owner of Vice Den" doesn't look too good on the c.v. does it? Or the assault convictions.'

'Convictions?'

Kuczynski nodded, even more ebullient. 'Found guilty at Reading Crown Court of assaulting Miss Amanda Rider. It was mentioned in the local paper, plus a photograph of Miss Rider. Very attractive blonde bird. Model. They'd been living together for four years, lucky sod.'

'And Reid got a sentence?'

'Suspended.'

'Unusual?'

'Judge said there were mitigating circumstances.'

'What?'

'Miss Rider was, it seemed, a very volatile young lady. There'd been an argument when he said he wasn't going to buy her an MG. She'd started smashing up his place – Meissen vases that had been in the family, that sort of thing. He told the court he *had* to hit her to make her stop. Judge seemed to agree.' Kuczynski studied Chris for a moment before exclaiming, 'But that's not the point, is it?' He jabbed him in the ribs. 'The point is, he done it. Beat up his little woman. Hit this beautiful, vulnerable woman. Plus he owns a brothel. Not just violent, but exploits women. Not a pretty picture, is it?'

'I don't see how any of this has the slightest bearing on Project Silo.' Chris didn't try to conceal his annoyance. 'So what if Bob Reid got involved with some temperamental bitch, or was conned by a hooker into renting her his flat?'

Kuczynski's eyebrows twitched above his sunglasses. 'Well, old son, I'm sure Elliott could do something with it.'

Chris was still shaking his head when, unable to help himself, Kuczynski continued, 'As for Ed Snyder at Active Red, well, that's just another case of your high-flying businessman being led by his balls instead of his brains.' He glanced over to see if Chris was listening. 'Just eighteen months ago, his secretary sued him for sexual harassment. He used to touch her up in the office, the dirty sod. Said he'd make it worth her while getting her kit off for him. Company car, holidays in Spain, that kind of thing. He decided to pay her off, out of court, before the media started crawling all over him. Settled for fifty grand. No liability, of course, but it doesn't sound good, does it?'

They had paused, Kuczynski fiddling in his pocket for a packet of cigarettes and a lighter. Just being with this man made Chris feel squalid, as though he'd fallen in a cesspit. The supposed crimes and misdemeanours Kuczynski had dug up didn't impress him. They only made him wonder what in God's name he was doing talking to this spiv. After Kuczynski had lit up, they about turned and headed back in the direction they'd come.

'It's even worse for Snyder when you discover he'd had an affair with a previous secretary which went on for two years. He's a married man, you know, three kids. Lots of late nights at the office. While Mrs Snyder's at home cooking his tea, Mr Red is being very active doing some horizontal jogging.' Kuczynski laughed uproariously, before resting his hand on Chris's shoulder for a moment. 'See, mate, I'm worth every penny of my outrageous fees, aren't I?'

Chris felt like exploding – telling this jumped-up bovver boy precisely what he thought of him and his outpouring of sleaze. But he judged it wiser to keep schtum. For all he knew, Kuczynski was in charge of monitoring his own activity; the guy who could, at will, have him put into a wetsuit with a dildo up his ass. So instead, Chris only replied, 'You sure have dug up a lot.'

'And I'm sure it's going to be very useful.' Kuczynski had obviously expected more enthusiasm. 'If it's anything like the last investigation I did for Elliott, it will be very useful indeed.'

Chris didn't begin to wonder what that might have been. Instead, he was remembering the night of his encounter with Jacob Strauss. How he'd been standing by the lifts at Lombard, a towel looped round his neck. 'I'm going to lap up every last detail,' he'd said. Chris knew now the kind of details Strauss had been expecting, and why he'd found it so disturbing. Strauss, North and Kuczynski. They all mucked in the same gutter.

Now he turned to Kuczynski and said sincerely, 'I'm sure the client is going to love your report.'

Kuczynski chuckled. 'Reward in itself.' Then, opening his coat and extracting a ring-bound document, 'You know, I never thought I could call myself a bona fide public relations man but here I am,' he grinned, handing the document over to Chris, 'a vital cog in the great Lombard machine.'

Chris tried to pull a smile. 'Thanks for your work.' He shook the proffered hand.

Kuczynski bowed elaborately, tipping his hat. 'Thank you for your custom, old son.'

At her bay window overlooking the courtyard of St John's College, Ellen Kennedy had been daydreaming for a full half minute before she realised it, and stopped, with a word-less expression of self-reproach. She'd caught herself away with the fairies increasingly of late, much to her annoy-ance. So little time and so much to do, the thought of wasting precious moments on idle fancies vexed her.

The starting off point was always the same, of course: what if the GlobeWatch money came through? What if she found herself with eighty thousand pounds of funding to put into action the many programmes that had only ever been cherished ideas? The whole scale of her non-academic activ-ities would suddenly change. The balance between her teaching and research would change too. These thoughts excited her enormously. But she was also apprehensive. What a curious feeling, being on the brink of being able to do all she'd dearly wanted to for so many years – and now finding herself nervous about taking the plunge. She supposed the nervousness would soon disappear once she started planning the detail of the programmes she'd be embarking on. She'd already spent some time going through the document she'd presented to the GlobeWatch Executive Council, writing in the margins names of the various assistants she would approach, making a note of rooms available for hire which could constitute the base of her new operations. She'd never indulged in this kind of detailed planning before – she had no time for wandering about in realms of pure fantasy. But now it was all tantalisingly close.

She'd had no doubt that her proposals had gone down well with the Executive Council, just as the other Council members' suggestions had struck her as eminently reasonable. Many of their ideas, like hers, had been developed and discussed over several years, in various different forums, always in search of a suitable sponsor. Not only did Claude Bonning hold the key to realising her own dreams, he could also make real the cherished dreams of others. She'd heard stories of his fundraising credentials while he was at Family First, an organisation that had grown exponentially while he'd been at the helm. But his performance with GlobeWatch had been masterful. The list of companies donating to the new body couldn't fail to impress – they read like a *Who's Who* of corporate Britain. And although the individual amounts donated by each company weren't revealed, the total was; £250,000 was an astonishing sum to have raised for an organisation that was just starting up.

However, Ellen couldn't overlook Claude's somewhat

lower credibility in other areas of GlobeWatch's organisation. Although the Executive Council had been convened in an orderly fashion, all very democratic and consensus-orientated, it seemed to her that, in his impatience to get things off the ground, Claude had chosen to ignore procedures that she considered important. Three days after the Executive Council meeting, minutes had arrived in the post. Unlike some of her more lackadaisical colleagues in voluntary organisations, Dr Kennedy was punctilious about reading minutes of meetings. And she couldn't help noticing, in the note about 'GlobeWatch Awards', that Executive Council members were to tell Claude if they disagreed with any of the proposed companies he'd shortlisted for the awards, or it would be assumed they were happy with his choices.

That was all very well, to speed up the process, thought Ellen, but it wasn't what had been said at the meeting. There, it was simply the categories for awards that had been mentioned. Any Executive Council member not paying close attention could easily find that they had unwittingly agreed to something they hadn't even been aware of. If she didn't know him better, Ellen might have suspected Claude was trying to gain Executive Council approval by the back door. It was naughty of him, and she meant to bring it up next time they spoke. He had a lot to deal with, she realised that, and she was well aware that other people weren't such sticklers for accuracy as she. But it was the principle of the thing.

She glanced at her watch. Exactly nine-thirty a.m.; the time, she had long since decided, after which it was professionally acceptable to telephone someone. Picking up her receiver, she began to dial. Since the Council meeting she had been watching the post with much greater than average interest. Every day she'd venture down to the porter's lodge, trying to suppress a flush of excitement at the prospect of a letter from Claude, saying that her proposals had been agreed to. But, alas, there had been nothing. After a week of such mornings, she had decided that ten days was a reasonable waiting time. If she hadn't heard anything by then, she'd be perfectly within her rights to call up to enquire. And today was day number ten.

'Oh, Claude, Ellen Kennedy here,' she announced when, to her relief, he answered the phone.

'Ellen, so good of you to call. There's something I've been meaning to discuss with you.'

Oh dear, she thought, bracing herself for disappointment. If he wanted to discuss something, it sounded far from straightforward. Would it mean some form of revision, perhaps? Or a great reduction in activity?

'I expect you're calling about the funding?'

'Well, if it comes through it will mean quite important changes to my timetable,' she explained. 'I like to plan—'

'Of course. Quite understand. I've spoken to quite a few of the Council members so far and your ideas have received a great deal of support.'

'I see.'

'But the consultation process is continuing. I hope to have it completed within a week or so.'

'Good.'

'Rest assured I'll telephone you straight away when I have something definite.'

She couldn't help wondering what it was he wanted to talk to her about. Evidently it wasn't to do with her proposals which, she supposed, was something of a blessing.

'You received the minutes?' he asked her now.

'I did. It all seemed straightforward – except for the awards scheme.'

At the other end, Claude Bonning closed his eyes wearily. Of all the committee members, Ellen Kennedy had been the one he'd most expected to pick him up on it. He hadn't been wrong.

'Award categories were discussed very briefly at the end,' she said now, 'but nothing was said about shortlisted companies. I'm sure I would have remembered.'

'You're quite right.' He realised nothing was to be gained by arguing the point.

'Some of the Council members,' she continued, 'might find they'd agreed to giving prizes they knew nothing about. That's my fear.'

'I see what you're saying.' He tried to be conciliatory. 'My reason for doing it this way is simply to do with timing. Our sponsors, who are donating substantially, want to see some evidence that GlobeWatch, as an organisation, actually exists. Now, you don't need me to point out that it's going to take a very long while before the various programmes proposed bear fruit. An awards ceremony is one way to make impact very quickly. But even so, there are function rooms to be booked, administration to be worked out, and then there's the media . . .'

'I see,' she said, in a dry tone that suggested she quite probably didn't.

Claude kneaded his forehead with fingers and thumb. Ellen Kennedy was someone he needed on board, perhaps more than any of them. She was the one Elliott North had been so desperate to sign up from the very beginning. She was vital to the plan.

After a pause she said, 'I suppose it's not what's being

done that concerns me, so much as the way it's being done.'

'Well, I am discussing this very point with each Council member individually.'

'Nominations for the awards?' She wanted to be clear.

'That's right. I'm c-canvassing for opinions.'

The reality was he'd been tiptoeing around the issue, trying to get agreement with as little real discussion as possible. Most of the Council members had obliged.

'Well, so long as everyone has had their say.' She sounded placated.

'Of course. Do *you* have any comments?'

'The list seemed fine to me. I did notice that you've proposed Starwear for the Best Developing Nations Employer prize.'

At the other end, he felt his heart pound in his throat. Please, dear God, don't object to Starwear.

'An excellent choice,' she told him. 'I knew Nathan. So sad.'

He sighed, with real feeling. 'Actually, that was what I wanted to discuss with you. As you can see, Starwear has been nominated for several categories. So a few members have suggested putting Starwear forward for the main prize. Would you have any objections?'

'Not *per se*. But isn't this something we really ought to discuss at Council?'

'Under normal circumstances—'

'I realise you're under time pressure. But, as you say, this will be a high-profile event – the first time most people will ever have heard of GlobeWatch. It's important to me that we're as transparent in our workings as possible.'

Transparent. Claude thought instantly of Jeannie. Poor,

mad Jeannie. His whole life had been founded on deception. Well-intentioned deception, but deception nonetheless.

'I agree, an open forum would be more, as you put it, transparent; but, Ellen, I can't tell you the huge pressure I'm under from our sponsors to get this thing finalised.'

She couldn't mistake the frustration in his voice, like a deep and unexpected groan of weariness. It seemed so unlike Claude, who was always so upbeat and energetic. It made her pause for thought.

It hadn't escaped Ellen that Claude was seeking approval from her for a proposal at the very same time that she was seeking funding approval from him. If she'd had a more developed sense of paranoia, she might even have imagined there was a direct correlation between the two: let Starwear get the big prize, and you'll have your funding; if you don't agree, forget it. But Ellen wasn't paranoid and, besides, despite the procedural irregularities, she didn't think, for a moment, that Claude would ever get tangled up in anything like that. What she did say, however, was, 'Tell me, Claude: I notice that Starwear is on the list of GlobeWatch sponsors; was their donation significantly bigger than any of the others?'

'I'd have to look at my files to see how much they gave,' he lied. He knew, perfectly well, that Starwear was the only real donor. All the other companies had come from the client list of some PR agency, and had agreed to chip in £100 apiece. It made for an impressive list, nonetheless, which concealed the true purpose of the exercise. Having come to the nub of the matter, Ellen's question now was excruciating.

'Obviously, if they were one of the bigger sponsors—'

'Of course.'

'And I think I deserve a direct answer.'

18

Judith paced about the sitting room of her Earl's Court flat in jeans and bare feet, a glass of red Château Cardboard in one hand, and a cigarette in the other. Laid out on the carpet around her were piles of all the documents she'd collected during the past five and a half weeks for her Starwear investigation. This Wednesday night, the flat was her own. Simon had gone off with some tough old queen from Hamptons, the gay pub just around the corner. He wouldn't be back till at least three a.m., which meant she had the place to herself, thank God. Time and space to think. Laying out all the documents in carefully ordered piles was the way she liked to put things together. Physically walking around the ideas, preferably with a glass of something alcoholic by way of a relaxant, was how she preferred to work out her stories. Once she had the big picture in her mind, she found, the story would write itself.

Sipping deeply from her wineglass, she glanced across at all the evidence she had assembled. The first pile was what had got her started out on this investigation – printouts of company accounts from the disk Denise Caville had backed up from Merlin's computer. The Ultra-Sports and Trimnasium accounts, with Merlin's annotations, provided all the evidence she needed of Jacob Strauss's disastrous career prior to his joining Starwear. In the next pile was the press pack issued by Lombard on Strauss's appointment as CEO of Starwear, with all the glowing prose extolling his business prowess, as demonstrated in his track record with Ultra-Sports and Trimnasium.

One pile along from that were the Forbes reports on the Quantum Change programme, showing all the business re-engineering that was necessary to arrive at certain ambitious factory outputs. The outputs were all forecasts, of course, as the Quantum Change programme had still to be implemented. But next to this were Starwear's own annual reports and accounts showing the real figures once Quantum Change had been put in place – figures that far exceeded even Forbes's most optimistic expectations. The cuttings showing press reaction to the Quantum Change results were all there too. Judith couldn't help marvelling at how few questions had been asked about why the fruits of Quantum Change had been so abundant – having more, rather than less, seldom aroused curiosity in the City.

Then there were the notes of her meeting with Matt Lester, and his explanation of why actual profits had been so far in advance of the Forbes figures. It was all to do with the disposal of assets – to be precise, the sale of an office block. But in that same pile was a recording of her inter-view with Prince Abdul, who confirmed that no such disposal had ever taken place.

The final pile consisted of transcripts from last night in Southfields: pages and pages of first-hand accounts by chil-dren, now living with their families in London, who had literally been incarcerated for months at a time in a corru-gated-iron shed in conditions that equalled the most

Dickensian excesses. These children had been forced to sleep under workbenches – never having more than six hours' sleep a day – and had been fed on slops and made to work, supposedly to pay off family debts. Last night, as she'd sat with her tape recorder on the floor in front of her, she had barely been able to believe the matter-of-fact way in which the children had recalled the most appalling experiences of abuse.

From ages as young as six, children would be forced to sit on production benches, under a blaze of bright, fluorescent light, working their nimble fingers tirelessly to stitch the identical seam on a hundred garments an hour. Production was constantly monitored and the punishment for those who fell behind their target was instant and severe. Seats would be taken away from them, so that they had to stand for hours at a time, sometimes days, while they continued working. Those who complained were administered severe beatings. The slave masters who ran the factory were careful never to hit them on the arms or face – instead they'd be forced on to their stomachs and flogged until they bled from their backs and buttocks and legs. Some of them, including Vishnu, had rows of ugly weals to prove it.

Pleas to be allowed to go home to parents or other relatives were met with news that they were no longer wanted at home. So there they would stay until they were thirteen or fourteen, by which time they would have outgrown their usefulness. No illness of any kind was tolerated – nothing must interrupt production. When children collapsed from exhaustion or any other condition, they were removed, never to be seen again.

The results of this appalling cruelty could be seen in a huge shed near Jaipur which housed dozens of emaciated children, many of whom were pathetically small for their age, and who knew nothing except work and brutality. Physically scarred and emotionally traumatised, many had forgotten any other kind of existence, or were too exhausted to care. They were children living a barely human existence, the victims of abject, Indian poverty – and cut-throat retail pricing in the shopping malls of Europe and America; small, dark shadows living in the twilight who'd had their childhoods stolen from them.

The ones Judith had met were the lucky ones, God help them. At least they'd had, through family networks which extended into Britain, some hope of having debts paid – as little as £300 was all that was needed to release a child from six years' bondage to his 'owner'. But what about all the others – the pathetic little scraps of humanity who were, at this moment, slaving under the fluorescent glare, stitching Starwear garments to be sold in British shops in a fortnight's time? There was no escaping the reality of their tortured existence.

Never had Judith's emotions been engaged as strongly as they were on this story. Twenty-four hours after meeting the children, she could still barely believe what they'd been through. Not only was this a story that would rock the headlines, she thought, it was also one demanding to be told. But how should she tell it, and where did it fit in with all the other information she had pulled together? As she paced between the piles of paper, taking occasional sips of wine and drags from her cigarette, she tried to get her head around it; to decide from which angle to come at it.

Usually, it didn't take much working out to decide how to approach a story. Most investigations were single-pointed. But this one had so many different strands to it.

The main story, of course, was the exploitation of child slaves by Starwear. Here was a company which professed to be a leader in the area of corporate citizenship and business ethics, enslaving poverty-stricken six-year-olds in order to be able to sell tracksuits from Los Angeles to London. Here was a company whose leader, corporate guru Nathan Strauss, in explicitly denying using slave labour, had clearly lied. This was more than just another business story: it was front-page material. The moment it was published in *The Herald*, it would be picked up by every other news channel, television included – and not only in Britain, because this was an international problem.

The consequences for Starwear would be instant and apocalyptic. Every shop stocking Starwear merchandise would have to dump it – or risk a consumer boycott. Sales of Starwear goods in the developed world would collapse – and so, too, would Starwear's share price. The Starwear brand, today worth a supposed $10 billion, would overnight become valueless, regarded, if anything, as a symbol of evil. The company would be forced to close its child slave factory in Jaipur – and wherever else it was exploiting cheap labour. If there was anything left of Starwear by the end of it, and if it managed to hold on to any market share at all, the company would be ripe for takeover.

A secondary string to the main story was the financial manipulation of Starwear executives like Matt Lester, in their efforts to keep the truth from shareholders. Through the Company Report and Accounts, Starwear had clearly misled shareholders about their source of profits – that alone would have been enough to cause a furore in the business press, and deal the share price a devastating blow.

Then, of course, there was the personality angle: the

story of Jacob Strauss, handsome, privileged, idle and corrupt; a ne'er-do-well who, despite his wealthy background and Ivy League education, had proved himself utterly incapable of running a business on the level. A combination of greed and impatience had seen the demise of Ultra-Sports and Trimnasium. Somehow he'd climbed aboard Starwear, where his grotesque errors of judgement had continued – except that, instead of bringing down his own self-made enterprise, he was now tearing the guts out of a family firm that had been in operation since the 1950s. In so doing, he was also destroying the world's biggest sportswear manufacturer, and rendering utterly valueless what had once been the second biggest brand in the world.

It was while Jacob Strauss had headed up Starwear's International Division that Quantum Change had been implemented. During its initial failure, he'd virtually gone into hiding. Then he'd turned to child labour to solve the problem and, when the graphs had started pointing upwards again, he had been the first to take the credit for the huge increase in production. The mystery, as far as Judith was concerned, was: why had Nathan let him join Starwear in the first place?

Nathan's probity had never been in any doubt. Not only had his Starwear I and II policy declarations quickly become regarded as cornerstones of global corporate ethics but also, as a man, he had been transparently sincere. Like most business journalists she had met him, though briefly, on several occasions, and soon concurred with her colleagues who decided that, for all his awkwardness with the media, Nathan Strauss had one of the finest minds, and most developed ethical sensibilities, in the corporate world. When he had appointed Jacob as Managing Director of

International Division, didn't he know about Jacob's business track record? When he had stood in front of blazing television lights and told the world that Starwear would never contemplate using child labour, had he knowingly lied then? She couldn't believe that was possible. She could believe, however, that Jacob had used Nathan to buy credibility, knowing that a few words from Nathan were all that was needed to halt any further questions on the issue.

Judith finished her wine, and wandered into the kitchen, where she pulled a ready-made lasagna out of the freezer, pierced its plastic-film wrapper, and popped it in the microwave. She set the timer for the required four minutes and thirty seconds, and as the microwave hummed into action, she poured herself another glass of wine from the box and took another swig. There was no doubting this was the most explosive story she had ever embarked on; the kind of story that came up only once or twice in a journalist's entire career. But, for all her discoveries, there was still something missing from the big picture; a gap, an important part of the puzzle without which the whole story wouldn't be told.

She thought of William van Aardt's 'suicide'. She wasn't the only one who was suspicious – Merlin de Vere had been too. But no sooner had he got hold of the evidence that fuelled his suspicions than he also died, in the 'sexual experiment gone wrong'. Then there'd been the lookalike 'burglary' of her flat. And the late-night phone call from Chris to say he was being followed. There was a major cover-up going on, and she didn't know who was responsible for it. Of course, somewhere behind the scenes, Jacob Strauss must be pulling the strings. But who was orchestrating everything? Which spider was at the centre of the web?

Chris knew. Even if he hadn't believed her at first, he seemed to have changed his opinions. Being trailed as he drove through town must be freaking him out. But there was more to it than that, Judith couldn't help thinking, much more. And she'd be seeing him in two days' time.

It was strange, she thought, how the world turned. When they had been younger, Chris and she had been going to conquer the world together. They'd had such high hopes and dreams for themselves; dreams that had unravelled in the years after university, never to be realised. Now, a decade later, here they were in the same corner. But one fact, more than any other, dominated her thoughts: Chris was now a Lomboid. She was still far from certain she could trust him.

'Big typing job, I'm afraid.' Chris stepped into Charlotte's office and handed her the Solly Kuczynski document he'd received earlier that week.

She flicked through it. 'Which bits do you want?'

'The whole lot.'

Reaching the last page she did a quick mental calculation. 'That's one and a half hours . . . should have it done by six. Is that OK?'

Chris couldn't help smiling. He still marvelled at Lotte's 'can do' attitude. At MIRA there would have been squeals of indignation, and complaints about workload from his secretary who would have taken three days or more.

'Six is more than OK,' he told her, 'mid-morning tomorrow would still be fine. I need you to insert the document into Project Silo. How many appendices are we up to?'

'Six.'

'Make this seven.'

'Do you want copies made?'

'Three, please.'

She scanned through the document and glanced up briefly, meeting his eyes. 'Is this . . .?'

'Uh-huh.'

Ever since he'd got the report from Advance Security, he'd been conscious of every syllable he'd uttered – and not only at home. There were probably bugs in every phone he used. As for this place . . .

Now Lotte started reading phrases aloud. '"Mr Reid's ownership of the brothel",' she raised her eyebrows, glancing down the page, '"sued for sexual harassment by his secretary. He promised her a BMW . . . sex in the stationery cupboard". Well!' Her eyes gleamed. 'You can't be accused of being too academic with this lot.'

He had given her the gist of North's criticisms in the days before he realised every word he spoke was being monitored. These days, though, he was more diffident, so he just smiled.

'Take it you've seen the announcement?' she asked, putting Kuczynski's document down.

'Announcement?'

'General agency meeting, Friday morning. Eight-thirty in Reception.'

He'd been there less than two months and hadn't heard about a general meeting before. 'Does this happen often?'

'Only once while I've been here. So it must be big news.'

She was calling the announcement up on to her screen. He moved beside her to read it. It had come from Mike Cullen's office. Attendance at the meeting was compulsory, it said; Mike had some important news he wanted to communicate directly and in person. There was no clue as to what that important news might be.

'Strongly worded,' remarked Chris.

'It's caused an uproar downstairs. There's been a circus down there with people cancelling flights and rescheduling meetings, you name it.'

Chris was curious. 'Mike would have known the inconvenience . . . must be really important.' Then, after a pause, 'You said you went to one before?'

She nodded. 'Must have been about two years ago, just after I'd joined.'

'What was that one about?'

'You know Lombard used to have the IGO account?'

Chris rolled his eyes. IGO was one of the world's largest chemical manufacturers, and a British company. For years it had cultivated an environmentally friendly image – a 'greenwashing' job in which Lombard had played a key role. But then, a Government-commissioned report had shown that not only were IGO's green credentials decidedly suspect, it was actually the country's worst polluter. IGO had reacted swiftly, promising to clean up any of its plants that had fallen short of its own stringent standards, etcetera, etcetera – but the damage had been done. A genuine clean-up would have cost more than IGO's shareholders were prepared to stomach, so it was never going to happen. The company was fighting a PR battle that was impossible to win and had become an embarrassment to Lombard. Associating with a company whose credibility was so irreparably damaged was bad for Lombard's own image. So, despite a monthly retainer which was in the generous six figures, Lombard had resigned the account.

'Mike announced that we were resigning IGO. It was a big shock – we had a lot of people who were working on

IGO full-time. He did his best to calm nerves, you know, tell people there would be no redundancies, that kind of thing. At the same time that he was telling us, the announcement went out on the stock exchange – it knocked fifty pence off IGO's share price.'

Chris suddenly felt the muscles in his face relax. 'Very interesting.' Would Friday morning's meeting also be a client resignation announcement? If Kate had shown Mike the Ultra-Sports and Trimnasium accounts, maybe he now felt the same way about representing Jacob Strauss as he had about IGO. He turned and began making his way back into his office.

'By the way, did Kate catch you?' Charlotte called after him.

He shook his head.

'She wanted to see you. Had just been in with Mike, but you were away from your desk. Seemed important.'

Broadgate Circle is the City of London's answer to New York's Rockefeller Plaza – minus the flags. An ice-rink in winter, during the summer months the skating circle is covered over and used for displays and performances, from jazz bands to croquet. Overlooking it, in restaurants and wine bars, City suits enjoy the entertainment as they pitch for business, shake on deals, or simply catch up on the latest gossip. In Corney & Barrow wine bar, Kate Taylor was having a Thursday pre-lunch-time spritzer with Patrick O'Neill of J. P. Morgan. Patrick was an analyst who followed media companies, and Kate had known him for a couple of years and often spoke to him about her media industry clients. Large, curly-haired, with a Limerick lilt, Patrick had always seemed more publican than analyst;

Kate tried not to let his appearance distract her from his incisive mind. She'd set up today's meeting ostensibly to discuss the latest interim results of United Magazines – but their conversation would, of course, be far more broad-ranging.

Apart from their professional contact, they had met socially a few times with Patrick's late colleague, Merlin de Vere. In fact, it was Merlin who had introduced them. The last time they'd seen each other had been at Merlin's funeral. The J. P. Morgan team had been well-represented, and had included several of the company's top brass. There could have been no clearer signal, thought Kate, of the high regard in which Merlin had been held by his colleagues – however bizarre the circumstances of his death. Now Kate asked, 'Tell me Pat, I know Tim Packard is holding the fort at Morgan's on the manufacturing side, for now, but do you know what's happening to Merlin's remit?'

'There's been some interviewing going on.' He swigged his Guinness. 'But I don't know for sure. The golden hellos are getting pretty steep.'

Luring potential employees had always been a pricey business in the City – especially at a senior level. Merchant banks regularly churned out million-pound 'golden hellos' just to get signatures on the dotted line. That was before the generous seven-figure salary, and even more generous bonus structures.

'Going to be hard to replace,' Kate responded.

'To be honest,' his expression was serious, 'we're all still recovering from the shock.'

There was a pause as they both looked out of the window, gazing out, unseeing, at the putt-putt competition currently in progress down in the circle.

'It was a very strange business,' she mused. 'I'm still trying to get my head around it. Just seemed so completely unlike him.'

Conversation was moving towards the real reason she'd set up today's meeting. She had been well aware, at the time of Merlin's death, that a conspiracy theory was doing the rounds: something to the effect that his death was murder, not accidental suicide. At the time, she hadn't paid it too much attention. Under the circumstances, she reckoned, it was to be expected that stories of that kind would circulate; none of Merlin's friends wanted to believe he was some kind of sicko pervert. She hadn't even wanted to think about how he'd died. In fact, she'd tried to put the whole thing out of her mind.

It was after Chris Treiger had shown her the documents on Ultra-Sports and Trimnasium that an alarm had sounded. Sitting in her office, going through the accounts, she had suddenly remembered her last telephone conversation with Merlin. It was a call she'd replayed in her mind many times since his death, wondering about the significance of it. They had been arranging to meet the following week. But what made the arrangement different was that Merlin had phoned her to set up the meeting. Usually she, as the PR person, called him to arrange things. And something else was odd too – the reason he gave her, over the phone, for wanting to meet: 'There's something really quite important I need to speak to you about. Serious implications. I'd rather do it face to face.'

Now that she knew the truth of Jacob Strauss's disastrous business past, and knew, also, just how desperate Elliott North was to suppress any suggestion of it, Kate was struck by the horrifying possibility: what if it was Jacob Strauss that Merlin had wanted to discuss with her? What if he, like Chris Treiger, had decided to investigate Jacob's track record – only to discover the same can of worms? And what if Elliott North had got to him first?

It was at that point that she decided to do some asking around for herself – starting with Patrick. Meeting his eyes now, she asked, 'Is the conspiracy theory still doing the rounds?'

'You know, the thing about conspiracy theories is they usually die down after a while. But this one just keeps going down new avenues.'

'Oh?'

'When it first came out it was all circumstantial. It had to do with things down in Merlin's cottage not being quite right. He'd put red wine in the fridge; he'd forgotten to wind a clock. But no one can build a case on that.'

She nodded, grimly.

'Now the story is that Merlin knew too much.'

Her heart quickened. 'About?'

'Some skeleton in a corporate closet. He'd been digging around and uncovered something.'

She tried to disguise her alarm. 'Does anyone know which company?'

Patrick shrugged. 'Who knows. Could be anything in the manufacturing sector.'

Then, taking another gulp of Guinness: 'I don't set very much store by the stories. If they're true, it'll be the first time that murder was used as a financial PR technique.'

She tried to smile at his gallows humour. 'Do you have any idea where the stories are coming from?'

'You know how it is, they just do the rounds. But I did see Merlin's girlfriend not so long ago. She had to come into the office to collect his things.' He shook his head. 'Not very easy. We only spoke briefly. She's convinced there was more to it than there seems. It wouldn't surprise me if some of the stories have come from her.'

Kate shook her head in sympathy. 'That was . . . Denise?'

'Denise Caville,' he confirmed. 'Runs her own catering firm.'

Back behind the closed door of her office, later that afternoon, Kate put down the phone. She had just spoken to Denise Caville, and it hadn't been an easy call. She'd vacillated for several hours before even making it: could she, an outsider whose name Denise may not even recognise, really justify intruding into the woman's grief? But on the other hand, it seemed that Denise was searching for certainty. Not knowing what had really happened would be the worst of it. And perhaps, somewhere down the line, Kate could help.

As it happened, Denise did remember who Kate was, but remained guarded. Yes, she told Kate, she believed it was murder. Merlin had uncovered some controversial facts about a company, and she reckoned he'd been silenced. But she wouldn't say which company it was, or how much more she knew. All she did say was that, having exhausted all possibilities with the police, she'd put the matter into the hands of an investigative journalist whom she knew Merlin had trusted. She didn't say who the journalist was. But, by then, she didn't need to. Replacing the receiver after her brief conversation, Kate stared ahead of her, the alarm bells ringing loud and shrill. She and Merlin often used to talk about the different financial reporters and what they'd written about various companies. They'd concurred on some writers and disagreed on others. And there was one reporter, she knew, whose investigative skills Merlin rated highly. The same reporter, surprise, surprise, who had recently been asking questions about Starwear.

She got up from her desk, and strode straight from her office up the stairs to Monitoring Services on the third floor. Although the fact wasn't generally known in Lombard, Monitoring Services had originally been Kate's idea. When the agency had still consisted of a dozen consultants in three rooms, she'd come up with the thought of having a dedicated executive to monitor media output and keep tabs on journalists who were frequently changing their jobs.

Monitoring Services was established and subsequently mushroomed in scale and scope. Since starting out as an administrative function, it had long outgrown that role. Kate had no particular interest in its day-to-day workings; all she ever sought from Bruno d'Andrea and his team was a good steer on journalists. Although she found his manner unusual, he'd never disappointed her.

She found him now, as always, sitting behind his desk in his semi-dark office, reading through a document.

'Judith Laing?' she asked, stepping inside.

He rolled his eyes. 'What now?'

'What do we know about her?' She perched on the edge of a chair opposite him.

'You've seen the intranet biography?'

She nodded. 'Has it been updated since then?'

He leaned back in his chair, so that his eyes were in shadow. 'Why do you ask?'

'At the last Starwear traffic meeting someone said she was interested in the company. We arranged for her to see

Matt Lester. I was just wondering if anything's come of it? There's been no coverage so far . . .'

For a long while d'Andrea stared at her without saying a word, before gesturing ponderously with his spotted hands. 'We're monitoring Judith Laing very closely at the moment.'

'On behalf of Starwear?'

'Not only that – although you are right, she does have a keen interest in the company.'

'Do you know what exactly *about* Starwear interests her?'

He tilted back his head. 'I couldn't tell you.'

'You said "not only that"?'

'Ah, yes.' He leaned back over his desk, meeting her expression with those pale grey eyes. 'But you will have to keep this to yourself. Your new boy . . .'

She looked puzzled.

'Chris Treiger. He and Judith Laing.' He held up his hand, two fingers twisted together. 'Like this.'

'What?'

'Since university.'

'You mean . . . ?'

'Lovers.' He pulled a slow, sly smile, observing her surprise, before continuing, 'I don't know what the . . . relationship is now. But they still seem very close occasionally, if you follow me.'

She gaped at him, wide-eyed.

'We're keeping an eye on Mr Treiger. We feel he hasn't been entirely above board with us.'

Kate was fighting for her composure. 'Let me get this straight,' she said. 'Chris was involved with Judith Laing at university. They still get it together from time to time.'

'Correct.'

'So if he has nights of passion with an old flame, does that make him a security risk?'

'Well . . .'

'I'm . . . surprised he never mentioned her to me. But it's his private life.' She regarded d'Andrea closely. 'Has he done anything at all to arouse suspicions?'

D'Andrea shook his head. 'Not my suspicions. But', glancing up to check his door, 'I can't say the same for our American colleague.'

'That man is paranoia incarnate.'

D'Andrea fixed her with a serious expression. 'He's also dangerous,' he said gravely, 'extremely dangerous. I'd be careful of him if I were you. And Chris Treiger should be especially careful. North has him in his sights.'

'He's already made his feelings plain over the Project Silo report.'

D'Andrea shrugged. 'I don't know about that. But North is convinced that Treiger and Laing are cooking up the exposé of the century on Jacob Strauss.'

'That's what all this is about, isn't it?' Kate fought to control an urge to scream, and instead kept her voice down. 'Jacob Strauss?'

D'Andrea snorted. 'Well, let's just say that things were a lot more simple when Nathan was in charge.'

That Thursday afternoon's Starwear traffic meeting was like no other that had gone before. Mike Cullen always chaired the meetings – but this afternoon he had sent his apologies. Kate Taylor had said she was unable to attend, sending her deputy, Stewart Watkins, on her behalf. Marilyn Rhodes seemed unusually preoccupied and Bob Wang's main worry was a major, five-year sponsorship deal he was in the middle of negotiating on Starwear's behalf. Nicholas King was inscrutable and bespectacled, mid-table. Elliott North sat, as ever, doodling on his briefing pad.

The Agenda followed the same format it always did for these meetings, going through all the PR disciplines – Financial, Corporate, Consumer, Sponsorship, Political and Special Projects. Usually, Mike Cullen would make a deliberate point of referencing activities to the Four-Point Plan. But today, with no Mike Cullen, there was no mention of the Four-Point Plan. And there was little appetite among those present for dwelling on the Agenda, although there could be no escaping the importance of the Textiles Bill, due to be debated and voted on in the House of Commons next week. Reporting to the meeting, Nicholas King seemed almost relieved that some of his more senior colleagues weren't there to witness his discomfort.

'It's not all bad news,' he tried to sound upbeat to begin with, 'we have a Member of Parliament prepared to sponsor an amendment that specifically excludes sportswear manufacturing from the Bill. And we have several other MPs prepared to give voice to their support of the amendment. But in the end, it's a numbers game.'

He glanced round the table at his colleagues, all of whom seemed lost in other thoughts. 'We're fighting against a Bill which the Government says is a major plank of its legislative reform. The Government won't be derailed and will resist having the Bill killed by a thousand amendments. There are all kinds of special-interest groups out there wanting to climb on the bandwagon, to be excluded from the Bill in the same way that Starwear does. It's the present view of the Minister that if you give in to one group, you have to give in to them all.'

Marilyn Rhodes did her best to suppress a yawn.

'Of course, we've considered taking this outside Parliament, directly to the public, but it's not an issue that plays well.'

'Surely,' Stewart Watkins tried to contribute, 'if the public can be persuaded that including sportswear manufacturers in the Bill is bad for the industry and bad for Britain ...'

'The cost of such persuasion would be huge – and would take considerably longer than a week.' Nicholas King delivered a patrician expression over his half-moons. 'It is also the least effective way to achieve legislative change. Besides, you're up against those arguing for free competition. There's a knee-jerk public reaction that open competition is good, and restrictive trading is bad. Whatever arguments you marshal, they tend to fall on deaf ears. Most MPs have a slightly more sophisticated understanding and, believe me, we've conducted an intensive lobbying campaign among them.'

North looked up. 'What's their reaction been to the "responsible management" line?'

'Keen appreciation among the Opposition, lukewarm on Government benches. Not enough, so far, to support an amendment, let alone a full-scale revolt.'

'Just so long as the "responsible management" story has been gotten over.'

'They've all heard it till they're climbing the walls,' King was firm. 'They've been individually wined and dined. There have been presentations to the Select Committee and a succession of letters both to MPs and the Ministry. They are all acutely aware of the points we're making. It's a matter of achieving consensus for our point of view.'

Ending now, he glanced about at the sombre faces. There was no doubt in his mind that his lobbying efforts on Starwear's behalf were doomed to failure. What the company was trying to achieve simply went against the current of public opinion. It would take a lot more than 'Bad for the Industry, Bad for Britain' clichés to swing this one.

'Just as well I've got some positive news,' North commented from the end, moving the meeting on.

King glowered down the table.

'GlobeWatch has nominated Starwear for several awards, including Best Developing Nations Employer. Starwear is also among three nominees for the overall GlobeWatch Company of the Year Award.'

There was a pause while the others digested this. Then Marilyn Rhodes asked, 'Big splash event, is it?'

North nodded. 'Grosvenor House. All the trappings. It will be a big night out.'

'Must be costing a bit – for a charity organisation,' she couldn't resist observing.

'I'm sure there will be no difficulty raising sponsorship,' North tried making light of it, 'for such a good cause.'

Marilyn fixed him with a hard expression; a steel-eyed, penetrating cynicism. He didn't like the look of it at all.

19

Mike Cullen didn't much care for general agency meetings. Assembling every Lombard consultant in one, cavernous chamber might do wonders for the ego, but it played havoc with time-sheets and disrupted the servicing of clients. Which is why he resorted to meetings of this kind only when he considered it absolutely necessary.

Now he looked out across the massed ranks of Lombard consultants gathering in Reception. It was just a few minutes before eight-thirty a.m. on Friday, 31 October. Kate Taylor's recent revelations had left him with absolutely no alternative. Having considered matters at length, he'd realised that he had to act decisively. The announcement he was about to make was one he'd been considering for some months now. It was the timing of it that he'd decided to bring forward abruptly.

After checking his watch, he held up his hand for silence. He didn't have long to wait. The intensity of anticipation was almost palpable.

'Thank you all for making the necessary arrangements to be here,' he began. 'I know it hasn't been easy for some of you. I have an announcement to make which, although brief, is nonetheless critical to all of us who work at Lombard.'

His expression was serious as he glanced across his dark-suited, private army.

'During the past few days I have had important discussions with Kate Taylor; discussions which continued again last night. During the course of them, we talked through a number of issues which have concerned me for some time, and which affect the future of this agency.'

The silence in reception was electric, all those present hanging on his every word.

'As many of you are aware,' he said now, 'I have always taken the view that PR is a young person's business. I've never seen myself running Lombard *ad nauseam*. There comes a time when one needs to make room for those who are younger, hungrier, and more able than oneself. However, this process has to be carefully managed, to ensure a strengthening, rather than weakening, in market position. Succession planning is vital. So', he turned now to where Kate Taylor was standing on a step next to him, 'I am delighted to announce that Kate Taylor has been appointed Deputy Chief Executive Officer of Lombard with immediate effect.'

One of Kate's team began the applause, which quickly became a thunderous wave, echoing round the cavernous marble hallway. Kate was as popular with her colleagues as she was respected by the market. The logic of the announcement was self-evident; by installing her as his deputy, Cullen was preparing for the future. As always, he had caught his colleagues by surprise. But few would find fault with the decision.

Joining in the applause, there was only one Lombard

consultant who found the announcement utterly bewildering. Chris had come downstairs expecting a very different
kind of announcement. Pleased though he was for Kate, he
couldn't help wondering: *What about Starwear and Jacob
Strauss? What about the evidence that their biggest client was a
crook? None of this made any sense.*

'The logistics make it a bit difficult for us all to celebrate
the news together,' Cullen continued once the applause
had abated, 'but during the course of the morning, a case of
champagne will be delivered to each one of you to enjoy
over the weekend.'

To the applause was added much whooping and cheer-
ing.

'Thank you.' Cullen signalled he'd finished. 'That's all
for now.'

Chris struggled through the crowded room towards Kate,
but by the time he'd reached the front, she had already left
with Cullen and a group of other Lombard directors.
Making his way up the stairs to the first floor, he strode past
the jangling telephones of the Pit towards where Kate's secretary was taking a message. Kate had been trying to get
hold of him since yesterday evening, her secretary told him,
hand over the mouthpiece. She'd wanted to see him before
this morning's announcement. But she'd be tied up in a
management meeting until twelve o'clock, then she had a
lunch engagement, after which she was going straight on to
a two-thirty at London Wall. She'd be back around five.

Chris booked in to see her, the moment she got back.
Then he returned to his office, emotions churning. Mike
Cullen's announcement – together with the promised case
of champagne and the fact that it was a Friday – had put

everyone in an upbeat mood. On the way out of the Pit, and up in the lift, Chris had to act as pleased as everyone else. But he couldn't help wondering what in hell was going on. This was all just inexplicable.

He spent the day restlessly going through project work, trying to get started on things but never able to settle down. Tonight he was seeing Judith. He'd been looking forward to it all week. He'd hoped – naively, it now seemed – that when he saw her he'd have found a way out of this, for both of them. When he'd given the Ultra-Sports and Trimnasium accounts to Kate, he hadn't thought everything through. But he had anticipated some effect, other than Kate getting a promotion. He had imagined that Mike Cullen would do something about Starwear in general, and Elliott North in particular. But how had Mike reacted? What had he said? Right now, there was no way of knowing. Suddenly, it was as though the accumulated stress of the past few weeks descended on his shoulders; he began to feel heavy with weariness.

'Congratulations!' he said to Kate, stepping inside her office just after five.

'Thanks,' she said, smiling briefly. 'Coffee?'

He nodded.

She collected up her handbag. 'Let's go round the corner. Will you need your coat?'

'I'll be fine.'

They made their way downstairs and out of the building. It was another grey afternoon, and above them the clouds were leaden.

'I've been trying to get to see you,' she began as soon as they were outside.

'What did Mike say about the accounts?'

'He was furious.' She glanced across at his anxious expression. 'They were the last straw for him. Don't, for God's sake, tell anyone, but he's going to resign Starwear.'

Large drops of rain began spattering on the pavement around them.

'I thought that's what this morning was going to be about.'

She shook her head. 'Not till after the annual results are posted. It's only a week away. Starwear's biggest profits ever. He wants to go out on an up.'

She retrieved a compact umbrella from her handbag, which opened out at the press of a button. The rain was pelting down now.

'A week seems an awfully long time,' he said, as she raised the umbrella over them both.

They walked briskly and close together, crammed under the small umbrella. He didn't know what to say next. How could he begin to explain everything that was going on? Then, glancing up at him sharply, she said, 'Tell me, what do you know about Merlin de Vere?'

He didn't hide his surprise. 'Only that it may not all be what it seemed.' He decided this was no time to be coy. 'There are some who think he was murdered because he knew too much.'

'And would those some include Judith Laing?'

There was no need for him to reply. The alarm in his eyes said it all.

'Elliott North knows the two of you are involved—' she began to explain.

'*Were* involved,' he protested, 'ten years ago. At university. I've seen her twice in the last year.'

'Well, he's convinced otherwise,' Kate told him.

The rain was hammering down so hard now that she turned into a doorway where they stood under a protective arch.

'Look,' she said to him gravely, 'there's something you should know. Judith has been doing an investigative job on Starwear. When Nathan was in charge, that wouldn't have been an issue, but I can't say the same for Jacob. The guy's obviously a crook. He's got a lot to hide. And Elliott North's job is to make sure it all stays hidden.'

He was following her every word intently.

'I've been doing some asking around about Merlin for myself,' she continued. 'It may be that he also got hold of these accounts.'

'Are you saying North gave the orders?'

'I'm saying that, seeing how he's acted over other things, it wouldn't surprise me.'

It came as no relief to have his suspicions confirmed; no relief to know that he had on his tail the guy who'd arranged for Merlin de Vere to be found, ass-up in a garbage can.

'That's not the worst of it, I'm afraid.' She glanced about them briefly, before looking back up at him. 'You should also know you're being watched.'

'Who by?' It was the question he'd been desperate to have answered.

'North has d'Andrea tapping your phone conversations. It wouldn't surprise me if he's got some private dick tracking you after office hours.'

'But why?'

'Because he thinks you're intimate with Judith Laing. He sees her as a threat.' Her face was filled with concern. 'I assume you haven't given Judith the same information you gave me.'

He shook his head. 'Didn't have to,' his own expression was weary, 'Judith was the one who told me about Jacob Strauss. I didn't believe her, so I had it double-checked. You're right about Merlin de Vere. He'd found out the same stuff.'

'Jesus!'

For a while they stood, staring out at where the rain pummelled the pavement, before Kate turned to him and said, 'Chris, please be careful. Until we get shot of the Starwear account you're in very serious danger.'

They held each other's eyes for a while until he asked her, 'What should I do?'

She shook her head. 'Nothing. Just watch yourself. Don't do anything to arouse suspicion.'

He couldn't help reflecting on the irony of her advice; the same advice he'd given Judith; the advice he'd been living by ever since discovering he was being followed.

'But whatever else you do,' Kate was grave, 'don't have anything to do with Judith Laing.'

He'd carefully planned his route to see Judith. Instead of going home by car, as he nearly always did, he left the building among a group of other Lombard consultants who were making their way to a nearby pub for a Friday evening drink. He reckoned that whoever was trailing him would be expecting to drive. And sure enough, no sooner had the Lombard gang set off along the pavement than he caught sight of a figure in a dark coat emerging from a car parked conveniently close to the Lombard basement exit.

He didn't follow the gang to the pub; instead, as they

passed the nearby Underground station, he darted down the stairs, making his way briskly among the rush-hour crowds, through the barriers, on to the escalator, and along a corridor to the Central Line. It was impossible to tell how far his pursuer was behind him. At that time of night the place was bedlam. Passing a newspaper stall, he thrust some coins in the vendor's hand and grabbed an *Evening Standard*. It came in useful once he'd got on to the platform and edged his way right along it, to a strategic spot amongst the crowd.

Shielding himself among a group of large brokers wearing loud ties, he opened the paper and buried himself in its business pages. As he waited for the first train, he kept a sharp eye on movement down the platform. Of course, he didn't know what the guy looked like. But, moments after taking cover, he spotted a figure bursting through the platform entrance, hurriedly glancing up and down the packed crowds in each direction. In just an instant Chris took in a dark coat and swarthy features, a close crew cut and heavy eyebrows. Behind his newspaper, he had no idea if his pursuer would home in on him, though it was less than twenty seconds before a blast of acrid air heralded the arrival of the next train.

Heading west on the Central Line at rush hour on a Friday meant jostling and shoving your way into a carriage already way past capacity – or quite possibly having to wait for the next train, or the one after that. But waiting wasn't an option. Chris crammed himself into a doorway so bulging with bodies he was hanging outside the carriage – which was when he caught a glimpse of the other. Same carriage. One door along. Following his every move.

When the doors slid shut, Chris had to cram his way

into the train and the pinstriped forest of disgruntled commuters. Pressed to the side of the carriage, neck bent against the door, there was no evading his pursuer just a few yards away. At the next station, when a large exodus of passengers was replaced by a frenetic inward surge, he positioned himself behind a group, so that he was at least out of direct view. This would all be about timing, he knew. Timing and bluff.

When he got to Chancery Lane he moved further into the carriage, all the while following his pursuer out of the corner of his eye. The dark figure was matching his every step, and now moved deeper into the carriage too – which was precisely Chris's intention. At the next station, Holborn, he made his break, moving stealthily back to the door behind the jostling passengers – just as it was sliding shut. He jammed it open with his elbow, wrestling with all his strength to keep it open just long enough to jump. Then he was out of the carriage and walking down the platform. The train was grinding away, his pursuer trapped on board.

So far, so good. Though it wasn't over – not by a long shot. Now he made his way to the Piccadilly Line, which would take him to South Kensington, the nearest station to the Oyster Bar. Crushed on to yet another overcrowded platform, he glanced again at the newspaper and this time his attention was suddenly seized by a photograph. Front page. It was of Dale Nesbitt. 'Police Search for Missing St Stephen's Boy', blazed the headline. He quickly read the three-paragraph article. Dale Nesbitt had been reported missing two days before. He'd disappeared during the middle of the day, and when last seen was wearing his school uniform. None of the staff or pupils had any idea where he'd gone and he had no living relatives. Police were appealing to members of the public to come forward if they could help.

The article went on to link Dale's disappearance with that of another St Stephen's boy eighteen months earlier. He'd been missing for three weeks before his body was found in the undergrowth near Virginia Water railway station in Surrey. He had died of asphyxiation, and a coroner's report indicated that sexual assault had taken place.

Chris forgot he was on a packed platform during Friday's rush hour. For a few minutes he stood there lost in thought, heart pounding and mouth dry. He remembered standing in the deserted porch at St Stephen's, Dale frozen to the spot, terror on his face and a puddle at his feet. In the distance was the priest with his black robes and white face. Chris could hardly believe he was living with such evil.

*

He'd chosen the Oyster Bar, in the Bibendum building, because he knew Judith would be arriving by tube, and there was only one street she could use to get there from the Underground. A long, straight road, ideal for observation. By the time she emerged from South Kensington station, just before eight, his plans were set. Concealed in the entrance to a block of flats, he watched as she started out towards Fulham Road. He wasn't scrutinising her so much as the fellow passengers making their way down the pavement behind her. His actions were less a precaution than a confirmation of what he half suspected. And after a minute or so, when she crossed the road, his fears were confirmed. Ten yards behind her, a dark-suited man crossed the road too, his eyes fixed on her.

Things moved quickly after that. Arriving at the Oyster Bar, Judith glanced about for Chris, before sitting at an empty table. A waitress came to take her order, and asked Judith her name before handing her the note Chris had left. Moments later, Judith emerged from the side entrance of the bar, where a taxi was waiting, door open, with Chris sitting in the back seat.

'What's going on?'

'Just get in. Quickly.' Then, as she climbed up, 'I came alone. You didn't.'

'What d'you mean?'

The cab had already pulled away and was heading round the corner past the main entrance to the Oyster Bar. Chris seized Judith by the shoulder and pulled her down as he ducked to window level.

'There's someone on your tail. I watched him follow you from the tube. Just a couple of moments ago he was standing right there,' he jerked a thumb in the direction of the Bibendum building.

As they sat up again, he tried to fathom the look in her eyes. He couldn't avoid seeing that she still doubted his motives.

'And while we're on the painful subject, it might be an idea to have your flat swept for bugs. They found twenty-five listening devices in my house.'

She was shaking her head, the edge to her expression only heightened by this latest revelation.

'Look, Judith . . .' he knew he had to win her over, 'I don't blame you for being suspicious of me. But, for God's sake, d'you think I'd be putting myself on the line if I wasn't serious?'

'Last time we met—'

'I know. I didn't believe a word you said.' He glanced up at the open window to the driver's cabin before leaning over to slide it shut. 'But, like I told you on the phone,' he lowered his voice, 'a lot has happened in a very short while. They've connected the two of us. They're convinced we're working up a story that'll blast Strauss out of the sky. That's why they've got both of us monitored twenty-four hours a day.'

She was chewing her lip, which he took as a good sign. Maybe he was getting through to her.

'Plus, after this all started, I checked out the stuff you told me about Strauss. I found it's true.'

'What stuff?'

'Ultra-Sports. Trimnasium.'

'Oh that!' She was dismissive. 'Ancient history.'

'You mean there's more?'

Instead of a reply, she just rolled her eyes; a response which suddenly irritated him. 'I think I have a right to know what's going on.'

'I might say the same thing,' her tone was caustic. 'I had my flat trashed two weeks ago. Now you tell me the place is crawling with bugs and there's some creep on my tail.'

They glared at each other across the back seat. Then, after a pause, while she looked out of the window at the shops slipping past them, she turned to him. 'I'll do a deal with you,' she said. 'You tell me exactly who's following us. And I tell you why.'

It was only a moment's thought before he nodded. 'Shoot.'

Moments later they were climbing out of the cab and walking down a street in the direction of the river. Speaking quickly, Judith told him about her investigations, starting with the discrepancy between the Forbes forecasts and the outputs shown in Starwear's Annual Reports. How

Quantum Change had bombed out when it was first implemented. The rumours of a threatened takeover, with shadowy offshore companies taking up positions. And Jacob Strauss going into hiding until the turnaround, at which point he had emerged to take the credit.

But it was when she started on the child slavery story that he followed her with mounting incredulity. Of course he knew about past rumours, but as she told him about all the first-hand evidence she'd assembled, he realised that Strauss's American crimes and misdemeanours were paltry by comparison. Child slavery put him in an altogether different league. This was corporate apocalypse.

'No wonder they're so paranoid about us,' he exclaimed in a low whisper, after she'd finished.

'Just like they were paranoid about Merlin de Vere?'

He looked at her seriously. 'Why haven't you run the story?'

'I plan to. Early next week. The piece that's missing is where you come in.'

He raised his eyebrows.

'You know what happened to William van Aardt and Merlin de Vere—'

'The past few days I haven't been able to think of much else.'

'Then who are these people? Who trashed my flat? Who's on our tails? Who's Jacob Strauss's minder?'

They walked on a few paces, curving round a bend in the street which narrowed to a one-way lane leading to mews entrances. It wasn't so well lit, and there was nobody else walking the cobbled pavements. In a low voice he said to her, 'Have you ever heard of a guy called Elliott North?'

Her expression was blank. 'Mr Fixit?'

Chris nodded. 'Jacob Strauss's minder.' He told her how North had been recruited by Strauss in New York, when he was Managing Director of International Division. He went on to detail the tensions that had accompanied his arrival at Lombard – North's controlling behaviour, his sitting in on journalist briefings, his attempt to bribe Jim Ritchie. Then there was his use of Bruno d'Andrea for monitoring and Solly Kuczynski whose activities, Chris was certain, went way beyond digging up dirt on the personal lives of Starwear competitors.

It was the first time Chris had told anyone about this. Next to him, Judith was following him intently, his revelations making sense, for the first time, of why it was that Merlin had been such a key player – why she had had her flat searched. Jacob Strauss's minder knew, better than anyone, about the power of the media. He understood exactly how the system worked and how to exploit it. His choice of targets; his timing; it all added up now. Of course he had to be in public relations.

After Chris had finished, they walked on awhile in the semi-darkness, the sound of traffic receding with each minute. Then she asked him, 'So. What next?'

He glanced over at her. 'Obviously, you have to get the story out.' Then, shaking his head, 'It'll be the most sensational corporate scam in years. If I were you, I'd file it and high-tail out of town.'

'That seems all very easy.'

'What does?'

'Giving the story to Carter, going to Wales for the week, and when I get back it's hey, ho, back to normal.'

He flashed her a look of irritation. 'Do you have a better idea?'

She shrugged, 'Anyway, what are *you* going to do?'

It was a question he never got to answer because, in that same moment, they both became aware of footsteps in the distance behind them – careful, self-conscious footsteps that made them both suspicious. Judith glanced over at him with a look of recrimination.

'Do we run?' she whispered urgently.

'Too late. If it's anyone, we've already been seen. I reckon we turn around. That way we'll know.'

'But—'

He was already turning. She had no choice but to follow suit. Then they were looking back up the dim-lit corridor to where, ahead of them, a figure had paused, motionless in the shadows. As they made their way towards him, he seemed frozen for a few seconds, before turning suddenly fugitive, racing up the cobbled pavement towards the distant lights of Fulham Road.

When Judith turned to face Chris, her eyes were filled with anger.

20

Kate pressed the 'Send' button at the top of her e-mail and made sure her message with its attachment had gone, before pushing back her chair from her desk, picking up a half-empty glass of champagne, and taking a swig. It had been a real roller-coaster of a day, beginning with the agency announcement at eight-thirty that morning, and non-stop activity ever since. There'd been wall-to-wall meetings, then, late in the afternoon, panic in New York, with one of her clients' American subsidiaries needing her urgent help with an American Stock Exchange release. She'd had no time to bask in the glory of her new title, or to think about how the new job would affect her life. At nine-fifteen p.m., she glanced across her paper-strewn desk, towards the opened magnum of Bollinger; just as well she hadn't planned to go out to celebrate, she couldn't help observing, wryly.

Before she left for the day, she wanted to make sure New York had received the information she sent them. 'Never assume,' was her personal mantra. She'd call them in five minutes. In the meantime, she needed her evening shot. Stepping into her bathroom, she closed the door behind her. Force of habit. Outside her office, the Pit was deserted.

No one had been around for the past half hour except for a security guard on patrol.

In a few, easy motions, she had filled a syringe, given herself the needle, and disposed of the used equipment. Going back into her office, she walked over to her meeting table, and opened her Filofax, even though she already knew what she had planned for this weekend; in marked contrast to her crowded schedule from Monday till Friday, Saturday and Sunday were empty. The prospect wasn't completely depressing – nor was it one she wasn't used to. She'd make a plan. Tomorrow morning she'd call a girl-friend and they'd meet for lunch, maybe take in a movie. And whatever else she did, she was most definitely going shopping, to reward herself as the new Deputy Chief Executive Officer of the UK's largest and most powerful PR agency, with something wonderful from Burlington Arcade, perhaps, or Mappin & Webb. She could certainly afford it on her new package. Just because she didn't have a man in her life didn't mean she couldn't still enjoy self-indulgent treats.

She was just stepping away from the table when the wave hit her. A sudden dizziness which made her crumple, and almost lose balance. It was followed within seconds by another, heady surge. She hadn't had an insulin rush in years – but she knew, in an instant, what it was – the crazy giddiness and disorientation; the feeling of being almost physically struck down; and, within seconds, the rising nausea. She had to get to her bathroom. *What was happening to her?* she wondered, bewildered. *Why now?*

The bathroom door seemed a long way away. She knew she couldn't walk there. Somehow she managed to fumble on to her desk chair, and lurch across the floor towards the door, throwing herself forward in her seat, desperate to get to the point where she could reach out for the door handle; lift herself up. She managed to grab it, and haul herself up into the bathroom before another, blinding wave of dizziness, threw her to the floor. *Please, God, stop this! Give me time! Oh, God! Just one, single minute!* Clawing for the toilet bowl, she managed to prop herself up so that the rim of the bowl was cool on her forehead. She was conscious of nothing but pain. Her head felt as though it would explode. She wanted to throw up, but when she retched, nothing came up. She hadn't eaten for hours.

She knew what she had to do. She kept sugar tablets in the medicine cabinet. Insulin was rushing through her system, plundering all her sugar reserves. She needed to replace them. Immediately. She waited on the floor of the bathroom, trying to summon the strength to stand up, to open the cabinet, to reach for those tablets. When finally she did, staggering to her feet with all the energy she could muster, she swung open the cabinet door and reached out her shaking hand to where she kept the tablets. But they were gone. *Oh, Jesus, where had she put them? She hadn't needed them for ages. They just used to sit there. She'd stopped even noticing them. Had she moved them? Had the cleaners been in?*

Her lips were trembling now and her eyelids twitching. Her whole face felt as though it was crawling with insects. She could barely control her hands. They were like claws, shuddering, and being jabbed with the torment of a thousand needles. Somehow, though, she managed to grab hold of the vials she used to inject herself. Standard 100-unit insulin. It said so, there on the labels. But as she fumbled with the vials, they flipped over so that she was looking at their glass bases. The number 1,000, was printed on the bottom of each one. *It must be her vision.* She held them right up to her face. *How many zeros were there? It had to be two! She'd been on 100 units for the past twenty years!* But she looked and looked until there could be no mistaking. They were 1,000-unit vials. *Someone had switched the labels.*

Her whole body was shaking now, and she felt herself sliding down against the wall. *She'd had ten times her dosage. There was no sugar replacement. She'd go into a coma in just a few minutes if she didn't get help.* The pain in her head was excruciating now – the whole world seemed to be spinning at a thousand miles an hour, and it was all she could do to get on all fours, to start crawling across the carpet back to her desk.

She was way past the point of worrying if she vomited on the carpet. She couldn't think about anything. *Just get to the phone!* She felt her muscles shuddering in uncontrolled spasms as she scraped across the floor. Her face was wet with silent tears of agony. *Please God, let this be over!*

She couldn't get up to the desk, of course. So she tugged the cord of the telephone. It crashed to the floor. Fumbling with the receiver, she pressed for an outside line. But it was dead. No dialling tone. *Oh, Jesus! Something must have happened when it fell!* She tried again. Same result. *This wasn't working. She couldn't get out.*

What about security? She pressed the red button. *Thank Christ it was ringing!*

Ringing and ringing. She lay there, her whole body shaking violently, as though with fever, willing for an answer. *Willing, please God, make him pick it up. Make him get back to his desk.* She knew he went on patrols throughout the night; patrolling through all five floors of the building. He might be in the middle of one of his patrols. Or just starting. He might be another twenty minutes. She couldn't last that long.

Sobbing, she kept the phone clutched to her head and floundered towards her office door. Maybe he'd be on the first floor. Or she could get to one of the phones in the Pit. *Fuck Elliott North! She wasn't going to let him do this to her. He wouldn't get away with it. She was going out there to get help. She'd survive this. She was going to live!*

It was only instinct that kept her going, with every muscle, every sinew, racked with pain, and her mind a swirling cauldron of dizziness and torment. Using up the last of her rapidly depleting energy, she shuddered and fumbled her way across the carpet. *She had to get there! She had to live!* When, finally, she made it to her office door, she threw herself up to wrench the handle. But she failed to open it, and only collapsed back on the floor, in a bruised, weeping heap.

Only sheer desperation drove her to make the second attempt, thrusting upwards and reaching out. She seized the handle and tugged it down and towards her with every last strength of which she was capable. But once again, she failed and fell, broken and sobbing. Just before the last wave of agony exploded her from consciousness, she was struck by the knowledge that she'd been locked inside her own office.

Judith spent the whole of that weekend writing up the article. She was still in her dressing gown when she sat down behind her computer on Saturday morning, a mug of coffee at the ready and a lit cigarette in the ashtray. She began typing. The start of articles was always the hardest, but she already knew how she was going to open this one: a description of one day in the wretched existence of a child slave in India. Having described that, she would establish the facts to prove that this was only one of dozens of similar stories of child slaves used to manufacture Starwear products, to be sold in the high streets and shopping malls of Britain, Europe and America.

Once started, she found it hard to stop. It was a stream-of-consciousness exercise, and the whole story flowed out with an effortlessness she'd seldom experienced before. All the weeks of thinking and planning seemed to click into place, and her fingers rattled over the keyboard at high speed as she included all the different dimensions to the story. Slave labour was the main focus, but she also highlighted the financial irregularities; how Starwear had misled its shareholders about the source of its income and profits; Jacob Strauss's previous business disasters – versus the way he'd projected himself as the 'entrepreneurial genius'. And then there was the cover-up, the deaths of William van Aardt and Merlin de Vere. Completely absorbed in her work, the next time she glanced at her watch it was three forty-five p.m.

Blobbing out, exhausted, in front of the TV, she had an early night, before continuing her work the next day, finishing the story, editing it, polishing it and saving it on to disk.

On Monday morning, she didn't bother dressing in a miniskirt or Wonderbra. Sensible black trousers and a white blouse would do. She was at work early, planning to catch Alex Carter the moment he appeared. But it wasn't until nine-thirty that he arrived, bleary-eyed and in a foul mood after getting caught on the M25 on his way back from a weekend in the country. So much for her big moment, she thought. The grand delivery of her investigative triumph.

He grunted when she knocked on his office door.

'Remember how you asked me about Starwear last week?' She walked over to his desk with her ten-page print-out.

His right eyelid twitched. 'What about them?'

'Well, I dug up a lot more about them than I thought I would.'

'What?' He reached out, seizing the article from her, flicking through the pages. There was no doubting she had his full attention now. 'This isn't research?' he demanded.

'It's got past the research stage,' she said, meeting his eyes. He seemed peculiarly agitated. 'It's a six-thousand-word article. I spent all weekend writing it.'

He glanced back at her pages, random phrases leaping out at him: 'Starwear's squalid child slave factory', 'Jacob Strauss's trumped-up business credentials'.

'I think it could be the corporate exposé of the year,' she said evenly.

Behind his desk, Alex Carter blanched. 'Leave this with me.' He shook her article. 'Close the door on your way out.'

Back at her desk, she couldn't stop watching him out of the corner of her eye. She could see everything through the glass walls of his office: how he sat, utterly engrossed in the article, holding his face – she reckoned he could probably hardly believe what he was reading. Then he pulled out a cigar, ripped off its wrapper, and lit up – no fiddling and fussing, no savouring the moment. He was puffing huge clouds of smoke for quite some time, then he was at her article again, pen in hand, scribbling furiously. Next he was making a phone call, pacing up and down behind his desk and jabbing his cigar in the air as he only ever did in moments of high drama. And this was drama all right, she thought. This was the business news equivalent of the atomic bomb.

She tried to distract herself with routine tasks: expenses form, personal filing, going through that morning's voluminous pile of media releases from PR agencies. Every few minutes she would glance sidelong towards Carter, who seemed to spend the whole morning stamping up and down his office on the telephone. She found it hard to keep her excitement reigned in. He knew, and she knew, this was no ordinary exposé. This story would be picked up, instantly, by all the national and international media. Television, radio, you name it. This story would see the demise of Jacob Strauss and the collapse of Starwear – the world's second biggest brand.

Eventually, some time after eleven, he called her in.

'This is the most astounding investigative reportage I have ever seen,' he told her, once she was standing opposite him, in a fug of cigar smoke. 'Congratulations! You've proved that my decision to hire you for *The Herald* was absolutely right. I don't think I've known of a case . . .' He was scanning through her pages again, shaking his head, 'Incredible. Quite incredible.'

As he glanced up at her she noted now that his whole right cheek seemed to have given way to a nervous tic.

'I have just one suggestion to make – and I think you'll agree with me. The central story, the child slave thing . . .'

'What about it?'

'It needs to be stronger.'

'Stronger?' She could barely believe it. 'But, I mean, how could it *be* any stronger than it already is?'

When she emerged from his office, two minutes later, she was in a state of shock. Alex Carter had come out with the last thing in the world she'd ever expected.

'Ellen? It's Claude here.'

'Oh, Claude.' Behind her desk, she felt herself rising to her feet with anticipation. 'How are you?'

'Very well, thank you.' He didn't return the salutations. The truth was, he felt an awful burden of guilt after so blatantly lying to her during their last conversation. Now he just wanted this over with. 'I'm delighted to say, your proposals have got the go-ahead. Unanimous funding approval. I've just posted you a letter to that effect.'

'Oh, Claude, I *am* thrilled!' She didn't disguise her excitement.

'So am I,' he agreed heartily. 'I know you've been forced to keep a lot of those ideas on the backburner for years, but they've always deserved funding.'

'I've already given some thought to the next steps,' she enthused. Then she was telling him about the staff she planned to recruit, and administration arrangements, her budget forecasts and planned timetable.

Bonning heard her out, and they talked for a while about future Executive Council Meetings, before he got to the real reason for his call.

'Last time we spoke, you mentioned how pleased you were about the recognition we were giving Starwear at our awards ceremony.'

'I remember.'

'Well, how would you like to be the one to present the

GlobeWatch Company of the Year Award?'

'That's . . . some kind of speech?'

'Just a short one,' he told her. 'Of course, all the media will be there. Good chance to get your message across.'

'But, I mean, this is a great honour. Are you sure I'm the best person . . .'

'The honour would be Starwear's to have someone of your calibre making the presentation.'

'Oh, Claude,' she chuckled happily, still aglow with delight, 'flattery will get you everywhere.'

When Chris arrived at Lombard the following Monday, the mood in Reception seemed subdued. He put it down to the way he was feeling. By now, Elliott North would know he'd seen Judith last Friday night. He would probably have known by Saturday morning. During the weekend, Chris had been constantly surrounded with people. He'd played golf and watched cricket and eaten out in restaurants and every minute of both days he'd deliberately kept himself protected among friends.

The first thing he noticed when he stepped into his office was the envelope on his otherwise empty desk. He picked it up and tore it open. It was issued from Mike Cullen's office. In two short paragraphs it announced that last Friday night, at about ten, Kate Taylor had been found by a security guard in her office, in a coma resulting from sugar deprivation. She had been rushed to hospital, but had died on arrival.

'I cannot find the words to express my profound shock and sense of personal loss,' read the second paragraph. 'My grief is overwhelming. Apart from the highest regard in which I held Kate as a professional colleague, about which

I spoke to you all on what turned out to be her last day among us, I also counted Kate as a dear, much-loved friend. Her death is an appalling tragedy.'

Chris put down the paper, in a state of shock, before sliding into his desk chair and putting his head in his hands. He could hardly take in what had happened. Could this really be an accident? Kate had had diabetes since she was a teenager. She'd kept her sugar level balanced for the past twenty years. So why had this happened now? Surely sugar deprivation didn't strike diabetics down in just a few minutes – not, that is, unless they'd suffered an insulin overdose. Could it be that Kate had paid the price for exposing North's cover-ups? Maybe, if he, Chris, hadn't shown her those company accounts, she wouldn't have voiced her misgivings to Mike Cullen, and North would have left her alone. If he hadn't shown her those accounts, she wouldn't have made enquiries about Merlin de Vere. The cold hand of guilt settled over Chris. Maybe he was to blame. William van Aardt. Merlin de Vere. Now Kate Taylor. Another murder dressed as a tragedy. And this time, he was involved.

Somehow, it just didn't seem possible. It was only on Friday that she'd been made Deputy Chief Executive Officer, a title that made her seem more in control, more invincible than ever. And now this. As he sat, staring down at his desk, he began to realise how much reassurance he'd drawn from her – not only because she was his Personal Manager but also, and much more importantly, because he knew he could trust her. He had taken his fears to her. She had kept his confidences – she had kept faith. Today, right now, he needed her more than ever. As he sat, pondering over what had happened, and still in a state of shock and sadness, he wondered what he should do about his suspicions. If Kate *had* died of an insulin overdose, surely that would show up in a post-mortem? If someone had tampered with her medication, wouldn't the police soon be round, asking questions? But then, they hadn't been inclined to ask too many questions about Merlin de Vere. And what should he do about Mike Cullen? Didn't he have the right to know what Elliott North was doing to his company?

When Charlotte appeared at his door, she didn't need to ask if he had seen the note. Making her way over to him, she briefly squeezed his shoulder. 'Like a coffee?'

'Thanks.'

He looked up as she made her way out again. At the door she turned. 'By the way, when you're ready,' she wore a sympathetic expression, 'Elliott North was up here looking for you a few minutes ago. He'd like to see you in the Boardroom at nine.'

He didn't know what to expect from North. Some kind of interrogation about his relationship with Judith? Or what he knew about her Starwear story? Or how much she'd dug up on Jacob Strauss? As he made his way upstairs, he felt weary. If North went off at the deep end again, he was tempted just to cut him short. Come right out with it and tell him that by the end of the week, his campaign of murder and deceit would be headline news. But he knew he had to keep quiet and endure. He must ride out the storm – for Judith's sake, and Kate's too.

North was on his mobile phone when he knocked on the Boardroom door and stepped in. Standing by the window, he gestured that Chris should sit down. He seemed to be discussing some planned outing with a friend to a

West End cabaret – there were snide references to show-girls, and much laughter. Then, snapping the phone shut, he turned to Chris. 'Mike would have been here too,' he began, studiously rearranging his features from sly grin to a sombre expression. 'He asked me to pass on his apologies. He's upstairs at the moment,' he gestured towards the pent-house, 'inconsolable.'

Chris nodded.

North's put-on sorrow lasted about five seconds as he sat down opposite Chris, placing his mobile on the table in front of them. Then, in a very different tone, he declared, 'He wanted to join me in congratulating you.' He was upbeat.

Chris was puzzled.

'Project Silo really hit the mark,' North thumped the Boardroom table with gusto, 'really did it!'

This was crazy! Could North possibly be describing the same document he'd described only a couple of weeks ago as 'a crock of shit'? The only difference had been one appendix.

Trying to find a voice, Chris asked, 'You reckon the new stuff will be—'

'The new stuff is great,' beamed North. 'Well briefed.'

Why was he bothering? They both knew who had told Kuczynski to dig through the personal lives of Bob Reid and Ed Snyder.

'In fact, the whole report is going to form the corner-stone of future Starwear strategy.'

Chris stared at him, dumbstruck. Then he couldn't resist saying, 'I – I don't know . . . last time we spoke about it, you said—'

'Oh, that.' North laughed mirthlessly. 'Management technique.'

'What?'

'Encourage peak performance. I really wanted to make sure you were giving your best.'

This conversation had turned into something from *Alice in Wonderland*. He couldn't even begin to understand it right now. So he just said, 'I see.'

'So. How do you feel about the report now?'

It was the first time, Chris realised, that North had ever asked him for his views on anything.

'Fine.' He nodded once. 'I think it's fine. It will help position the brand—'

'Exactly. Positioning.' There was a pause before North said, 'Mike thinks it's a brilliant report too, by the way. So, in recognition of the great job you've done,' he stared at his mobile phone as he began fiddling with it, 'we've decided to reward your hard work.' He glanced up at Chris abruptly. 'Got a valid passport?'

'Yes.'

'Good. You'll be needing it. We'd like you to take a look at some of the Quantum Change factories in developing countries. First-hand experience. The idea is to develop a strategy on how best to present Quantum Change to the City. But let's be honest, it's a bit of a beano, too. You'll get time to have some fun.'

'Oh?' Chris was surprised. 'When did you have in mind?'

'There's a press tour arranged of Starwear's Jaipur factory, which means you'd need to leave London the day after tomorrow.'

Chris raised his eyebrows.

'D'you have a problem?'

'I don't suppose—'

'Good. You'll need to get down to the Indian High

Commission a.s.a.p. to sort out a visa. In fact, I suggest you get over there right away.' He was standing up and making his way to the Boardroom door. 'Mike really liked the report,' he repeated on his way out, 'really liked it.'

North returned to his office, took out the Swiss Army knife he always carried in his pocket, and began peeling an apple. He'd spoken to Treiger in the Boardroom because he hadn't wanted anyone else to tune in; no one else to listen to him grovelling to that little shit. Especially after learning that Treiger had spent Friday evening in the company of none other than Judith Laing.

He'd been radioed with the news first thing on Saturday and had gone ballistic. Apparently the two of them had spent half the evening shaking off Sol's boys before going for an intimate stroll in Chelsea. Then, first thing this morning, he gets a call from that shithead Carter; the call he'd been half-expecting ever since he discovered that Judith Laing was a lying little bitch. The only difference was, the call was a lot worse than he'd expected.

She'd dug up the lot: India; William van Aardt and Merlin de Vere; Matt Lester's cock-up; Jay's past business problems. It couldn't get any worse. Carter had come on the line, throwing toys out of the cot and demanding an explanation. An explanation?! Their 'understanding' was all very well when it came to presentational issues, he'd started out in high dudgeon, but as City Editor of *The Herald* he could not collude in the cover-up of a major international scandal. Jesus Christ, the way the fat ass was carrying on, you'd have thought it was someone else's spoilt brats they were packing off to Gordonstoun; someone else they'd paid to go on luxury holidays in five-star hotels;

someone else for whom they arranged to have the use of a box at the Royal Albert Hall to entertain his blue-blooded friends.

Carter got an explanation all right. North had explained that if Carter ran a single negative story about Starwear, it would be his last as the City Editor of a national paper. Receipts relating to every single 'hospitality' benefit he'd ever received from Starwear had been meticulously filed. They would be shown, without hesitation, not only to Carter's boss, but to his City Editor rivals at all the other papers. In twenty-four hours Carter's career would be blown. North had slammed down the phone on him.

That had knocked the crap out of him. Gone were all the demands and bluster. Next time he called, Carter was bleating, all sackcloth and ashes, all woe is me and what's to be done. Deciding he was in a more receptive frame of mind, North had told him exactly what was to be done and when it was to be done by. At the other end, Carter had listened, without even the mildest of protestations, though North could almost hear the pips squeaking.

He'd enjoyed it, thought North, enjoyed showing Carter just who had the leverage in the relationship, who had the power and who was calling the shots. But his pleasure was short-lived. His mobile went off again – and it was Jay. They'd already spoken to each other half a dozen times this morning, and it hadn't been easy.

'So, what's news?'

'I fixed Carter all right. You know all the shit he was giving me? Well, I sorted him out. Made him see who's boss. And I've just seen Treiger—'

'I didn't mean that stuff. I expect you to have sorted it. I'm talking about tonight.'

'Tonight,' North repeated, frowning.

'It's been over a week.'

'Jay, I just don't think—'

'You're like a broken fucking record. "I just don't think",' he mimicked, '"I just don't think". I just don't care what you "just don't think"! Talking of who's boss, I don't pay you for your advice, right? I pay you to fix things.'

'I know, Jay,' he whined.

'And I'm telling you to fix it for tonight.'

'You know what's been going on. Things are just so hot at the moment . . .'

There was a pause before, at the other end, Strauss said, 'What's the problem? Don't you like working for me any more?'

North fumed in silence.

'Well?'

'OK, OK. I'll see what I can do.'

He slammed shut the phone with a bitter expression. The time was coming, and pretty soon, when the show would be over, and he'd be unhitching his wagon from the international travelling circus that was Jacob Strauss. But there would be no unhitching before some bargaining took place. He'd come a long way from that roach-infested tenement in Brooklyn, and he wasn't about to throw it all up, not for anyone. He planned to continue living in the style to which he'd become accustomed. And Jay Strauss was going to continue to pay for it.

He'd had ample opportunity over the years to assemble his evidence. Plenty of time to work out his plan so that if he gave the order, or if anything happened to him, Jay would be sunk. One well-directed missile and it would all be over. He would only ask for ten million. Peanuts, to someone like Jay. Christ, he went through more than that in a year. Ten mill to keep his trap shut for ever. A small price to pay.

North thought he'd spend his first summer in Greece.

One thing she'd grown to love about London were the parks. Hyde Park especially. It wasn't far from where they lived, and she loved to stroll along the Serpentine in the evening. She found real peace and tranquillity there – especially among the late-autumn colours. The burnished golds and mellow reds offered a soothing haven away from the confines of her home and her disastrous marriage. By the end of each visit, after an hour of communing with nature, things didn't seem so bad.

Ever since she'd first met him, her husband had been surrounded by kids. Little boys in particular looked up to him. He was their hero – always arranging adventures for them, like trips to football games, gymnastics, motor racing. And he was constantly fixing for them to have the things that little boys so liked to have – the latest trainers, tracksuits and trendy golf peaks.

For a long time she had seen nothing untoward in it. In fact, it had been one of the things she'd found most attractive about him when they'd met. Many men didn't much notice children, too wrapped up in their own worldly concerns of money and power. But he'd been different. They were both different – that's what she used to think in the early days, when she still used to believe his PR. They were the golden couple, embarked on a glamorous adventure, he with his entrepreneurial business career, she there to support him, to bear his children and ensure the future of the dynasty. Silly fool that she was.

The physical side of their relationship had never really been what she'd hoped for. It certainly hadn't been anything like what his many fans probably fantasised about. She had been disappointed, of course; despite being hugely energetic in other areas of his life, when it came to the bedroom he just didn't seem to have the drive or the interest. But she'd tried to be practical about things. Sex was only one dimension out of the many that made up marriage, she'd told herself. When all the others were going so well, why get hung up on it?

She had thought it strange when she'd found him, just after their fourth anniversary, helping a ten-year-old boy into a Starwear tracksuit he'd just given him. The kid was stark naked and her husband had had his hands round the front as he pulled up the pants. It had had her worried the moment she saw it. The boy was quite old enough to be capable of pulling on a tracksuit. But when she mentioned it afterwards, he'd just laughed. The kid was a bit clumsy, physically, he explained. He'd been having problems with the knot.

She supposed she'd rationalised it away. It wasn't something she'd even wanted to think about, but she hadn't been able to avoid doing so. It had been undeniable the time she'd come home from a date unexpectedly. The friend she was due to meet for lunch had been struck down with a migraine. She'd walked into the games room which he'd fitted out with all the latest computer games and electronic toys. This time, they were both naked and he had the boy under him. There could be no mistaking what he was doing.

She'd gone upstairs immediately, packing her bags and those of their two children. She'd stormed out, picked the kids up from school, and spent the night with her parents in a state of deep shock. She hadn't been able to tell them – especially not them – or anyone else, what had happened. She'd questioned the children closely about their father – but he didn't seem to have interfered at all with them, thank heavens.

He'd pursued her, arriving on her doorstep and pleading with her to come back. When she had calmed down enough to speak to him, he didn't try to deny what had happened or where his urges lay. But he said he didn't want to wreck what they had. He would go for counselling. He would change.

It was the oldest come-back line in the book, and, even sillier fool that she was, she'd gone back to him. For the sake of giving the kids a family life. For the sake of appearances. But things had never been the same between them again. He'd made a great show to her of going for counselling. But he also spent increasing amounts of time away on business. Their lives had become more and more separate, and she didn't question what went on when he was away. She couldn't take his lies, but she feared the truth even more. Over time, she'd made up her mind to leave. She was only staying for the two girls, now. Once they were finished at school she would move out. That, at any rate, was her plan.

All the same, there were times when the light, which she tried to persuade herself was at the end of the tunnel, seemed all but extinguished. Times when she couldn't avoid being reminded of the dark side of her husband's nature – and became deeply unsettled. Right now she was going through one of those periods. It had been sparked off by an article she'd read in the papers about the disappearance of a young boy, Dale Nesbitt, from St Stephen's Children's Home. St Stephen's wasn't far from where they lived – she had driven past the school grounds, always filled with boys in their instantly recognisable purple and gold uniform. She knew that her husband had been involved in corporate donations to the Home. She knew too that when a St Stephen's boy had disappeared before, he'd later been found dead, his sexually abused body concealed in the undergrowth beside a railway line, like some discarded toy.

Of course there was nothing at all to link her husband either to that event, or to the more recent disappearance. Even the prospect of it was too horrifying to contemplate. But, no matter how she tried to suppress it, she couldn't help thinking the unthinkable, driving herself mad with worry. She'd been to the doctor about her agitation – though hadn't dared to hint at the cause. He'd prescribed her pills and told her to come back in a month if she wasn't feeling calmer.

But either the pills weren't working, or her deepest fears were just too hideous to be blocked out by drugs. If anything, in the past few days she'd felt under even greater pressure, the dread of it colouring everything else in her life, so that her whole world was miserable with foreboding. As Hyde Park sank slowly into twilight, and a chill wind swept a flurry of leaves off the branches, she paused for a moment among the ancient trees: one of these days, she felt, she was just going to crack apart.

21

Judith hurried towards the British Airways check-in desks at Heathrow Terminal 4. Unlike the remaining passengers in Economy, she didn't have to wait. Rushing her trolley across the Departures hall, she made her way directly towards the blue, Club Class carpet to the Delhi flight check-in, and handed over her ticket and passport.

Carter's reaction to her story had been the very last thing she'd expected, and eight hours later, she still wasn't quite sure what to make of it. Fulsome with praise, he'd told her that Starwear would be the business scoop of the year. The City desk would have its finest hour. He'd promised her a major byline when her article appeared, late this week or early next. Given the scale of her revelations, he said he was sure *The Herald*'s editor would pluck the story from the business section, and paste it across the front page. And if Judith didn't get at least one investigative journalist of the year award out of this, he told her, he would eat his deer-stalker.

Which was all well and good. It was what he'd then proposed that raised her doubts. Her central allegations, he expounded, concerned a factory she had never visited, three and a half thousand miles away. First-hand interviews with kids back in London were one thing. But if she had been there and seen things with her own eyes, and got more photographic evidence, the story would be all the more compelling.

The cost of flying her to India for a few days, in the context of such a major exposé, was a mere trifle. Though she'd still been surprised when he'd told her to book her ticket and sort out a visa, the latter something she already had. She'd been even more surprised when he'd said to go business class. It was a sign of approval she'd never expected. Or was it? This was where her feelings were ambivalent, as she wondered if Carter was setting her up for something. Getting her out of town to take all the credit for her story himself? Or, much worse, operating in conspiracy with North? She'd considered that possibility once before – and dismissed it as paranoia. Now it kept returning, an unknown, potentially treacherous undercurrent about which she felt decidedly apprehensive. Not, she realised, that there was so much as the flimsiest shred of evidence to support her fears. In the end, she decided she didn't have much choice but to act on the basis that Carter was genuine, and see this trip through.

Starwear arranged press visits to its Quantum Change plants, and she'd be joining a tour of their Jaipur operations on Thursday afternoon. She had no doubt it would be all happy workers, upward-pointing graphs and impressive diagrams accounting for new efficiencies. But even that would be useful – it would set up a vivid contrast for her other, unofficial factory visit, which she'd already arranged with the help of the Jaipur Abolitionist Group. One of R. J. Patel's cousins ran a stall in the bazaar just two blocks away from The Royal Jaipur Hotel, where she was due to stay. He knew exactly where Starwear's real mass-production centre was to be found, and would take her there before the Thursday-morning tour. Of course, security around the child slave plant might be tough to penetrate. There were no guarantees at all that she'd witness anything to arouse suspicions in the limited time she was there. But at the very least, she'd pick up on some local colour to work into her story. And maybe more evidence would be forthcoming.

There had been a lot of arrangements to make in the past eight hours – not only setting up her flight. She'd phoned up Bernie to tell him about the sudden turn of events, and asked him to pass the news on to Chris as a matter of urgency. She could hear the puzzlement in his voice as he took down her message, but Bernie, being Bernie, didn't press the issue. He was good that way.

The BA lady handed over her boarding pass and pointed in the direction of International Departures. It was the very first flight on which she'd travelled in such exalted circumstances, and she'd have loved to wallow in every indulgence that was going, but time was against her. She'd arrived at Heathrow with no time to spare and the 'Boarding' sign for her flight already flashing. Hurried along by the staff at the hand-luggage check, she made her way through the warren of corridors at a half walk, half trot, before finally making it to her flight.

'Good evening, madam.' She was ushered through to her Club Class seat by an air steward whose cool poise couldn't have been more different from the sense of controlled panic she'd felt all day. 'Would you care for a welcoming glass of champagne?'

That, more or less, set the tone for what was to follow.

Kicking off her shoes, Judith realised she had nothing left to do right now except enjoy the trip. She decided a little alcohol might help her relax into things. Several glasses of champagne were followed by wine over dinner, and then a few tumblers of Baileys-on-the-rocks.

By eleven o'clock she was beginning to feel quite sleepy, but decided to watch the in-flight news. It was broadcast live from the BBC in London and was running some of the stories that had been through the newsroom the previous day. She watched the bulletin through half-closed eyes, listening to the familiar round of news items. About halfway through, her attention was suddenly caught by a story just breaking. The Chief Executives of two leading UK sports manufacturers, Sportex and Active Red, were at the centre of a scandal involving allegations of sexual misconduct and business impropriety. Robert Reid and Edward Snyder were shown denying the accusations, while scrambling from cars outside their homes, being pursued by large groups of tabloid reporters and paparazzi.

The news piece wasn't long, though it had Judith wondering as she swilled the remaining Baileys in her crystal tumbler. During the course of her own enquiries she'd checked out Reid and Snyder but hadn't found anything on them, certainly not in the child slave department. But these new allegations were a bit too much of a coincidence – especially with stories about both Reid and Snyder coming out at the same time. She couldn't help wanting to know where they had come from. And why.

Chris didn't get to see the newspapers until eleven thirty on Tuesday, having spent all morning till then at the Indian High Commission. The situation there had been far from satisfactory. Yesterday, after queuing for an age, he'd been told that visa applications took a standard four days. They'd try to process his in two if he came down in person the following morning, but they were making no promises. This morning he'd waited and waited his turn in the queue, but when he finally got to the front, the official told him, categorically, that he must wait until Thursday morning. At this rate, there was no way he'd get out in time for the Jaipur plant tour on Thursday afternoon.

Arriving back at his office, frustrated by this latest turn of events in a day that already felt like a surreal nightmare, he began flicking through the newspapers, and was hardly able to take in what he saw. Every single one of them, broadsheet and tabloid, was full of the stories Kuczynski had dug up about Reid and Snyder. Even from the most cursory glance, it was clear that both men were up to their necks in sleaze. 'Active Red's Three-in-a-Bed' was *The Globe*'s front-page lead article. According to Shayla Maxwell, Snyder's ex-secretary who'd charged him with sexual harassment, Snyder had once suggested she bring along a friend for 'a bit of slap and tickle after hours'. Of course, Snyder and Maxwell had never so much as kissed, nor had Maxwell even proven that sexual harassment had taken place – a point *The Globe* studiously ignored. Instead, the newspaper had paid Snyder's former mistress £25,000 to 'spill the beans' on their affair of three years earlier. A deluge of voyeuristic detail on where, when and how they'd had sex was laid out for the prurient consumption of over four million readers, including the information that Ed's mistress had had her pubic hair coloured red and specially shaven in the shape of the Active Red logo for one of his birthdays.

The Dispatch's front-page piece was headlined 'Britain's Biggest Sneakers' and reported not only on Ed Snyder, but Bob Reid too. Not content with his £450,000 salary from Sportex, *The Dispatch* told its readers, Reid also had an income estimated to be in the region of £150,000, tax free, from the proceeds of immoral earnings. Without actually calling him a pimp, the paper ran photographs of well-groomed, attractive women entering and leaving his Belgravia flat. One such woman, propositioned by an undercover reporter, had listed her charges, which were published in a separate box – £50 for oral sex, £100 for regular sex, £150 for bondage and domination, with other services negotiable.

In case this character assassination hadn't quite finished him off, out came the assault conviction made against Reid at Reading Crown Court. Amanda Rider, the former model – whose volatile temperament and vase-wrecking escapade were not mentioned by the paper – had, for a generous financial consideration, no doubt, posed topless on an exercise bike like the one on which she said she and Bob Reid had once had sex.

The broadsheets had also gone to town on the Reid/Snyder stories, providing a fig leaf for the lurid details by explaining that both men were among the most vocal supporters of the Government's proposed Textiles Act, to be debated in the next few days in the House of Commons. The same stories as those run by the tabloids were pattered out, together with extra, business-related reportage. Bob Reid was a man with a violent temper, said one disgruntled ex-employee, who, if provoked, went completely off the rails. Staff were so terrified of him when he went on factory visits that they used to hide in the cupboards. When Reid snapped back at reporters who phoned him for a reaction to the stories, he only seemed to prove the point.

As for Snyder, morale at Active Red was said to be at an all-time low. The downturn in south-east Asian markets had seen orders collapsing, and Snyder was implementing enforced redundancies. 'It's like the end of the coal industry,' said an embittered Derby worker, who'd lost his second career. 'These days it's not a question of "if" Snyder will sack you, it's a question of "when".'

But it was the *Financial Times* story, which included none of the salacious sexual details about Reid and Snyder, that was the most worrying of all. Allegations about the two men, it reported, had first emerged from a confidential analysis of the sportswear market undertaken by a leading public relations company. 'The analysis, intended for internal consumption, identifies serious allegations of sexual misconduct and errors of judgement.' Reid and Snyder had both been contacted for their reactions to the report. Both had said the stories were heavily one-sided, and that they were seeking legal counsel. But there were no outright denials – and the protestations of bias only served to underline their apparent guilt all the more. Bob Reid and Ed Snyder had been tried, found guilty and hanged by the national press before they were even aware of what was happening. Whatever else they did in their lives, the damage to their reputations would be serious and irreversible.

Chris surveyed the papers, coldly furious. How could he have been so naive about the real purpose of Project Silo? From the moment North had told him to go digging up dirt he should have realised. Instead, he'd been the innocent all along, unable to understand why the personal lives of

Starwear's competitors should be of the slightest interest. Blind to where it was all heading. No wonder North was packing him off to India the very next day. The stories about Reid and Snyder weren't one-day wonders. They'd go on and on for the next week at least. The tabloids were already racing about with fat cheque-books, handing out money to whoever had a bad word to say about the two men. The flood of sleaze and allegations would continue. And all at a time to inflict maximum damage to Sportex and Active Red. Members of Parliament, having been lectured repeatedly on the merits of 'responsible management' by Nicholas King, would now be made vividly aware of the kind of people pressing for greater competition. When the amendment making an exception of sportswear was put to the House, all the headlines about Reid and Snyder could hardly be ignored.

With the exception of the small number of *Financial Times* readers, the vast majority of people had no idea where all this information was coming from. They weren't to know it was a smear campaign deliberately orchestrated to occur at the moment of maximum impact, that it was a confection of half-truths designed to be deliberately misleading. Until today, Reid and Snyder had just been two men running sportswear companies; from now on, whenever their names came up, there would be smirks about their sexual peccadilloes, question marks about their sense of judgement.

So much, thought Chris, for the report of which he'd been so proud – his finest piece of strategic planning to date. It had been hijacked and used by North for a dirty-tricks campaign. Yet another reason why Kate's death was just too much of a coincidence. She would never have countenanced this kind of activity. Apart from its colossal tastelessness, it could, in the long run, only be bad news for Lombard. Since the mid-nineties the corporate world had had to become more transparent and accountable; an agency that dealt in muck and sleaze was hardly going to prosper.

His immediate impulse was to try to see Mike, but he didn't even know if Mike was in his office. He had spent yesterday closeted in the penthouse, having cancelled all meetings. According to Rosa, her boss had been utterly distraught. Running to him now with the papers, complaining about Elliott North, somehow didn't seem right. Besides, he told himself, whatever tales were coming out about Reid and Snyder now would soon be eclipsed by a far bigger story. When Judith's piece came out in *The Herald*, journalists would have a far grander story of deceit and malevolence to explore.

Deep in thought, Chris didn't even hear his telephone ringing – till Lotte put her head round the door. He picked up the receiver.

'C. T. It's Bernie.'

'Oh.'

'Look, I've got a nice little case of claret in,' he used the code phrase, 'would you like to come round to sample it tonight?'

Chris paused. 'I wouldn't mind sooner.'

'When were you thinking?'

'What about right now?'

'I've got Mr Snyder on line two,' Rosa's voice came through on Mike Cullen's intercom, 'shall I put him through?'

Mike Cullen looked at his watch. Eleven-thirty a.m. He was surprised it had taken so long.

'Sure,' he told Rosa. Then, after a pause, 'Good morning, Ed.'

'What in the hell is going on over there?'

Mike Cullen raised his right hand to his brow, massaging his eyebrows with forefinger and thumb. 'It would seem that a report has been deliberately leaked to the national media.'

'I had TV cameras outside my office yesterday afternoon, the things they were saying were just so ludicrous I thought it was some flash in the pan. So I came to Berlin, as planned, for a meeting. Now my Corporate Comms guy has been on the phone saying there's crap all over the papers.'

Mike Cullen sighed. 'On a personal level, it is very regrettable.'

'Regrettable! I don't know if I'll still have a marriage when I get home.'

'Believe me,' Cullen spoke with feeling, 'I'm going to get the bastard responsible.'

'You'd better. My Comms guy says the whole thing came out of Lombard.'

'I can understand why he might think that,' interjected Mike Cullen, 'but it's not entirely fair. We *did* produce a report on the sportswear market, a bona fide marketing strategy. All this . . . personal detail was in an appendix to the document commissioned by Jacob Strauss's PR hit man. I suspect he was the guy who leaked it.'

'The day before the Textiles Act is debated in Parliament?'

Mike Cullen closed his eyes. 'The intention was pretty clear.'

'He's going to completely derail us!' Snyder's voice rose.

'The chances of that sportswear amendment sticking now are at least fifty-fifty!'

'I agree it's bad news for Active Red right now,' Mike Cullen said after a pause, 'but look at the big picture. What's bad news for Ed Snyder today is very good news for him tomorrow.'

'Are you seriously telling me I'm supposed to ignore the national media?'

'I am,' murmured Cullen, 'on this particular occasion.'

'Well, excuse me for sounding ungrateful, but I'm just finding this all a bit of a mind-fuck.'

There was a pause before Cullen responded. 'Look, Ed, I can completely understand the way you're feeling. And believe me, my heart goes out to you,' he tried his best to be reassuring. 'I just want you to be sure of two things. First, this isn't coming from Lombard, it's coming from Jacob Strauss. And second, despite all this crap, we still have our understanding.'

There was silence at the other end.

'In just a couple of days, things will look a lot different.'

It was a long while before Snyder finally said, 'You'd better be right.'

'Oh, I am right,' Cullen told him. 'Nothing in the world is more important to me.'

Bernie came downstairs to Reception in shirt sleeves, and swiped Chris through security with a guest card.

'We can use this for two minutes,' he led him to a ground-floor meeting room, closing the door behind them and glancing over at where Chris stood, expectant. 'Judith called late yesterday afternoon. I left a message on your mobile, but you obviously didn't get it.'

'Answering service is playing up,' Chris grunted. 'What's up?'

'She asked me to tell you that Carter's sent her to India for the rest of the week.'

'What?'

'Staying at the Royal Jaipur Gardens Hotel. Something about a press tour and getting first-hand evidence for an article.'

'Christ Almighty!'

'What's going on?' Bernie was bemused.

'Wish I knew.' Chris stared at him for a moment, before shaking his head. 'Yesterday morning I was given orders to join the same tour. Starwear's Jaipur plant. Bit of a coincidence, isn't it? And the guy giving the orders is the same guy who's been having me followed. The same guy—' He halted in his tracks. No. He couldn't tell Bernie about Merlin de Vere. William van Aardt. Kate Taylor.

Bernie was following him intently. 'So how d'you reckon this chap got Carter to send Judith?' he asked.

'That's what's bothering me.'

'Well, he's got to have Carter in his pocket, hasn't he?' Bernie pointed out the obvious.

Chris quickly recalled Judith telling him about the time Carter had wanted to know what she was writing up on Starwear. How, she had wondered, had he got wind of that? He also remembered Judith saying how Carter had demanded a 'sympathetic portrait' of Jacob Strauss on his appointment as CEO – and the resulting hagiography produced by one of his lackeys.

The possibility that Carter was taking money from Starwear had, of course, crossed Judith's mind – but she had dismissed it as preposterous. Paranoia. Surely not even

Carter would allow himself to be so compromised? Right now, however, it seemed far from paranoid. As Chris thought rapidly through what had happened, the sequence of events was shockingly self-evident: yesterday morning she had handed in her piece to Carter. Carter had immediately been on the phone to North. North had come up with the scheme to send both of them to India.

'Why d'you reckon this chap wants you out of the way?'

Chris glanced back at him, fear in his face. *A tragic accident*, he couldn't help thinking. *Some appalling incident in Jaipur* . . .

'I've got to warn Judith,' he told Bernie urgently.

His friend gestured to a telephone. 'Want to try?'

'Her room'll be bugged.' He met his friend's expression of concern. 'No. This is something I have to do myself.'

Hurrying back to Lombard, Chris had just one thought on his mind: how to get that visa stamp in his passport so that he could get out to India immediately. He didn't know anyone in the Foreign Office, let alone the Indian High Commission, nor could he think of anyone who did. Phoning the High Commission from his mobile, he asked yet again about speeding up visa applications – this time on compassionate grounds. A telegram would be needed from a police station or hospital in India, he was told. Which ruled out that option. It was only when his thoughts returned briefly to the news of Kate's death, that the memory surfaced, sudden and unbidden from the past: Kashmir Development Agency. It had been one of Kate's clients.

Back at Lombard he made his way immediately to the first floor, where Stewart Watkins, Kate's second-in-command, was working behind his desk, ashen-faced and still coping with the shock of yesterday's news. After exchanging condolences, Chris told him, 'I've just been ordered to India to look at a Quantum Change factory. I need an Indian visa – problem is, it takes the High Commission three days and I need one a lot sooner. Do you know anyone at the Kashmir Development Agency who could pull strings?'

'KDA is a one-man operation,' Stewart replied, 'Anant Singh. He's a player all right, but he's known round here as the client from hell.'

Chris raised his eyebrows questioningly.

'Seems to have a lot of time on his hands. He won't let us so much as phone a journalist without having to be bought lunch to discuss it first.'

Chris glanced at his watch. Twelve forty-five p.m. Looking back at Stewart he asked, 'May I have his phone number?'

A few minutes later he was in his office, and had dialled KDA. 'Mr Singh. Chris Treiger here from Lombard. I realise this is extremely late notice, but I was wondering if you might be able to join me for lunch today. I need to discuss an issue of some urgency . . .'

22

Chris had never been to India before, nor had the country ever featured on his wish-list of holiday destinations. One billion people, many living in abject poverty, had always struck him as a good reason to stay away. Now though, as he made his way through the streets of Delhi in the back of a twenty-year-old Mercedes Benz taxi, he couldn't help being struck by the astonishing human drama unfolding before his eyes – lorries, rickshaws, bicycles, Brahman cattle, Rolls Royces, scooters, and everywhere people, a great mass of humanity in motion; he had never before been caught up in such a vivid panoply.

He could do with more speed though. He'd managed to get out to India a day earlier than expected. Thanks to the kind services of Anant Singh, secured over a two-hour lunch in the country house ambience of Rules, he'd picked up a stamped passport from the Indian High Commission the next day, then headed to Heathrow airport for the Wednesday night flight shaking off his shadowers *en route*. He'd already told North about his visa troubles, and North had got Starwear to shift their press tour from Thursday afternoon to Friday morning. But he hadn't told anyone, not even Charlotte, about his early departure. Delhi time was five hours ahead of London, and right now everyone back home would be fast asleep in bed. When they got to the office they'd be expecting him in. By the time anyone knew he was in India, he'd have been here more than half a day. For a few hours, at least, he had time on his side.

On the flight over he'd had plenty of time to think, and to follow the consequences of the Project Silo bombshell. BBC World News had carried an item about that day's debate on the new Textiles Act in the House of Commons. A Government backbencher, no less, had referred to that day's newspapers, and questioned the wisdom of opening up the sportswear to companies run by men 'whose scruples are those of the gutter'.

There had been a commotion on Opposition Benches with much jeering and waving of papers, at the scent of dissension in Government ranks. When George Thannet, MP, proposed his sportswear amendment, he'd found support from both sides of the House. 'It was an embarrassing day for the Government,' announced the newsreader, 'and the likelihood of the Textiles Act being passed in its entirety now looks increasingly remote. An amendment excluding global sportswear manufacturers is expected to be passed tomorrow.'

Chris had leaned back in his aircraft seat, trying to get a grip on the scale of events, and the speed at which they were happening. Elliott North had successfully hijacked first his report, then the British parliamentary process, to get a law passed that would cover Jacob Strauss's back and which would further entrench Starwear's commercial advantage. And that translated directly into bigger profits. There seemed no end to his power.

Though it was North's malevolence, much closer to home, that he found so troubling. Knowing what had happened to William van Aardt and Merlin de Vere was one thing; but losing his most trusted colleague was quite another. Time and time again his thoughts had returned to Kate's final hours. Exactly how had it happened? What had North's operatives done to blast her blood sugar levels out of control? She must have known what was happening to her. There must have been some time – was it seconds, or minutes? – when she realised, and tried to do something about it.

And in Chris's mind, at least, it wasn't too hard to replace Kate with Judith; to imagine her trapped in some Indian nightmare from which she'd never escape. There she was, thinking she'd been sent out to Jaipur to put the seal on the biggest story of her career, when the reality was horrifically different. *Please God, make it not be too late!* As his plane sped through the night, the cabin lights dimmed and all the passengers around him under their blankets and eye masks, Chris had tried to work out what to do when he got to Delhi. How he'd make contact with her. A plan for their escape. His mind racing through all the options, he'd considered every step, every last detail, to bring this surreal drama to an end.

The trip to Jaipur took just over two hours and he told the driver to drive straight past the Royal Jaipur Gardens Hotel, into which he'd been booked, and towards The Forum, another hotel he'd been assured at the airport was 'for world-class executives'. There was no problem checking in, and as soon as he was alone in his room, he put through a call to Judith. She wasn't there, and after an interminable wait, his call was picked up again by

Reception. 'She went out this morning, sir,' he was told. 'Would you like me to pass on a message?'

'No.' He had no intention of alerting North to his arrival. 'When is she getting back?'

'I'm sorry, we don't know.'

After hanging up he changed into casual clothes, tucking his passport into an inside pocket and his cash into a moneybelt around his waist. Then he made his way out of the hotel, trying to remain incognito, but painfully self-conscious of his colour and clothes. Walking back to the Royal Jaipur Gardens took just a few minutes. Across the road from the hotel entrance he found a few curio shops and a crumbling post office, as well as the inevitable collection of hawkers' stalls, with everything on sale from incense to fresh fruit to luminous rubber keyrings made in Taiwan. Buying himself a can of lukewarm Coke, he kept a close watch on the hotel entrance.

He hadn't been waiting more than forty minutes when an ancient Datsun taxi pulled up and Judith stepped out. He had no doubt she was being followed, although it was hard to see who by, there was so much traffic about. Having already prepared for this moment, he pointed Judith out to a small boy whose mother had been selling cheap brass vases at the roadside. As directed, the child made his way across to Judith and handed her a vase which contained his note rolled up inside, before disappearing back into the chaos of humanity.

Ten minutes later, Judith emerged from the hotel, a camera slung round her neck and carrying a few postcards as she headed towards the post office. Once inside, she made her way towards a row of telephone booths. They were the old, colonial variety, with solid teak doors for privacy. Several were already occupied. She stepped into one that was empty. A moment later, Chris opened the door and squashed in beside her.

'What's happening?' She was irritated.

'North sent me over to go on tomorrow's factory tour.'

Eyebrows shooting up, her snappiness turned to agitation.

'Bit of a coincidence, isn't it?'

'You mean, Carter . . .'

'. . . was taking orders,' he finished for her.

'That must have been who he phoned.' She remembered how he'd been pacing up and down in his office, cigar jabbing in the air, after he'd read her article. 'What d'you reckon they're going to—'

'Not something I want to think about too much.' He was shaking his head. 'Some kind of tragedy in Jaipur. You know, last Friday night Kate Taylor died. Insulin overdose,' he grimaced.

'Oh, my God!' Her face was flooded with alarm. 'What's going to stop him?'

'*We* are,' he was definite. 'And you're getting your story out – that asshole Carter is in for the shock of his life. I've worked out a plan. The first thing we need to do is get the hell out of here right away.'

She looked reluctant.

'Tomorrow's the great factory trip,' he told her. 'You can be sure they've got something lined up for us that doesn't involve admiring Quantum Change efficiencies.'

'But I've come all this way. I've *got* to see the other factory.' She touched her camera. 'Photographic evidence. It's less than twenty minutes from here.'

'I don't know . . .'

'We could be there and back in under an hour. Are you saying we can't wait that long?'

This wasn't something he had anticipated, wasn't in his plan. 'How d'you know where to go looking?'

'That's sorted. Jaipur Abolitionist Group. I've already spoken to Ravi.' She jerked her head in the direction of the bazaar. 'He's taking me.'

'You know you're probably being followed?'

She nodded. 'Ravi thought of that.'

Less than fifteen minutes later they were each on the back of a scooter, winding their way through the congested streets at high speed. The scooters didn't follow the same route all the way as they wove in and out among market stalls and down side alleys, the tumult and mêlée of Jaipur passing by in a high-speed whirl of vivid colour and pungent aromas. Ravi and his friend Aziz had assured them the trip wouldn't take more than a quarter of an hour. But ten minutes later they were still caught in the urban sprawl with its bewildering contrasts of new office buildings, slum shacks, open sewers and satellite TV dishes all in the same block. They didn't seem to be getting any closer to an industrial area, thought Judith. Then Ravi turned down a side street and raced along for two blocks before pulling unexpectedly down a dark and narrow alley. He cut the motor.

'We are here,' Ravi told her in a low voice.

She looked bewildered. 'The factory?' she whispered.

'Yes indeed.' Turning, he nodded towards a large, corrugated-iron shed. It was about twenty yards down the road, diagonally opposite the entrance to the alley. Judith stared across. It wasn't instantly obvious that this was the same building she'd seen in the photograph in London, and she had imagined that the factory would be on the fringes of town, away from everything. But as she looked at it, she realised that it *was* the place. She couldn't get over it. Here it was, hardly any distance at all from the centre of Jaipur – a large, unprepossessing shed with a constant buzz of traffic rushing past it. And inside, untold misery.

Aziz's scooter, with Chris on the back, appeared at the other end of the alley.

'That's it.' She nodded towards the factory when he joined her.

He looked surprised. 'Not what I was expecting.'

'Me neither.'

'Do you think its guarded?'

At that moment, Ravi and Aziz hurried them down the alley and against the wall. 'Be careful or they see you,' Ravi warned them in a strenuous whisper.

'Who?'

Slowly, Ravi edged to the corner of the alley, before nodding towards two Indian men wearing khaki uniforms and leather boots, with holsters on their belts, who were sauntering round the building, glancing about them as they conversed.

'How many?' asked Chris.

Ravi held up two fingers.

'All the time?'

'Twenty-four hours,' he replied, once the men had rounded the corner.

Judith strained to look down the street. 'Can we get closer?'

Ravi set off into the street, gesturing for them to remain while he looked up and down through the traffic of bicycles, hand carts and ancient cars. Then he was back beside them. 'Not safe,' he told them.

A moment later, a loud, deep rumble reverberated down the street, with every strip of sheet metal and pane of glass rattling ominously. The noise was coming closer and closer until, from the darkness of the alley, they saw a large van roaring past, so wide it almost scraped the buildings on each side. As the gears ground down noisily, there was a sudden squeal of brakes, and a pneumatic gasp as the van pulled up outside the shed. Then a slamming of doors as the driver and his passenger climbed out and hammered on the shed door, before making their way round to the back of the truck. Peering round the corner from their hiding place in the alley, Judith and Chris exchanged glances. *Had the van come for a consignment? Were they about to see Starwear merchandise being loaded up* in flagrante?

The two men had opened up the back of the van and were climbing in. As the huge, rear doors swung to each side with a resounding crash, Judith and Chris could see inside; it was packed with cardboard boxes. From floor to ceiling, they were crammed so tight they looked like a towering, impenetrable wall. Then from the shed appeared a group of adolescent boys, dressed in rags, a foreman behind them shouting orders. They weren't especially young, thought Judith – sixteen, seventeen – although they were scrawny and unkempt. Leaping up into the van in what was evidently a well-rehearsed routine, they began unloading its contents at high speed. The cardboard boxes, each the size of a tea chest, were rapidly taken out of the van and into the shed, the foreman and guards closely watching over the process, like prison officers supervising a gang of convicts.

What would happen when the van was emptied? Judith couldn't help wondering. *Were they going to pack it with the finished goods?* But the moment the last box was taken out of the van, the driver slammed the rear doors shut, and the guards herded the boys back into the shed. There was much revving and juddering as the driver turned the van to go back in the direction from which he'd come. Then with a thunderous roar, he was heading up the street.

Judith turned back to Chris and pulled a face. It wasn't quite the first-hand evidence she had hoped for. There'd been nothing obviously suspicious about what was unloaded. And the teenage boys were no younger than those to be found in factories anywhere else in the world. But, she supposed, they would hardly have sent out eight-year-olds to collect the boxes; they had other uses.

Ravi now looked from her to Chris, clearly expecting them to want to leave.

'I just wish we could get closer,' she said. 'I wish we could look inside.'

Ravi and Aziz were both shaking their heads vigorously. 'No go inside.' Ravi was firm.

'But *look* inside,' she gestured. 'I know it's dangerous. But I need to see if there are children.'

'Many, many children,' said Aziz. 'Many of them.'

Ravi had stepped into the street and was glancing about nervously before returning to them. 'There's a place . . . there.' He pointed across the road to a decrepit, two-storey building which had evidently long since been closed up. 'You can see the children there.'

Judith looked up to the flat roof of the building. Directly across the road from the shed, it looked straight down on to it. If there were any gaps in the roof . . .

'You want me to take you?' Ravi looked at her.

She nodded.

Once the guards were out of sight again, Ravi made his way across the street and approached the door to the closed-up building, now secured only by a padlock. Taking something out of his pocket, he fiddled with the lock for a moment before it sprang open. Then he waved to Judith.

She turned to Chris. 'I'll just be a minute,' she told him, leaving him with Aziz, before crossing the road and following Ravi into the building. The moment she had stepped inside she was hit by a stench of human excreta and decomposing garbage. Ravi was already making his way up a flight of wooden stairs, but she buckled, gagging on the foetid vileness of it, before covering her mouth and nose with her arm and following.

The staircase was falling apart and the balustrade in a state of collapse. She found herself hardly daring to put her weight on steps that were so rickety they felt about to cave in. The whole structure creaked and warped perilously as they made their way, first up three flights of steps to the upstairs floor, then up another, narrower series of stairs, in a state of even worse repair, leading up to the roof. She didn't dare look down at the putrid void beneath as they picked their way round missing steps, treading on rotten boards which slipped and cracked beneath them.

Finally they reached the top, and Ravi threw open a trapdoor which led on to the roof. Judith didn't think she'd ever felt such relief to escape from a building. As she clambered out on her hands and knees, camera dangling from her neck, she paused a moment, out of breath and heart racing. Ravi was a short distance in front of her, bent double as he approached the low wall running around the top of the roof. She followed suit a few moments later, joining him.

They both peered over the edge, checking out the position of the two guards, who were walking away from them. Tentatively, they stood, looking away from the guards and out across the roof of the shed. It took Judith a moment to work out what she was seeing. There were gaps in the roof, where sheets of corrugated iron had fallen away and hadn't been replaced – gaps into which she could see. But what was going on inside? It was a while before she could take it in, then, suddenly, it all clicked into place. She was looking down on the heads and shoulders of dozens and dozens of children squashed on to workbenches, their hands moving constantly, feeding the machines in front of them. It was the scale and densely packed squalor of it that she didn't, at first, comprehend. There were just so many of them, such a mass of tiny bodies and such a blur of arms – it was like staring into an ants' nest or a hive of bees. Hastily raising the camera to her eye, she focused the zoom lens as close as she was able, firing off half a dozen shots.

Ravi pulled her down as the guards began to come up the other side of the building. 'You hear the machines?' he asked.

With all the street noises, she hadn't been aware of noise from anywhere else, but now that she paid attention she realised there was a steady hum of turning motors – inside the shed it must be deafening. Ravi mimed feeding cloth through a sewing machine. 'They want children for the little fingers.'

She shook her head. 'Terrible.'

'Yes, indeed. But you will save them?' He looked at her with a searching expression.

'Well,' the task before her now seemed suddenly more daunting, 'I'm trying my best.'

He was peering over the wall again, before gesturing that she could stand. There was some commotion in the factory, which she had to stand up fully to see. The foreman she'd seen outside the shed had something in his hand and was viciously beating one of the children on the head and shoulders. All around him, she noticed, the other children continued to work, as though nothing was happening. Ravi looked over at her. 'That one is evil,' he said, pointing.

She nodded, outraged by what she was seeing, but realising there was absolutely nothing she could do to prevent it. Once again, she lifted up her camera and began shooting. So absorbed were they both by the scene that they realised, too late, that they also were being watched. An ageing Land Rover had pulled up outside the shed. In the passenger seat sat a large, uniformed Indian man with an automatic rifle resting across his knees. Behind him an Indian, in the same khaki as the shed guards, was pointing up towards them.

Judith and Ravi both saw them at the same moment.

'Quick!' Ravi turned and was tugging her away. 'They kill us!'

It was less a rooftop than a patchwork of planks, but she raced across behind him to the other side of the building, propelled by an instinct she'd never known she possessed. Suddenly, everything was happening in slow motion and she was anaesthetised from fear. They reached the edge of the building, and the next rooftop was one level down. She'd never dream of jumping from that height – usually. But now she didn't even stop to think. Ravi was already down there, and he paused, to help break her fall. Then they were running again.

Looking behind them, down into the street, she saw guards emerging from the building they'd just jumped from, shouting and waving their arms in confusion. Aziz and Chris had seen what was happening and had pulled out of the alley on the scooters. Reaching the edge of the second roof, Judith and Ravi had no choice but to jump again. Thank God for the fruit seller! They headed straight for a pile of mangos. The moment she hit the ground, Judith felt herself being yanked by Aziz on to the back of his scooter. Ravi was already back on his with Chris, racing up the street beside them.

She guessed she shouldn't look back, but she couldn't help it. They were all in the Land Rover now – four of them plus the guy with the rifle – homing down on them fast, firearms at the ready. Crunching through gears as it roared up behind them, the Land Rover was mowing down anything in its path. Pedestrians, bike riders and beggars were diving out of the way as it left a trail of destruction in its wake, smashing market stands to the ground, hoeing down the pitiful stalls of fruit and lamp oil and knick-knacks that were the livelihoods of their owners. It couldn't be more than twenty yards behind them now.

Aziz screamed out something to Ravi who was just behind them. Then they turned left into a much wider road. There was less traffic here, and looking back at the Land Rover, Judith saw it gaining ground by the second. This was a disaster! It would be on top of them at any moment! When she heard the first crack, Judith didn't immediately realise what it was. Then, as Ravi and Aziz wove crazily from side to side, she knew. She couldn't bear to look back. The firing came closer. She felt a bullet searing straight past her cheek.

Then the two scooters had swung a savage right down an alley which seemed impossibly narrow – too narrow for a Land Rover. Horns pressed firmly down, they plunged into the darkness at a crazy speed. Behind them there were screams of rage, and an intense volley of firing. Bullets ricocheted off the walls, blasted glass and splintered doors. Judith felt several more rounds whining past her, and felt a tug at her jeans. Ravi and Aziz were still zig-zagging from side to side, as the few other people in the alley cowered in entrances or behind dustbins.

As every moment passed, the firing grew more distant. Pursuing them on foot, the guards had been hopelessly outmanoevred. Then behind her, Judith heard Chris cry out. Looking round, she saw him clutch his side. Something was falling to the ground. Ravi and Aziz kept on ploughing up the alley, before roaring through an open barn and, miraculously, out into a main street.

It seemed they had left their pursuers behind. But they rode on at high speed for several more blocks before turning again into a side street and, finally, dodging into someone's back yard. Judith was immediately off her scooter and over beside Chris. She didn't have to ask what had happened; he was clutching his right side. A large patch of his shirt was already dark and wet with blood.

'My moneybelt!' His face was contorted with pain.

'Fuck the moneybelt.' Judith looked over at Ravi. 'We need a hospital.'

'No,' Chris winced, 'too easy for them.'

'Well, we can't have you dying of blood loss—'

'Red Cross?' said Aziz. 'There is a clinic.'

'Can they deal with bullets?'

'Yes. They have doctors,' Ravi confirmed, looking anxiously at Chris. 'Not too far.'

'Let's go.'

Ellen cleared her desk of all her academic papers, placed a blank pad of paper in front of her and, at the top of the page, in the neat, copperplate handwriting she'd learned almost sixty years ago, wrote 'Starwear Prize – speech.'

She'd set aside the next hour to prepare the speech which Claude had told her should last no longer than five minutes, maximum. Successful public speaking was, she knew, ninety per cent preparation. And she was determined to use her five minutes at the podium to maximum effect. She was, of course, quite used to standing up in front of people and talking at length – she'd been lecturing since her late twenties. But the GlobeWatch Awards Ceremony was a rather different environment. And of special importance to her were all the VIPs who'd be there. It would be a high-profile evening, and apart from GlobeWatch's own Executive Council – which constituted many of the most influential not-for-profit organisations in Britain – there would also be major corporate donors and captains of industry, plus public relations agencies whose blue-chip client lists spanned most global businesses. And, of course, the media. Television cameras from all major and satellite TV networks would be there, providing feeds right around the world. Reporters from all the national and international press would take up a tranche of seats. While the event was unlikely to make prime-time news, Claude had assured her that because GlobeWatch's award scheme was the first of its kind in global industrial relations, the ceremony would be used in business news broadcasts right around the world. Edited highlights meant that the words she chose would probably be seen and heard by tens of millions of people. She would choose them with care.

Focusing her thoughts on Starwear, she inevitably remembered Nathan, and the last time they'd met – such a stimulating discussion about new trends in corporate citizenship! Dear man. She was doing this for him, also, she told herself. Too late, alas, for him to witness in person. But it was a recognition of his values, which had become the values of his company. Claude had had some literature on Starwear sent over to her – she'd never realised just how much good the company was doing in some of the world's poorest countries. Quite apart from employment, which was the greatest gift of all, Starwear was providing housing, and schools, and putting money into clinics. Starwear was, in many ways, a model company, she thought, and other big businesses would do well to emulate it. She thought she'd make that the key message of her speech.

23

The moment they had arrived at the Red Cross hospital, Chris had gone straight into Casualty. There they found that he'd lost over a pint of blood, but was only suffering a flesh wound. Another inch to the left, the American doctor told them seriously, and the bullet would have punctured his kidney. A nurse had stitched and bandaged him, and given him instructions to take it easy. He and Judith had exchanged glances. Take it easy. Yeah. Right.

His original plan had been to get Judith out to Delhi airport and back on a home-bound plane as soon as he made contact with her. Now, of course, that was out of the question – their pursuers would be on the lookout. Outside the Red Cross hospital they had quickly discussed new arrangements with Ravi and Aziz before deciding to drive to Bombay. It was seven hours away and, they reckoned, the airport there was unlikely to be covered. Ravi knew someone who could drive them. Judith had the cash.

That had been over seven hours ago and now, as they saw the first signposts for the airport, Chris felt a certain relief. Looking at Judith, he squeezed her hand. They'd already discussed what they'd do when they got there. It wasn't something Chris was looking forward to. They both had passports, but no money. Chris had lost all his cash and credit cards with his moneybelt. All the money Judith had would be spent on this car trip. Judith did have a credit card – but it had less than £100 credit on it. Not enough for two one-way tickets out of Bombay.

They'd gone through the options. All they needed was someone at the end of a phone with a credit card – which included just about any of their family or friends. But in the back of the car, still scarcely able to believe what they'd just been through, Chris had said to Judith, 'You know, whichever way I look at it, he's got to be told.'

'Told?'

'Mike. About what's happening – Kate Taylor, Merlin de Vere. Now you and me. Someone's got to tell him.'

Judith regarded him carefully. 'And what would you expect him to do then?'

'Call in the police, for starters. Fire North. Resign Starwear – which he's planning to do anyway.' Chris's expression was serious. 'Mike can't afford to have Lombard associated with . . .' he gestured generally, 'all of this.'

Judith glanced away and thought for a moment before saying, 'I don't know. It's high risk.'

'You mean, his phone being tapped?'

She shook her head. 'No. I mean, do you really trust him?'

'Trust Mike?' He shook his head, with a smile of disbelief that she was even asking. 'That's not even a question. I mean, I know you're suspicious of PR people, but if you'd met him . . .'

'I just don't think we should be taking any more chances.'

Looking across the back seat, he met her eyes grimly. 'It'll be all right.'

Inside the airport terminal they'd looked for telephones – and were relieved to find a calling centre, where phones were available in private booths, payable by credit card. In minutes he'd got an outside line, had dialled up Lombard, and was through to Rosa. 'I need to speak to Mike.'

'He's in a meeting right now.'

'Well, interrupt it. What I've got to tell him is extremely important.'

Responding to the urgency in his tone, Rosa put him on hold for a few moments before there was a click and Mike was on the line. 'Mike, I'm calling from Bombay airport,' Chris began. 'I have to tell you something, and I need your help.'

Forty minutes later, they emerged from the centre. Over the past half hour, a bedazed-sounding Mike Cullen, reeling from Chris's revelations, had been toing and froing, with Rosa on the other line, trying to work out the best way to get them out. Lombard had a correspondent agency in Bombay, and Mike knew the Managing Director there. He'd spoken to the MD who would come out to the airport and arrange payment of the tickets. After they'd checked in they were to let Mike know what flight they were on; he'd come out to Heathrow personally to collect them.

It would be more than an hour until Mike's Bombay contact arrived. Chris had arranged that they'd meet him outside the International Departures gate, under a prominent billboard for Cathay Pacific. Meantime, the only comfortable place in the whole airport was the upstairs bar.

'I could do with some anaesthetic,' Chris said wearily, as they made their way inside.

'Mine's a double,' ordered Judith.

Soon, they were perched on bar stools sipping gin-and-tonics, discussing in low voices what exactly they'd do next. It was only when they'd been there some time that they became aware of the signature tune of Sky News being played. The barman told them there was a TV lounge next door. Both wanted to know about the Textiles Bill amendment; picking up their drinks, they went through to the other room.

Conflict in Afghanistan dominated a bulletin which carried very little in the way of domestic UK news. If the Textiles Bill was going to get a mention, it would only be near the end. But although they watched the bulletin right through, there was no mention of the Bill. It was only when international weather came up that Chris glanced at his watch – and realised they had less than five minutes to go until their rendezvous.

Whether it was the combination of alcohol and blood loss, or the effects of his bullet wound, Chris suddenly found it harder to walk. His whole right side was stiff and he felt depleted of energy. His progress down the stairs from the bar was painfully slow – he found himself having to swing his right side with his left. When they got to the bottom, Judith fetched him a baggage trolley to give him extra support. As they made their way across the airport hall, he checked his watch again. 'We're going to be late.'

Judith looked over at his worried expression, before glancing at her own watch. 'Not by much. He'll wait.'

Eventually they came out of the International Departures hall and were making their way towards the Cathay Pacific poster. There was the usual airport hustle about the place – porters, taxis, travellers and buses all intent on getting somewhere else. By the Cathay Pacific poster, they noticed, stood a European couple about their age. Cause for confusion, thought Chris, trying to move faster.

Then a taxi came screeching round a corner, heading directly towards the rendezvous point. There was a sudden burst of automatic gunshot. Then screaming as people fled inside the terminal. The European couple were covered in blood, the woman writhing in pain, the man clutching her to him. Then another burst of rounds from the back of the taxi. This time the force of it blasted the couple off their feet, slamming them hard against the billboard four feet behind. They slid to the ground, collapsing in a heap like bleeding rag-dolls. The taxi was already speeding away.

Judith and Chris stood, frozen with horror, witnesses to their own execution. It was only after a long while that Chris turned, hollow-eyed, to Judith, and managed in a dry whisper: 'Is he in on it too?'

Mike Cullen replaced the telephone receiver on his desk with a look of grim satisfaction. Kuczynski had just been on the line.

'Confirmation from my Bombay operative,' he'd said. 'You won't be hearing further from the two problem children.'

'Are you *absolutely* sure about that?' Cullen had pressed him.

'Completely sure,' Kuczynski reassured him. '*Finito*.'

Cullen had paused a moment before saying, 'Congratulations, Sol. Another job well done.'

He got up from his desk now, and walked across to the floor-to-ceiling windows with the most expensive view in

London. Getting what he wanted hadn't turned out to be
easy. But making a hundred million pounds cash was never
going to be. With Treiger and Laing out of the way, however, he'd removed the final obstacle. Soon he'd be
savouring the fruits of his Four-Point Plan. He'd soon be
selling the considerable shareholding he'd secretly amassed
in Starwear, through Zillion, Kraton and Quivelle. With
Starwear shares trading at their highest price ever, the deal
would amount to £104.5 million. The proceeds were to be
sheltered in a Liechtenstein trust fund, well beyond the
reach of the taxman's grasping fingers.

He'd set up the three offshore entities to protect his
anonymity soon after his first meeting with Jacob Strauss in
New York. Nathan's younger brother had, singlehandedly,
taken the entire Starwear empire to the brink of commercial suicide with his failure to implement Quantum
Change. Every other major sportswear manufacturer had
succeeded in setting up primary production centres in
developing countries, but even with the highly paid help of
Forbes, Jacob Strauss, through a combination of overwhelming arrogance and colossal stupidity, had ensured the
programme was a disaster for Starwear.

When Cullen had met him, Strauss had been desperate.
He needed a quick fix. And Cullen had given him one;
subcontract on a massive scale until Quantum Change is
sorted out. Use the cheapest possible suppliers. That meant
the sweatshops of India, Thailand and Indonesia; it meant
eighteen-hour days for a bowl of rice; it meant exploiting
women and kids. All of which couldn't be further removed
from big brother Nathan's ethical stance. But what Nathan
didn't know couldn't hurt him, and ethics were a luxury the
company couldn't afford.

While bargain-basement producers were being set up, Cullen had taken advantage of Starwear's collapsed share price. He'd bought in at rock-bottom, borrowing money against his ownership of Lombard to buy twelve per cent of the company. Using Zillion, Kraton and Quivelle to conceal his identity – the names had been chosen, one at a time, by his Liechtenstein-based lawyer, using a telephone directory and a Mont Blanc Meisterstück – Cullen had derived droll amusement from watching both Strauss brothers run around like headless chickens at the prospect of seeing the family firm taken out.

Over time, their fears had receded. They'd decided that future profit-taking, rather than corporate control, was the motive behind the substantial buy-up of shares. Cullen had watched productivity figures soar and the share price recover. He'd bided his time, waiting to pick the best moment to sell, but it hadn't been straightforward. When the rumours about child slaves came out, Nathan had given Jacob the third-degree. Jacob had stuck to his line – there was no truth to the rumours at all. Nathan's public statement denying the child slaves had been as forceful and conclusive as you could get – Cullen had written it himself. Such was Nathan's moral authority that his denial had squashed the rumours more effectively than if there'd been a DTI investigation. Then Nathan had discovered the truth – and been unable to live with himself. It was Nathan, after all, who had appointed Jacob to the Starwear Board – at the behest of their dying father to whom he'd always felt a powerful sense of filial duty. Just as it was Nathan who'd saved Jacob from his failing businesses by setting up Sprintco offshore and buying out Ultra-Sports and Trimnasium for a dollar apiece.

Nathan's suicide had been a huge inconvenience. Nathan was the perfect CEO, eminently capable and credible. His lack of media savvy seemed only to underline his guru-like status in the corporate world. Jacob, on the other hand, PR'd well, but his incompetence couldn't be hidden for ever, which was why Cullen had come up with his Four-Point Plan: an intensive PR campaign with one single objective – to drive up Starwear's share price in the short term.

Getting the amendment in the House of Commons had been a key part of the plan. Blocking the prospect of opening up competition would give the share price a major boost. Analysts had already marked the company down on the basis that the Textiles Bill would go straight through. Late this afternoon, when George Thannet's amendment had been accepted by the House, Starwear's price had rocketed by ten per cent. Project Silo had done the business, though not quite as Cullen had planned. He'd hoped Treiger would have dug up some dirt on the operational inadequacies of Sportex and Active Red, but both companies had seemed clean as whistles. So he'd decided to go after personal stuff to bomb the bastards out of the water – and it had worked.

He'd had even more difficulty keeping alive the myth of Jacob Strauss – the 'entrepreneurial genius', as North had described him in a fit of excess. He'd decided to eliminate William van Aardt long before, to stop stories of Strauss's personal life circulating through the media. Then Merlin de Vere had got hold of Strauss's early track record and he'd had to be silenced too. But the worst of it had been Judith Laing, who'd rapidly whipped up the most lethal of cocktails, and involved Treiger in it too. Then, as if that wasn't bad enough, Kate Taylor had been sucked in; Kate, for whom he really had had big plans. He'd had to get rid of her, of course, but not before carefully distancing himself from the operation by promoting her twelve hours earlier.

It had all been very messy – not his style – but it needed to be done. Jacob Strauss's reputation would remain intact for another week from now. Which was all the time he needed. The Starwear share price, riding high on the Textiles Bill amendment would be receiving an even bigger boost in a few days' time when the company's annual results were presented. Analysts were already moving their forecasts northwards in the expectation of strong earnings. Then, the icing on the cake, Starwear would have a clean sweep at the GlobeWatch awards next week, culminating in the grand prize for 'Company of the Year'. With the company at its very zenith, Cullen would sell out his shareholding. He'd already lined up a very willing buyer, one who'd ensure that Jacob Strauss, egotistical asshole that he was, would instantly be ejected from corporate life, never to be heard of again. There was a certain poetic justice about it, thought Cullen.

Glancing at the share price monitor in his office, he looked at the Starwear figure, blinking a reassuring green. He didn't need a calculator to work out that he'd made over half a million pounds today. He was feeling decidedly celebratory. With the ease of habit, he arranged his features in an appropriately earnest expression and made his way through Rosa's office.

'I'm just going upstairs for an hour to relax,' he told her. 'Hold all calls.'

24

Chris had never experienced such relief as he did the moment the door of Lufthansa Flight 261 to Frankfurt was closed, and the plane began taxiing to the end of the runway. After the unbearable tension of the past twelve hours, he felt exhausted as he eased himself back in his seat. Glancing over to where Judith sat beside him, expression weary and eyes closed, he didn't doubt she felt the same way too.

Just over an hour before, they'd witnessed the murder of the couple mistaken for themselves. As the airport crowd had reacted in a screaming turmoil of panic and hysteria, they'd stood in a daze, scarcely able to take in the reality, numbed to silence and too stunned to move. Then, less than a minute later, sirens were sounding, police cars and an ambulance screaming into view.

The two of them had drawn their arms round each other, and returned inside the terminal building in a state of deep shock. The killing put everything in a dramatically different perspective. Knowing it should have been them out there, that two innocents had been caught up in their own, desperate drama, provoked overwhelming feelings of horror, outrage, guilt. It also, in a strange way, brought the two of them suddenly closer, like the sole survivors of some appalling disaster. Reeling from emotions on a scale they'd never experienced, at the same time they realised that now, even more than before, they couldn't lose their grip. They had to get the hell out of this place.

Heading for the departures screen in the airport building, they found the first flight to Europe was by Lufthansa in an hour. Ground crew at the Lufthansa desk told them seats were still available. A reverse-charge to Judith's cousin Michelle, in London, and her credit card details, secured them two places in Economy. They scrambled through customs and immigration through to Boarding, which was already under way.

Now as Chris looked over at Judith, he reflected that they'd just been through the most harrowing experience of their lives together. There was no question now of not trusting each other, and no room for hostility. They were both in it together. As if in response to his thoughts, she reached out and took his hand in hers, drawing it into her lap as the plane thrust down the runway. Both of them looked out of the window as they took off, watching the sprawl of Bombay beneath them as the plane curved upwards in sharp ascent.

Then, as the plane reached its cruising altitude, Judith turned to Chris, her expression wan. 'These past couple of weeks . . . I know I've been . . . difficult.'

He shook his head, before reaching out and tracing the line of her cheek with his finger. 'It's your job to be suspicious.'

'I didn't just mean that.' There was a tenderness in her voice he hadn't heard since the old days. Taking both his hands in hers, she told him, 'I've basically been a total bitch.' Her eyes were filled with sorrow. 'The things I said, I didn't . . . you know.'

He didn't trust himself to speak. Instead he reached over and took her in his arms. She wrapped hers around his, and they held each other, a familiar embrace unleashing a flood of feeling.

'I'm sorry,' she managed eventually, nuzzling back into his shoulder.

'Oh, Jude!' He stroked her hair, the way he always used to.

He was the only one who'd ever called her Jude. Hey, Jude. Her *nom d'amour*. After they'd broken up, he had avoided using her name altogether, though when he had to, it was always the more formal Judith.

'It's a long time since you called me that,' she whispered.

'It's a long time since we've spoken. Really, I mean. But it's been hard for us both.'

She leaned back in her seat, wiping her eyes. 'I wish you weren't always so bloody reasonable,' she sniffed, embarrassed.

He smiled. 'I'll try to be less reasonable in the future.'

She grinned. 'Yeah.' Then, confiding in him after a pause, 'You know, I'm not so sure what to do now – about my article, I mean.'

His eyes met hers with an intimacy they hadn't shared for years.

'We know that Carter's on the take. If I give him the photographs it'll be a repeat of what happened with Cullen.'

He shook his head. 'You know, I'm still not convinced it was Mike. North has so many phones tapped.'

'You think there's someone down there at the airport with an envelope full of rupees for us?'

'Could be. It's just so utterly out of character that Mike should be involved.'

She paused a moment before saying, 'I guess the evidence *is* only circumstantial. If North was listening . . .'

'Not that that helps with your Carter problem.' He stroked her hand before suggesting, 'What about taking it a level up?'

'Tilyard?'

Carter's boss and the Editor of *The Herald* was a remote figure with whom she'd had few dealings.

'Carter would go ballistic. I don't even know if he's told Tilyard about Starwear.'

'It's such a huge story, he should have. And if he hasn't, you'd be doing your career no harm by going direct,' he mused for a moment, 'unless you took it back to *The Guardian*.'

Judith nodded. 'I'd thought of that. They'd love to have it, but if I did that no one I worked for in the future would ever trust me again.'

Their conversation was interrupted by an air hostess offering drinks. They both ordered Cokes, before Judith continued, 'What I'd really like to do is get the story out to all the media. Maximum exposure.'

The phrase triggered a memory for Chris. The last time he'd seen it had been in a Starwear traffic meeting note. 'Something like GlobeWatch,' he mused.

Judith frowned. She'd heard of the organisation before, but right now couldn't place it. 'What's that?'

He pulled a wry expression. 'Starwear's in line to win a whole lot of awards from them. I know North's making sure all the media are there.'

As he was talking, Judith was following him intently.

'Some kind of think-tank on global industrial relations. Wouldn't surprise me if they're just a set-up—'

'But it would horrify Ellen Kennedy.' She'd worked it out now.

Chris's expression was puzzled. 'Dr Kennedy from St John's?'

She was nodding.

'What's she—'

'I phoned her three weeks ago. She's big on the child labour issue. I checked her out as a lead. Said she was involved with GlobeWatch. In fact, she's handing out the awards.'

In that instant, the same possibility occurred to them both. They searched each other's eyes with excitement. 'Imagine if she turned up at the awards ceremony with the real story.' Chris spoke quickly. 'When are the awards?'

'The eleventh. What's today?'

'We arrive in Frankfurt on the seventh. Cutting it fine.' His tone was urgent. 'We'd still have to get to Oxford.'

Judith met his look of doubt with a sudden determination. 'It's too big an opportunity to miss. I just hope to God my photos come out, and we get to her in time.'

'I hope she plays ball.'

'She will.' Judith was certain. 'How can you argue with photographic evidence?'

The Great Room of the Grosvenor House Hotel is one of the largest and most opulent salons in London, long established as the capital's pre-eminent venue for gala banquets and awards ceremonies. The evening of the GlobeWatch Awards Ceremony saw the hotel's banqueting staff swing into well-oiled routine, to ensure that each one of the four hundred invited luminaries was made to feel important. A red carpet swept across the pavement to receive men in black ties and women in elegant evening wear as they stepped from the backs of chauffeur-driven Bentleys, Jaguars and London cabs.

Once in the hotel, gathering on a balcony that over-looked the Great Room, guests were offered sparkling flutes of Moët et Chandon and trayloads of exotic canapés by circulating staff. Glittering beneath them were fifty can-dlelit tables, covered with immaculately starched white tablecloths, and laid with silver and crystal and sumptuous floral centrepieces. Seven-thirty for eight p.m., the invita-tions had instructed, and the balcony was filling all the time, the buzz of excited conversation and laughter growing rapidly, so that by ten minutes before the hour, the pre-dinner drinks party was roaring.

Tonight's gathering was certainly of the turbo-powered variety, with more heavyweight businessmen gathered here than at a UN economic summit. Lombard had exerted its considerable corporate influence to ensure that the Chief Executive Officers and Managing Directors of the world's largest global businesses were assembled here in one room. Industry leaders and the money men who bankrolled them, high-profile entrepreneurs and business gurus, all the major brokerage houses and merchant banks were represented – the atmosphere positively reeked with corporate testos-terone. They'd flown in from New York and Chicago, from Tokyo and Sydney, from Berlin, Paris, Moscow and Milan.

And the power wasn't purely economic. There were senior politicians too: Tory grandees and Labour peers, three former Prime Ministers and two former US

Presidents, cabinet ministers from around the world. To a room heaving with *gravitas* had been added a sprinkling of celebrities to add glitz to the occasion: blue-blooded English aristocrats and exiled European monarchs, golf stars and supermodels and several private Gulfstream-loads of Hollywood power-brokers.

They were all here for a night at the top. Because Lombard had persuaded them, or their advisers, that the GlobeWatch Awards Ceremony was the place to be seen at. It represented the very essence of the new millennium's business values – global corporate citizenship and enlightened self-interest – values that all of those attending wished to be associated with. It presented an opportunity to bask in reflected glory, if not to capture it for themselves. For Lombard had also exercised the full might of its media influence to ensure that anyone who was anyone in the business media had been coaxed or cajoled into attendance. Here tonight were the City Editors of every national British newspaper and major press agency, as well as the *Wall Street Journal* and *International Herald Tribune* from America, the *Frankfurter Algemeine Zeitung* from Germany, France's *Le Soir*, Italy's *Il Mondo* and a raft of reporters from China and south-east Asia. Television cameramen from the BBC, ITV, BSkyB, CNN, Bloomberg and CNBC had set up on a special TV platform, able to get footage right around the room. The effect had been carefully choreographed so that no one arriving could fail to be impressed by the company in which they found themselves – and, by association, impressed by themselves, for being among the élite corps of global power-brokers and tycoons whose money made the world go round.

At the centre of one of the most star-studded groups in

the room stood Jacob Strauss and his wife Amy, both resplendent in their evening finery. Flash-cubes had been going off all around them from the moment they stepped from the back of their Bentley. And one thing they both knew was how to play the media – a smile here and a handshake there, saying the right word in the right ear, and standing by the right people for group photocalls. Standing back a few feet from the Strausses, apparently unnoticed but orchestrating much of what Jacob and Amy Strauss were doing, stood Elliott North. He was cool and svelte in his dinner jacket, his face freshly shaven and cologned, and moustache neatly trimmed. Behind those flashing lenses, he didn't miss a thing. There were a number of people he needed Jay to circulate among, and he had only a limited time to work the room, in accordance with the plan already worked out by Mike Cullen.

Because tonight was all about Jacob Strauss. Under the auspices of GlobeWatch and the ethics of the new millennium, the reality was that this was Jacob Strauss's coming-out party; his first major public occasion as CEO of Starwear. It was a bit like a débutante's ball – and everything was in place so that a more spectacular endorsement of his corporate vision, leadership and values would be impossible to imagine.

As North guided Jay and his wife first in this direction, and then that, he took special satisfaction from his role, feeling like the gambler who'd already bought off the croupier. Little did any of these guests realise that it was Jacob Strauss who would be setting off for the stage four times during the course of the evening to collect a GlobeWatch award. Jacob Strauss would make the trip the final time for the greatest prize of all – GlobeWatch's

Company of the Year. It was Jacob Strauss who would come out of it all as the golden boy of corporate America who had conquered the world.

All of which suited North fine. The higher Jay flew, North reckoned, the further he had to fall – and the less inclined he'd be to take the trip. He had already decided this would be his last official engagement as Jacob Strauss's PR adviser. For, despite tonight's impeccably organised ambiance of *bonhomie*, Strauss's demands were becoming more reckless than ever. And, along with his increasing demands, it was becoming harder and harder to cover up for him. Treiger and Laing had been put out of action, thank Christ, but there would be others. You couldn't hide the truth for ever. When Jacob Strauss was basking in the glow of tomorrow's headlines, he'd decided, he was going to ask for his share of the success. Ten million dollars.

That island in Greece was beckoning. He could see it in his mind's eye.

One of the elegantly clad guests at the GlobeWatch Awards Ceremony didn't head for the Great Room entrance along with the other guests, but made his way, as instructed, to the main hotel entrance. Presenting himself at Reception, he was directed to a suite on the seventh floor. He knocked on the door, which was opened by Mike Cullen himself.

It had required all of Cullen's considerable persuasive skills to get Ed Snyder along tonight at all. Outraged by the sordid revelations of the tabloid press, and the damaging accusations of the broadsheets, he'd been fighting a rear-guard action all week. It had been frustrating and exhausting – going well beyond the usual stresses of his business schedule, intruding deep into his personal life too. His wife had stuck by him, thank God. She'd realised the sleaze was being orchestrated deliberately to blacken his reputation at the very time he needed all the corporate credibility he could muster. She was damned if she was going to let Jacob Strauss wreck her marriage. And, pre-dictably, the moment the Textiles Bill amendment had been passed, the stories disappeared, the telephone stopped ringing, the photographers decamped from outside their house.

At the end of the most bruising week of his career, it required all the confidence Ed Snyder could muster to walk into a room filled with his business peers and act as though he was taking it all in his stride. Yet this was precisely what Cullen had persuaded him to do. Though there was, of course, a very great incentive.

'Drink?' offered Cullen.

He glanced at his watch before shaking his head. 'Ten to,' he replied. Then he fixed Cullen with a look of enquiry, to which the other immediately responded.

'I'm ready to trade,' Cullen said.

'When?'

'Now.'

'In the next ten minutes?'

'We can shake on it in the next ten minutes. Carry out the transaction first thing tomorrow.'

Snyder was taken aback by the unexpected suddenness of it. But no less interested.

'How much?' he asked.

'One twenty.'

He regarded Cullen closely. He'd been following Starwear's share price as intensively as Cullen himself. That evening's price had closed up, putting Cullen's holding, he'd worked out earlier that evening, at just over £120.5 million pounds. 'Sounds reasonable,' he responded.

'I'm a reasonable man.'

Shaking his head with disbelief, he walked across to the window that looked down on Park Lane, to where guests were still arriving for the ceremony. 'After everything that's happened this week . . .' he mused.

It would be the most incredible turnaround. To his thirty-nine per cent holding would be added the twelve per cent, which no one knew Cullen owned – all that was required to give him full control of Starwear. Having been dragged through the dirt by the national press, he'd soon be king of the castle, CEO of the world's largest sportswear manufacturer, owner of the world's second biggest brand. The first thing he'd do would be to fire Jacob Strauss, for whom he had a well-developed contempt. He'd clear out Strauss's cronies; he'd merge in the Active Red operation and have in his control a business empire three times the size of its closest competitor. All with the entrenched commercial advantage that Starwear had won by its amendment in the House of Commons that week. He couldn't suppress a smile.

Catching the expression from across the room, Cullen grinned. 'I did tell you to keep focused on the big picture.'

He nodded. 'You did.' Then, glancing directly at Cullen, 'I suppose you'll be wanting me to keep on Lombard as Starwear's PR advisers?'

Cullen raised the palms of his hands equivocally. 'It's a no-strings deal. If you decide to keep us on, of course, we'd be delighted. Though I would propose a certain restructuring.'

Snyder agreed.

'Just remember,' Cullen reminded him, 'whatever success Starwear enjoys tonight will be yours, by virtue of ownership, tomorrow.'

Snyder shrugged his shoulders dismissively. 'You don't need to sell me on it. I've been working for this moment my whole lifetime.'

'You and me both, Ed. So, we have a deal?'

'We have a deal.'

The two men shook hands.

Ellen Kennedy was wearing the same black dress she wore for all her 'evening do's', as she called them. It had cost her a small fortune at Laura Ashley's ten years before, but it was very flattering – black lent her petite frame a certain *je ne sais quoi*, she'd always thought. She particularly liked wearing the dress with her grey hair up, as she was wearing it tonight, and complemented by the twin strand of pearls she'd inherited from her mother. Arriving at the Grosvenor House by cab, she carried under her right arm a plastic folder containing her three-page speech.

Claude had assured her she needn't worry about bringing a copy of the speech. All of the speakers' addresses, including the one she'd sent him, had been prepared for an autocue machine, so that speakers needed only to focus on their delivery. Ordinarily, Ellen would have been only too happy to take advantage of the technology. But tonight it was out of the question; the speech she was about to give was very different from the one she'd faxed over to Claude three days ago. It couldn't be more different. In fact, what she planned to say was the very opposite of her original intentions.

What had changed it all had been her visitors last Friday night. A knock on the door at ten-thirty at night was unusual to begin with, but still more unexpected was the discovery, on opening the door, of Judith Laing and her young man, Christopher. As she showed them in, she'd recalled her telephone conversation with Judith a few weeks ago, when she'd said she was investigating a child-labour story. Was the visit in connection with that, she wondered, or was it purely social? After sitting down, Judith had confirmed that Ellen was to be the keynote speaker at the GlobeWatch Awards Ceremony in two days' time. Then she and Christopher told their story.

Ellen had, of course, been shaken to the core by their revelations. But there was no time for disbelief. Quite apart from her remembering Judith as a student with a particularly acute intelligence, the two had brought evidence – including photographs of Starwear's slave factory in Jaipur. Christopher had told her about the *modus operandi* of Mike Cullen and Elliott North – the deaths, in suspicious circumstances, of William van Aardt, Merlin de Vere, Kate Taylor; the dirty-tricks campaign against Starwear competitors; and how he suspected GlobeWatch was merely a front set up by Starwear to give itself prizes.

Recovering from her shock, Ellen Kennedy didn't know what made her more furious – the horrific abuse to which Starwear was subjecting children in India, or the fact that she'd almost been deceived into giving the company her full endorsement. Almost – but not quite. She had been tempted to phone Claude Bonning, then and there, and have it out with him. But Judith and Christopher had persuaded her otherwise. They had proposed a very different tack indeed, and one which, she conceded, would have far more impact.

The three of them had talked into the early hours before Judith and Christopher left – they were staying at a friend's cottage in the Cotswolds. Next morning, Ellen had started making a few discreet enquiries, using the list of GlobeWatch sponsors Claude Bonning had originally sent her. One advantage of having been a lecturer for the past forty years was that generations of students had passed through her hands. Some, like Judith, had stayed in touch, and had gone on to scale the dizziest of corporate pinnacles. By now, Ellen knew a fair number of senior executives at various companies, including some on the GlobeWatch sponsor list. She managed to track down a few at their homes during the weekend. She was sorry to trouble them, she explained, but she hoped they could answer a quick query, or give her the name of someone who could; was it the case that their company had made a substantial donation to a non-profit-making group called GlobeWatch?

A couple had known the answer straight away. Others phoned her back. In three out of five cases, there had been no record of any donation, although amounts below £250, one of her former students explained, were not individually listed. In the remaining two cases, a donation had been confirmed. In each case, the company had made a donation of £100 on the recommendation of their PR advisers, Lombard.

It was all the proof she'd needed. But she still wanted confirmation from Claude himself. Making her way now into the hotel, she found him resplendent in his penguin suit, greeting more movers and shakers than she had ever seen in one place.

'Claude, I need a quiet word,' she had told him, unsmiling.

'What – now?' He'd appeared startled.

'Yes.'

She seemed very serious, he couldn't help noticing, which was strange. She didn't seem the type to suffer from nerves.

'Well, I . . .' He glanced about the crowded room rather helplessly, before remembering the security room just off the lobby. Swiftly leading her to it, he showed her inside, before closing the door behind them.

'In the past few days,' she began immediately, 'I've been on the telephone to five of my former students now working for companies who *supposedly* sponsor GlobeWatch.'

Her emphasis had him suddenly, and visibly, crumpling.

'It turns out that none of the companies has paid more than £250. In fact, it's more like £100 each. And unless I'm very much mistaken, GlobeWatch has only one corporate sponsor. The same company that's in line to win four prizes tonight, including the Company of the Year Award. Is that the case?'

Claude was, by now, white-faced, his jaw trembling. There was no need for him to answer.

Stepping closer to him, she looked despairingly into his eyes. 'Claude – *why*?'

Raising his hands to cover his face, he shrank before her, until he finally managed to gasp, 'I was blackmailed.'

'Elliott North?' She was brisk.

He glanced up at her, astonished.

'Huh!' she snorted. 'As I thought.' Then she was making her way across the room.

Behind her, he called out, plaintively, 'You'll still be . . . making your speech?'

At the door she turned. 'Oh, yes, Claude,' she told him, 'you can be sure of it.'

The motorbike courier pulling into *The Herald*'s Wapping offices winced as he swung off the bike and made his painful way across to Security. He'd been on the bike for the past three hours, racing up the M4 from the Cotswolds, ignoring the developing cramp in his legs. Speed was of the essence, the young lady had said. And he had promised her he'd get the envelope delivered before seven. Looking at his watch now, he noted with satisfaction that it was just ten to. He raised the visor of his helmet, looking at the woman inside Security.

'Delivery for—' he squinted at the envelope, 'Carol Anderson.'

Within a minute, Carol had come down to collect the envelope. PA to the Editor of *The Herald*, she rarely received envelopes addressed to her personally. Tearing it open on her way back to the office, she read Judith's hand-written note, glanced over the accompanying piece – and gasped. She began running towards the Editor's office.

Judith and Chris walked hand-in-hand down the cobbled pavement from the pub where they'd just eaten dinner. Bernie's Cotswold bolt-hole was conveniently located just a few hundred yards away from one of the most congenial hostelries in the shire – one with which the two of them had grown rapidly acquainted in the past two days.

Following their visit to Ellen Kennedy in Oxford, they'd arrived around three o'clock on the Saturday morning. Neither of them having slept properly for over forty-eight hours, they'd collapsed in Bernie's double bed and slept solidly till mid-afternoon. They had phoned Ellen again, and she had told them of her investigations confirming GlobeWatch's true status as a mere front for Starwear – and about the speech she'd planned for the following night. Then the two of them had set off for a pub dinner.

It had been an evening of red wine and candlelight, reminiscences about their times together at Oxford, and an outpouring of their lives since then. There had been such intimacy, such emotion. It was as though the barriers holding them apart for so long had, after all the events of the past few days, been tossed aside, unleashing an intensity of feeling neither of them had felt since they were last together. On their way home, on that crisp, November night, they had paused outside a chapel where Christmas carols were being practiced; they were both transported back to the first time they'd been together, after carols at St John's. Drawing Judith close to him, Chris put his arms around her and kissed her. Raising her face to his, Judith responded to his passion, their bodies melting together.

What happened when they returned to the cottage was as inevitable as it was utterly ecstatic. High on good feeling, the moment they stepped inside the door they hadn't been able to wait to tear off each other's clothes. Leaving a trail of coats and jeans and underwear all the way from the front door to the sitting room, they'd knelt down in their nakedness before the glowing embers of the fire, lost to each other as they kissed. Then, drawing back, with his forefinger Chris traced the smoothness of her cheek, pale beneath her dark, tousled hair, down her neck, all the way to where her pert, beige-tipped breasts were taut beneath his touch.

'I just want you so much.' His voice was husky.

She responded to his expression of unashamed lust, lying

back on the carpet and drawing him on top of her, between her parted legs.

There'd been none of the hesitancy or self-consciousness of first-time sex, but all of its breathless edge. Unable to resist his urgency, his driving demand for satiation, Judith had been crazy with passion. Their rising cries became noisy and unrestrained, as their rhythm grew faster and faster. She had urged him hoarsely on, through territory so well known and so loved – and yet so utterly exhilarating.

And afterwards, when they had both been to the edge and over it, they lay together in front of the fire, flooded with bliss. As she basked in the afterglow, a silent tear trickled down Judith's cheek. Wrapped up in him, she hadn't felt so safe, so sure of herself, for years. For Chris, holding her folded into his body, it had been like coming home.

Tonight, as they opened the front door of the cottage, after another day of country walks and fire-lit passion, they were both stirred by an anticipation of a different kind. Chris walked across the sitting room and switched on the TV. Glancing at his watch he saw it was half-past eight – Claude Bonning was doing an exclusive, pre-ceremony interview live on the balcony of the Great Room, while behind him GlobeWatch's high-profile guests were dining.

Turning to Judith, he slipped his arm around her waist. 'So,' he murmured, 'we're on countdown.'

Making chit-chat with captains of industry was not generally something that came easily to Ellen Kennedy, and that night was no exception. She found herself at a table of corporate warriors with a combined net worth greater than that of the continent of Africa, and whose sole obsession, it seemed, was the latest activity of international stock markets. Usually, she would have seen this as a networking opportunity, a chance to broaden her professional horizons and, who knows, maybe stimulate interest in the research work she did. But not tonight. To begin with, she was feeling daunted by the task she faced. And besides, after tonight, she realised, she would have no shortage of opportunity to explain to people what she did outside the lecture theatre.

The mood in the Great Room, which had started out as one of high spirits, moved up a key as guests began dinner. Wine flowed freely, as first the *hors d'oeuvres* were consumed, then the *entrées*, a detectable buzz of anticipation developing as waiters swooped and fluttered about the tables and the minutes ticked closer to the main event. In front of each guest was an Order of Ceremonies card, bearing the GlobeWatch logo, and outlining how, after coffee had been served following the main course, the awards ceremony would begin. Up at the front of the room, on stage behind a podium, a massive, wall-to-wall screen flanked by *faux* Doric columns and towering flower arrangements, bore the GlobeWatch logo projected in blue and green. All very theatrical, Ellen Kennedy couldn't help observing. Around the room, as the noise level steadily increased, there was one table in particular that seemed to be enjoying itself. Seeing her looking over, the businessman to her left followed her gaze.

'Jacob Strauss,' he noted, 'and that Lombard guy, what's his name? Mike Cullen.'

'You know them?' she asked.

'Know of them.'

'Hmm.'

It wouldn't be long, she mused, before very few people couldn't make the same claim.

Finally, coffee had been served, the lights dimmed, and after a hush of anticipation had descended, came a blast of 'Thus Spake Zarathustra' from massive speakers in all four corners of the room, together with a spectacular display of projected computer graphics on the front screen. Then, across to the podium strode Claude Bonning. His opening address was upbeat and assured. Despite a few nervous glances in the direction of Ellen's table, he explained bravely what GlobeWatch was, and why it had been created, before welcoming the first celebrity speaker of the evening to present the first award. He was, pronounced Claude, the world's leading motivational guru, a man who closely advised the US President, who had helped BMW achieve fifteen per cent performance increases, and who had coached British swimming champion Chris Parry, who went on to win five gold medals at the Olympics.

'Your majesties, my lords, ladies and gentlemen,' Claude drove up the excitement, 'will you please welcome to the GlobeWatch Awards Ceremony this evening, Dr Anthony Black.'

There was more music and a tumult of applause. This whole thing, thought Ellen, had all the razzmatazz of an Oscars ceremony. On her Order of Ceremonies card she'd noted that a production company had been brought in to ensure the evening's flawless progress. In fact, before sitting down for dinner, she'd been approached by a young man bristling with mobile phones, to be asked about her preference for the height of the podium, and did she have any other needs. She'd surprised him by handing over a series of photographic slides she wished to use. He hadn't expected them, he said, but would ensure they were all set up ready for use.

Now, as she took in the music, the lighting, the dramatic setting, she realised it had all been designed to create maximum excitement. The first speaker, Dr Anthony Black, had no doubt been selected for the same reason. A highly effective speaker, he broke the ice with some well-directed humour, before seizing control of the audience with a few of his key motivational concepts. In a few spell-binding minutes he succeeded in communicating a vision of corporate success limited only by the imagination, of global interconnection bringing the human race closer together, and of a future of transformation and enlightenment. By the end of it his audience were, metaphorically, if not literally, on the edges of their chairs. When he announced the winner of the first category – Human Potential Development – the result was greeted with triumphal applause.

And so the evening went on. Speech after speech. Prize after prize. All building up to the grand finale. Jacob Strauss's first appearance on stage to collect the prize for Best Developing Nations Employer was greeted with an applause so great it had the chandeliers clinking. On his second and third appearances, his reception seemed even more thunderous still. But Dr Ellen Kennedy was not one of those clapping. Ignoring the curious glances of her fellow diners, she sat watching the proceedings with an expression that was deliberately blank. All would very soon be revealed, she decided. Her time would come.

And come it did. The triumphal music leading up to the ultimate prize of the evening was even more extravagant than all that had preceded it. Claude Bonning once again took to the stage, pronouncing Dr Kennedy to be 'One of the foremost thinkers of our time. A celebrated academic. A global leader in the field of corporate citizenship. Acclaimed internationally for her work in developing countries. Author of three important books . . .'

When she stepped up to the stage, a diminutive figure amid the massive floral bouquets and Doric columns and GlobeWatch logo, the applause was deafening.

Opening out her folder on the podium, she carefully donned her reading glasses and glanced about the cavernous room. After forty years of addressing large, and not always well-disciplined gatherings, she had an extremely well-developed instinct for ensuring the undivided attention of all present. And right now she used the power of the pause: a period of silence, longer than most speakers would feel comfortable with, standing with calm assurance for long enough so that when she spoke her first words, every single person there was desperate to hear what she had to say.

When, finally, she did begin, she started in a most unexpected fashion.

'Yesterday I spoke to a young lad called Vishnu,' she told her audience. 'He was surprisingly cheerful for a boy living in circumstances which, I suspect, are a lot less fortunate than the average twelve-year-old in Britain. Vishnu has no idea where his parents are, or even if they are alive – he last saw them when he was seven. He lives with his aunt and uncle, and shares a cramped room with three cousins in a semi-detached house in London. The family can't afford bus fares, so he has to walk three miles to school every day. He has no spending money except for the £5 a week he makes on his paper round. So there's no question of video games, or designer trainers, or trips to the movies – all of which are considered, these days, to be a normal part of growing up.

'But Vishnu considers himself to be extremely fortunate. In fact, he thinks his life is one of luxury. All the more surprising, when you consider what terrible injuries he has suffered.'

As her first slide appeared, there was a massive, collective gasp from the audience, which had no idea where this speech was heading, but was utterly engrossed nonetheless. The slide showed the back of a naked child, horrific weals scorched across his back, buttocks and thighs, as though he'd been branded with a steel bar.

'These burns were no accident,' Ellen continued calmly, 'they were deliberate burns inflicted by the man who owned Vishnu, so that he couldn't sit down.'

Expressions of shock had turned into a rumble of outrage.

'Vishnu's crime was to complain, after working for fifteen hours, that he could no longer thread a needle because his hands were shaking. He wanted a rest. His owner decided to teach him a lesson he would never forget.

'But Vishnu is quite right to consider himself one of the lucky ones,' she continued. 'He has relatives in Britain who came to the rescue. For the sum of just one hundred pounds, very much less than the cost of each of our meals here tonight, he was saved from another four years of slavery. The same can't be said of the children he left behind.'

Her second slide had been taken from the roof of the building across from the Starwear shed in Jaipur. Blown up across the whole of the screen, it showed dozens of child slaves bent over benches, a scene of unimaginable horror. Children were clearly shackled to their benches, with scarred backs and bruised faces, it was an image of the most Dickensian squalor. This time, there was more than simply a gasp from the audience. Voices were raised in indignation, above a rising tide of disapproval.

'We can't know how many children work as slaves in Vishnu's old factory,' Ellen continued, 'how many are tortured, raped or simply worked to death. But I would guess about two hundred at any one time.'

She paused for the flurry of indignation to subside, regaining the audience's full attention before she announced, 'This photograph was taken last week in Jaipur, India. The factory costs less than four hundred bowls of rice a day to operate, and as such is one of the most productive garment manufacturers in the world. Its location, indeed its very existence, has been one of the most ruthlessly guarded secrets of recent times. But I can reveal tonight that this factory, and others like it, is knowingly and all too willingly operated . . . by Starwear.'

At that moment, the Great Room erupted in emotion, undignified bellows of denunciation sounding above a chorus of outrage. Across the room from where Ellen Kennedy stood beneath the image of unimaginable misery, cameramen on the television platform had broken away from her address to follow proceedings below. There was shocked bewilderment on the faces of famous politicians; tears on the cheeks of a supermodel; alarm as businessmen called out in incredulous voices.

The table of Jacob and Amy Strauss was the very epicentre of a volcanic explosion. Completely abandoning the pretence of charming civility he'd adopted all evening,

Strauss had leapt to his feet and, face purple with fury, was screaming at North, 'What the fuck are you doing?'

North's expression was one of wild panic. The vein in his forehead had swollen to dark crimson.

'I had no idea!'

Opposite North, Cullen experienced a rare moment of complete bewilderment. Then his survival instinct kicked in. 'Jacob, sit down!' he shouted above the cacophony. 'There are TV cameras everywhere. Don't draw attention to yourself!'

But Jacob Strauss had lost it. 'What the fuck is going on?' He picked up a wine bottle and smashed it on to the table.

North looked over at Cullen. 'Should I get Bonning?'

Cullen had already glanced across the room to where Bonning had been standing – but he'd disappeared.

'Too late,' he correctly surmised.

All about them, diners who only minutes before had been congratulating Jacob Strauss on his third ascent to the stage were now staring at him in shock and confusion. There were bellows from tycoons, City Editors and merchant bankers:

'Explain yourself, Strauss!'

'That's how he's getting those figures!'

'Unbelievable!'

Ellen Kennedy waited a while for the waves of outrage to peak, before she held up her hands. For all the exploding passion in the room, her gesture commanded rapid respect. It was as though her scandalised audience could hardly wait for further explanation.

'I fully realise the seriousness of the accusation I am making,' Ellen said, 'but Starwear is guilty of very serious crimes. While carrying out the systematic abuse of children in India, the company has been completely misleading its shareholders about the true source of its profits.'

Her next slide showed Starwear's last annual report, with a red circle around the figure for India.

'This figure is attributed to Starwear's Quantum Change factory, which is also in Jaipur. A very impressive figure, I'm sure you'll all agree. But even at maximum output, the Quantum Change factory was never designed to produce even half of the output shown.'

She now showed the relevant page from the Forbes report, a substantially lower figure also ringed in red.

This time, the reaction in the room was of even greater ire. If anyone had been in doubt before about her accusations, they were evidently convinced now. All heads were turning in the direction of the Starwear table, where an undignified slanging match had ensued between Strauss and North. Amy Strauss, who had arrived resplendent in Versace, was making a hasty exit from the room in floods of tears, Helen Cullen following closely after to provide moral support. Starwear's guests at the table were standing, throwing down their napkins in disgust and making their way towards the stairs. All this time, Mike Cullen sat, absolutely silent, shaking his head with an expression of stern disapproval.

When Ellen Kennedy raised her hands again, her audience seemed less inclined to calm down. Furious taunts and bitter recriminations rebounded across the room. 'Quiet, please.' She had to raise her voice. 'Please let me continue.'

Then, as the noise subsided, 'I regret that Starwear's deceits do not end there,' she said loudly above the continuing row. 'In fact, *we are all* unwitting participants in the company's attempts to present a false image to the outside world.'

That had the effect of alarming her audience to a chastened silence.

'When I accepted a position on the Executive Council of GlobeWatch, I was reassured by the breadth of corporate support for the objectives of the organisation. I am sure you will share my sense of outrage to discover, as I did a few days ago, that in fact GlobeWatch has only one major donor – the company which, by coincidence, has been awarded three of tonight's prizes, and which I was due to present with a fourth. Your majesties, my lords, ladies and gentlemen, I'm afraid that GlobeWatch is nothing more than a phoney front group set up by Starwear to give itself prizes, thereby distracting our attention from the horrors it is perpetuating in the developing world right at this moment.'

There was no stopping the storm of protest unleashed now. Dignitaries behaved in the most undignified fashion as they stormed out of the Great Room, hurrying for the staircases amid howls of acrimony directed at the Starwear table – all captured by television crews and newspaper reporters who could scarcely believe the scene unfolding around them. There were demands for Claude Bonning, who was suddenly nowhere to be found. Even the production company lost control of their slick, audio-visual management – the image of child slaves appeared once again on the screen and was jammed there, whipping up still further agitation, until someone found the switch for the chandeliers, and turned them up to maximum brightness, so that the Great Room was suddenly bright as day.

Ellen Kennedy stepped down from the podium and made her way directly to a concealed exit with as much dignity as she could muster. She had just made, she knew, the address of her life. Amid the chaos of hasty evacuation, the few Starwear directors remaining had slunk off into the crowds, leaving only Jacob Strauss and Elliott North to face the scorn and wrath of those same people who, only minutes before, had been applauding Starwear with vigour. Strauss was now incandescent with rage, the 'golden boy' of American business transmuted into a seething cauldron of violent resentment.

'You're fired, you dumb fuck!!' he screamed at North, before shoving his way through the crowd of appalled cabinet ministers, film stars and City Editors. 'I had no idea,' he bayed to anyone who would listen, 'I had no idea it was going on.'

'It's your company, Strauss,' someone called out.

'I had no idea,' he repeated, lamely.

His only instinct was to get out – but he wasn't heading for the main staircase, that was for sure. Instead he made off in exactly the opposite direction, away from the departing crowd, back across the Great Room, and down a corridor until he spotted an Emergency Exit sign. He threw all his weight against the door, shoving it open – bursting into the hotel kitchen. A number of staff turned to look in astonishment at their black-tied visitor, before a waiter quickly approached him. 'Can I help you, sir?' he asked, giving no hint that the guest's entrance had been somewhat *outré*.

'Just get me out of this fucking place!' Strauss screamed.

Mike Cullen, meanwhile, had made his way directly towards the television platform with as much smooth aplomb as he could muster. Cameramen were still taking live footage of the many famous faces, producers were on their mobile phones talking excitedly to their stations, and the platform had become a natural centre of gravity for every City Editor and press agency reporter in the room.

'Gentlemen, I'm Mike Cullen,' he introduced himself in a loud voice, trying to garner as much attention as possible. 'My company, Lombard, advises Starwear on public relations issues.'

He was braced for the inevitable jeers and taunts. But at least he had them all paying attention to him now.

'I want you all to know that I am as devastated by the revelations we've just had as you. I realise you will have a lot of questions. So I propose holding a full media conference, right here, in fifteen minutes' time. I will have a statement for you by then, and I will be glad to answer all the questions you no doubt have.'

Summoning a one-man media conference with such haste was unprecedented, and he'd certainly caught them by surprise. But then this evening had been the business news event of the decade. As he stepped away from the TV platform, Cullen found Ed Snyder looming in front of him, his expression turned in a sardonic smile.

'You know, Mike,' he said to him, 'if it's all the same to you, I don't think I will buy those Starwear shares tomorrow.'

Cullen scowled.

'But I'm sure you won't have any problem selling them – if the price is right.'

Cullen resisted the temptation to lash out at the smug little prick as he walked away. *If the price was right!* In the past twenty minutes he'd seen his £120 million shareholding destroyed. Right at this minute, fund managers in America who'd watched the proceedings on Bloombergs or CNN, would be offloading their Starwear stock for whatever they could get. The price would be collapsing by the second. Investors would be bailing out like rats from a sinking ship. It was all over for Starwear. By the time the London market opened tomorrow morning, his Starwear shares would be reduced to less than the level he'd bought them for. Overnight, the ubiquitous Starwear brand, once valued at £1 billion, was dead.

Adrenalin charging through his system, Cullen realised, though, how much he still had to play for. It was Starwear's reputation, not Lombard's, that had been destroyed tonight. But guilt through association would quickly follow – he'd seen it a hundred times before. He needed to cover his tracks; he knew exactly what he had to do. In the next fifteen minutes he'd marshal his thoughts, sell his shares, speak to his lawyer. Polish his spin.

25

Making his way swiftly along the fifth-floor corridor of the Grosvenor House, Elliott North unlocked the door of his suite. And groaned. Sitting in the lounge, sipping champagne in their gossamer gowns and lace underwear, were the four teenage hookers he'd arranged with the agency: blonde, brunette, redhead and oriental; the way Jacob always liked them. He'd completely forgotten he'd ordered them.

'Just fuck off, the lot of you,' he barked, jerking his thumb towards the door.

They glanced at one another, startled, before one got up and sauntered over to him. 'Sure we'll go, Mr Bigshot, but you have to pay first.'

North snorted, pulling out his wallet. He was in no position to argue. He needed them out. He counted £800 into her outstretched hand.

'Two hundred each? Please, you insult us.'

Eyes blazing with anger, he flicked out another £400. 'That's it,' he snapped his wallet shut. 'You've got half the night left to go fuck some asshole.'

The hooker had already stepped away and was slipping into her overcoat. 'Who's the asshole?' she retorted, before jerking her head towards the door. 'Come on, girls. We're out of here.'

North walked through to the bedroom, closed the door, and pulled out his mobile phone. It was his first moment to himself since the meltdown; his first chance to think. And he knew he didn't have long. He also knew Plan A was out of the question. He didn't have a hope in hell of getting £10 million out of Jay Strauss. Not tonight. Not ever. But he did have a Plan B, just in case something like this ever happened. All the corporate dirt had been dished tonight, but there was still the personal stuff. And he had the evidence safely stashed.

Now he pressed one of the memory buttons on his mobile.

'Barron,' came the hurried answer from the *News of the World* editor.

'Keith, it's Elliott North.'

'Hey! I've just been watching it on TV. It's a fucking madhouse down there!'

'Tell me about it.'

'So what can I do for you?'

'Jacob Strauss,' he began, 'I've got some stuff on him you'll be very interested in.'

'I've just seen it all on TV!'

'No. Not that stuff. Different stuff. Kinky sex with prostitutes. Drugs. You name it; I've got the photos.'

'Is that right?'

'And videos. I'm willing to go exclusive with you. But I'll need a lot of money.'

'How much?'

'One million.'

There was a loud guffaw at the other end. 'He's only a

businessman, for God's sake! Not some movie star. Where's your perspective?'

North swallowed. 'Well then, seven-fifty.'

'You're wasting my time. Even if this stuff is as hot as you say, I'd never pay more than half a mill – and that's assuming there's enough material to take several runs at the story.'

'OK, OK! Half a mill. But I need cash.'

'That's never a problem.'

'And I need it tonight.'

There was a pause. 'Not planning to be around very long?'

'What do *you* think?'

After arranging a meeting place not far away, in one hour's time, North pressed the 'Off' button, and headed for the door.

Across town, in the semi-darkness of his office in Monitoring Services, Bruno d'Andrea had followed the entire night's proceedings on television. He had also just listened, with the greatest of interest, to Elliott North's conversation with Keith Barron. Action was called for, he decided, and on this occasion he didn't think he needed to trouble Mike Cullen to make the necessary arrangements.

Alex Carter surveyed his appearance in the mirror of *The Herald*'s executive bathroom. It met with his approval. He'd always felt good in a dinner jacket. The crimson cummerbund about his waist had a flattering, slimming effect, and as he leaned towards the mirror to inspect his face and the lines around his eyes, he decided he was looking good for his age. If anything, he reflected, he was growing more handsome with each passing year. Though it wasn't only a physical thing – he supposed he had also developed a certain charisma as he'd ascended to his position of power in business media.

He was a survivor all right. The upset earlier in the week had been his biggest test: how to deal with that prick North. In the end, he'd had to go along with North's plans for Judith Laing. He'd sent the deceitful little minx off to India, never to be heard of again. Which suited him fine. And there, Carter had reassured himself, was the end of it. He'd made it clear to North that they were evens. He didn't expect any more trouble from him. The stress of it had had him really worried. The Starwear story was one he'd have given his left ball to break as an exclusive. Suppressing it had gone against his every editorial instinct. But he had to think of putting the kids through school. And, he supposed, he did enjoy his trappings – the country home, the Jag, the rather good wine cellar. Dabbing eau de toilette behind his ears and on his forehead, he patted the leather cigar case in his top pocket and stood to attention. He was all set for a big night out. He intended to enjoy himself.

Making his way back through the office, still a hive of activity at seven forty-five at night, he found Carol Anderson hovering at his office door.

'Harvey would like a word,' she told him.

Carter rolled his eyes. 'I'm on my way out, right now. Can it wait . . .?'

'It's urgent,' she said briskly, before heading back to her desk, just outside the Editor's office.

Typical Harvey Tilyard, fumed Carter, stalking across the newsroom. Everyone agreed on Harvey: brilliant journalist, hopeless manager. Just didn't have the right 'people

skills' – didn't know how to win his subordinates' support
and respect in the way that came so effortlessly to Carter.

'You wanted to see me?'

Harvey turned away from a screen covered with material for the next morning's edition.

'Yes.' A frown appeared as he glanced over his littered
desk, before finding the envelope that had recently arrived
by courier. 'I've just had sight of this.' He extracted Judith
Laing's Starwear article from the envelope, and flicked it
towards Carter. 'I believe she filed it eight days ago?'

His eyes met Carter's with a look of fierce enquiry.
Harvey Tilyard was not a man to beat about the bush, and
this latest delivery had confirmed a number of suspicions he
had long harboured about his City Editor.

Reaching for the Starwear article, Carter was suddenly
aghast – though he tried to disguise his feelings. He glanced
at the front page before flicking through the rest. 'Yes,' he
replied, meeting Harvey's eyes for the first time with as
much confidence as he could muster.

Harvey leaned forward in his seat, glaring at him. 'Must
I ask the obvious question?' he snapped.

'I didn't think it was strong enough,' tried Carter.

'Not strong enough? Good God, man, what do you
mean?'

In his dinner jacket, Carter felt himself perspiring like a
guilty schoolboy. 'The central allegations concern a place
three and a half thousand miles away which Judith Laing
had never visited.'

'A place our Delhi stringer could have checked out in
two hours flat.'

'Given Judith's involvement—' protested Carter.

'Ah, right,' Harvey nodded facetiously, 'given Judith's

involvement you decide to sit on the biggest story you've ever seen, to give all our competitors a sporting chance.'

Much to his mortification, Carter felt the colour rising in his cheeks.

'In the meantime, you decide to do sweet FA about the other stories that could have been run as stand-alones – Jacob Strauss's track record; the discrepancy between Forbes forecasts and the Annual Report—'

'Well, maybe that was an error of judgement,' Carter conceded.

'And not your judgement to make!' Harvey retorted angrily. 'This is a front-page story. You knew that damned well. And you didn't even do me the courtesy of running the piece by me. At the very least it shows incompetence on a spectacular scale.'

He paused, glaring at Carter. 'Of course, there's another explanation I don't even want to think about.'

Carter grew rapidly alarmed. 'What are you talking about?'

'Carter, don't ask me to spell it out.' Harvey fixed him with an expression of extreme distaste. 'Suffice it to say that as of this moment I am relieving you from your position as City Editor of *The Herald*.'

'You can't just fire me on the spot!' exploded Carter, shaking with rage and shock.

'Why not?'

'I have family obligations—'

'And I have an obligation to my readers.' Harvey was caustic. 'Would you prefer me instead to suspend you and order a full-scale enquiry? Firing you is the very least I should be doing. I'm still considering the grounds for criminal enquiry.'

Carter stood a moment, his face frozen with disbelief. Then he turned to the door.

'I want you straight out of the office and downstairs,' Harvey called after him, as the final indignity. 'Carol will clear your desk and send personal items to your home tomorrow.'

It was more than twenty minutes before Jacob Strauss managed to flag down a taxi outside the Grosvenor House. In the normal course of events, Elliott North, or one of his Starwear flunkies, would have phoned ahead for his driver, and the Bentley would be waiting for him as he emerged from the hotel. But he had no hired help tonight. Standing on the pavement, flailing helplessly at every passing cab, only added to his towering resentment. And mounting anxiety.

When a taxi finally did stop for him, he shouted his address through the window, telling the driver to 'step on the gas', before he slumped in the back. They were soon speeding past the hotel entrance to the Great Room, where a great crowd on the pavement were climbing into chauffeured cars, or trying to hail taxis, after an evening abruptly curtailed. He supposed his wife was among them. Stupid bitch for deserting him at the table. She could walk home for all he cared.

He was utterly dazed by the events of the evening. Never in his life had he been so humiliated. Blood still pounding in his head, he glanced over his shoulder through the back window of the cab, half expecting to see the red and blue lights of a police car. He knew it was all over for him now. Thanks to that complete fuck-wit Elliott North, the family firm was down the tubes. There would be criminal investigations; lawsuits fired at him from every quarter; jail sentences pronounced. All *in abstentia*, if he had anything to do with it. He wasn't hanging around in this shit-hole of a country waiting for the noose to close round his neck. He'd get the hell out to Switzerland, where he'd long since stashed some money. Then he'd decide what to do next.

Glancing at his watch – ten twenty-five – he knew he'd have to move fast if he was going to get out tonight. The Starwear Citation jet was in New York. And he had no PA to shop around for a scheduled flight. So when the cab pulled up in front of his Boltons home, he handed the driver a £50 note and told him to wait. He ran up the steps and, once inside the house, made his way directly to the study, where he threw his passport, bank cards and other financial documents in his briefcase. Then to the bedroom where he'd never changed so fast; he dumped the evening suit and changed into more casual clothes, not wanting to draw attention to himself later at the airport. Looking around the extensive wardrobes of his dressing room, it didn't even occur to him to pack clothes – he could always buy them at the other end. Then he was hurrying downstairs.

He'd reached the hallway when the front door opened and in stepped Amy. Hair clinging damply around her face and eyes blotched with mascara, she couldn't have looked more different from the song of elegance who had arrived at the Grosvenor House earlier that evening. Across the hallway, she took in her husband's change of clothes and briefcase at a single glance.

'On your way somewhere?' She was weary.

'What the fuck d'you expect?'

It was a moment before she shrugged. 'I expect you to run away. Like you always do. But you can't this time. There's nowhere to go.'

As she met his eyes, she recalled the wall-to-wall image that had so distressed her earlier that evening – the photograph of all those kids in his factory. 'How could you?' she demanded hoarsely.

He pushed past her. 'No time to stand around listening to your crap.'

'Just so you know,' she turned as he opened the door, 'tomorrow I'll be speaking to lawyers about a divorce.'

He threw back his head and let out a short, frantic cackle. 'I hope you're not expecting any money out of me.'

She shook her head. 'It's not about money.'

For a moment he regarded her with narrow-eyed disdain before telling her, 'Everything's about money.'

Then he was rushing down the steps to the waiting cab.

An hour later he was sitting in the First Class lounge at Heathrow Airport, waiting for the midnight flight to Zürich. The lounge was surprisingly full for that time of the night. So he found himself a corner and propped the *FT* up in front of his face, keeping an eye on the door.

He didn't give a second glance to the tall, balding man in the Burberry who stepped into the lounge five minutes after him – he seemed like any other businessman. A short while later, though, he was disturbed by a clearing of the throat. 'Excuse me, Mr Strauss, are you travelling to Zürich?'

Strauss folded down the paper with a look of irritation. 'Yes.'

Confirming his target, George Blake of Scotland Yard introduced himself, flashing his ID.

'What d'you want?' Strauss glanced around – Blake seemed unaccompanied.

'The stock exchange authorities are very anxious to speak to you, sir.'

'Well they can speak to me when I get back from Zürich,' Strauss retorted angrily.

Blake's expression was withering. 'You have no intention of coming back from Zürich. You only bought a one-way ticket.'

Strauss stood up, his fury rising. *Who was this imbecilic paper-pusher to order him about?*

'Are you saying I don't have a choice?' he smouldered.

'You do, actually.' Blake didn't even try to hide his contempt. 'You can come away quietly, or make your life even more difficult than it already is.'

That was too much for Strauss. 'Don't you tell me what to do, you fucking idiot!'

He lashed out at Blake, catching him full in the chest, sending the detective flying back on to the sofa behind him, currently occupied by two Japanese businessmen, before rushing for the exit. But he wasn't halfway across the room before five uniformed policemen were running towards him from all sides. Simultaneously seized by three of them, he heard a fourth begin reading him his rights in a loud voice while everyone in the First Class lounge stared.

'You can't do this!' he screamed, as Detective Inspector Blake approached him. His hands were now behind his back, and cuffed. 'You can't arrest me for stock exchange irregularities! There's a whole process—'

'You're quite right, Mr Strauss,' Blake grimaced. 'And I couldn't have forced you to stay. But, you see, we rather counted on your behaving foolishly. Assaulting a police officer *is* a detainable offence.'

Then, as the policemen began leading Strauss to the door, he added, 'Though I daresay you'll have visitors from the stock exchange during your spell on remand.'

At ten-fifty p.m., ten minutes before the appointed hour, Elliott North watched the car appear around the corner of Berkeley Square and pull over outside the building. From behind the wheel, a man stepped out and, briefcase in hand, made his way to the entrance of the building. He was there for less than twenty seconds before North walked over to him.

'Elliott?' the man confirmed, as North approached him.

He nodded.

'Frank Williams.'

They shook hands briefly before Williams gestured. 'In the car.'

North glanced at the briefcase. *Half a million pounds cash.* Williams opened the passenger door for him, and he stepped inside. Then when Williams joined him he said, 'I want to see it.'

'Sure.'

He handed the briefcase over to North, who clicked open the two catches simultaneously. And there it was. Neat piles of crisp, £50 notes.

They were driving off now, heading out of Berkeley Square towards Piccadilly.

'We're going somewhere a little more private.' Williams's round, florid face was creased into a grin. 'Do the deed, like.'

North hadn't met this guy before. But the turnover in

tabloid staff was over fifty per cent a year, so that meant nothing.

'So what have you got for us?'

From under his evening suit jacket, North pulled out a large padded envelope containing the most incriminating photographs he had of Jacob Strauss and a variety of different girls in porno outfits. There was also a detailed list of Strauss's sexual adventures, and the madames who'd variously indulged him.

As they drove on, he described what he had, hyping up the contents of the envelope.

'Sounds like a real corker of a story. Real corker,' enthused Williams. Then, as they pulled into a quiet, Belgravia mews, 'You sure you haven't shown this stuff around to anyone else. Mr Barron won't be pleased . . .'

'You have my word on it.'

Williams winked. 'Good enough for me.'

Williams pulled the car over to one side of the mews, and turned off the engine. It was suddenly dark and very quiet.

'Now,' he said, 'let's see what you've got in there.'

No sooner had North handed over the envelope than he was aware of something flicking in front of his face – then the sudden, violent tug of a cord around his neck. Eyes popping in agony and hands frantically reaching up to his throat, he struggled and writhed in his seat for a silent thirty seconds before slumping, motionless. The driver was still looking over at him when the smell of faeces began to fill the car.

'Gordon Bennett!' He rapidly wound down the window and started the engine. 'Waste of a posh suit, eh, Harry?'

Moments later, the car was heading east, and Williams was pulling out his mobile. He dialled a number.

''Ello Mr d'Andrea,' he said after a few seconds. 'Mission accomplished.'

Never in his whole career had Mike Cullen addressed such a large gathering of the world's media – and never had he spoken on a subject of such supreme personal importance to him, or with so little time to prepare. But he knew he had no choice. He who lived by the media must die by the media – and he had no intention of dying just yet.

As he stood outside the Grosvenor House facing blazing TV lights, a battery of over a dozen microphones and Dictaphones thrust in his face, the constant whir and flash of photographers all about him, he marshalled all the persuasive power and sense of shaken outrage of which he knew he was so eminently capable.

'When I took Nathan Strauss on as a client ten years ago,' he began, at once siding with the angels, 'I was proud to count him among Lombard's biggest corporate clients. In due course, he also became one of my most valued personal friends.'

He described the closeness of his working relationship with Nathan, and how the development of Starwear I and II had been a joint endeavour. But sensing a certain restiveness among the media, he quickly moved on.

'You will remember Nathan's statement, over a year ago, in which he denied that Starwear had any involvement in child labour? I certainly remember it. I wrote that statement . . .'

There was an instant volley of questions. Cullen gestured for silence. 'Please. Let me finish. I wrote that statement at Starwear headquarters following a lengthy telephone conversation during which Nathan asked his brother Jacob, explicitly and several times, whether any of the stories then circulating about child labour could be true. Jacob denied the possibility of it each time. Like Nathan, I found it, quite frankly, unimaginable that a senior executive of a global company like Starwear would even countenance using child labour. Like Nathan, I didn't think his own brother would tell an outright lie. Like Nathan, I took Jacob at his word.'

Cullen went on to relate how Jacob's appointment as CEO, following Nathan's death, had created immediate problems at Lombard. It was not only Jacob's 'erratic' behaviour, it was also the imposition of Elliott North on Lombard, creating tensions both inside the agency and out. North, Cullen told the press, had made 'crude and aberrant attempts to manipulate the media' and had had to be disciplined. And it had been North who was the prime link with GlobeWatch which, Cullen told the rolling TV cameras, he had assumed to be a bona fide not-for-profit organisation.

Having staked out his defence in the clearest possible terms, Cullen glanced about the assembled throng before raising both hands in the air, sending off a fresh explosion of flash-cubes.

'Having said all that, I am not trying to shirk my responsibility,' he said. 'Lest you think I protest too much, let me say this: I was wrong to accept so unquestioningly the information my client gave me about his business; I was wrong not to dismiss Elliott North when his outrageous behaviour first became apparent; and I was wrong not to resign the Starwear account when it became clear that Jacob Strauss was intent on self-destruction.

'I apologise now, fully and without reserve, for my agency's unwitting support of Starwear's horrifying crimes against children. And I promise that I will do my utmost to try to right my client's wrongs. Quite apart from anything else, tonight I pledge one million pounds from Lombard to be used with immediate effect to free the child slaves abused by Starwear. And I'd encourage other City businesses to contribute to the Lombard Free the Children Appeal.'

His voice growing hoarse, and eyes shining, he ended, 'When I think of those images we saw tonight . . .' he shook his head, lips trembling with emotion, 'who could not be moved?'

Watching all of this on television, Chris turned to Judith. 'You know, I just can't believe he'd be involved.'

She was staring at the screen. 'If he is, he's very plausible.'

'D'you reckon he's got us all fooled?'

She pulled a droll expression. 'Well, he *is* in PR.'

At that moment the telephone went. Apart from Bernie himself, there was only one person who had their telephone number: Harvey Tilyard. Picking up the cordless receiver, Judith glanced at Chris significantly, before taking the phone into the bedroom. Chris carried on watching Cullen deftly fielding the inevitable barrage of questions, shouldering just the right amount of excusable blame while pointing the finger firmly at Jacob Strauss and his malevolent personal spin-meister.

When Judith came back into the room, she was wearing a broad smile.

'Tell me!' Chris was impatient.

'Front-page spread tomorrow, with extra reporting on GlobeWatch. Bylined Judith Laing – Deputy City Editor.'

'Whey-hey!' He leapt to his feet, put his arms round her and pirouetted her around. 'Congratulations!'

She couldn't stop grinning.

'And what did he say about Carter?'

Leaning back from him, she drew a line across her throat.

'What?'

'Summarily dismissed three hours ago.'

'So who's taking over?'

'We'll all have to cover for him till they get a replacement.'

Chris stared down at her, shaking his head. 'I'm so thrilled for you. This calls for a major celebration.'

'It'll have to wait for the weekend.' She rolled her eyes. 'They want me in tomorrow morning. Short-staffed.'

'Yeah, I guess.'

They sat down on the sofa, opposite the fire. Judith turned to Chris. 'But what about you, darling? Will you talk to a lawyer tomorrow?'

That was another thing they'd discussed during the past few days: what would happen when the two of them made their sudden reappearance back in London? How would Chris protect himself from North and his operatives? Now he looked pensive. 'You know, I just want to sweep away the bugs and put all this behind me.'

'But they tried to kill you!'

'You too.'

'Journalists are supposed to get shot at. Anyway, look what it's done for my career.'

Which left the unspoken question hanging: what about *his*?

'I know.' He looked up at her sympathetic expression.

'But I'll find something. Maybe set up on my own.' He glanced over at her quizzically. 'Of course, the overheads in my new place are up a bit. Perhaps I should find someone to house-share.'

'Oh? What sort of someone?'

'Let me think. Single, white female—'

'Attractive?' She played along.

He shook his head. 'Not just attractive. I'm thinking sex appeal – dripping with it.'

'Dripping even?'

'Sex on legs.' Then with mock seriousness, 'A professional lady, of course. Maybe something in the media.'

'Like a Deputy City Editor?' She laughed.

'That would be perfect.'

Lying back on the sofa, they kissed and he rolled on top of her. 'You know, I've never made love to a Deputy City Editor before.'

'Oh, really?' she whispered with a grin, reaching down and fiddling with his belt. 'First time for everything.'

EPILOGUE

Helen Cullen surveyed the exposed branches in Hyde Park as she followed her usual route around the Serpentine. By mid-November they were stripped bare of all leaves, forming dark silhouettes against the winter sky. Even in their nakedness they had a peculiar beauty, a stillness she usually found soothing to the spirit. But not this evening. She doubted anything was capable of soothing her – not even the powerful new tranquilizers her doctor had prescribed the day before, designed to keep her emotions wrapped in a numbing, chemical cocoon.

Later this evening she was to join her husband at a State Banquet at Buckingham Palace, in honour of the visiting President of France. When Mike had phoned her with the news some time ago, he hadn't concealed his excitement. It wasn't so much the prospect of an evening of starchy formality with chinless wonders from the Foreign Office that appealed; it was more that the invitation itself sent out a signal of recognition. It would have been motivated and endorsed by people in high places. It was an encouraging sign that Mike Cullen was being noticed with approval. A first step, perhaps, towards an eventual knighthood? Arise, Sir Michael?

Mike had been in the news a great deal in recent days. Having previously maintained a rigid code of invisibility at Lombard, after the Starwear débâcle he'd suddenly been everywhere, talking up his Lombard Free the Children Appeal. The appeal had been a great success, having raised over £20 million in two weeks. The newspapers had been full of photographs of Mike Cullen in India, surrounded by emaciated and pathetically grateful children.

All of a sudden, Mike Cullen was the conscience of the City, the man with the heart of gold. Although a few critics pointed out that he had been all too willing to collude with Jacob Strauss – not only during Strauss's brief period as CEO of Starwear, but for several years before that, when Strauss was Managing Director of Starwear's International Division – the attacks had been fragmented and drew little support.

Following his vintage performance outside the Grosvenor House, the consensus of most media commentators, several of them numbered among his closest friends, was that Mike Cullen had been a victim of Jacob Strauss's despicable duplicity.

Several senior journalists had stepped forward to confirm Cullen's contention that Elliott North was the real PR villain. Jim Ritchie described North's crass attempt at bribery. The hasty departure of Alex Carter from *The Herald* gave substance to the theory too. And with Jacob Strauss's 'no comment' policy contrasting sharply with Mike Cullen's openness, a momentum was soon established; it wasn't long before opinion formers among the huge number of blue-chip companies represented by Lombard were stepping forward to voice their solidarity with Mike Cullen.

It seemed to Helen that she couldn't open a newspaper without reading about her husband, or seeing some carefully placed press photograph. Bruno d'Andrea had been phoning their home every night with news of the next day's papers. The only Lombard executive for whom she had a visceral dislike, d'Andrea seemed to be riding high at Lombard. Mike had awarded him a one-off bonus amounting to several hundred thousand pounds – exactly what for, she shuddered to think. She knew there had been all kinds of shenanigans at the office. Having overheard her husband's muttered late-night phone conversations, she knew that his new Research and Planning Director, a young man with whom he'd been much enamoured, had returned his company car with a letter of resignation to take immediate effect, after just two and a half months at the company. It was so out of keeping for Lombard, Helen couldn't help wondering what had prompted the sudden departure, though she suspected it was directly linked to the Starwear débâcle – and all her husband's furtive telephone conversations in the nights that followed.

She hated it all. It was one thing trying desperately, for the sake of the girls, to keep up the pretence that theirs was a happy marriage; and it was quite another to keep up the façade with her husband revelling in the full blaze of publicity as a saviour of children. She found the whole thing abhorrent; a travesty so utterly cynical it made her feel even more disturbed than she already had been. Whatever anyone else thought of her husband, she knew that under all that charm was a well-developed core of evil.

And of course, stories about the disappearance of Dale Nesbitt continued to circulate. Just a few nights ago she had happened to turn on the television when *Crimewatch* was covering the case. She'd stood there, staring at the reconstruction with her heart in her throat, as the programme showed an anonymous stranger arriving at St Stephen's to collect Dale. A police detective said he believed there was a good chance Dale might still be alive, perhaps being held captive somewhere. If that was the case, he concluded, someone, somewhere must know about it. *Please would they come forward with information!* There were interviews with several teachers from St Stephen's, and with Dale's fellow pupils from school. Dale was described as exceptionally good-looking, a committed athlete, a sensitive boy. There were pleas to call *Crimewatch* with any clues, however tenuous they might seem. It was only after the piece was over she'd realised she was crying.

Of course, she still had no evidence at all to link the disappearance to Mike – only the knowledge that her husband had, once before, engaged in acts of paedophilia; that he'd had some kind of sponsor's relationship with St Stephen's. And, of course, her deeply troubled intuition. But was that cause to pull the whole world down around her?

She paused awhile, as she always did at the end of her walk, looking across the mirror-still water. An evening wind sent a shiver through the stark branches, and she clutched her coat to herself. This evening, as always, the only conclusion she had reached after her walk was to press on; keep putting one foot in front of the other. Deeply reluctant though she was to take part in tonight's charade, she felt she really had no choice.

Two and a half hours later she found herself being led through the reception area of Lombard House towards the lift which would carry her to the penthouse. She was always treated as something of a deity when she arrived at

Lombard, with much bowing and scraping accorded to the Chairman's wife. Tonight was no exception, as one of the exquisite Sloaney girls at Reception complimented her on her beautiful gown, before stepping into the lift beside her, and pressing the top button.

She'd arrived deliberately late so that she wouldn't have to endure too much of the pre-Palace cocktails. Mike had arranged celebratory drinks with some of his fellow directors, and by the time she stepped into the penthouse sitting room, there were about thirty people already there – Mike himself looking even more darkly splendid than ever in white tie and tails. She accepted a fresh orange juice from a caterer, and spent a few minutes talking to Nicholas King. It wasn't long before Mike pointed out that it was almost time to leave.

Excusing herself for a moment, she went through to the *en-suite* bathroom leading off the master bedroom. It was as gleaming and luxurious as ever – Italian marble sparkling under concealed downlighters in the ceiling. Putting the finishing touches to her make-up, she washed her hands and dried them on one of the small hand towels provided, before raising the lid of the wicker basket to dispose of the towel.

It was only when she'd closed the lid of the basket that she realised the significance of what she'd seen. Opening the lid again, she looked inside carefully; there was definitely something that wasn't a towel, curled at the bottom. Reaching down, she pushed aside a few other towels to check what it was. As she lifted it up, she felt her heart suddenly racing. Sure enough, it was what she'd suspected. Creased and soiled, very much the worse for wear, it was, nonetheless, a boy's tie. In St Stephen's colours.

She felt as though she was caught in a surreal drama. She stepped out of the bathroom and into the bedroom, depositing the St Stephen's tie on the bed. Like an automaton she found herself picking up the telephone receiver on the bedside pedestal, dialling the emergency services, and asking for the police.

When a police officer came on the line she said, 'I'm phoning about the boy who was abducted from St Stephen's – Dale Nesbitt.'

'You have some information you'd like to give me?'

'I know who abducted him.'

Sensing a movement, she looked up to find her husband standing across the room from her, pointing at his watch. 'His name is Mike Cullen.' She ignored her husband.

'And what is your relationship with this man?'

She sighed. 'He is . . . was . . . my husband.'

Dale was found in Ledford Style, a small village in Suffolk, a few days later. He'd appeared at the kitchen door of the local coffee shop begging for food. Marj Wilkins, the proprietor, had taken one look at the bedraggled little urchin, shivering from cold, before installing him at the kitchen bench with bacon sandwiches and a mug of hot chocolate. Then she had called her brother-in-law Jim, the local police constable.

Jim had been round in minutes. He'd always had a way with children, and after a short while had persuaded Dale, revived by his meal, to tell him how he came to be in rural Suffolk. The story that followed had been like something out of a weekend tabloid. It involved a London orphanage run by priests, who were bribed by a businessman to allow access to their boys – the paedophile who had showered

Dale with gifts before molesting him. Dale spoke of his fear, every time he was summoned to the man's flat. Finally, Dale described his incarceration there, and nightly abuse for nearly a month. His chance to escape had come when the man had transferred him to a basement storage room as the flat was needed for a party. In the storeroom Dale had found a piece of wire and, using a trick he'd learned from the boys at school, had managed to unpick the lock. Wandering the unfamiliar streets of the City, he'd found his way to Liverpool Street station, and jumped on the first train that was leaving.

Jim and Marj Wilkins sat listening, trying to conceal their horror. While Dale had been talking, Jim was thinking about the missing persons directory down at the station. He was almost certain a boy from a London orphanage had been reported missing not so long ago. He could easily check. Then he asked gently, 'D'you know the man's name?'

Dale screwed up his face. 'He made me call him Santa. I've forgotten his real name'.

Jim was nodding. 'We'll soon find out.'

'Just look in the papers. He's in there a lot.'

'Oh, really?'

Marj was already making her way through to the coffee shop, from which she retrieved a pile of that week's *Daily Mails*. They flicked through the pages and it didn't take long before Dale pointed, expressionlessly. 'That's him.'

The photograph showed a beaming Cullen in his shirt-sleeves, with a large group of Indian children clutching his arms.

'Mike Cullen?' Jim read the caption.

Dale nodded.

'"Spin-doctor saves child slaves from misery",' Jim and Marj read the headline aloud together.

Then Jim was shaking his head. 'You just never know, do you?'

An extract from David Michie's latest thriller

PURE
DECEPTION

PURE DECEPTION is available
from 18 January 2001
in Little, Brown hardback

Prologue

London
Monday 30 August

Alan Brent had never felt such terror in his life. Even half an hour later, hurrying through the night with shoulders hunched and collar raised, he had to fight to control the nausea, to keep down the acid rising from his stomach. *Clink, clink, clink,* came the sound from his trouser pocket. Steel on glass. He tried to block it from his mind.

In twelve years undercover he'd seen some sights – all manner of depravities and perversions and horrors. But none like tonight. Christ, no! Even though it hadn't been him trussed up on the floor and subjected to Larson's barbaric surgery, he'd scarcely been able to comprehend the sheer, stupefying viciousness of it. Behind their thick lenses, his eyes were still wide with shock. In his jacket pockets, he'd clenched his hands into tight fists to stop them shaking.

They were moving as fast as possible without drawing undue attention. One of the dark shadows was fifty yards ahead; the other man, fifty behind. This was Alan's first time out and they were taking no chances. They had been ruthlessly effective from the start, their actions planned meticulously to cover all scenarios, drilling each sequence in rehearsal, again and again, so when it had come to the actual operation, they were doing it for the hundredth time, and had carried it out with digital precision. Searing, heart-stopping torment had been inflicted with Teutonic efficiency. No wonder Larson thought he was untouchable.

As they rushed past shop windows lit up in the night, Alan told himself he should derive some satisfaction from the fact that he had at least been accepted. He'd broken into the inner circle. They would never have let him anywhere near this if they'd had the slightest doubt. Going operational was a mark of trust, recognition – he needed that if he was going to penetrate the highest level of the organisation, though he hadn't counted on the cost. What had happened tonight outstripped his most lurid expectations, and there was nothing he could do about it now. He was way past the point of no return. Bile rose in his throat. It was all he could do not to retch.

They turned into his street. He paused, as he'd been instructed, while the front escort checked the way before signalling all clear. Alibis had been established and weren't to be wrecked by chance encounters – that was their reasoning and he played along with the game, knowing that, if it came to it, he could get one of the women from HQ to pretend to be his girlfriend.

The house was a typical Victorian terrace, indistinguishable from the other sixty in the street. He made his way quickly from pavement to front door, keys in his hand, and as soon as he was inside he shed his jacket, threw it over a coat-hook and headed immediately for the stairs.

The sound from his trouser pocket as he ascended was a loathsome reminder. *Clink, clink, clink.*

AIan's kitchen was large and scattered with the detritus of bachelorhood, cast in sepia by the grubby yellow glow from the streetlamp outside. Standing in the centre of it, spectacles glinting, he raised shaking fingers to push back the dark, wiry locks that fell dishevelled about his face. This was his first moment alone since the attack. It felt surreal to be back in the midst of familiar territory after what he'd just been through. As he stood there, heart pounding, and mouth vile, he still found it hard to believe. God Almighty, what had he let himself in for? In all the time he'd been working his way into the group, they'd never gone this far.

As he took a step forward, there came the sound from his pocket again – a single, unbidden *clink* – and with it, the unavoidable knowledge that the moment had come for him to deal with it. Trying to ignore it just wasn't an option any more. Wearily, he picked up a paper serviette from among the salt and pepper sachets and other remnants of numberless fast-food meals scattered across the kitchen bench. Unfolding the serviette over his right hand, he reached down into his pocket.

An hour before, the jar had been empty and clear; now, its glass sides were sickeningly smeared. He set it down at the far corner of the bench without looking at it. He 'd been down on his knees when they had made him pick them up. His skin-tight gloves were so fine, it had been like touching them with his bare hands. He hadn't felt nausea at the time – only shock. His fingers had shaken so violently he'd only just got them in the jar and was screwing the lid tight when he'd been ordered out.

Turning, Alan made his way from the kitchen, trying to dismiss the jar from his mind. He wanted, more than anything, to leave it all behind – to forget about it completely. Climbing a final flight of stairs, he made his way into the long attic room he used as his combined office and bedroom; the place where he spent most of his days and all his nights. As always, it was lit by the ghostly purple glow of his screensaver, which was reflected in a series of Velux windows that ran along the ceiling.

He slumped into the sofa and turned on the television with the remote control, at the same time picking up a half empty can of Sprite from the floor and taking several, greedy swallows to flush the bitterness from his mouth and throat. He flicked through the television channels trying to find some absorbing distraction. But there was no distraction, he soon discovered, from his own raging turmoil. No matter what images appeared on television, he couldn't get what was in the jar out of his mind. Nor could he avoid the realisation, which came suddenly and nagged at him insistently, that he would have to go back downstairs again. There was no way he could avoid it. He would have to return to the kitchen, pick up the jar, and put it away in the fridge.

It was a warm night, after all. He couldn't risk the contents decomposing.

<u>GIDEON</u>

Russell Andrews

When they asked him to be a ghost writer, he didn't realise
they wanted him dead.

Struggling writer Carl Granville is hired to turn an old
diary, articles and letters – in which all names and
locations have been blanked out – into compelling fiction.
But Carl soon realises that the book is more than just a
potential bestseller. It is a revelation of chilling evil and a
decades-long cover-up by someone with far-reaching
power. He begins to wonder how his book will be used,
and just who is the true storyteller.

Then – suddenly, brutally – two people close to Carl are
murdered, his apartment is ransacked, his computer stolen,
and he himself is the chief suspect. With no alibi and no
proof of his shadowy assignment, Carl becomes a man on
the run. He knows too much – but not enough to
save himself . . .

'A fast-moving thriller in the Grisham genre'
Sunday Telegraph

POSTMORTEM

Patricia Cornwell

A serial killer is on the loose in Richmond, Virginia. Three women have died, brutalised and strangled in their own bedrooms. There is no pattern: the killer appears to strike at random – but always on Saturday mornings.

So when Dr Kay Scarpetta, chief medical examiner, is awakened at 2.33 am, she knows the news is bad: there is a fourth victim. And she fears now for those that will follow unless she can dig up new forensic evidence to aid the police.

But not everyone is pleased to see a woman in this powerful job. Someone may even want to ruin her career and reputation …

'Terrific first novel, full of suspense, in which even the scientific bits grip'
The Times

HART'S WAR

John Katzenbach

Life isn't easy when you should have died . . .

Tommy Hart, whose B-25 was shot down over Germany, is burdened with guilt that he is the only surviving member of his crew. He is just another PoW at Stalag Luft 13 waiting for the war to end. But the tedium of the camp comes to a halt with the arrival of a new prisoner, Flight Lieutenant Lincoln Scott, a black pilot who instantly becomes the target of contempt from his fellow prisoners. His most vociferous adversary is Vincent Bedford, a decorated bomber captain, and the hatred between them is as volatile as a primed grenade.

When a prisoner is brutally murdered, all the evidence points to the killer being Scott, and Hart is 'volunteered' to defend him. While Scott steadfastly maintains his innocence, Hart senses that he has been chosen merely to make a show of defending the accused in what is presumed to be an open-and-shut case.

In a trial rife with racial tension and raw conflict, where the lines between ally and enemy blur, there are those with their own secret motives – and a burning passion for a rush to judgement, no matter the cost.

'Katzenbach's best book by far . . . a novel about honour and heroism'
Philip Caputo

FINAL JEOPARDY

Linda Fairstein

The days of Assistant D.A. Alexandra Cooper often start off badly, but she's never faced the morning by reading her own obituary before.

It doesn't take long to sort out why it was printed: a woman's body with her face blown away, left in a car rented in Coop's name in the driveway of her weekend home. But it isn't so easy to work out why her lodger – an acclaimed Hollywood star – was murdered, or to be sure that the killer had found the right victim.

As Coop's job is to send rapists to jail there are plenty of suspects who might be seeking revenge, and whoever it is needs to be found before her obituary gets reprinted.

'Raw, real and mean. Linda Fairstein is wonderful'
Patricia Cornwell

Other bestselling Warner titles available by mail:

☐ Gideon	Russell Andrews	£5.99
☐ Postmortem	Patricia Cornwell	£5.99
☐ Hart's War	John Katzenbach	£5.99
☐ Final Jeopardy	Linda Fairstein	£5.99

The prices shown above are correct at time of going to press. However, the publishers reserve the right to increase prices on covers from those previously advertised without prior notice.

WARNER BOOKS

WARNER BOOKS
P.O. Box 121, Kettering, Northants NN14 4ZQ
Tel: 01832 737525, Fax: 01832 733076
Email: aspenhouse@FSBDial.co.uk

POST AND PACKING:
Payments can be made as follows: cheque, postal order (payable to Warner Books) or by credit cards. Do not send cash or currency.
All U.K. Orders   **FREE OF CHARGE**
E.E.C. & Overseas   25% of order value

Name (Block Letters) _____

Address_____

_____

Post/zip code:_____

☐ Please keep me in touch with future Warner publications

☐ I enclose my remittance £_____

☐ I wish to pay by Visa/Access/Mastercard/Eurocard

Card Expiry Date

_____

TERMS AND CONDITIONS

WIN £1,000
WITH
CONFLICT OF INTEREST
BY DAVID MICHIE

To win £1,000 just answer these questions:

1. Where did Chris and Judith first meet and begin their romance?

2. What medical condition does Kate Taylor suffer from?

3. Where does Helen Cullen especially like to walk in the evenings?

Write your name, address and the answers to the questions on a postcard and send it to:
Conflict of Interest competition,
Marketing Department,
Little, Brown and Company,
Brettenham House,
Lancaster Place,
London WC2E 7EN

Competition closing date: 30th November 2001